PRAISE FOR PATRICIA A. JACKSON

"Jackson modernizes Christian lore in her action-packed debut… urban fantasy fans will be happy to charge through to the end."

Publishers Weekly

"Crafted with skill, featuring an array of unforgettable characters and breath-stealing action, *Forging a Nightmare* is one hell of a ride. Highly recommended."

Julie E. Czerneda, award-winning author of The Gossamer Mage

"Just about anyone can get published and call themself a writer, but Patty Jackson is that much rarer and finer thing, a true writer, master of her craft. In *Forging a Nightmare* she has created a brilliantly plotted, hard-hitting fantasy deeply rooted in the mythos of the human, the divine, the angelic and the equine."

Nancy Springer, author of 'The Enola Holmes Mysteries'

"Christian, Greek, and Norse mythologies combine to create a stunning depiction of Heaven and Hell in this action-packed novel about an apocalypse angel and a special-ops officer turned warrior horse. You won't want to miss this hell of a ride!"

Reese Hogan, author of Shrouded Loyalties

"Patricia Jackson's *Forging a Nightmare* is a deep dive into a world of angels and magic that lies right under the surface of reality. Filled with well-drawn characters that become a part of your heart and a tightly woven plot that is carried through the entire novel, this is one book where the action moves the story at a thrilling pace."

Ginger Smith, author of The Rush's Edge

Patricia A. Jackson

FORGING A NIGHTMARE

ANGRY ROBOT
An imprint of Watkins Media Ltd

Unit 11, Shepperton House
89-93 Shepperton Road
London N1 3DF
UK

angryrobotbooks.com
twitter.com/angryrobotbooks
Oo-rah!

An Angry Robot paperback original, 2021

Cover by Daniel Kamarudin
Sigil Artwork by Gabrielle Tranchitella
Edited by Rose Green and Gemma Creffield
Set in Meridien

ISBN 978 0 85766 922 3
Ebook ISBN 978 0 85766 923 0

Printed and bound in the United Kingdom by TJ Books Ltd.

9 8 7 6 5 4 3 2 1

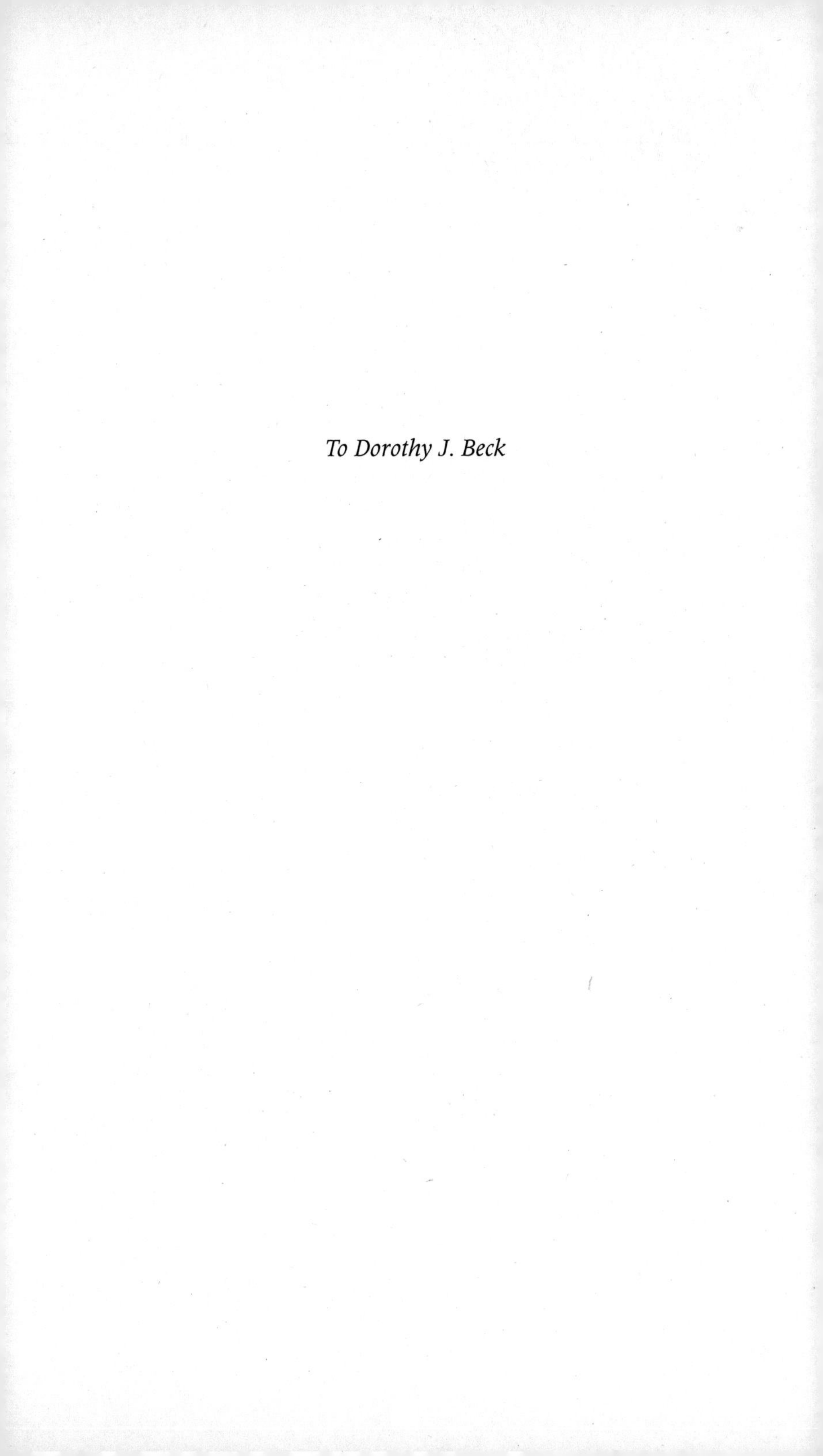

To Dorothy J. Beck

PROLOGUE

The woman was an abomination. Ababalond. A whore. Not by deed or profession, but by nature of birth.

Prone, she crawled on her belly, attempting to drag herself through the gravel and detritus beneath the Greywacke Arch on the eastern side of Central Park. Bleeding profusely from her mouth, she moaned like a gutted heifer on the floor of a slaughter house.

Her efforts were in vain. Her destiny as certain as the last leaves clinging from the branches of a dead tree.

The blade in his hand danced across her flesh with the artistry of a master butcher, adroitly carving strips of flesh in varying degrees of thickness and length... without entirely severing them from her body. Being mostly human, the woman could not appreciate the eloquence of his strokes nor comprehend the exquisite precision required for the Ritual of Descarbia.

She whimpered. It was all the control she had left. He had cut out her tongue first, leaving her bereft of a voice. *As it should have been,* he thought. Her kind were undeserving. The qeres coating her throat prevented any other vocalization as it seared the sensitive lining of her esophagus from the inside out. Thick gouts of phlegm clogged her throat. She was dying already, but her body kept fighting that reality. He had to admire her strength of will, even if he held no respect for her tainted lineage.

He stood over her, straddling her body as the initial convulsions started, and grinned at his handiwork. Rolling the woman onto her back with a callous kick, he leaned down and pulled at the outer corner of her eye. He held onto the lashes like the fragile legs a spider, then giving the lid a sharp yank, he cut it free with the bloody dagger.

Though the silver blade was razor sharp and the cut explicitly precise to avoid cruelty, the injury could not be without some discomfort. She tried to squeal in pain, but the cry was strangled by the fluids rising in her constricted throat. Drowning in them, her body writhed in agony, her lungs yearning for a final breath.

Dropping down on top of her, he drove his knee into her chest to restrain her flailing form. What little air there was in her lungs escaped in a frightened gasp, accompanied by a spray of bloody spittle. While she was thus distracted, he cut off the other eyelid with the adeptness of a monk plucking a fly from the air. He thought the quick action was a mercy, like stepping on a child's foot before removing a splinter.

The dying woman stared up at him in horror. Without eyelids, she had no choice but to stare. He smiled. It was nearly time. He placed the clipped lids in an earthen jar with her tongue and set it aside for later.

In the brief moment that he had turned away, she died. As deaths go, it was a quiet one, unlike the first two. He was disappointed to have missed her passing, but knew that the brain was still receiving and processing information. He leaned over her and carved another obscenity into her cheek.

The woman was an abomination. Ababalond. A whore. Not by deed or profession, but by nature of birth. And now, she was no more.

CHAPTER 1

"And lo, a black horse; and he that sat on her had the name Famine!"

Michael Childs tossed a five-dollar bill into the homeless preacher's cash box and kept walking. It was 7pm on a rainy Monday night. The Park Avenue sidewalks were packed with crowds of boutique shoppers and tourists. Shoulder to shoulder, they moved through the city like cogs in a timepiece.

The historic boulevard was jammed with traffic due to a convoy of parked vehicles, consisting mostly of New York City police cars, ambulances, forensic vans, and a hearse from the coroner's office. The brilliance of the city by night was barely noticeable against the intermittent flash of blue and red emergency lights.

Manhattan was in the midst of a midwinter heat wave. The mercury was expected to climb into the high sixties and peak at a record-breaking seventy degrees by the weekend. Just in time for Valentine's Day.

Eager to preach to a generous congregation, the homeless man hurried after Michael in bare feet. Michael quickened his pace to elude the vagrant. He was getting warm from his brisk, mile-long walk from Wollman Rink. Buried beneath tons of stone dust, the ice-skating venue had been converted into a riding ring for a week of Renaissance pageantry. Michael's boots were covered with it as he stepped off the curb to merge with the flow of official traffic.

With no time to change into a business suit, he made his way to the police barrier wearing a chainmail gorget around his neck. The weighted maille rattled as he walked despite the padded black gambeson beneath it, which clothed him from shoulder to mid-thigh. Reinforced with buckles and straps, it complemented his suede leggings, boots, and spurs.

As a Black man, dressed in medieval ensemble, he received more than a fair share of strange looks from pedestrians and the first responders on the scene. Dodging an ambulance, Michael swept his suede arming cap from his head and ran his fingers through his short, coarse dreadlocks. They rasped loudly against his gloves.

Ignoring the heavy police presence, the old preacher continued to pursue him. "From whom shall the wicked seek comfort, for Famine shall kill their root, and the Black Horse shall slay their remnants."

Michael firmly pressed a ten-dollar bill into the vagrant's grimy, calloused hand. "Get lost before you get arrested."

An unhinged, toothless grin surfaced from a matted beard. "The greatest plague God unleashed upon the world was His angels. You'll see." With that, the transient preacher retreated back down the street to his cardboard tabernacle.

"Sir," a uniformed officer said as Michael approached, "there's an active police investigation going on here. I'm going to have to ask you to step back." Wearing a yellow raincoat that barely covered his paunch, the policeman held up his pale hands to halt further encroachment.

"FBI." Michael flashed his badge and ducked beneath the wooden barricade without waiting for permission.

"Bureau sure has a funny dress code these days."

"You should check us out on dress-down Fridays. Onesies and lingerie."

"Mike?" Elijah Pope poked his head around the back doors of a forensic van. "Let him past, Larry."

Michael stepped aside to give way to a passing team of CSI

techs in blue lab coats with evidence collection bags in their hands. The three women hesitated long enough to stare at him before returning to their vehicle on the street.

"What the hell are you wearing?"

Michael flashed a mischievous grin. "EJ, I was at joust practice when you called. I was galloping in full armor with a lance and an eighteen hundred-pound Clydesdale named Buttercup bearing down on me."

"A crazed murderer running loose in the city, and you're out playing Knights of the Round Table? And at your age?" Larry stuffed his thumbs into his gun belt and rolled his eyes. "What do you want to be when you grow up someday?"

"I don't know, Larry. I have a Master's degree in Archaeology from Harvard. Another in Medieval Studies from Oxford. And I was third in my class at the FBI Academy." Michael held up his badge and credentials again, mocking the cop. "When you want to compare academic pedigrees, let me know."

"Damn, Mike, let that man breathe. We've got work to do." Elijah led Michael away from the sullen cop and directed him to a white tarp laying on the sidewalk. "Meet Miss Mary Klinedinst."

"Same MO?"

"See for yourself. Hope you had a light dinner."

Tucking his own leather gloves into his belt, Michael retrieved a pair of latex ones from a forensic kit and drew back the tarp. The pallid face of a Caucasian woman stared up at him, lying supine on the damp concrete. She was young, in her mid-thirties, and dressed in a bloody silk blouse and slacks. Her eyelids had been cut away with a sharp instrument, forcing her vacant eyes to stare into nothingness.

With an adept degree of precision, the killer had carved her face with occult symbols. While the rudiments of the language looked vaguely familiar, Michael could not immediately identify it. Bare and discolored, her arms were stretched over her head, hands reaching for the small clay jar placed beyond her fingertips.

Michael sank down on one knee. “Her tongue?”

“Judging by the smell coming from that jar above her head?” Elijah shrugged. “Cut out and burned along with the eyelids. Just like the others.”

A set of wings lay unfurled behind the victim’s shoulders, artistically sculpted with care for the aesthetic. They might have been beautiful had they not been carved from the very skin and muscle of the dead woman’s back.

“It’s him again. This is the third one.” Michael rubbed the back of his hand across his stubbled chin.

“Time to upgrade our perp to a serial killer then.” Elijah glanced around to see who might be listening. “The unofficial name on the streets is the Harbinger.”

“Dried blood in the wounds suggests she was alive when he carved her up. Took his time, too. No apparent bruising like the last victim. Something tells me the torture didn’t kill her, did it?”

“ME’s preliminary report points to anaphylaxis. Judging from that nasty yellow shit coming out of her mouth, she choked to death on her own fluids.” Elijah pulled a pen and notebook from his coat. “I ordered a tox screen, but I’ll bet anything it comes back the same as the others. Sorry to get you involved in this, man. I really thought we’d have better leads after the last two victims, but we’re coming up empty. There’s also this.” While attempting to juggle his notepad and pen, Elijah let a small vial slip through his fingers. He reflexively grabbed for it and caught the tube before it could hit the ground. “Shit!” he swore as the unctuous contents dribbled onto his fingers.

“Way to contaminate the crime scene, EJ.” Michael stepped back, bumping into a portable light fixture.

“Nothing to contaminate!” Elijah shook the excess liquid from his hand. “This shit’s all over the ground and her. Just like all the other vics.”

Michael took the vial from Elijah’s hand, tightened the lid, and dropped it into an evidence bag. “I’m gonna request the

Bureau send your ass back to the FBI Academy." He peeled off a glove and tossed his partner a bottle of hand sanitizer.

"We know it's not a corrosive agent. It's some kind of perfumed oil."

Michael pulled the tarp farther down to examine the lower torso and then scrutinized the dead woman's hand. "Six fingers."

"Six toes too." Elijah leaned over a stack of equipment crates while taking notes. "Our boy definitely has a type."

Perplexed, Michael shrugged. "How's this asshole finding his targets?"

"The coroner clued me into a few databases that focus on polydactyly. I checked into them, but so far, I got nothing."

"OK. So where's my love note?" Michael grabbed a blacklight from the forensic kit. Carefully angling the light source, he examined the ground beside the body. The ultraviolet beam lit up a hidden message written with the oil in the same strange script carved into the victim's face.

"Old English again? Like the previous two scenes?"

Michael shook his head. "The same script, but like I told you before, Old English uses the Latin alphabet, partner. This is something else. A dead language. But it clearly has more of a pulse than our victims."

"All them fancy letters behind your name, and you can't read it?" Elijah rolled his eyes. "Will the real Dr Childs please step up."

"I never finished my doctoral program, remember? My mother's the expert with the Ph.D. I settled for the FBI." Michael clenched his jaw in envy. "You have her number. Call her."

"I called *you*. Your degrees didn't fall out a Crackerjack box." Elijah glared at him. "You're a damn good cop, Mike. That's why I brought you in as the lead on this thing. Stop living in your mom's shadow."

Michael nodded, accepting the criticism. "I'd be a liar if I said I wasn't a little jealous of her. Rumor is, her new book's been nominated for a Pulitzer." He held the light out for his partner to hold over the script as he snapped pictures with his phone. "If anyone can decipher this writing, it's her."

"Michael Childs!" Elijah perched the glasses on the tip of his nose. "You did not send that shit to your mom!"

"You brought me in for my expertise *and* my resources." Michael challenged his partner's disapproving glare with a grin. "My mom wrote the book on obscure pagan rituals. Why wait around for some half-baked expert to tell us what she probably knows?"

"She left your ass alone in one of those underground crypts when you were a kid, didn't she? That's what's wrong with you, Mike!"

"What else you got on our vic?"

"Miss Klinedinst was a city school teacher. First grade." Elijah sidestepped the forensic photographer and her assistant as they attended to the task of cataloging the scene under blacklight.

"Tomorrow's a school day," Michael groaned. "Have somebody from the local precinct contact the principal. Right after they notify next of kin."

"I know my job, Mike. It's what I was getting ready to do when you rudely interrupted me dressed as Aragorn."

Pulling the tarp back up, Michael caught sight of a rolled tip of newspaper beneath the victim's hand. "Remember when you said we had nothing?" He gently tugged it from beneath the body.

Elijah held out an evidence bag. "What is that?"

"A racing form." Michael scrutinized the perfect print handwriting on the back page. "There's a name written on it. *A. Raines*. Any idea who that is?"

Taking the bag from him, Elijah examined the back page. "I got nothing, son. What are these numbers beneath the name?"

"Look like stall numbers in the shed row," said a CSI tech, glancing over Elijah's shoulder.

"Shed row, Palmieri?" Michael asked. "Since when have you seen the backstretch of a racetrack?" He chuckled at Elijah's confusion. "It's where they keep the horses when they're not racing or training."

"My ex-husband's a trainer at Belmont Park. Every other weekend, my kids stay with their dad. They like to pet the horses and feed them carrots and peppermints."

Straightening his gorget, Michael stood up. "A trainer, huh? Could be worth contacting him. You got a phone number for this ex-husband?"

Palmieri grabbed the notebook and pen from Elijah's hand. She scribbled on a blank page, tore it out, and handed it to Michael. "Top number's my ex. The bottom one's mine." She winked at him and walked back to her van.

CHAPTER 2

At 5am, despite the absence of sun, the shed row at Belmont Park was teeming with activity. An army of stable hands labored at mucking stalls, throwing feed, and scrubbing water buckets. Grooms juggled lead ropes, halters, and brush boxes while bracing the powerful but fragile legs of their equine charges who resided on the backside of the famous track.

The shed row was lit with fluorescent bulbs and lined up like tenant housing. The intense lighting bled into the night skies. Horses neighed or kicked impatiently at their doors. It was breakfast time. The racket echoed beneath the wide rooftop eaves that protected their stalls from the elements.

Michael hid in a corner stall leased by Palmieri Racing. It was difficult to be inconspicuous with a seventeen-hand racehorse breathing down your neck. He had made the mistake of giving the bay gelding a Lifesaver Wintermint. One is never enough, especially for a Thoroughbred with a sweet tooth.

In the shed row across from him, three stalls down, Anaba Raines stood in the doorway. Shrugging into a weathered, black duster, she ran her hands beneath the collar to free her shoulder-length mane of dreadlocks. They fell across the back of her leather coat. Her black skin defied the harsh light. The peculiar effect made her appear darker, as if she were a mutinous shadow refusing to be expelled.

Michael recognized her from a boot camp graduation picture taken six years ago. He looked down at an image he'd been sent on his phone. Her hair was shorter then, not worn in dreads. She was dressed in the distinctive Marine Corps dress blues. While her hairstyle had changed, the fierce, unrelenting gaze had not.

The word *DECEASED* was stamped in red at the bottom of the photo, yet she was alive and breathing. Or so the early morning tendrils of breath wafting above her head proved to his eyes.

"Are you sure you sent me the right file?" Michael whispered into a receiver at his neck.

"Raines, Anaba T., Gunnery Sergeant." Elijah's voice came through over the earpiece. "United States Marine Corps. MARSOC. Killed in action: Aleppo, Syria."

"For a dead Marine, she looks awfully healthy."

"You want her social security and serial number again? Cause that's about all I can give you. Every other line in her goddamned jacket's been blacked out and sent to redaction heaven."

Michael heard a rustling of paper on the other end of the line.

"To be honest, I'm waiting for the spooks in black to come get my ass for even pulling this shit off the server. So give me a situation report on this Raines and get out of there, Mike."

"Hold that thought." Stroking the gelding's neck, Michael used the horse as cover to peer farther down the shed row.

A team of grooms and riders assembled in a narrow junction between the barns. Four Thoroughbreds stood obediently among them. Chain shanks clanked noisily against the horses' metal bits. Unlike the other trainers gathering to take their horses to exercise, this group's attire was tattered, their equipment piecemeal and weathered.

An elderly man came out of a nearby stall and approached them with a slight sway in his gait. His face and head were covered by an indigo veil with only his eyes visible. The loose end of the veil hung from his stooped shoulders and talismans made of silver and cowrie shells swung from the fabric near his temples.

Carrying a crude, flat drum, he bowed his head respectfully to the group. They bowed to him in return, but prolonged the gesture, recognizing his station. Rhythmically, he drummed on the skin with crooked, arthritic fingers and began to sing in a low, mournful voice.

Michael held his breath to listen. Though he could read and speak Ancient Greek and Egyptian, he had not paid enough attention to the obscure languages of Africa.

The shaman ceased his drumming and handed the instrument to the nearest groom. Reaching into his gris-gris – the leather shamanic bag at his side – he pulled out a small bundle and then passed a lighter over it. The sweet scent of tobacco wafted into the air from a plume of smoke that rose from the dried leaves. Fanning the smoke over his head and in the direction of the group, the old man paused for a groom to settle a spooked horse.

"I call to the kel essuf." His voice was potent, stronger than the doddering old body from which it came. "I stand in your light for judgment, unburdened from this mortal weight by the wind that is your breath." He went to each supplicant and fanned the smoke over them. "Make me humble for I am weary from pride. Give me strength against my greatest enemy, who is not my brother, but myself." The shaman prayed the longest over Raines.

The wind shifted. Michael saw the flags over the security building flutter from an easterly to a westerly direction, dissipating the concentrated column of tobacco smoke that spiraled above Raines's head.

"I give you the four corners of the world, daughter," the shaman whispered.

Staring him in the eyes, Raines replied, "Because one cannot know where one will die."

"Yes. Now go and bring the thunder."

Assisted by grooms, four exercise riders got a leg-up onto the backs of the horses and headed for the track. Taking the reins of the rear horse, Raines looked up at the young rider. She stared at him until not only the boy, but Michael also, grew uncomfortable.

"This mare can't afford a jockey who doesn't believe in her." Raines caressed the Thoroughbred's neck. "Last chance, Ziri. Bring her in, or I bring you in."

A groom brought a wooden mounting block to Raines and a dark-colored horse. She placed a foot in the stirrup and confidently mounted in one fluid motion. As an avid equestrian, Michael was accomplished enough to recognize her level of familiarity and skill. Pausing only long enough to tie a few strands of her dreadlocks from her face, the Marine donned a crash helmet, tightened the girth, and followed the other horses onto the track. The horses and riders disappeared from view behind the maintenance office.

Michael slipped out of the stall and hurried through the labyrinthine paths between the shed row barns to the upper decks of a private spectator promenade. A network of dynamic stadium arrays flooded the nearby track, creating a false semblance of daylight.

"EJ, is it possible Raines has a twin sister?"

"She's the only child of Ira Lee Dixon and Annie Mae Raines of Mobile, Alabama. Both deceased," Elijah replied. "The New York Racing Association has no record of her: not as an owner, not as a licensed trainer, not even as a groom or jockey."

"Yet everybody here seems to know exactly who she is."

"Any record of her ceased three years ago with her death certificate. She's a ghost, Mike."

Michael scrolled through the Marine's file information on his phone. "With this many combat ribbons and service commendations, I don't see a motive, partner."

"Don't need a motive when you work for the CIA. Her file has spook written all over it."

A high-pitched whistle pierced the night, followed by the muffled thunder of hooves on turf. Michael watched the closely packed herd of three horses fighting for position along the inside rail. They were trailing behind a fourth horse, ridden by the youngster Raines had chastised. Leading them by nearly five lengths, the boy stood up in the stirrups and pumped a fist in victory.

"We need her for questioning, EJ," Michael said. "I'm bringing her in."

"Agreed, but maybe you need to hang back. Let me call in a team to back you up."

"No, no, partner, too loud." Michael made his way down from the bleachers and back toward the shed row. "I'll handle this myself."

The four Thoroughbreds cantered on down the track to cool out. Raines trotted up to the security gate behind them. A fine steam rolled off the horse's flanks as she dismounted and handed the reins to a groom. She removed her crash helmet and tucked it beneath her arm before retreating into the training yard.

Michael followed her at a distance. He considered himself an expert at surveillance, adept at the art of blending in, but she was better. Though he kept to the shadows, Raines eluded him. Peering through the darkened windows of the maintenance office, he caught a glimpse of her through the paned glass as she stepped into a building labeled as a quarantine area.

"Mike, what's the sitrep?" Elijah said.

"I think she made me."

"Not too late to hang back."

"I'm too close."

Michael slipped through the doors to the quarantine barn. The four stalls inside were vacant. The vet's office in the corner was dark. Stacked straw bales blocked the rear door. There was no way out except the way he had come in. Raines was nowhere in sight.

"Hello?" Michael called to the darkness. "Miss Raines?"

"Who the hell are you? And why are you following me?"

Michael could not get a bearing on where she was hiding. He cleared the four empty stalls and stared into the wooden eaves above him. "FBI Special Agent Michael Childs." He produced his badge and held it up as he slowly circled the floor of the small barn. "Just want to talk, gunny."

"About what?"

"There's been a murder in Manhattan."

"There are several hundred murders in Manhattan every day, Special Agent Childs," she replied. "It's called the stock market. You can read the obits in the Wall Street Journal."

"The victim was a school teacher named Mary Klinedinst. Your name was written on the back of a racing form found with her body." Michael looked cautiously about him, unable to discern where her voice was coming from. "I just have a few questions, gunny."

"Stop calling me that."

"Okay, how about Anaba?"

"Now you're just being rude."

Michael heard movement in the eaves above him, but was too slow to react. She landed behind him and caught him with a roundhouse kick to the jaw. He reached for his service weapon, but his right hand went abruptly numb when the Marine jammed her elbow into his collarbone, almost dislocating his shoulder. Michael threw a left hook, but she blocked with a forearm and slammed her crash helmet into his face.

Moving with preternatural reflexes, the Marine locked Michael's arm at the elbow to use as leverage. He was at her mercy. She turned her back on him, pulled him against her, and threw the back of her head into his face. Blood splattered from both his nostrils. She followed up with an elbow strike between his eyes.

The acrid taste of blood brought a sense of urgency that cleared the stars from his vision. But only momentarily. Raines flipped him with a foot sweep and swung him about like a rag doll. Michael collided face first into the metal trim of a stall door. Stumbling into the stall, he collapsed in the ankle-deep sawdust inside.

Raines was unrelenting. She grabbed Michael by the neck with both hands and slammed him against the wall.

"Anaba, don't!" It was the boy from the exercise yard. "What if he doesn't know?"

"Doesn't know what?" she hissed.

"Doesn't know what he is. If you kill him, you're no better than the amanɣi hunting his tribe."

Michael felt her grip slacken. Slamming her knee into his balls, she left him gasping in the sawdust.

"If you know what's good for you, Special Agent Childs, forget my name. Forget that I exist." She raised her boot over his head, then viciously stomped him in the face.

It was midmorning when he awoke. What little light there was came filtered through the windows of the quarantine barn and cut through the darkness behind his eyelids. Ears ringing, Michael rolled to his side and sat up in the sawdust.

"EJ?" he said. There was no response over the comm. He pulled the mic closer to his mouth and repeated, "EJ, you there?" The connection was lost. With the earpiece now useless, he yanked the unit out of his ear and jammed it into his coat pocket.

He stood up, gripping his knees for balance, and took slow, deliberate breaths before straightening. Archaic symbols were now scrawled in blood on the back wall. The glyphs surrounding the rudimentary image of a cross looked similar to those found at his previous crime scenes.

"What the hell?"

"You all right, mister?" Glancing over his shoulder, Michael saw a freckle-faced girl in a pink crash helmet peering at him through the stall bars. And then he noticed a dozen anxious faces also gawking at him from the barn aisle.

"What the hell are you doing in there?" shouted a security guard. "We piss-test horses, not people!"

His mouth was dry, but Michael found his voice and his badge. "FBI," he croaked. "This is a crime scene. I need to call for backup."

"Your backup's already here," the guard replied.

"Mike!" Elijah yelled, hurrying through the barn entrance with three NYPD officers.

"EJ, thank God!" Michael was relieved to see a familiar face. He leaned against a stall door, exhaustion swamping him. "Get these people out of here. We've got another crime scene."

"You heard the man. Back the hell up out of here!" Elijah ordered. He pointed to the nearest cop. "I want names, addresses, and witness statements on everybody who was in here." He turned back to Michael, examining his bloody face. "I let you question a person of interest, and you decide to go three rounds with her? Have you lost your damn mind?"

"She got the jump on me."

"What part of *special forces* did you not understand? I'm calling a bus."

"For a black eye and a busted lip? No." Michael sat down on a stack of hay bales and gingerly dabbed at his lip. "Do me a favor. Get some pics of those symbols on the wall while I clean myself up." Michael stumbled over to the sink outside the vet's office. Turning on both spigots, he let the water run over his hands and splashed it over his face.

Elijah adjusted the magnification on his phone to capture the glyphs on the wall. "These markings look similar to the ones carved into our victims' faces. Maybe Raines *does* have motive after all." He shrugged. "We just don't know what it is yet."

"Anaba Raines isn't our killer, partner, but she's connected. She knows something."

"Of course she knows something," Elijah replied, glaring at him. "That's why your face looks like that."

"Raines is a blunt instrument. She's a Marine. She gets the job done." Michael stretched his bruised neck to alleviate the stiffness at the base of his skull. "Our killer likes to take his time. It's the torture, not the kill."

"I'm putting a BOLO out on her."

"No." Closing his eyes, he fought down a wave of nausea. "That'll just spook her."

"She could have killed you, Mike."

"But she didn't." Michael cupped his hands in the water and drank. He swished it around his mouth then spat the bloody water out in the sink. His phone chimed with an alert. He glanced at the screen. "Shit!"

"What's up?"

"It's my mom." Michael leaned over the sink and did his best to keep from vomiting. "I'm supposed to meet her for lunch to talk about those pictures I sent from the crime scene."

"With your face looking like that? Better think about cancelling."

"She may have some answers. I have to go." Michael reached into his pocket and popped the last Lifesaver Wintermint into his mouth. "Find out whose blood is on that back wall."

"I got this. Go before I decide to kick your ass, too."

"Thanks, EJ. Text me the results."

CHAPTER 3

Michael was twenty minutes late, a cardinal sin in the book of Dr Serra Childs. Despite it being midday, traffic on First Avenue was gridlocked. At the entrance of Little Corsica, he tossed his keys to the valet and hurried inside the Italian restaurant, bracing himself for the maternal interrogation.

She was sitting at their usual table, overlooking a rose garden with a basket of breadsticks and a cup of freshly brewed Earl Grey tea. Her graying sisterlocks were immaculate, braided and coiled about her head like a crown. At the sight of him, she frowned. "Michael Jered Childs, what has happened to your face?"

"I caught a lance in the helmet." He leaned over and kissed her cheek. "It's nothing."

She ran her fingers delicately over the bruise beneath his eye. "If you're going to lie to me, at least make it a *good* story. Honestly, Michael. What have you gotten yourself into this time?"

"Mom, please." He sat down in the chair across from her. "My job at the Bureau isn't always sitting behind a desk."

"Don't you *mom* me." Having ordered for them, Serra lowered her voice as the waiter arrived to serve their meal. When they were alone, she scowled at him. "Does the arrangement on your face have anything to do with these?" She laid out a file folder on the table between them.

"It's an unusual case, and I needed an unusual perspective." Michael thumbed through the familiar images of his crime scene. "Ever seen a ritual like this in your field work?"

"I have." She unwrapped her silverware and laid the cloth napkin over her lap. Michael waited for her to expand on her statement, but she did not. His mother always enjoyed an intellectual guessing-game.

"Ancient Sumerian?" he prompted.

"Much older. Antediluvian Period – a time that predates the Great Flood," she said, sipping her red wine. "The script here is Enochian."

"Any chance you can read it?" Michael grabbed a breadstick and dipped it into his lasagna.

"It's the Ritual of Descarbia, an ancient rebuke: *Father, I humbly undo what was defiantly done against Your Holy Word and cast this corrupted flesh from the Light forever.*"

Michael felt the same chill he'd experienced when entering a recently unearthed tomb as a graduate student. "Sounds ominous."

"The carvings on the face are profanities meant to denigrate the victim, torturing them in this life and marking the soul for persecution in the next. The outstretched arms suggest she is reaching for something that can never be obtained. The clay jar represents this world – absolution, mortality. I'm guessing there were remains inside?"

Michael confirmed her question with a nod. "He burns the tongue and the eyelids."

"Without a tongue, the soul can never confess its sins or ask forgiveness. But that isn't what killed her, is it?" Dr Childs stared into his eyes, reprimanding him in a way that words could not. "What is it you're not telling me?"

"Alright," Michael said, deciding to ignore all protocols against sharing the sensitive details of an ongoing investigation. "She died from some kind of severe allergic reaction."

His mother raised an eyebrow. "Go on."

"What I'm about to tell you hasn't been released to the public, so I need you to keep it quiet, Mom. Not even idle talk in the university faculty room, okay?"

Her eyes narrowed at the insinuation. "I wouldn't dare."

"Good. Last night, the perp claimed a third victim," he said. "As far as I can tell, the only connection between them is that they were born with twelve fingers and toes. And that they're dead."

"Nephilim," Serra breathed, her nostrils flaring subtly. It was a tell that betrayed her keen interest.

During his graduate work, Michael had studied biblical myths with his mother at Oxford. Sects of the Christian faithful believed that after the fall of Adam, a few of God's angels visited His Creation. Seduced by the beauty of human men and women, the angels transgressed the natural law and mated with them. Their children were the Nephilim, born with twelve fingers and toes.

"One of the victims had surgery as an infant to remove the sixth digits," Michael continued. "The other two, including the woman murdered last night, did not." He watched the perplexed expression on her face.

"The surgery was so they could fit in without calling attention to themselves." Serra held up the crime scene photos to scrutinize them. "You know how people can be cruel when someone stands out as different."

Michael pulled her arms back down to the table to prevent fellow diners from seeing the graphic images with their dinner. He smiled at the annoyed glares of the maître d', who walked by at that moment.

"Not every Nephilim was born human," Dr Childs explained. "Many were grotesque giants. Misshapen cannibals. The more radical Christian factions believed that God sent the flood, in the time of Noah, not only to punish mankind, but to rid the world of these aberrations and His wayward angels who lived among them."

Michael saw the distant, pensive look in his mother's eyes as she studied the pictures. "Mom, what's wrong?"

"There shall be no burial for them nor any to mourn their passing, for they shall be as the Father intended, never to have existed."

"Is that a line of scripture?"

"From a Book of Genesis that few have ever seen."

Michael rolled his eyes. "Not that Vatican conspiracy again."

"It's not a conspiracy, Michael. Because of the sins of their parents, the Nephilim can never go to Heaven. They walk between worlds." Serra folded her napkin and laid it on the table. "There are few mercies granted to sinners in the afterlife. Closing the eyes to block out the vision of suffering is one of them. By removing the eyelids and burning them, the killer has taken that away." She pointed to the photo. "The wings carved from the victim's flesh are a mockery of the Nephilim's angelic heritage." She paused briefly. "It's odd, you know? *You* were born with twelve fingers and toes." Serra took Michael's right hand and massaged the nearly imperceptible scar. "Your father insisted on amputation so that you wouldn't stand out. I didn't argue." She tilted her head and smiled, twisting her finger around an unruly dreadlock near his face. "In my eyes, you were perfect."

"Not perfect enough to keep him from walking out on us."

Her eyes narrowed, the affection stripped away by his candor. "Our parting was a *mutual* agreement. It was made in our best interests *and* yours."

It was not an argument he would win. Eager to change the mood and the topic, Michael pushed his phone across the table. "Do you recognize these symbols?"

"You have the minor in linguistics. You figure it out." His mother adjusted the napkin on her lap and picked up her utensils, switching her attention to her plate. She had an uncanny ability to change gears like that, suddenly blocking people out.

"Mom!"

"Michael Childs, either you start leveling with me, or I'm not saying another word. You can start with an explanation for your face."

Her eyes were cold. Michael looked away, but surrender was inevitable. "I got into a fight this morning while investigating a lead at Belmont Park. I lost. Badly." He took a swallow of his wine and his ruined pride. "When I came to, I was lying in a horse stall. This symbol –" he handed her his phone "– and these glyphs were written in blood on the back wall."

Serra paused and let the silence settle around them. "Remember when I asked you to do your internship with me in Mali, instead of London?"

Michael blinked, unsure of the relevance.

"You should have listened," she finished, dryly. Serra turned her attention to Michael's phone and studied the digital picture with interest, zooming in and out. "This is the Tuareg Cross of Air. The writing is Tifinagh, the signary of Tamasheq. Beautifully rendered."

"Tuareg?" he asked, still feeling like an intern in her presence. "I saw an old shaman blessing the riders and the horses at Belmont. He was wearing a blue tagelmust. He started the invocation by calling on the kel essuf."

"You, my son, stumbled across an ămud," she whispered. "A prayer to summon the spirits and curry their favor." Ignoring her pasta alla norma, she carefully studied the images.

"You almost sound jealous," Michael said with a chuckle. "I thought the Tuareg were Muslim, not Pagan."

"I am quite envious, and yes the majority are Muslim. But there's a small population of Tuareg who hold to their shamanistic beliefs, which pre-date Islam and Christianity." She slid the phone back across the table. "This has nothing to do with your case."

Unconvinced, Michael re-examined the photos from the quarantine barn. "So, it's not like the Enochian at my crime scenes?"

"Whoever drew this ălbăraka – the Tuareg cross – wasn't trying to harm you. This is a blessing: *let him not be abandoned.* They were trying to protect you."

"Why the blood?"

"An attempt to make the ălbăraka more powerful. If I had to guess, that isn't human blood. Probably a goat."

Michael buried his face in his hand and closed his eyes. "This is why I didn't follow you to Mali. Cataloguing medieval weapons and armor was way easier than keeping up with your understanding of obscure cultures."

"Michael, this is not a competition. There's too much for one person to know. Think of Enochian as a complex alphabet of signatures. The sigils come from an ancient grimoire known as the *Keys of Solomon*. By themselves or combined, they trigger specific arcane effects." Serra reached into her purse for a magnifying glass. "The innermost circle is dominated by the Sigil of Iofiel, the same seal of resurrection that was found on Christ's tomb. But it has been intentionally perverted. As written here, the signature represents banishment."

"Whose signatures?"

"The Elohim."

"Angels? Mom, seriously? This sounds like a plot for a new Harry Potter book."

"Michael, whoever committed these unspeakable acts has an intimate knowledge of Enochian lore." Serra set down her magnifying glass. "Was there an oily substance found at the scene?"

"How did you–" He pulled the evidence bag from his pocket and handed it to her with a latex glove.

She put on the glove and picked up the vial. Then, with the deliberate care of an experienced archaeologist, twisted the lid off and peered inside.

"We keep finding this substance at the scene and on the victims. Toxicology says it's a harmless mixture of herbs–"

"Hardly harmless. This is what caused the severe allergic

reaction in your victims. Anaphylactic shock, I'll wager?" Serra sniffed the cap. "This is qeres, an ancient funerary oil. You'd no more rub this into your skin than embalming fluid. It's toxic."

"Didn't older women in the eighteenth century use embalming fluid to improve their looks?"

"And they looked great – *at their funerals.*" Tightening the cap, she wrapped the glove around the vial as if the contents were radioactive. "Get this to a qualified, *academic* lab for analysis, and whatever you do, don't touch it."

"Mom, a qualified, academic lab *has* seen it, and it's a harmless–"

"Michael Childs, do not touch that substance!" Serra said. "Forget that you're married to your job and listen to your mother! Promise me that you will not touch it!"

The random chatter in the dining area dimmed in response to her raised voice. Fellow patrons cast curious glances in their direction. Her agitated manner unsettled him. "Fine!" Michael said, throwing his napkin on the table in frustration. "I promise."

"I mean it, Michael."

"Mom, I promise you that I will not touch the goddamn qeres."

Michael's phone rang, thankfully interrupting their heated discussion. The caller ID read: *St. Joseph's Rectory*. "I need to take this," he said, leaving the table and escaping to the coatroom. "Special Agent Childs," he answered.

"Agent Childs, this is Father Patrick Paige from St. Joseph of the Merciful Heart."

"What can I do for you, Father Paige?"

"I was wondering if we could talk. Here at the church. Sometime this evening? Say, six?"

There was a confidence in the priest's voice as if the decision had already been made. "Can I ask what this is about?"

"Mary Klinedinst was one of my parishioners."

The name of one of the murder victims piqued Michael's interest. "I'm sorry for your loss. How long had she been part of the church?"

"All of her life. Which makes it imperative that I see you right away."

"Father, I've got some important paperwork I need to attend to, and I'm on a deadline." It wasn't a lie. He needed to put in a call to a federal judge to get a subpoena for hospital records that were imperative to the investigation. "Can I send another agent or an officer from your local precinct?"

"Agent Childs, I'm also very well acquainted with one Anaba Raines."

Michael's chest tightened. "What do you know about her?"

"She's not what you think she is. Can I count on seeing you at six? Come early if you like. The confessional will be open until 5:30."

"I'll be there."

Michael hung up and returned to the table. He sat down heavily in his chair.

"Michael?" his mother asked. "You look like you've seen a ghost."

"I may have," he replied, looking up to meet her worried eyes, "and if I play my cards right, I may see her again."

"*Her*?" The cold demeanor of the academician faded at the potential prospect of an unknown girlfriend. "Something I need to know, son?"

"No, Mom. Would you mind if we skip dessert? Something's come up. I need to head uptown." Michael tossed a hundred-dollar bill on the table and signaled the waiter.

"Only if you promise to spend some quality time with your family this the weekend."

Michael frowned, about to protest but Serra cut ahead of him. "Otherwise," she said, "I see that Chef Ramsey has some lovely carrot cake on the dessert tray over there. I know how you much you love his carrot cake." Grinning impishly, she took a sip of tea from her cup.

Defeated, he threw his head back and closed his eyes. "You win, Mom. See you this weekend."

CHAPTER 4

Surrounded by academic degrees framed in African blackwood, Moses Rathan sat in his office contemplating the whim of irony. The vain accoutrements were modeled after his predecessor, the former FBI Director-In-Charge: a faithless human seeking godhood through the acquisition of power. Even as the last breath was wrested from his body, the fool believed he had control of his destiny.

Levithmong, Rathan thought. In Enochian, the word was a divisive term for mankind. *There is only one true God,* he lamented. *And He is deeply flawed. Blinded by His love for a lesser creature made of clay.*

A remarkably handsome being – as most angels were – Rathan was fastidious about his appearance. His black skin cast a dark illumination that rivaled his custom-tailored suit. The subtle wash of gray in the precise trim of his goatee accentuated his noble features and matched his closely cropped hair.

The surname Rathan was a misnomer. Rathaniel was his given name. He was the Fifth Commander of the Grigori, a disgraced legion assigned to oversee the Creation – the world that God built – after the Fall of Man. *Glorified janitors.*

Brushing a thumb pensively across his wide lips, he studied the crime scene pictures of the most recent homicide. From the refined calligraphy of the Enochian profanities to the surgical removal of the eyes and tongue, the killer's handiwork was quite exquisite.

A knock at the door distracted him. Rathan closed the file folder and looked up as his administrative assistant peeked inside the door. "Sorry to disturb you, Assistant Director."

"What is it, Chelsea?" He sat back in his chair and pretended to be annoyed by the intrusion.

"Special Agent McKabe is here to speak with you."

"Send him in." Rathan sat motionless, betraying no emotion as the agent stepped into the office and closed the door. "Agent McKabe," he said, rising from his chair to offer his hand.

"Assistant Director Rathan, I got your message." McKabe accepted Rathan's greeting, clasping his forearm. "I trust you're pleased?"

Rathan opened the file folder and spread the photos across his desk. "Another excellent display, Kokabiel. You've become quite the consummate practitioner of the Ritual of Descarbia."

McKabe adjusted the perfect symmetrical knot of his tie and brushed aside a strand of blond hair, feigning modesty. He scanned the gallery of pictures with the eye of a smug artist looking for imperfections. "Another filthy Nephilim laid low. It was my duty and my honor."

Rathan sat down and studied the top photo, holding it up to the lamp at the corner of his desk. "I've not seen this kind of expertise since the Battle of Mahorela."

"When our garrison slaughtered Lucifer's frontline? Good times. May the urches be forever damned." McKabe sat down on the chair opposite the director and crossed his legs. "Still, Rathaniel, the Ritual of Descarbia was meant for the Fallen. True angels. Its use gives far more ceremony than these half-breeds deserve."

"So long as the Nephilim suffer – in this life and the next. That's all that matters."

McKabe rubbed his hands together. His smile took on a sardonic, almost sadistic countenance. "The last one suffered greatly, clinging to her faith and her prayers like a shield as if the Father would protect her." He scrutinized his manicured fingernails. "She had far more spirit than the first. *He* died whimpering and begging for his pitiful life. Took the joy right out of it."

"And the soldier?"

"The urch had the audacity to fight back. Nearly took Valac's eye. Must be true what they say of these Marines." His grin deepened with malevolence. "I took special delight in carving a few *extra* obscenities into his flesh. Nearly depleted my stores of qeres too." McKabe leaned forward, propped an elbow on his thigh, and massaged his chin. "What about Childs? When will it be his turn?"

"In time, brother. The Grigori have only recently established our presence here in the FBI. No need to risk it by being too ambitious."

"Is it wise keeping him so close? What if he actually manages to catch a lead and uncovers what we're doing here?"

"We'll continue feeding him just enough to keep him and his partner chasing their tails," Rathan said. "They have proven themselves useful hounds in flushing out the others."

"You're playing a dangerous game, Rathaniel. What if he is the Qaaon? We should kill him now."

"You give him far too much credit."

"Perhaps you give him too little. His presence is an affront to the entire garrison." McKabe lowered his eyes to avoid Rathan's glare. "I do not mean to overstep my boundaries, Fifth Commander. But if Childs should inadvertently discover his lineage–"

"He won't."

"Which is why we should kill him and eliminate any chance of that happening! Don't forget the prophecy! *A Nephilim will rise to the ranks of the Four Afflictions.* All he needs is the weapon–"

"Do you hear yourself, Kokabiel!" Rathan slammed his fists against the desktop. "You sound like the very levithmong we have been forced to live with! Always looking for signs and omens! Always misinterpreting them to what best suits their pathetic desires."

"Perhaps the matter should be brought before the other garrison commanders?" McKabe suggested.

"Their vote put me in charge of the legion, Kokabiel! I don't need their permission to act as I see fit. Now clear your mind of such troubling details. There is work to be done."

Dabbing at his forehead with a silk handkerchief, McKabe took a deep breath and exhaled. "Forgive me, brother."

"There is nothing to forgive. Your fear is understandable, but misplaced. We will fulfill the edict handed down to us. The Nephilim will be eradicated."

"I did not mean to question your judgment," McKabe said, his tone subdued. "Maoffras restil."

"Yes, brother, we shall praise Him and our praise shall be immeasurable." Rathan raised his chin, stretching his neck to relieve the tension in his shoulders. "I understand your trepidation and I am not beyond your counsel, Kokabiel. If you truly feel Childs has outlived his usefulness, send Nuriel and two others, but not to kill him. We need to discuss the next sacrifice."

McKabe grinned, the spark returning to his eyes. "Thank you for your trust."

Rathan nodded. "Go. Make the necessary preparations."

CHAPTER 5

Michael glanced at his watch. The local streets were deserted. It was nearly 5:30pm, and he was running late with no chance of beating the uptown traffic from SoHo to the Bronx. Exasperated, he hung his dry cleaning on the garment hook in the back of the Jeep. The heavy, custom-made surcoat and gambeson bent the wire hanger, tumbling onto a pile of leather armor and jousting equipment.

Precariously perched on the edge of the back seat, his practice sword fell out of the car. The hilt clanged noisily on the asphalt at his feet. When he stooped to retrieve it, he saw a pair of weathered, black paddock boots by the corner of the rear bumper.

"Anaba Raines, you're under arrest!" He snatched the Glock 19M from its holster and stood up, taking aim. "Hands up where I can see them!"

"I'm not the one you need to be worried about," she said, keeping her hands in her pockets. "They are."

Pressing his back against the Jeep for cover, Michael kept the gun trained on her. He glanced over his shoulder and saw two white men and a Black woman approaching from the other side of the street. Casually dressed in jeans and sneakers, the pedestrians appeared to be out for an evening of bar-hopping, with one exception: the gray wings rising above their shoulders.

Keeping the gun raised in warning, Michael turned to face them. *The fuck?* He shook his head in disbelief and squeezed his eyes closed to readjust his vision. Clearly he had suffered a concussion while fighting with Raines. But... the wings did not fade away.

The trio advanced, tactically, in a semi-circle formation, pulling curved talwaars from their concealed scabbards on their backs. Etched into the fuller of the blades, Enochian glyphs glowed with a fierce, golden illumination.

"We're not here for you, ripir," the woman said to Anaba. Her hazel eyes and face were framed within a mane of intricate braids and gold talismans. "Flee while you still can."

Michael flashed his credentials. "Federal Agent! Stay where you are!"

Exchanging an amused glance, the two men continued walking toward him. When the first raised his sword, Michael fired two shots into his chest. The hollow-points caused no more than a reflexive hesitation from the impact. A thin trickle of blood dripped across the man's gray Black Veil Brides t-shirt.

The second man tackled Michael, slamming him against the Jeep's open door with enough force to knock the wind out of him. "Come along quietly, half-breed."

Gasping for breath, Michael collapsed to the ground. The gun was knocked from his hand and clattered to the street behind the front tire of the Jeep. He strained to reach it, desperately, but could just feel the grip against his fingertips.

"Gun's not going to work," Raines said, her hands still in her pockets. "Not against them." There was a hint of a smile in one corner of her mouth as if she were enjoying the spectacle.

Michael grabbed the only weapon within reach: his sword. "I'm open to suggestions." He curled into a fetal ball beneath the SUV's door as a talwaar landed in the street where his feet had been. Sparks and shattered asphalt peppered his face from the force of the impact.

"Running works." Raines forced back the assailant standing

over Michael with a spinning wheel kick to the chin. Reeling from the blow, he stumbled back into his companions. She yanked Michael to his feet and ran for the alley.

"This morning you tried to kill me," Michael panted. "And now you're helping me?"

The Marine was fast, navigating the concrete labyrinth with agility and confidence like she was in a combat zone. He struggled to keep up with her.

"If it weren't for Ziri, you wouldn't be breathing," Raines said, crouching down at a corner to assess the area ahead. "You can thank him later, if we survive this."

"Who are those people? Some kind of homicidal cosplayers?" Michael sank down beside her to watch for signs of pursuit behind them.

"Did the wings and the resistance to hollow points not give it away?" Raines skirted a privacy fence, signaling with a closed fist for him to stop. "They're angels."

"Angels? I'm having a little trouble believing–"

"I don't give a shit what you believe. I couldn't care less if these guys gutted you and left you in the street. Father Paige sent me to make certain you got to the church. Just need to play a little fox and hound to give Ziri enough time to hotwire your Jeep."

"Hotwire my Jeep?"

"Got your key with you?"

Michael fumbled in his pocket. His apartment keys rattled against the Jeep's ignition fob. "Yeah, why wouldn't – oh fuck."

"Like I said, the kid needs a little time." Anaba pulled the vibrating phone from her back pocket. "Yeah? I got him. No, stay clear. There's three of them," she said in an authoritative tone. "I don't care if you're out of practice. Get that Jeep started and get your ass over here!" She shoved the phone back into her jeans.

"Raines, what the hell is going on?"

"Should have fucking killed you when I had the chance," the Marine swore under her breath. With no warning, Raines was on her feet and shoved him against the wall. "You better nut up, Special Agent Childs. We're not role-playing here!" She cut her eyes to the left as a shadowy, winged figure stepped from the darkness into the street light.

Michael followed her eyes to the right and saw the other two angels; they were trapped.

"They're going to take you and kill me, if they get the chance. I hope you know how to use that," Raines said, glancing down at the longsword Michael held.

Michael drew the sword from its scabbard. He adjusted his grip on the hilt by curling his index finger over the guard and assumed the boar's tooth stance with confidence. "I can handle myself."

"No matter what you see, fight as if your life depends on it." Raines stood back-to-back with him.

"Are you even armed?" An overwhelming stench of rotten eggs circulated in the damp air. Michael coughed, breathing in the noxious odor. "What's that smell?"

The Marine didn't respond. She roughly bumped him, almost knocking him to the ground. He shrugged off her silence as the angel with the gunshot wound moved on him.

"You don't want to do this, partner," Michael warned.

Brandishing the talwaar in his left hand, the angel twirled the exceptional blade over the back of his hand and lunged at him. The forward thrust was aggressive, not seeking to test, but to directly penetrate his defenses.

Michael blocked him. Caught off guard by the explosive power behind the strike, he clenched his teeth as his wrists were wrenched into a painful position to absorb the impact. The talwaar gouged the edge of his longsword and left a deep groove in the steel. He parried the next blow with the flat of the blade to protect it from further damage. Feinting a retreat, he pirouetted and deftly slipped behind his opponent.

Narrowly avoiding the angel's thrashing wings, Michael sliced his sword across his left flank. Sparks flew from the contact like flint drawn across steel.

Michael stared through the tear in the t-shirt, gawking at the prime, pink flesh beneath it. There was no sign of injury. No blood. Only a simple line of red marked his stroke. "What the fuck?"

"Levithmong. Time to die!" The angel lunged with the talwaar.

Michael spun on his heel and deflected the heavier blade. Falling to instincts honed in unarmed combat, he reached beneath the crossed blades and twisted the angel's wrist. Superior strength meant little without the proper leverage and the joint lock forced the angel to relinquish the sword.

Before the talwaar hit the ground, Michael grabbed the hilt and buried the blade in the angel's torso. Mouth agape, the angel faltered, dropping to a knee.

"Yield!" Michael shouted. It was the safe word, the prelude to the tap out that ended every match.

Blood spilled from the jutting lip of the wound and from the corners of the angel's mouth. His eyes widened, not in fear, but recognition. "Kill the Nightmare! He draws strength from it." He yanked a dagger from a sheath hidden beneath his pant leg.

Michael countered by burying the talwaar's blade up to the hilt in the angel's abdomen and gave it a savage twist. With his face skewed in pain and disbelief, the angel collapsed to the damp asphalt at Michael's feet.

Hands trembling, Michael stepped away in horror. He had fired his service weapon at numerous perpetrators, even wounded a few. But he had never taken a life. The experience was everything he had ever read about in Psychology at Quantico, the FBI academy, and the Ancient Greek texts in his mother's library – personal, visceral, binding.

The angel's body flushed with a strange, ethereal light and then crumbled inward on itself as if his flesh were a sandcastle left to the mercy of the tide. Michael dropped the talwaar, and, after a brief spark of light, it also was rendered unto dust.

The scent of sulfur still permeated the air. Its source came from a creature now occupying the place where Raines had stood. A magnificent black horse walked from a cloud of brimstone and molten flecks. Striking her hoof against the asphalt, the mare's legs burst into flame. The blaze sent waves of light and heat through the alley and ignited a conflagration in her mane and tail. *"Kill the Nightmare,"* the angel had said to his companions. Michael stood transfixed, only now understanding what he meant.

With a squeal that reverberated in the confines of the alley, the mare charged the remaining angels. Momentum and her greater mass knocked both to the asphalt in a jumble of wings and arms and legs. Losing his balance in the assault, the male angel found himself pinned beneath her fiery hooves. He gasped beneath the weight and tightened his desperate fingers on the hilt of his sword to slash at her legs.

The warhorse reared back, more in defense than in pain, and the angel took to his wings to escape. One downstroke launched him six feet into the night. Leaping after him on her powerful hind legs, the mare caught him by the ankle with her teeth. She threw her head down and sideways, bludgeoning the female angel with the body of her companion.

With a savagery that made Michael wince, the mare slammed him against the cornerstone of the building. The brick support-column cracked under the violence. The angel went limp, his back bent in an unnatural angle. The mare dropped him. His shattered body fell to the street with the sound of rocks rattling in a plastic bottle.

"You are an abomination!" the female angel gasped, glaring at Michael, sputtering blood with every syllable. "You were never meant to be!" She raised her sword in a gesture of defiance, looking down at her fallen companion, but hesitated to cross paths with the warhorse standing between them.

Disdainfully, the horse sniffed the air above the dying angel's face. One of the mare's large, black eyes rolled back in Michael's direction to see if he was watching. With a guttural squeal, she arced her powerful neck, lunged downward, and snatched the angel by the throat. Charged brimstone billowed from her nostrils into his anguished face.

The celestial's neck blackened, severely charred by the suffocating vapor. As he coughed up bile and smoke, one flailing wing cuffed the horse in the head. When this feeble attempt did not break her hold, he clawed at the mare's face. In retaliation, the warhorse shook him viciously, like a hound shaking a hare. Muzzle covered in gore, she relinquished her hold. The angel's corpse was reduced to ash in a blast of flame from her legs.

"They will be avenged!" the remaining angel growled. She sheathed the curved sword between her wings and leaped into the darkness. The sound of her wings beating against the night air echoed faintly in the alleyway.

Cowardly cunt.

Michael heard Anaba's voice distinctly, though it felt like no more than a scratching in the back of his mind.

A cloud of brimstone enveloped the warhorse, consuming her in a funnel of shadows and fire. When the spirited flames dissipated, Anaba emerged from the dense black smoke in human form.

"Anaba?" Breathing deliberately through his nose to control himself, Michael stared at her in horror. "What in the hell is going on here!"

"I don't have any answers for you, Agent Childs," Anaba replied with evident contempt. "But congratulations on popping your cherry. You just killed your first angel."

The screech of skidding tires nearly drowned out her voice. A familiar Jeep Cherokee careened around a convoy of parked cars and came to a halt in the mouth of the alley. Michael recognized the driver – it was the young rider he saw at Belmont Park.

"If you can't tell me what's going on, then answer this," he said, pointing the longsword in her direction. "What the hell are you?"

"Complicated," she replied with menace. "Now get in the car."

"Just wait a minute," he protested, grabbing her arm.

The Marine pivoted in an instant, twisting his arm until he was on his knees. When he dropped his sword hand to the ground to slow his fall, she deftly stepped on the blade to prevent him from using it. "Don't touch me! Don't you *ever* fucking touch me! I will kill you!"

He believed her. Michael held a hand up in surrender, gritting his teeth as she wrenched the tendons in his shoulder.

"Get in the godddamn car." She released him and walked behind the Jeep.

Shoving his jousting gear out of the way, Michael tossed his practice sword onto the floorboards and climbed into the backseat. He slammed the damaged door and wedged it into the frame with some effort. "Are you even old enough to legally drive?" he asked the boy sitting in the driver's seat.

"Government man has jokes," he said with a smirk. He peered into the rearview mirror, the insincere grin fading. "I'm old enough to jack this piece of junk, ălfăsseq."

"What did you call me?" Michael leaned forward to get in the boy's face, but Anaba intercepted him.

"He called you a hypocrite," she growled. "You're a fucking Fed, so I'm inclined to agree." Spotting the glint of the ka-bar knife laying on her thigh, Michael sat back. If Anaba was as good with the knife as she was with her hands, he was unwilling to stake his life on provoking her. Especially after what he had witnessed.

As they sped away from the alley, his mind raced through the absurd logistics. The crime scene was in two locations, complicating any follow up investigation. Other than a bit of blood – mostly his – there would be little evidence to collect or process. Except for a handful of ash and degraded DNA, there were no bodies to send to the morgue for examination. The sole witness to the assault had flown away. The only hard evidence Michael had was sitting in the front passenger seat of his Jeep.

He imagined writing the report: *Suspect turned into a black horse with fiery hooves. The perp then engaged one of three winged suspects, killing one by tearing out his throat with her teeth. His body burst into flame, leaving just ash.* He cringed, imagining Rathan's acrimonious glare after reading it. Within twenty-four hours, Michael would be a laughing stock, sitting in the Bureau's psychiatrist office.

"She's not what you think she is," the priest had said on the phone. This was certainly true. A decorated Marine listed as killed in action, though no body was recovered. A person of interest in a high-profile murder investigation. A potential serial killer with multiple bodies left in her wake. It didn't add up. Intrigued, Michael could not take his eyes off her.

Barely turning her head, Raines cut her harsh eyes back to glare at him. "Is there a reason you're staring at me?"

"I think he likes you, anna." Ziri grinned, tapping out a beat on the steering wheel.

The Marine's stern eyes fell on the young driver. "When we get to the church, I think you need some time in the confessional."

"Why?" Ziri frowned.

"Because by then I'll have decided if I'm going to bury you in the same grave as the Fed."

CHAPTER 6

"Anaba, I got your message." Like the stoic, two hundred year-old Bronx church he served, Father Patrick Paige was a fit man for his age. Dressed in a black shirt and pants and a white clerical collar at his throat, he wore a threadbare, green cardigan. A gold cross and an attached medallion of St. Christopher was pinned to the breast. His unruly gray hair gleamed wet in the fluorescent lighting. "Thank the Almighty, you're safe!"

"The Almighty had little to do with it."

"I will not have you blaspheme, Anaba. Not here." As Michael warily walked into the rectory office, the priest hurried to the front of his desk. "Agent Childs, I presume?"

Michael accepted his offered hand and greeting. "Father Paige."

"I'm done here," Anaba said. She flippantly saluted the priest and turned to leave. "Bravo Zulu. I'm out."

"You're not going anywhere." Michael intercepted her. "You killed a man tonight!"

"They weren't men. I already told you. They were angels."

"You never mentioned Grigori!" Father Paige said. "Did you engage them?"

"Not like I had a choice. They were after him," Anaba said, pointing at Michael. "All he brought to the party was a Glock and some hollow points." She then glared at Ziri and flicked the boy's ear. "Give it back."

The boy flinched in surprise. Sighing, he slipped the Glock 19M from his pocket and contritely handed it back to Michael.

"You little delinquent!" Michael snatched the gun from his hand. Releasing the magazine, he cleared the chamber before jamming it into his holster. When he stooped to retrieve the ejected bullet, he saw blood splatter on the floor.

The trail was nearly imperceptible against the dark grain of the wood floor. The trace drops led from the rectory threshold to Anaba's paddock boots, where it was collecting in a small pool beside her left foot.

"You're hurt?" Michael reached for her shoulder.

The Marine punched him in the mouth. "Last warning! Don't ever touch me again!" She callously stepped by him and retreated into the corridor.

Michael shook the fog from his head. "Is she always like this?" He massaged his throbbing jaw.

Father Paige leaned back onto the edge of his desk, lips pursed in a thin line. He could not, however, hide the hint of a smile. "Tread lightly, Special Agent Childs. Where Anaba walks, peril usually follows."

"I like peril," Michael replied, briefly hesitating in the doorway. "That's why I joined the FBI."

St. Joseph's was a labyrinth of narrow corridors that smelled of stale incense, candle wax, and Murphy's Oil soap, the latter being the preservative that gave the wooden walls and floors of the church their luster. A light in an adjoining corridor led Michael to a women's restroom. Without any hesitation, he chased her into the lavatory. "What the fuck is your pro–"

Anaba was propped against the wash counter, standing in front of the mirror dressed in nothing more than jeans and a black sports bra. Her arms were lean and sinewy, her lower torso well defined with muscle. Carved into her flesh was the etching of two feathers forming an incomplete pinwheel that rose prominently from her left shoulder. One of the elaborate renderings was old and scarred. The other was fresh, inflamed, and still bleeding.

"Do you fucking mind?" She scowled at his unannounced intrusion.

"That's Enochian," he said, recognizing the distinctive script etched into the skin between each feather.

"Your point?"

"Similar glyphs were found at three recent murder scenes."

"And you think it was me?" Anaba snorted, cocking her head to one side. "I *am* a killer, Special Agent Childs, but I'm no murderer. If I was offing people born with twelve fingers and toes, your dumb ass wouldn't be breathing." The tone of her voice was caustic. "But if you keep popping up on my radar, I'll rectify that mistake."

Michael chuckled softly. The Marine's words were as potent as her fists. "You may not be the perp, Raines, but you're a part of this. I know it." He wiped at a tickle above his lip, not surprised to find his nose was bleeding.

She shrugged back into her bloody shirt and the duster. "I've never been shy about being half-naked in front of men *or* women," she said, narrowing her eyes, "but the least you could do is knock next time." Incensed, she roughly shoulder-bumped him on the way out of the bathroom.

"Raines? Wait a damn minute!" Michael burst through the door to pursue her, frustrated with her noncompliance.

Ziri was waiting for him, blocking the corridor. "Leave her alone!"

"What's your problem, kid?" Standing a few inches taller than the boy, he tried to use his greater size to intimidate Ziri and maneuver him out of the way.

"Ălfaăsseq!" Ziri replied, undaunted. "Deceitful men like you who think they can wield their power with no consequence!"

Still dressed in their ecclesiastical vestments, a trio of altar boys came around the corner oblivious to the tension rising.

"Hurry along, gentlemen," Father Paige said to them. "Father Thomas is holding vespers at 9 o'clock."

The children slipped sideways to get past them before hurrying down the hall to a flight of stairs that led down from the first floor.

"Mrs Winters was looking for some help in the kitchen." Father Paige smiled down at Ziri, taking him by the shoulder. "Would you be so kind?"

Ziri glared at Michael. "Yes, Father." He reluctantly bowed his head to the priest and averted his eyes to avoid disrespecting the clergyman. He retreated into the hallway and promptly trotted down the stairs after the altar boys.

Father Paige took a Kleenex from his pocket and handed it to Michael. "Anaba has learned to speak with her fists first and deal with the repercussions later."

"Does that kid know his crush is a blooded sniper with over fifty kills? And those are only the ones they can confirm." Michael dabbed at his bloody nostrils. "Who knows how many others she put down."

"To the Tuareg, she was a freedom fighter engaged in a war against a corrupt government that is determined to bring their people to heel. A government of men who put politics before faith. Men like you." Father Paige looked away contritely.

"He doesn't know anything about me–" Michael remembered the Tuareg cross scrawled in blood on the back wall of the quarantine barn. "Wait, Ziri's Tuareg?"

"Do you know what the term Tuareg means in Arabic?" Father Paige asked.

Michael allowed his silence to answer for him.

"Abandoned by God," Father Paige continued.

The blessing, as translated by his mother: *Let him not be abandoned* had been Ziri's handiwork, not Anaba's. Michael regretted being so hard on the boy.

"Three years ago, under the ruse of a border dispute, Malian soldiers attacked a Tuareg encampment, executed the tribal elders, and proceeded to slaughter the entire tribe. Ziri was part of that tribe, and they would have killed him, too."

"That's about the time Anaba was declared missing. Somewhere in Northern Africa, right?"

"Anaba wasn't missing. She was in hiding among the Tuareg as a man. Ziri believes she is the embodiment of a kel essuf – a desert spirit summoned by his grandfather to protect him. She's a Nightmare."

"Finally!" Michael rejoiced. "We can agree on something."

"No, Agent Childs, you misunderstand me. Anaba Raines is a true Nightmare – an infernal destrier, a war horse, trained for hunting and killing angels. She saved Ziri's life by slaughtering the soldiers who murdered his tribe, just as she saved yours tonight." Paige smiled, his blue eyes appearing gray in the dim light. "You're not a religious man, are you?"

"I'm a qualified archaeologist. I believe in science and fact." Exasperated, Michael closed his eyes and massaged the bridge of his nose. "She killed that man – that angel – without so much as blinking an eye. It was... brutal." He turned to the priest in shock. "And she enjoyed it. Every minute of it."

"Anaba takes no pride in it, no more than her record as a sniper. It's what she was forged to do."

Michael cleared his throat and exhaled forcefully through his mouth to ground himself back in reality. Distracted, he wiped anxiously at his nose to check if it was still bleeding. "Father Paige, if you know anything about this murder investigation, and you're withholding information, you are in violation of federal law. Regardless of any religious tenets."

"Remember, Agent Childs," Paige murmured, "I was the one who called you."

"Fair enough." Bowing his head to the rebuttal, Michael added: "For the next ten minutes, I'm a believer. I'm listening.

Father Paige led Michael down a wooden staircase. The interior lighting was poor, making the way precarious in the shadows. Michael kept a hand on the rail for balance. The priest paused on the landing and looked up at him. "As a man of letters, I trust you are familiar with the story of Lucifer's fall?"

"Biblical lore is my mother's specialty." Michael shrugged, unable to hide his skepticism. "I get the gist of it: jealousy and betrayal, a failed coup, ending with the rebellious angels being cast from Heaven."

"God did not cast them out. Think of Heaven as a womb. Lucifer and those angels who sided with his disobedience were aborted. Pride had so altered their nature that Heaven could no longer sustain them. So they fell," Father Paige explained. "While they maintain some of their divinity, their grace was diminished. To even the odds, they took up the practice of forging Nightmares from the souls of the damned."

The priest continued down the final flight of stairs to a large recreation area. Michael followed him across the room to a longer, narrower flight of concrete steps leading into a subbasement. "St. Joseph's was remodeled during World War II to serve as a bomb shelter in case the Nazis got the upper hand."

He walked into an oblong concrete dormitory. Cramped in rows, military-style bunks lined the walls. Fifty people sat huddled among them beneath a low ceiling. Though they appeared well fed and healthy, their tattered clothing spoke loudly of their hardship.

"I didn't know St. Joseph's was a homeless shelter?" To keep up with the priest, Michael sidestepped footlockers, garbage bags filled with personal possessions, and people. Their frightened eyes looked to him with a semblance of hope.

"You'll find their names on the NYPD's missing persons list. Disappearances going back the last three months. They're here to avoid becoming victims like Mary Klinedinst."

Michael's eyes narrowed as he stepped through a heated game of spades. "If these people really are in danger, the safest place for them is in police custody."

"Police custody? If I hadn't sent Anaba, you might have been the next victim. And you're an armed federal agent. These people don't stand a chance." Smiling and shaking hands with the residents, Father Paige worked his way to a kitchen in the back of the dorm.

"Why was Anaba's name written on a racing form found on Mary Klinedinst's body?"

"Protection," the priest promptly replied. "If caught in the open, unable to return to the sanctuary of the church for fear of exposing the others, the Nephilim had only two options. Finding Anaba."

"And the other option?"

"Death." Unlocking a steel door with a key on his rosary, he stepped into a walk-in refrigeration unit and switched on the lights. The bulbs hummed in the cold. "Special Agent Childs, meet Nathan Ponds." The priest pulled back a white sheet to reveal a corpse laying on a table.

Michael stared down into the face of a young Black man in his mid-twenties. His face had been carved up with Enochian profanities. His eyes were closed, the lids intact. Despite the mutilation of his features, he appeared at peace. A dried, yellow discharge had crystallized from the cold, crusting in the corners of his mouth.

"Twelve fingers," Michael counted. He went to the end of the table and uncovered the victim's feet. "Twelve toes. His tongue?"

"Still intact. We were able to stop them before they finished the ritual."

"We?"

"Anaba and me, but..." Paige fell silent, his lips pursed together in a thin line of regret. "We did not arrive in time to save him."

"Father, keeping this body here in the church is an obstruction of justice. You should have called the police the moment you found him. I could have you arrested," Michael said. "Or take you into custody as a material witness."

"You could do that, Agent Childs, but instead of being any closer to capturing these butchers, you would be three steps farther away from the answers you so desperately need to stop them."

"You're going to tell me angels did this?" Michael shoved his hands into his pockets and paced the room. "Who are they?"

"They are known as the Grigori – the Watchers, once sworn to protect the Creation," the priest replied.

Michael pointed to the corpse on the table. "What motive would anyone have for this kind of sick brutality?"

"Their motive? The absolute Word of God. A word so powerful it can create worlds and the life that inhabits them." Undeterred by the skepticism in Michael's eyes, Father Paige continued, carefully weighing his words. "The Grigori were an esteemed rank among the Three Spheres of the Elohim. They are now a disgraced legion tasked with eradicating the Nephilim. These murders are part of an ancient edict to finish what the waters of the Great Flood did not."

"A disgraced legion? What did they do?"

"The Great Flood was a cover up for an unsanctioned experiment gone wrong. After the fall of Adam, the Elohim sought the answer to existence by copulating with humans… a forbidden act and for good reason. Two hundred Grigori broke ranks and defiled themselves by taking human lovers."

"Minus a petri dish and a few water droppers, you make it sound so clinical." Michael massaged his forehead as a migraine throbbed behind his eyes.

"The history of mankind is riddled with the catastrophic results. The progeny of these Angels fell into two distinct categories," Paige said, holding up his fingers for emphasis. "Children born with twelve fingers and twelve toes, who possessed limited divine ability: telepathy, pyrokinesis, astral healing. Or, horrific monsters, deformed creatures of such violence they could not be sustained without destroying the Creation. You're familiar with the Minotaur and the Cyclops?"

Michael felt his jaw slacken in shock. "You're telling me that Pasiphaë and Poseidon were real? They were angels?"

"You know your Greek mythology, Agent Childs," the priest said with a chuckle. "Impressive."

"Comes with the territory. My mother is a biblical archaeologist, remember? She insisted."

"Pasiphaë was a Virtue of the Second Sphere. Poseidon was a Seraphim of the First, the highest order of angel," Paige continued. "*Both* were members of that original legion of Grigori."

"So, in retaliation," Michael said, "God sent the flood? Not to punish man, but to destroy *all* the Nephilim, good and bad."

"*The crops shall be as stone, and the soil like unto dust. There will be no bread, for Famine shall consume all the land, and all but the righteous shall perish.* Yes, it did not matter to Him in his fury." Father Paige reverently pulled the sheet over Nathan Pond's face. "Even after God granted His forgiveness, the Grigori continued hunting the Nephilim."

"But why?" Michael demanded, his cynicism falling to ire. "Even a serial killer derives some pleasure from his deeds. This is senseless slaughter. And why now?"

"While they represent a tiny fraction of the Elohim, the Nephilim are a lesser sphere of angel. There is no denying that fact. The Grigori hope to restore their tarnished honor by annihilating them," Paige replied. "As to why now?" The Priest shrugged. "These killings have been going on for thousands of years, Agent Childs, masked as natural disasters, random acts of violence, and atrocities of war."

Michael checked his watch. Three more minutes. "So, these people are the descendants of angels, who somehow managed to survive that flood?" He pressed the heels of his hand against his eyes. "How do you *know* all of this?" Michael pointed at the priest. "And if you say faith, I swear I'm arresting everyone in this goddamned church, starting with *you*."

Father Paige chuckled. "Let's just say I have a unique perspective."

The situation for the priest didn't look good. He had a basement filled with missing people, including children, who fit the killer's type, a murder victim laying in the cold storage locker of his church, and a potential suspect upstairs in his rectory.

"Father, I have to call this in. I'm sorry." Reluctantly, Michael retrieved his phone, staring at the screen. There were more questions than answers, which gave rise to even more complicated questions. He hesitated. "You claim that you got to Nathan Ponds before the ritual could be finished, so explain how he died?"

"Poisoning. Qeres killed all three of your victims and Nathan."

"Right, an ancient funerary perfume? You're starting to sound as paranoid as my mother." He pulled the evidence bag out of his pocket. "My partner spilled half this vial on his hand. Nothing happened."

"He's not an angel, nor the descendent of one." Father Paige crossed his arms and leaned against the wall. "Superficial exposure causes burns and blistering on the skin. If ingested or introduced to the bloodstream, qeres is a deadly toxin to angels, including Nephilim."

Michael stared at the body. "I shot one of those Grigori tonight. Dead center in his chest. With hollow points. It had no effect. I slashed him with my practice sword. Barely left a mark."

The priest looked at him sadly. "The weapons of man have no effect on angels. If you're to help these people, *your* people, you'll need to master a weapon forged by an archangel."

"*My* people!?" Michael snorted, snapping out of his trance.

"You are the only son of the Archangel Mikha'el–"

"My father is a deadbeat who abandoned his family ten years ago." Michael balled his hands into fists to keep himself from grabbing the priest's neck. "Hardly an archangel."

"Listen to me, Michael. You are a very unique Nephilim, an apocalypse angel," Father Paige said, deliberately accentuating his words. "This is why you have been targeted by the Grigori."

Michael unconsciously rubbed his fingers over the small scar where a sixth digit had been amputated when he was an infant. Trained to detect deception, he recognized the truth in the priest's words and the sincerity in the older man's eyes. "This can't be happening."

"When they realize that *you* are the Qaaun – His Chosen – they will redouble their efforts to kill you. Which is why I must get you to Samiel as quickly as possible. Anaba can take you to him."

"You slippery bastard!" Anaba stood in the doorway with Ziri looking over her shoulder. "This was your plan the whole time?"

"Anaba, please!" the priest pleaded. "You *must* take him!"

"I'm not going back! I'm not *ever* going back!" She glared at Michael with murderous intent in her eyes and stormed out of the room.

"What the hell's she talking about? Go back? Go back where?" Michael looked for answers first from the priest and then from Ziri.

"Hell, tezz." Ziri stared at the priest from beneath a lock of black hair that had fallen into his face. With silent accusations welling in his eyes, he stepped back into the kitchen and retreated into the dormitory.

Paige handed Michael another tissue. "Your nose is bleeding again."

"Shit. Is there a bathroom down here?"

"Down the hallway to the right." He took Michael by the shoulder. "You might want to use the men's room this time. You gave Sister Agnes quite a start when she heard a man's voice in the women's lavatory."

CHAPTER 7

Irritated by the sickly-sweet odor of urinal deodorizer pucks, Michael pressed his nostrils together to block the smell and stop the bleeding. He sat alone in one of three stalls in the men's bathroom. Haunted by the image of Nathan Pond's face, he stared into the tarnished mirror above the wash counter. His mind wrestled with fantastical subplots drawn straight out of the Ancient Greek and Roman epics that lined the built-in shelves in his mother's study.

The only son of the Archangel Mikha'el.

He retrieved the evidence bag from his pocket and eyed the qeres sealed within the vial. Was there something his mother had overlooked? Maybe exaggerated? He pulled out his phone to call her, then thought better of it. There was only one way to shatter the priest's ridiculous claims. But was it worth breaking a promise?

Michael opened the container and touched the inside of the cap with the tip of his little finger. He stared at the dab of amber oil, even raised it to his nose to sniff it. The scent was a heavy, persistent musk. Shrugging his shoulders, he rubbed the oil across his palm until it was absorbed into his skin.

When he tried to seal the vial, he fumbled and dropped the cap, losing all dexterity in his fingers. A painful itch crept beneath each nail bed. The discomfort grew into an excruciating burn like a welder's torch applied to his fingertips.

The affected skin grew hot with fever and bubbled with blisters as if he'd been splashed with hydrofluoric acid. Michael stood up to make a run for the sink, but fell to his knees and collapsed in the stall. He opened his mouth to cry for help, but the rapid swelling in his throat kept him from uttering a sound.

Twisted by seizures, his stomach forced an acrid bile into in the back of his throat. It seared up the sensitive lining of his esophagus and made him gag. He crawled toward the sink but only managed to drag himself a few inches.

"That was a very foolish thing to do, Michael," said a familiar voice.

As he laid shivering at the foot of the commode, Michael's mind was flooded with memories from his childhood: trail riding with his father, sword-fighting in the dojo garden, long drives in the country between joust competitions...

A loud commotion scattered these tranquil recollections. Anaba's livid face leaned over him. She dragged him across the floor, nearly dislocating his shoulder, and shoved his hand beneath a running spigot. "Do you have a fucking death wish?" With no regard for his comfort, she scrubbed the wound with soap, rinsed it, and let him drop to the floor.

"What's happened?" Father Paige shouted, rushing through the door, Ziri behind him.

Anaba pointed to the vial of *qeres* and its spilled contents.

"Ziri, get him some cold water and fetch the first aid kit." Father Paige knelt down beside the wash counter. "That was a very foolish thing to do, Agent Childs."

"I heard you the first time," Michael wheezed. He was grateful when the priest eased him into a sitting position.

"Was anyone else in here?"

"He was alone," Anaba replied.

Michael grasped at his hand to stifle the pain. Second-degree burns and blisters covered his little finger and palm. "I just touched the inside of the cap."

"One drop is sufficient to incapacitate a *full* angel," the priest chided.

"Stupid asshole!" Anaba stormed out of the room.

Clutching the first aid kit to his chest, Ziri pressed himself into the door frame to get out of her way.

Though relieved by her departure, a violent wave of nausea hit Michael in her absence. He scuttled like a crab across the bathroom floor, slammed his forehead against the paper dispenser, and threw up in the toilet.

"One of the angels that attacked tonight called me a half-breed," Michael spat once the heaving had subsided. He slumped against the stall divider wall, sweating profusely. Sickened by the smell rising from the toilet bowl, he flushed it. "I really am a Nephilim," he whispered.

Father Paige took the water bottle from Ziri and offered it to Michael. "Slowly. Slowly."

"I thought I was dying." Michael's teeth chattered in the stillness.

"You came close. Too close." Father Paige draped his cardigan about his shoulders.

"I heard a voice. I thought it was you."

"Your father." The priest wrapped a roll of gauze from the medical kit around the aggravated burn. "I served with him before I was called to join the Grigori. My given name is Pagiel."

Michael's mouth watered with a bitter, metallic aftertaste. "Your unique perspective? You're one of them."

"I don't share the views of my brethren. I remember what good the Father did for mankind, and what good mankind did for the Father." He smoothed down the gauze and taped it.

"So, you know my father?"

"I was standing at his side when the Father presented Adam

to the ranks of the Elohim. Your father was the first to kneel. I was the second."

Michael let his head fall back against the wall with a resounding crack. "This isn't happening."

"I'm afraid it is," Father Paige said. "While you may deny a higher calling, Michael, a higher calling has not denied you. But come, let's get you to the infirmary. There's a cot where you can lie down and rest."

Michael didn't have the strength to resist him. Leaning on Father Paige for support, he allowed the priest to assist him out of the bathroom and into the corridor, one shuffling foot at a time.

The infirmary was nothing more than a refurbished coatroom. Pale, lime-green wallpaper had been hastily applied to the walls in mismatched sections. The peeling drywall beneath showed through in places, revealing a decade's worth of war wounds: fingerprints, scuffs of coat racks, and dents from hangers.

To make up for the slapdash appearance, pictures of Christ, angels, and saints were taped over the imperfections. Colored by children, the artistry ranged from heavily applied crayon scribbled well outside the lines to the meticulous perfection of glitter pens.

Still feverish, Michael collapsed on the cot. He winced while painful shockwaves of vertigo ricocheted through his skull. Rubbing wearily at his forehead, he closed his eyes to escape the glare of the ceiling lights.

A bitter sentiment rose in the back of his throat. He longed to hear his father's voice again, even after a decade. But sentiment quickly turned to resentment as he considered the last ten years and the betrayal. Not just his abandonment, but his mother's stoic loneliness.

"Here, drink this." Father Paige handed Michael a disposable cup filled with a sour-smelling liquid. "Go on before the scent gives you second thoughts."

Michael complied, throwing back the concoction like a shot. He had hoped to avoid the inevitable bad taste, but it lingered on the back of his tongue. Retching, he grabbed the waste can at the end of the cot and hunched over it.

"Oh, you mustn't bring it back up," Paige said, patting him on the shoulder.

"What the hell was that?"

"Pickle juice. Best cure for a hangover, according to Sister Bernadette."

"I'm not drunk. I accidentally poisoned myself." He took in a desperate breath over the trash bin, his throat still burning from the irritation.

"The symptoms are similar." Grinning, Father Paige poured a second treatment into the cup and held it out to him.

Refusing the distasteful remedy, Michael set the trashcan down near the edge of the cot and laid down on the thin mattress. The flannel blanket smelled of cheap cologne and cigarettes. He was too exhausted to care. "You mentioned my father? Do you know where he is?"

"You judge him too harshly, Michael. He has always been close at hand, watching over you and your mother."

"Why did he leave us then?" Michael felt his mouth watering again and reached for the can, holding on to the lip until his knuckles cracked.

"He had his reasons," Paige replied. "Your safety being among them."

"My fucking *safety*?" Michael spat, rolling his eyes. "*This* is being safe?" He pointed to the purpling bruise on his cheek, suffered from a Grigori wing strike.

"The attack tonight was a lesson. You're no match for an angel. Not quite." Father Paige shook a scolding finger at him. "Not until you master a weapon worthy of your heritage."

Michael sat up and tossed his cell phone onto the pillow. "Let me type in a search for celestial weapons," he scoffed. "Maybe I can take advantage of the free two-day shipping."

Father Paige chuckled. "There is a war lance once carried by your father. While it may not make you the equal to an angel, it will certainly even the odds."

"Where can I find it?"

"Where your sire left it. Mount Victus – the site of Lucifer's last stand."

"In Hell?" Michael closed his eyes and let his head fall forward in defeat. "Seriously? What do you expect me to do? Break out Google Maps?"

"The only GPS you need is a Nightmare."

Michael opened his eyes and stared at the priest. "Anaba?"

"Nightmares have the ability to find roads and travel to places never meant to be found."

"Where is she?"

"Sulking in the sanctuary." Father Paige took Michael by the arm and helped him to his feet.

"Does she know about all of this?"

The priest nodded with a half-hearted shrug. "Why do you think she's sulking?"

"You mentioned a Samiel. Who is he?" Michael held on to the wall as Father Paige held on to him. His sense of equilibrium was completely gone.

"God has never wielded His hand against the Creation or any being within His works. Every catastrophe wrought upon the Earth has come at the hands of His Afflictions," the priest explained. *"There will be many widows and orphans in those days when a third shall fall stricken with Pestilence, a third by War, and another third by Famine, and those who remain shall live only to know the fear of the shadow of Death."*

"You're talking about the Four Horsemen of the Apocalypse?" Michael bit his lip, reminding himself to remain calm. "And what am I supposed to do? Chat about the weather? What am I up against? Is that why Anaba is my backup?"

"Not your backup. Your way in," Father Paige replied. "Samiel leads the Horsemen. No harm will come to you in his presence."

They made their way upstairs and into the main sanctuary of the church. Partially hidden in shadows behind statues of dead saints, Michael noticed Enochian sigils on the church's walls. Others were drawn beside paintings along the Stations of the Cross. The seals were rendered almost imperceptibly in fresh white paint. Only a subtle shift in the variance of the lighting revealed them.

"If I scratched that paint off, would I find blood?"

Father Paige's smile never faded. "No one was harmed, if that is your worry. It was the only way to shield the church from discovery."

"Which one is your signature?" Michael asked.

"That one." The priest indicated an obscured signet above a pair of short swords crossed over a shield. "My sigil is a seal of protection, but it is not especially potent. There are others, but one signature here is more potent than all the rest. Do you recognize it?"

Michael squinted through the dim candlelight of the sanctuary and scrutinized the signature inscribed above the church's front entrance. He slumped down into a pew. "That's the logo for my family's farm."

"That is the Sigil of the Archangel Mikha'el; God's greatest general, my dearest friend, your father." The priest put his hand on Michael's shoulder. "It will not be enough to keep the Grigori from eventually discovering us. When they do, they will slaughter every Nephilim beneath this roof. You must find a way to stop them."

"I thought these murders were the work of one deranged man – a homicidal psychopath. But now you're telling me it's a whole host of angels?" Michael took a deep, weary breath and exhaled. "Because I'm the son of the Archangel Mikhae'el? And I've got to go to Hell to get a weapon to stop them? I'm at the end of my rope with all this, Father Paige. How am I supposed to do this?"

Near the front of the sanctuary by the raised dais, Anaba stood like a sentinel at the foot of the altar. She stared up at the twenty-five foot statue of Jesus Christ on the crucifix. "You asked me to watch over some of your flock," she said, speaking loudly enough to be heard in the back of the church. "I did my best. Nothing I could do about the ones who got killed. You asked me to come to you if I saw anything out of the ordinary. I told you about *him*." She glared at Michael from over her shoulder. "I wanted nothing to do with any of this shit, and yet I'm hip deep. Now you have the fucking audacity to ask me to go deeper."

"Anaba, be reasonable," the priest pleaded. "Take him to Samiel before it's too late."

Michael put his hand on Father Paige's arm and returned the priest's cardigan. Still faint, he walked up the center aisle, leaning on the pews for support.

"You're afraid of going back to Hell." He took a cautious step back when she did an abrupt about-face to confront him. "I'm not questioning your courage, Anaba. But I want to stop whoever is murdering these people. Whatever that takes. Will you help me?"

Anaba stared into the darkened choir loft. "If you want something done, send the Army. But if you want it done right, send a Marine."

"Is that a yes?"

When her fierce gaze fell on him, Michael held his hands up in surrender. "Yeah, I know. You should have killed me when you had the chance."

He slowly made his way to the side exit leading to the alley beside the church. "Where are you going?" Father Paige asked.

"My Jeep."

"You need a Nightmare to get to Hell, Michael, not an SUV."

Michael laughed, wincing at his strained abdominal muscles. "If I'm going to Hell, I want my jousting gear. Something tells me I'm going to need it."

* * *

Outside, Michael shrugged against the stiff shoulders of his jousting gambeson, opting to leave his platemail in the trunk. The heavy fabric resisted him, maintaining its integrity like a ballistic vest. Tightly linked chainmail sewn into the material beneath the padding added weight to the defensive jacket as well as a supplemental layer of protection against penetration. He instinctively secured the leather straps and steel buckles, which ran in an angle from his right hip up across his left shoulder and then wrapped the maille gorget around his neck.

It was cold in the alley and he shivered, despite the thick armor. He secured a stiletto dagger in his boot, then knotted the leather swordbelt around his waist and adjusted the frog to lay below his left hip before jamming the practice sword and its scabbard down inside it. His stomach fluttered, just like it did when he suited up in his FBI tactical gear before a raid.

Michael stared up at the church. From the side entrance, St. Joseph of the Merciful Heart looked like any other building in the older Bronx neighborhood, aging brick and crumbling mortar with the exception of the gargoyles glaring down at him from the rooftops.

"What the fuck am I doing?" he whispered, exasperated, drawing the Glock 19M from its holster. He placed the weapon in a portable gun safe and secured the lid, which activated the digital, fingerprint lock.

Tucking his gloves into his belt, Michael slammed the Jeep's hatch shut and resigned himself to this course. He wanted nothing more than to close the investigation. He was determined to bring the sadistic killers to justice; even if that meant running a sword through them, he was prepared to do it.

Comforted by the jingling of his roweled spurs, he trotted up the concrete steps and headed back inside the church.

The worship sanctuary remained dim, illuminated by ambience lighting from the ceiling, controlled by a dimmer switch set on low. Tiered galleries of lit candles spread a secondary glow through the interior twilight and created an atmosphere of solitude and reflection. The mood, however, was completely shattered; the sanctum for peace and contemplation was being undermined by the willful antics of a Nightmare.

"*Anaba*!" Father Paige shouted. "You were a *soldier*. Have you no sense of decorum?"

In her Nightmare form, Anaba towered over an ornate marble baptismal font mounted in the corner of the church before a life-sized statue of John the Baptist. Plunging her nose in the basin, she drank the blessed water.

"Anaba, please!" Paige begged.

She glared at the flustered priest, eyes narrowed with contempt, and then savagely shook her head. Water splashed out of the basin in waves, drenching the floor and the priest, who was standing on the opposite side. Thoroughly soaked from head to toe, Father Paige groaned and shook the excess water from his arms and hands. His sweater drooped across his torso, sagging listlessly below his belt. He wiped the water from his distraught face and rolled his eyes in despair. "Mikha'el, He Who Is Like God," he prayed, glaring at Anaba, "defend us in battle that we may not perish at the dreadful judgment."

A prayer of exorcism? Anaba snorted. *For me? I'm flattered.* She turned to the creaking of the rusted doorjamb as the exit door swung closed behind Michael. With her hooves propped on the single step leading into the baptismal sanctum, the Nightmare stepped back from the font, looking like a proud puppy after emptying the contents of an overturned wastebasket.

She was, in one perfunctory word, magnificent. Equally as beautiful as she was malevolent. The Nightmare would have been an ideal candidate for jousting in the lists. Distracted by his initial assessment, Michael allowed himself to wonder what handling a sword or lance would be like from her back.

What the fuck are you staring at? Anaba charged him at a gallop down the center aisle. In three strides, she was on him, baring her teeth and snaking her head like a cobra.

Michael fell back into a pew to escape her. He raised his arm, averting his eyes to avoid provoking her. "I can't help it, Anaba. It's just…"

Just what?!

"Nothing." Embarrassed, Michael stood up and straightened his gambeson. He had backed dozens of young horses, introducing bit and bridle, saddle, and ultimately himself as a rider. *How could one back a Nightmare without getting their neck broken?*

He ran his hand along her neck with genuine trepidation. The fact that she tolerated his touch without flinching was a good omen or his death warrant.

What are you waiting for? A formal invitation from the Pope? She bared her teeth at him as if intending to bite. *Mission clock is ticking, Childs. The sooner this is over, the farther I can get away from you.*

Tentatively, Michael reached for the sooty roots of her mane near the withers. Her ears went flat, pinned flush against her head. It was one of the most aggressive signals a horse could send, telegraphing fear, fury, or an imminent attack. Not wanting to get bitten or kicked, Michael hesitated. "Are we going to do this or not?"

Her ears lifted in reply, but remained back and wary. Michael hopped twice and vaulted onto her back. He kept his hand tangled in her mane for leverage in case she bucked. The absence of tack did not bother him. He had grown up riding bareback, bridleless, and preferred the close contact with his mount as nature intended.

Anaba lowered her head, her ears pivoting forward, and sighed. It was a sign of her tolerance, perhaps resignation, but not submission.

"Now what?" Michael asked, closing his legs around her barrel.

Anaba snorted, a slow staccato of exhalations that sent profuse cloud blasts of black and yellow brimstone into the air.

The dense vapor rose like a fog, swirling about her with molten flecks of fire floating within it.

The Nightmare scraped the tip of her hoof across the floor, pawing at the ground. The grating of horn against textured tile echoed in the sanctuary. A spark ignited into rabid flames, which virulently spread from her hooves up to her legs. The orange flames licked across her crest, igniting her mane. With a thunderous roar, her tail exploded in a fiery conflagration.

Michael felt the intense heat surging across his hands but experienced no pain from his close proximity to the blaze. He moved his hands to his thighs as a precautionary measure.

As the Nightmare's flames rose, a proliferation of shadows descended and gathered around her in defiance of the searing light and created a conduit between worlds. These shadows deepened and expanded, coalescing into a wheel of impenetrable darkness ringed by fire.

"Father Thomas is coming!" Ziri said breathlessly, as he rounded the corner from the corridor. "He and those altar boys are on the stairs."

Father Paige picked up the golden thurible sitting on the floor beside the altar. Opening the metal censer, he threw a handful of myrrh onto the burning coals inside. "Quickly, you must be off. They'll be here any moment."

A wall of fragrant smoke poured through a myriad of holes in the crucible. It cast a profuse cloud over the front of the church as the priest swung the censer in earnest to cancel out the stench of brimstone. With a grin, he looked up at Michael and nodded. "Balit'ádh, Agent Childs," he whispered. "Good luck."

Anaba broke into a canter and leaped into the portal, soundlessly vanishing into the darkness beyond.

CHAPTER 8

Anaba emerged from the portal, cantering onto a gravel road. She broke to a walk as the corridor of shadow and flame dissipated around her. Gnarled trees with bare, sallow branches and thorns formed a skeletal archway above the path. Friction from the horned bark rubbing together produced a rain of ash. It coated Michael's hair and armor in a fine gray powder and cut visibility.

Michael squinted into the darkness but the road ahead remained shadowy and formless. Feeling claustrophobic beneath the twisted canopy of the dead trees, he slumped down across Anaba's withers. "Where are we?"

The Gate to the Vestibule Road, she replied.

"The Vestibule of Hell? Isn't that where souls are imprisoned until Judgment Day?" Michael rubbed the ash between his fingers, curious about the texture. "Or, at least, the souls of those who aren't good enough to go to Heaven, but not bad enough to go to Hell."

That's Purgatory, genius. The Vestibule is more like standing in line at Starbucks on Black Friday. You're not going anywhere fast.

"The Opportunists – I remember now. Neither in Hell nor out of it." Michael looked around in confusion. "But there're no souls here."

Ever hear the expression all hell's about to break loose? You're about to find out where it came from. Anaba walked onto the road. With a snort, a large gout of fire escaped her nostrils. Split by the brilliance of the flames, the shadows retreated, revealing a throng of gaunt, naked figures covered in mud and soot and excrement.

Michael felt the hairs on his neck stand on end. His eardrums popped with the sudden change in pressure as the sensitive membranes vibrated painfully, assailed by the piercing, chaotic shrieks that rose from a crowd of people gathered in front of them.

The ghoulish mob moved like a disorganized swarm of wasps. In a crazed state, the specters clawed at themselves and each other, goring their nails as they clamored for position on the road. But no quarter could be found. There were too many of them crammed onto the mouth of the narrow pathway.

"What *are* they?" Michael asked.

Wraiths. Opportunists who have no chance of ever getting into Heaven, and Hell doesn't want them. So, they exist here, trapped between worlds.

Their maddened wailing ceased when they became aware of the Nightmare and the rider on her back. With renewed, dirgelike keening, the damned charged Anaba and Michael as a horde. Anaba blew a blast of brimstone from her nose and struck the ground with her hoof. The spark ignited the cloud and set off a detonation of flames that radiated outward in a twenty-foot arc. The frightened wraiths threw their arms up, covering their faces, to shield themselves.

"Is there another way in? I don't like these odds."

There's always a crowd at the gate. Recent arrivals. Ears pinned flat against her skull, the Nightmare bared her teeth, issuing a guttural squeal of warning. The restless souls hesitated but did not retreat. *We need to make a way through.*

Catching movement in his peripheral vision, Michael snatched his longsword from its scabbard. A wraith shambled toward him from the listless throng. Lacking eyelids, her bulging eyes were wide, twitching in perpetual terror. Mouth agape, the low moaning that escaped her lips stirred genuine fear in Michael's gut. He held back the killing blow that would have split her head, recognizing the oblong, ashen face as well as the Enochian profanities carved into the desiccated flesh.

Anaba swung around to face the soul. She lunged a few steps toward it, teeth bared, and threatened to strike with a fiery hoof. The aggressive stance made the soul hesitate, but it did not move back into line with the others. Running at the Nightmare, the wraith raked her skeletal claws across Anaba's neck.

Nearly unseating Michael, Anaba squealed in rage and spun to bring her hindquarters around. From a standstill, she leaped six feet straight into the air and kicked out with both hind legs. Michael grabbed her mane to stay with her. The movement sent the restless soul reeling to the ground. Without hesitation, Anaba trampled her and a second soul, incinerating them in her flames. A swish of her tail ensnared a third. As the deadly blaze swallowed it, she flung the hapless soul back into the mob as a warning to the rest.

In the presence of a true predator, the dead fell back. Anaba took advantage of their retreat and galloped through them, scattering their numbers as they fled to escape her volatile fire.

What the fuck's wrong with you, Childs? When you draw a weapon, you better use it! Hesitate here, and you die!

"Sorry." Michael sheathed his sword. "That thing… that was Mary Klinedinst, the last murder victim." He clenched and unclenched his jaw, struggling to breathe. His sternum ached from the rapid palpitations of his heart. Mouth dry, he exhaled with effort. He knew the Nightmare was listening. One petite ear pivoted back toward the sound of his voice. "How much longer do we have to be here? Where is this Samiel?"

You don't go looking for the Angel of Death. He usually comes looking for you. Anaba sniffed the stale air and stepped into the center of the stony path. As the condemned souls scurried back against the trees for shelter, she promptly cantered away from the gate, leaving the mob behind them.

* * *

Veiled in shadow and a haze of gray ash, the Vestibule Road had no discerning features, other than the dense canopy of twisted trees that bordered the path and blocked out any glimpse of the skies. Judging from the burning fatigue in his thighs, Michael guessed they had been cantering in a straight line for nearly an hour without passing a single intersection, crossroad, or marker to indicate their passage.

Michael tapped futilely at his watch. Since his arrival, the hour hand spun in a slow, steady circle, counter-clockwise, while the minute hand had ceased to move. "If God is all forgiving," he said, unaware that he'd spoken his troubled thoughts aloud, "how does someone like Mary Klinedinst end up here?"

Anaba's ears pivoted backward toward the sound of his voice, but she made no reply.

"She was an award-winning teacher, nominated as Teacher of the Year in recognition of her work with at-risk youth. She didn't do anything to deserve this."

Shifting her weight to her haunches, Anaba abruptly slid to a halt. Head perched high on her powerful neck, she studied the shadows.

Michael grabbed a handful of mane and secured his grip on the hilt of his longsword. "Anaba?"

A foreboding darkness spread across the Vestibule Road. Like a crawling mist, it moved with sentience through the trees. Keeping a hand knotted in her mane, Michael watched his breath wreathe above his head like a frosted crown.

A silhouette walked from the engorged shadows between the trees and onto the road. The figure was also mounted on a Nightmare whose pale hide emanated a faint, green hue, a stark contrast to the rider's tattered, black robes.

The horrific visage of a skull peered from beneath a heavy cowl and sent a chill through Michael's limbs. The rider propped the wicked-looking blade of a scythe over his shoulder. Skeletal hands pushed back the hood, revealing not a bare skull, but a surprisingly handsome, yet somber, black face framed by a tousled mane of brown hair which hung across his shoulders.

"Arezodi, Son of Mikha'el, Son of God." The rider bowed his head in reverent respect.

"I'm afraid I… don't understand," Michael said.

"It is an Enochian greeting: I wish you peace." The stranger smiled, never breaking eye contact.

Michael felt his skin crawl uncomfortably in the ensuing silence. "Arezodi, then."

"The prosperity of our fathers and our fathers' fathers was forgotten when Famine came into the land, and the wicked were brought to judgment." The rider crossed his hands over the pommel of his saddle. "You seem far kinder than the scripture portended. You have your father's eyes, Son of Mikha'el. Will you walk with me?"

"You're Samiel?"

"While I am called by many names, this is the one given by my Father."

Deferring to Anaba, Michael shifted his weight across Anaba's back. Her small ears pricked forward, and she took a reluctant step toward the Angel of Death. She walked beside the other Nightmare, occasionally eyeing the Rider on its back.

Samiel's Nightmare had a single feather branded on its left shoulder. An ankh, the ancient symbol for life, was carved into the flesh near the tip of the scar.

"Anaba has a mark like that."

"The Crest of Nanqueel, I know. It is the way an apocalypse angel permanently binds themselves to their Nightmare." Samiel rubbed his hand across his warhorse's shoulder. The brand glowed beneath his fingertips then faded into the pale hide. "When sealed, it allows a Nightmare to wield the powers of its master and grants the Rider the ability to summon his mount no matter where it may be." Staring at the brand, he added, "Two feathers means she's killed two angels in combat. No easy feat. If you look carefully, you can read their names."

Michael reached down to touch the mark on Anaba's shoulder, and soon found himself grabbing for mane to keep from being thrown. Head bowed inches above the road, the Nightmare violently crow-hopped beneath him. Her back undulated violently like the mammoth, white-capped hurricane swells of a storm surge in the deep sea. "Anaba?!"

Touch the mark, lose a finger. The Nightmare ceased bucking, but remained tense, her ears pinned flat in fury.

"Why is she so sensitive about it?" Michael asked. He was panting from his efforts to cling to the livid warhorse's back.

Samiel laughed, shifting the scythe to his left hand. "She has her reasons," the Horseman replied cryptically.

When Michael leaned forward again to examine the brand, the Nightmare bared her teeth, prepared to bite his hand. "I won't touch it! Damn it, Anaba!" He held his hands behind his back to reassure her of his intention. Wary of the Nightmare's ill-tempered disposition, he clenched his legs against her flanks in case she decided to buck him off.

The brand had healed, except from the most recent addition, which had scabbed over. The old scar was white, speckled with red splotches that reminded Michael of proud flesh, a granular tissue that complicated wound healing in horses. It stood out, prominently, jutting from her muscular shoulder in vivid contrast to her fine black coat.

Unnatural, the macabre crest had evident form and function, judging from the span of the feathers and intricate script written between them. "I can't read Enochian," Michael said, his curiosity giving in to a sense of dread as he examined the mark.

"It is the language of your father. Try."

He concentrated on the ancient glyphs, staring until the sigils formed syllables and then words in his mind. "Vel-Velendriel. Briathos."

"Every Nightmare who survives their forging has inherent

talents, but with each brand those talents become more powerful."

"Talents?"

"Have you not noticed that her hooves barely touch the ground? That is the Touch of Zephyr. Have you not observed the shadows? She can control the darkness, as well as any flame. These are highly valued traits found in most Nightmares," Samiel explained. "However, this Nightmare is unlike any forged beneath these forsaken skies. There were rumors one had escaped the boundaries of Hell without a master, and no one is quite certain how or why."

The Horseman reached down to caress Anaba's neck. Before his fingers could make contact, she delivered a savage cow-kick to his horse.

The sickly pale Nightmare reared and lunged with an open mouth in an attempt to retaliate. Samiel held tight to its reins to prevent the bite. "There, there, Khull," the Angel of Death said. "You may have met your match in this one."

Chewing anxiously on the curb bit in its mouth, the Nightmare obediently settled into the bridle.

Anaba snorted a taunt. Molten flecks of brimstone billowed from her nostrils and floated back over her neck. The fiery debris licked at Michael's fingers, but still he felt no heat from them.

"You need never fear her flames," Death said, reading his thoughts. "A Nightmare burns only what it wants to burn."

"Good to know," Michael said, slipping on the suede gloves he used in joust practice. "But you can never be too careful."

Samiel stared at him for a long moment. "Pagiel is ever the optimist, but this time… I share his idealism. Let's see if you are worthy, Son of Mikha'el, Son of God." Samiel galloped ahead on the Vestibule Road. "Follow me, if you dare."

CHAPTER 9

A sharp turn onto an obscured trail led away from the dismal gray of the road. The gravel path gave way to a sprawling savannah of purple, waist-deep grass. Despite the unnatural coloration, the distinct scents of timothy and alfalfa were unmistakable.

"This isn't the Hell my professors talked about in grad class." Michael plucked a gangly stalk from the ground. He could have almost been riding through the Scottish countryside, except for the blood-red skies and the jagged streaks of black lightning that ripped above them.

"Appearances can be deceiving." Samiel pointed to the steaming pitch seeping from the root. "Come, Son of Mikha'el, let me show you its wonders!"

Michael flinched as the viscous ichor caught fire and burned like a flare. Alarmed, he shook the stalk until the flame was extinguished and tossed it far enough away to avoid injuring himself or Anaba. The Nightmare regarded the smoking stem in sullen silence as it withered, and cantered after Samiel.

Death drew his heavy, black cowl over his head. Fiery eyes bled through the impenetrable darkness within as a grinning skull replaced his august face. The Horseman dropped the reins over the pommel of his saddle and spurred his Nightmare across the field. The grass rippled in his wake like water disturbed by a skipping stone. As volatile tongues of umber flames leaped from the warhorse's legs, Samiel gripped his wooden staff in his skeletal fingers and raised the scythe high above his shoulders.

Still wary of the Horseman and his intentions, Michael drew his longsword. The blade hissed as it cleared the scabbard.

"I am not your enemy, Michael," Samiel said, "but there are many entities in Hell that are."

Covered in black pitch, an amorphous creature reared up from the ground in front of them. It drew itself up to a height of nine feet. Smoking black ichor trickled from the behemoth's arms, starting small fires in the purple foliage. Before the flames could spread, they were snuffed out by the clouds of steam emitted from the grotesque, misshapen body.

Hollow eye sockets smoldered in rage, as a second humanoid creature fought its way through the pitch. It bellowed a thunderous challenge from its crooked, toothless maw. The declaration was answered by Samiel's scythe.

Severed from its hulking shoulders, the shrieking horror's head left a trail of gray smoke as it arced over the Horseman and landed in the grass. Samiel spun the scythe over the back of his hand with a clever flourish and sliced the remaining creature in half as he galloped by.

Riding wide of the Horseman's scythe, Michael watched the quivering gelatinous forms dissipate into the tall grass. "What are those things?"

"Titans. They lie dormant in the tar pits beneath us."

"As in *the* Titans? Of Greek legend?" Michael asked.

"The same."

"I thought Chronos, Zeus, and Hades were myths? They really existed?"

"Not myths, *contenders,*" Samiel said. "The Lord God suffers no rivals to His throne. Any and all who would lay claim to His works reside here in Hell."

Another Titan broke from the ground with a primordial shriek that reverberated through the air. Its cry was joined by a hellish chorus as two others reared up from the pits beneath the grassy veld.

Anaba dropped her head and charged. Michael braced for impact and drove the longsword into the Titan's neck. He drew back with a twist and severed the head. The corpse sank back into the grass, disappearing into the pitch. Two more rose to take its place.

"There are so many of them!" Michael cried.

"They have little interest in human souls, but the essence of an angel will bring them to the surface every time," Samiel explained. "There is no denying your heritage, Son of Mikha'el."

Samiel's Nightmare rolled an eye back to look at Anaba. Pricking her left ear forward, Anaba lengthened her stride and galloped ahead.

Fearing her ill-temper, Michael snatched at her mane. "Anaba, no!"

"Don't interfere! This is what they were forged to do! When the Fallen hunt, their Nightmares are not just mounts." Samiel laughed malevolently. "They're the hounds."

Billowing brimstone from their nostrils, the Nightmares galloped single-file for a dozen strides. The noxious cloud hung in the darkening air and grew dense enough to hide the Nightmares in the shadows. Emerging from that darkness without warning, the warhorses pirouetted to opposite sides and brought their riders onto the unprotected rear flanks of the enemy.

Michael leaned forward over her withers and slashed with the longsword in a downward diagonal that cleaved open a Titan's torso. Anaba delivered a passing kick that sent the defeated creature reeling backwards.

"Magnificent!" Dodging a wild haymaker from the lurching creature, Samiel hooked a Titan by the neck and galloped away. Caught on the curved blade, the creature was dragged through the grass for two strides before being summarily beheaded.

Flipping his longsword into an underhand grip, Michael shifted his weight over Anaba's wither. Perfectly positioned, he bent down low over her and held the blade behind him for maximum effect. The Nightmare stumbled beneath him. He grabbed her mane to keep from being thrown. "Anaba, what's wrong?"

"She's mired!" Samiel shouted. "Even with the Touch of Zephyr, a Nightmare can be mired if the pitch rises and becomes too deep!"

Michael stared down over Anaba's withers. The viscous resin sucked at the tips of her hooves, pulling the Nightmare down into the foul, bubbling slag. Bogged down to the ankles, she exaggerated her gait to break free. A slow-moving Titan closed in for a kill.

"I've got you, boy!" said a strange voice.

Brandishing a great katana, the new rider was dressed in gosoku samurai armor. The ornate, crimson breastplate was tinged with silver over a scintillating pattern of plates that resembled reptilian scales. A pair of elaborate pauldrons adorned his shoulders, crafted into the semblance of a dragon's maw and its coiled tail.

His ruddy chestnut Nightmare galloped up beside Anaba, bared its teeth at the Titan, and headbutted the monstrosity as the rider cut it in half with his great sword. Like Samiel's warhorse, it had the Crest of Nanqueel on its left shoulder, with one feather and a flaming sword carved near the tip.

"Drive her on, lad, and then let your Nightmare do her job." Snatching back on the reins in a protective funnel of red fire, the boisterous rider veered away to engage the Titans rearing up from the pitch ahead of them.

Free of the tar, Anaba fell into line with the chestnut. Galloping abreast, the Nightmares charged toward a line of five Titans. One after the other, the Titans reared up and then slammed their fists into the ground. The resulting concussion sent a wave of smoldering grass and pitch in their direction.

The putrid swell crested four feet above the ground and buried the flora beneath a stinking black tide of sulfuric tar.

Anaba tucked her legs and leaped to avoid the surge. The evasive maneuver left Michael exposed to attack. Michael threw himself over the Nightmare's croup, dodging the beasts' talons, and rested his shoulders on Anaba's flanks. He was unharmed, but she was not so fortunate.

The Nightmare flinched when one of the Titan's claws dug three bloody furrows across her rib cage. With a grunt, she struck back with a vengeful hind foot.

Michael sat up, drew back his sword, and sliced the behemoth's throat. The wild stroke sent pitch and ichor spewing from the wound.

Titan's blood! Don't let it touch you! A snort of brimstone from her nostrils caught fire, igniting her mane and tail in a conflagration.

Michael ducked beneath Anaba's fiery mane to escape the rain of gore, which was vaporized on contact. A drop survived the flames and landed with a loud pop on his glove. Swiftly eating through the suede, the venom sizzled into the flesh beneath it. He growled in pain and balled his hand into a fist.

Anaba landed unevenly. She desperately threw her head up for balance, but she fell to her knees. Michael, too, lost his balance and was thrown against her withers, slamming his nose against her crest.

"Get off her neck! She's trying to save your life!" A pale, freckle-faced woman with red hair drew back the string of a recurve bow where three obsidian arrows materialized between the riser and the string. She loosed them as her pale Nightmare galloped to Anaba's side, trailing a blinding comet tail of white flame. The projectiles struck three separate targets, lifting the Titans into the air and rocketing them backward. The creatures did not rise again.

Anaba got to her feet and craned her neck around to look up at him. *I smell blood.*

"Caught myself in the nose when you landed." Wiping the back of his glove across his bloody nostrils, Michael leaned over to examine the gashes on her flank. A light sheen of perspiration dampened her black hide. He pressed his fingers against the injuries.

The Nightmare pinned her ears and hunched her back.

"Anaba, quit it. You're hurt," Michael said, exasperated by her antics. He held his fingers up to show her the blood.

I've had worse. It's not like you have a band-aid for it.

"Arezodi, Son of Mikha'el!" The heavily armored samurai galloped his chestnut Nightmare towards him between rising plumes of black smoke. Like phantom tombstones, the columns marked the place where a Titan fell. The Rider sheathed his katana and raised an open hand in greeting to show he posed no danger. The red-headed archer galloped up beside the samurai until her gray Nightmare was abreast with his. The Crest of Nanqueel with one feather stood out prominently against its coat with a biohazard symbol near the tip.

Anaba pirouetted to face them. Flattening her ears, she lowered her head, aggressively snaking it from side to side in warning.

"You handle a sword as if born to it, but I would expect nothing less from the son of the Father's greatest general." The samurai bowed his head respectfully. "I am the Horseman War, but you may call me by my given name Raijin."

"I am Wyrmwood, the Horseman Pestilence," the red-head added. She narrowed her gray eyes and glared at Raijin. "For the record, I told you and Samiel this was a bad idea." She jerked her thumb over her shoulder.

The Angel of Death had been unhorsed. He walked through the waist-deep grass ahead of his Nightmare. The warhorse staggered after him on three legs, jagged splinters of bone jutting from the bloody remains of its left knee. Samiel waited patient every few steps to allow the Nightmare to keep pace with him.

"You urches never listen," Wyrmwood grumbled. "The Father should rename you Mischief and Mayhem. Only one solution to that mess."

"Bad luck, Samiel," said Raijin. "We would have gotten involved sooner, but the boy was holding his own, considering that pathetic piece of steel he wields."

"That pathetic piece of steel put down three Titans," Wyrmwood said. "You only bested two."

"Was this some kind of a test?" Michael asked.

"*This* was an initiation," Samiel replied. "You came to Hell to acquire your father's war lance. We came to acquire you."

Michael felt the air leave his lungs. "*Acquire* me? For what?"

"As the new Famine," Wyrmwood said.

"The new Famine?" Michael scoffed, smoothing the hair along Anaba's withers. "What happened to the *old* Famine?"

"Dead," Raijin replied. "Killed while trying to retrieve a war lance forged by the greatest of angels."

"My father's war lance?" Michael asked.

"It was never meant to be claimed by another," Wyrmwood said. "It is your birthright."

"Wait a minute." Michael shook his head in disbelief. "The Four Horsemen of the Apocalypse can actually die?"

"His name was Eligoriel," Raijin said, the menacing edge in his voice as keen as his great katana. "He was a Domination of the Second Sphere."

"An insufferable blowhard, used to barking orders," Wyrmwood added.

"A duty he continued when he became one of us. Even challenging Samiel's authority." Raijin rolled his eyes, shaking his head. The metallic skirt of his helmet's neckguard rattled across the pauldrons of his gusoku armor. "Good riddance, I say."

"Enough," Samiel said to quiet them. "All things come to an end, Son of Mikha'el. Death will prevail over all, including the Most High God one day. While there are never more than four

Horsemen, there have been other apocalypse angels that have served in these offices. I, alone, am the original." Samiel patted his Nightmare on the neck. "You've served well, Khull, my old friend, but I fear your time has come."

The blade of Samiel's scythe flashed like lightning, partially severing the Nightmare's neck at the base of the skull. With its head attached only by the remnants of a spinal cord, the warhorse dropped dead in the grass.

"Christ, Samiel! Was that necessary?" Appalled by the sudden execution, Michael pressed the back of his hand across his mouth to suppress the nausea rising in the back of his throat. Mouth watering uncontrollably, he wiped away the panic of sweat around his lips.

"Nightmares are mortal, Michael," Death replied. "It was the only *humane* thing to do." Pushing back his hood, Samiel looked out across the savannah with a human face, shadowed with remorse. "The Titans will be back and in significant numbers," he said. A dozen shambling figures were already rising from the grassland.

Michael raised his right leg and crossed it over Anaba's withers to dismount. "I'll walk with you."

"No!" Samiel's voice spiked in pitch with his anger. "Nothing is more formidable than a Horseman on his Nightmare. Anaba is your greatest ally and your greatest weapon. Never, ever leave the protection of your Nightmare's back, Son of Mikha'el."

"While killing Titans has always been a pleasurable pastime," Raijin whipped his reins against the flanks of his Nightmare, and the chestnut lunged forward and then reared back against the bit, "a dead Nightmare dampens the revelry."

"Come then," Samiel said. "Let's walk to the road where we can speak in safety."

CHAPTER 10

Enthralled by Hell's diverse topography, Michael stared up at a mountain shrouded in mist. A trail meandered across the craggy slope and vanished into the hazy veil of the upper elevations. The mist was not water vapor, as he initially suspected, but stone dust. Debris was cast from the corkscrew motion of the mountain as whole sections of it rotated in opposite directions on a hidden axis. The grinding of stone-on-stone was apparent in a low rumbling that reverberated through the stillness like thunder.

"What is this place?" Michael asked.

"If there was a Mount Calvary of Hell, this would be it." Samiel followed his gaze up the fractured peak. "It is Mount Victus."

"Lucifer and his minions made their last stand at the summit," Raijin said. "The mountain is a burial mound made from the ash and bones of the thousands of angels who perished during the battle."

A high-pitched yelping startled Michael. Standing at the edge of the tall grass, six hairless dogs watched from the road's edge. They were hideous beasts, their skin ravaged with mange, and sores yellow with infection. The only visible hair was on their paws, which were coated in tar pitch and grass seed.

"They're known as Yeth Hounds, the souls of unbaptized

children." Wyrmwood drew back her bowstring and fired an arrow into the dirt to scatter them. "They're harmless scavengers unless provoked in great numbers."

They continued on without further interruption before Michael could no longer hide his concern. "If a Horseman died trying to retrieve this lance, what makes you think I'll succeed where he failed?" Michael asked, doubting himself.

"You are the Son of Mikha'el. He left that lance behind for a good reason," Wyrmwood said.

Samiel set the staff of his scythe on the ground and wearily leaned against it. "This is the *real* test, Michael. The first of three."

Michael snorted in frustration. "I thought I passed the initiation during that dust up with the Titans?"

"That was to see if we like you." Wyrmwood winked at him. "I'm betting you survive the first trial. Can't speak for my companions."

"I'm willing to bet a gold shekel he lives to see the third." Raijin picked at his teeth with a dagger.

Like the new kid in the neighborhood, trying to find a way to fit in, Michael yielded to an intrinsic competitive yearning. "All right. Tell me about these tests?"

"The Trial of Lineage will determine if you are worthy of a weapon forged by an archangel. Followed by the Trial of Endowment, which is a test to see if you can withstand the power of a Horseman's authority," Samiel explained.

"And the third?" Michael asked.

An unsettling sorrow clouded the Horseman's eyes, as if he had made up his mind about the outcome. "The Trial of Torezodu – the Awakening."

Michael shifted anxiously on Anaba's back. "What are we waiting for?"

"Samiel has summoned an ostler." Wyrmwood peered down the road at an approaching rider. "And there he comes."

Astride a white Nightmare, a tall, willowy man cantered

down the path along the base of the mountain. He led a second pale-green warhorse by a leather rope. There was a grim obsequiousness in his expression, as perceptible as the soot marring his gaunt face. The newcomer wore a battered silver cuirass, and slowed to a walk as he approached them.

Anaba stiffened beneath Michael. The languid hue in the ostler's eyes dissolved into the fierce intensity of recognition when he saw her standing among the Horsemen.

"Fetharsi," Samiel said. "Caim Seere, you are a reliable fellow. I trust you've brought something promising."

"Arezodi, Samiel," Caim replied, holding up the leather lead. "This Nightmare just earned its first feather during a hunt three days ago. You'll not find a better mount in all of Hell to fit your station."

Accepting the lead rope, Samiel appraised the leggy Nightmare with admiration. "I am in your debt." He offered a leather purse to the ostler. It jingled with coins as it was exchanged between them. "What's his name?"

"I call this one Malis."

Following Caim's blatant stare, Samiel glanced at Anaba. "No better mount in Hell, you say?"

"Except for *her*." Caim dismounted and drew a saber from the sheath at his shoulder. "Get off of her, thief! That black Nightmare is my property."

"Anaba?" Michael questioned.

The Nightmare dropped her head and pinned her ears. A gout of brimstone escaped her nostrils.

Samiel lowered his scythe, barring the ostler from moving any closer to them. "You may be an archangel, Caim, but your tarnished rank in Heaven has little bearing here."

"She belongs to me, Samiel!" Caim said, pushing against the polished wooden snath.

"And you may yet possess her, if the Son of Mikha'el does not survive this day." Samiel gave him a firm shove. "If you wish to remain in my favor, you will leave well enough alone."

"What if *she* doesn't survive?" The archangel stumbled back against his Nightmare. "How will I be compensated?"

"You lowly urch." Raijin thumbed the guard of his great katana and let the hilt rattle against the scabbard. "Consider leaving with your life and limbs intact your compensation."

Jaw clenched in resignation, Caim slammed his sword back into its scabbard and leaped to the back of his Nightmare. Snatching at the reins of the war bridle, he yanked so violently the horse reared and threw its head. Bloody flecks of foam splattered across his cuirass. He cast a final glare at Anaba and then Michael before galloping away in the direction that he had come.

"Who in the hell was that?" Michael felt his heart racing in his chest.

"Caim is one of the Fallen." Samiel watched the furious ostler until he disappeared around a bend in the road. "His sin was not disobedience, but indecision. When he refused to choose a side in the war, he was cast out of Heaven, only to become a pariah in Hell."

"The fool has set his sights on wearing the mantle of a Horseman." Raijin kicked a leg free of its stirrup and casually crossed it over the pommel of his saddle.

"Regardless, he knows a thing or two about training proper warhorses. Only an archangel can forge a Nightmare," Samiel explained. "Caim's made quite a reputation for himself."

Michael licked his lips, his mouth gone dry. "He forged Anaba?"

"Collected the soul himself," Samiel said, with a wry grin, "and then she escaped."

"That's why you didn't want to come back," Michael muttered to her. "You might have mentioned–"

Need to know intel, asshole, and you didn't need to know. She kept her ears pinned and flicked her tail across his leg.

"Steady now." Samiel raised his scythe over his new Nightmare's shoulder and slashed across the Crest of Nanqueel.

"What's he doing?" Michael asked.

"Ssh," Wyrmwood hushed. "He's binding the Nightmare to his service."

The frightened Nightmare flung its head in terror and reared against the lead rope. Samiel held on tightly, even as the warhorse bolted backwards. He laid his hand across the bloody wound. The Crest of Nanqueel glowed, pulsing rhythmically like a heartbeat. As the ethereal light faded away, it left one delineating mark: an ankh freshly branded near the quill of the feather.

"Malis, niis."

"Niis?" Michael repeated. "Come to me?"

"Nightmares are powerful, willful creatures. The forging process is a difficult, often traumatic ritual," Samiel explained. "I am completing the Enochian rite that Caim Seere initiated."

Subdued by the invocation, the Nightmare bowed his head. Shadowy tendrils resembling freshly tilled soil slithered across his head to form the headstall and cheekpieces of a bridle. Chomping noisily on the bit that appeared in his mouth, the destrier rubbed his head affectionately against the Horseman's shoulder and nickered.

"May you serve well," Samiel whispered.

A moaning rose in chorus above the insistent grinding of the mountain. Michael watched in horror as the ground of Mount Victus undulated with movement. "Titans?"

"Worse... Revenants." Samiel checked his girth and climbed into the saddle. "Be wary, Son of Mikha'el, nothing that dies in Hell ever rests in peace."

Stirring clouds of ash from the uneven ground, eyeless, skeletal figures rose from the soil and stood erect. They swayed from side to side as if in a stupor from a long slumber. Withered, moldy wings flapped, but could no longer capture the air. Their faces were frozen forever in poses of agonized death, as they shambled down the mountain toward the Horsemen.

"They've sensed an awakening!" With great effort,

Wyrmwood drew back the bowstring to the fullest extent and unleashed a volley of seven arrows. Hovering in the skies above her, they split into pairs and then split again until the sky was black with incoming projectiles.

Spurring his Nightmare up the mountain road, Raijin drew his great katana. "Unfaithful urches. Lie back down and accept your fate!" He hurdled a crooked ridge and landed among the walking corpses. They quickly swarmed him. His Nightmare initiated a three hundred and sixty-degree spin, clockwise and then counter-clockwise, allowing the Horseman to swiftly cut down the mob.

"Samiel, this could go badly for all of us." Bracing her feet in the stirrups, Wyrmwood leaned back as her Nightmare crow-hopped and trampled the undead angels as they attempted to rise from the ground.

Michael drew his longsword from the scabbard. "Is this how the last Horseman died?"

"Yes. These lamentable creatures are not as powerful as Titans but their strength lies in their numbers." Samiel drew the black hood over his brow. "Your predecessor came here alone, against our wishes, to claim a birthright that did not belong to him. He proved unworthy of it."

"Which way to the tilt yard?" Michael asked, referring to the place where jousts were held. He was surprised by the courage in his voice.

"Ride to the summit. We will hold this position and lure them away from you."

"You're not coming?"

"We've already gone beyond our forbearance. We can go no farther. Without our Fourth, we are weakened." Samiel pulled back on the reins to test the Nightmare's obedience to the bit. Submitting to the pressure, the warhorse lowered its head. "Horsemen, prepare the way."

"Incoming!" Wyrmwood fired a single arrow into the air above her head. In response, a torrent of gale-force wind descended on the mountain. Carried on the hurricane gusts, the hundreds of arrows she launched cut through the current, stapling the Revenants' desiccated flesh to the stony ground.

Standing in the stirrups, Raijin gripped the great katana in both hands and brought it down in a fierce, sweeping arc. A defensive line of fire erupted from a fissure in the rock and engulfed the closest revenants. It morphed into a fireball that rolled up the mountainside, fueled by the wind, devouring everything in its path. "The road is clear, but it won't be for long."

"Then I will hold it." Samiel raised the scythe out to his side. Two walls of earth jutted upward to secure an unhindered path to the summit. It funneled Raijin's fireball within it. The revenants trapped inside were incinerated or buried beneath the crushing weight of the earthen columns.

"You must go." Death regarded Michael with a smile. "Maoffras restil. May you praise Him, and that praise be immeasurable."

"For what it's worth, thank you, Samiel." Looking up to the summit, Michael grabbed Anaba's mane and tightened his grip on the hilt of his sword as she galloped away.

Samiel stared after him. "I do hope to see you again," he said sadly, "Son of Mikha'el, Son of God."

CHAPTER 11

The summit of Mount Victus was a ruin: a sprawling graveyard of cracked walls, collapsed friezes and broken pillars that littered the scorched earth. Overlooking the ravaged peak from a shattered altar, a war lance cast its solemn shadow over the deserted battlefield, a memorial to the dead on both sides of the conflict.

Water trickled through a fissure beneath the embedded blade-head. It cascaded through the ruined granite and became a waterfall. Over time, the water had pooled and formed a creek that meandered across the desolate mountaintop.

"That must be it." Michael was so transfixed on the lance he did not react to the rush of wings descending on him. Anaba bolted sideways, nearly unseating him. The tip of a blade nicked his ear. He ducked over Anaba's neck, his hands tangled in her mane.

It's an ambush!

"Unclean seed! You will die like the rest!" The black-winged soldier hovered above them. "The Grigori will not fail!" he yelled as he descended on them.

Michael braced the hilt of his longsword in both hands and blocked the stroke aimed at his neck. The practice sword twisted in his grip, fracturing along the edge of contact. Balanced precariously across Anaba's withers, he kicked the angel in the chest.

Anaba charged but the angel evaded her, buffeting her with a wing. Anaba cow-kicked his hand, disarming him, and knocked the Grigori into a crevasse with a solid headbutt.

"We need that lance," Michael said. Mourning the damage to his sword, he tossed the ruined blade to the ground.

Copy that. Hang on.

Anaba galloped into a narrow passage beneath a collapsed archway. Two more Grigori soldiers landed in front of her, blocking the path. The Nightmare slid to an abrupt halt and retreated. Hurdling a shattered rampart, she scrambled up a steep embankment onto a dilapidated bridge. The middle segment of its stonework had collapsed, leaving a twenty-foot gap in the center. Anaba lengthened her stride and launched herself over the expanse, tucking her nose between her knees to make the distance. But hidden in the fallen ramparts below, a trio of Grigori lay waiting and tackled the Nightmare in midair.

Anaba hit the ground, bringing Michael down with her in a fury of flailing wings and fiery legs. The impact dug a furrow in the soil and left a fifteen-foot trail of scorched debris through the ruins.

With the wind knocked out of him, Michael fought to stay conscious, clawing at the ground. His right leg was firmly trapped beneath the Nightmare, and a stabbing pain shot up through his calf and into his thigh. He felt faint, nauseous with the grinding of bone on bone, but swallowed the bile rising in his throat.

Lying on her side, Anaba snapped at the Grigori and kicked frantically with all four legs. They were stabbing at her exposed belly in unison. Michael heard the visceral noise of their blades rending her flesh, a sound like sharp scissors cutting through denim. The Nightmare's guttural screams cut through the fog in his head.

"Anaba!" Michael tried to get into a defensible position but was trapped beneath her. Brimstone billowed from her nostrils and a well-aimed kick on a Grigori cuirass caused a spark that ignited the sulfuric cloud. It detonated with a resounding burst of heat and flames, emitting a potent, white-hot flash. The explosion threw the Grigori thirty feet away from the injured Nightmare.

Michael flinched, shielding his head from the noise. His eardrums popped from the pressure, leaving a dull ringing. Although the intense heat enveloped him, he was unscathed even as the flames licked over his skin. "Anaba?"

The Nightmare struggled to get to her feet but failed to rise. She grunted and squealed, repeatedly kicking at the dirt. Panting in desperate, shallow breaths, she collapsed.

Michael gasped in anguish with her every attempt to move. Fearing every bone in his leg was shattered from the fall, he gritted his teeth and dug his fingernails into his thigh.

Two Grigori returned for them, covered in soot but otherwise undeterred. "Anaba, your six!" Michael shouted.

She lashed out with her tail and set the closest angel afire. Engulfed in the deadly flames, the Grigori stumbled toward the Nightmare, determined to kill her. She kicked him in the leg, shattering the tibia. As the dying angel slumped onto her hindquarters, Michael wrested the talwaar from his grip and thrust the commandeered blade into his chest.

He yanked the blade free, mustered his remaining strength, and thrust it into the neck of the other angel poised over Anaba's head. The curved sword sliced through the fleshy folds of his throat. The Grigori soldier dropped the dagger in his hand and groped for the talwaar. He wrapped his bloody fingers around the sword hilt and pulled it from his flesh, gurgling on his own blood.

"Anaba, you've got to get up!" Michael stretched to reach the discarded dagger. The hilt was just beyond his fingertips. The angel swayed unsteadily on his knees and went to drive the blade down toward the helpless Nightmare's face. As she managed to roll up for a moment, Michael grabbed hold of the dagger and threw it.

The sharp weapon found little resistance in the angel's

eye socket. The Grigori grasped at his face until his quivering fingers went limp. He collapsed beside Anaba.

The Nightmare took a deep, shuddering breath. A light steam rose from her belly where the Grigori had gutted her. She trembled uncontrollably, succumbing to shock. Michael saw the pool of blood collecting beneath her. It trickled into the stream and turned the water crimson. He didn't need to see the wounds to know they were mortal.

"Sound off, gunny."

...going to roll... Her voice was faint and strained. *...pull yourself free... get away from these bastards...*

"Not leaving you, Anaba," Michael said. "Even if I could. Pretty sure my leg's broken."

Christ... you're annoying. Anaba laid her head on the ground and took a few shallow breaths. *Good initiative... bad judgment, Special Agent Childs...* With an agonized grunt, she fought to roll. *There's more of them... time to move out.*

"Samiel said never to leave the protection of my Nightmare's back."

That's if you're sitting on my back... not under it... idiot.

Michael's mind raced through various tactical scenarios, but each of the potential outcomes ended the same – badly, until he remembered Samiel's words: *Nothing is more formidable than a Horseman on his Nightmare. Anaba is your greatest ally and your greatest weapon.*

"You're right, Anaba, I *am* a fucking idiot. The answer's been right in front of my face this whole time. Samiel practically spelled it out for me."

Michael, they're coming...

Michael snatched the dagger from the dead Grigori's skull and wiped the blade on his pants. "Pagiel said I needed a weapon forged by an archangel. That weapon? It's *you*!" He grabbed the fleshy fold of her neck and pulled himself up to her shoulder. Wiping away the dirt and grime, he stared at the Crest of Nanqueel.

Anaba raised her head, rolling one black eye back to look at him. *If you do this... you become one of them... the Horseman Famine.*

"I'm not going down without a fight," Michael said. "And neither are you." He sliced across the brand, suffering a pang of guilt when she flinched in pain. Holding his palm against the wound, he felt her blood running hot under his fingers. Michael closed his eyes and put his faith in the impossible.

An explosion rocked the summit of Mount Victus, disrupting the mountain's corkscrew revolution. The mountain buckled under its own weight as violent, seismic tremblers rearranged the ruined landscape. In a deafening blast, the stone altar beneath the war lance shattered, hurling shrapnel five hundred feet in all directions.

The war lance was catapulted, spinning end over end, through the air. Narrowly missing Michael's head, the eight-inch blade-head embedded itself in the ground beside him. Water bubbled up from beneath it and rapidly formed a shallow pool around Anaba's body. It grew deeper as the surrounding stream added to its volume.

The Nightmare took a desperate breath, her muzzle slipping beneath the water. Michael recognized the pronounced death rattle.

"Anaba?" He squirmed desperately to keep his face above the rising water, but he was out of time and allies.

Three Grigori soldiers stood at the edge of the deepening pool. While Michael writhed, in danger of drowning beneath the lucid waters, they waded in and attempted to harpoon him like an eel tangled in a fisherman's net.

Michael gasped. The involuntary act filled his lungs with water. He fought to remain conscious despite the excruciating pain in his chest. Unable to free himself from the Nightmare's dead weight, he grabbed the war lance in a futile attempt to save himself and wrested it from the ground.

A pulse of electrical energy shot through his fingers and up his arm. It paralyzed him and disrupted his heart. He closed his eyes against a blinding white light only to find the piercing glare present in the darkness too.

"Od'a Es tria'noan tliob cirp'ca El." Michael recognized his father's voice, sounding in his own head. *"And the Four shall be separate, but as One."*

A vision flashed before his eyes. Michael saw a Horseman dressed in gold and green maille. Wings unfurled, the angel sat astride a black horse as it reared from a mountaintop. They were surrounded by a churning, white-capped ocean choked full of debris and corpses.

"Ah-Azarim Aziagiar – A Bitter Harvest," Michael whispered, claiming the lance through the utterance of the ancient, Enochian name inscribed on the blade. He opened his eyes.

The waters in the pool suddenly burst upward into a spiraling funnel, surrounding Michael and Anaba within the eye of the vortex. The impenetrable water-wall rotated with such velocity that it cut through armor, shredded cloth, and blistered any exposed skin that came into direct contact. The Grigori retreated, repelled by the vortex.

"Anaba, niis!" Michael commanded, his fingers splayed across the Crest of Nanqueel.

The Nightmare lifted her head and rolled to her side, and then stood straight up, rearing on her hind legs. A plume of green flames ignited, proliferating across her neck and mane and then erupting in a roar, which set her tail ablaze. Padded in gray lambswool, a Portuguese saddle with a high-back cantle formed beneath Michael. He grabbed the pommel with one hand, gripping the lance in the other, and shoved his feet into the newly formed stirrups. Teeth clenched in anticipation of the pain, he flexed his right leg, forcing his weight into the heel. He suffered no hint of pain because the bones were no longer broken.

Anaba shook from nose to tail to expel excess water from her gleaming hide. The Crest of Nanqueel glowed vibrantly with the symbol of ancient apothecary scales etched beneath the feathers. A thin trickle of water spilled down between her ears and through her fiery green forelock to form the headstall and cheekpieces of a bridle. Bowing her head in submission, the Nightmare chewed quietly at the curb bit in her mouth.

Staring at the war lance in his hand, he watched the water trickle from the tip of the blade, down the polished, mahogany shaft, and onto his glove. It beaded along the suede surface without dampening the fabric, ensuring a firm and steady grip. Like an incoming tide, the water surged across his chest and shoulders and coalesced into a coat of gold and green maille. The gorget fit snugly about his neck and the high collar of the green gambeson beneath it. Brown leather breeches formed about his legs, complemented by matching tall boots and silver spurs.

Each Horseman is master of a domain. Famine's is water, Anaba said. *All the waters of Hell are bound by your will.*

Michael spun the lance over the back of his hand. Three black feathers bound with a leather cord hung from the base of the blade like an ornamental war token. It felt made for him: lightweight and yet sturdy enough to withstand the impact of a full charge. He set the base of the lance on the armored toe of his boot. He glared at the Grigori fighting to get through the watery barricade. They slashed and cut with their talwaars, but were unable to penetrate the lacerating vortex. He tightened his grip on the war lance. "Show me," he commanded of it.

The wall of water collapsed and sent a three-foot surge in a circular pattern. The Grigori scattered, taking to their wings. Three tendrils of water reared up from the engorged creekbed and snatched the fleeing angels from the sky. The watery coils crushed their captives, repeatedly slamming them into the ground and against the stone.

The first tendril enveloped its prisoner in a spinning watery cocoon. With each revolution, a layer of skin and muscle was stripped away from the angel. He shrieked in agony as he was flayed alive, down to the bone.

Trapped inside a swift-moving funnel of water, the second angel's black skin grew gray, hardening like stone. His faint screams turned to dry rasping as all the water in his body was forcibly drained from him. His eyes hollowed and caved in as his body was reduced to dust.

The remaining tendril tightened its coils, savagely shaking its captive like an overeager hound, as it presented its prisoner to Michael for judgment.

Michael stared into the angel's bruised face. "The open season on the Nephilim is over. Tell whatever masters you serve, I'm coming for them."

The watery tendril slammed the angel to the ground, pressing him into the mud before dissipating. As the water washed over him, the angel got to his feet, staggering and stumbling back. He glanced anxiously at the talwaar laying on the ground between him and Michael.

"Go," Michael growled, "before I change my mind." Michael drew back the reins as Anaba snorted, pawing at the ground in anticipation of a charge. The Grigori soldier quickly spread his wings and retreated into the crimson skies above the mountain.

"And lo, a black horse; and he that sat on her had the name Famine," Samiel said as he brought his warhorse to a halt before Michael, bowing his head respectfully. Wyrmwood and Raijin cantered up the mountain pass and halted beside him. *"Od'a Es tria'noan tliob cirp'ca El."*

Michael glanced at the lance and back to Death. "Guess this means I made the team?"

"Tipping the scales of your office so soon?" Raijin chuckled, scanning the skies above them. "You've made some powerful enemies, lad." He thumbed the hilt of his great katana. "This could all get very interesting and bloody."

"You fought well, Michael." Wyrmwood winked at him. "And now you have a weapon worthy of an apocalypse angel."

Michael ran his hand affectionately along Anaba's neck and across the Crest of Nanqueel; her fur was still damp. The

Nightmare tolerated his touch, blowing a warm breath over his hand and rubbing her muzzle against his fingers. "You okay?" he asked her. "Had me worried there for a minute."

"Good to go."

"Do I even want to ask about these feathers?" Michael asked, examining the totem hanging from the lance.

"A war trophy," Samiel replied. "Taken from Lucifer, himself."

"A war trophy from a fallen angel? Great! No better way to make friends, right?" He rolled his eyes. "So what happens now?"

"You have a murderer to catch, of course." Samiel cocked his head to the side and grinned. "And now you have the resources of Hell at your disposal, on Earth."

"You?" Michael pointed to the Horseman. "You're coming with me?"

"There is a celestial hand at work in all of this. The FBI is going to get a special task force capable of dealing with it." Samiel handed Michael a leather satchel. "Prepare these credentials to present to your FBI leaders."

Michael examined the dossier and read the first document with raised eyebrows. "Dr Amanda Wyrmwood from the World Health Organization? Specializing in unusual, infectious diseases?"

"Malignant strains of STDs are my specialty," Wyrmwood said with another wink.

"Dr Jakob Samiel, state coroner for Kentucky? You worked with the Attorney General of the United States?"

"That's when he's not consulting at the largest funeral home in the tri-state area," Raijin said. "Samiel wants to brag, but he won't, so I'll do it for him."

"Colonel Hiro Raijin, United States Marine Corps – military attaché to the Deputy Secretary of Defense, formerly assigned to South Korea? How does the Marine Corps feature into this?"

"One of your victims was a Marine," Raijin said. "Testy lot, those Devil Dogs. Like to take care of their own."

Michael continued reading. "And one Gunnery Sergeant Anaba Raines, USMC, assistant to Colonel Raijin. Miraculously back from the dead."

Marines don't die. We go to Hell to regroup.

Michael shook his head. "The Assistant Director's going to have my ass for bringing in a team without him vetting the request."

"Insist on a press conference," Samiel said. "Put us in the public eye where he cannot save face. There will be no dispute."

"And the Grigori will know we're involved," Raijin added. "Might give them second thoughts."

"Sounds like a plan. Thank you. All of you." Michael slapped Anaba's neck. "Think you're ready for this, gunny?"

Have you ever met a Marine who wasn't ready?

"Well, those Grigori did get the drop on us."

Anaba pinned her ears and flicked her tail across the back of his leg. *Should have killed you when I had the chance.*

CHAPTER 12

"Sweet, baby Jesus, Mike! It's like you fell off the fucking Earth!" Elijah's voice reverberated in the stillness of the guest bedroom. "We're partners, right?"

Michael held the cell phone a few inches away from his ear. Though Elijah was his closest friend, the events of the last few hours were not for sharing, not without the risk of being committed. "Of course we're partners," he replied. Michael stood by a small bay window, staring out into the dark alley between the St. Joseph's parsonage and a rundown carriage house. "Why would you even say something like that?"

"Hmm, let me see…" Elijah mocked the innocent tone in his voice. "Maybe because *one* of the two special agents assigned to this fucked up case went dark for ten hours. Maybe because the Assistant Director chewed the ass of the *only* agent available to him. Usually my partner, *my best friend,* is standing beside me. Getting his ass chewed, too. Making the experience less miserable."

"EJ, I'm sorry. I was taking care of some things."

"Like what? If we're partners, don't I deserve an explanation?"

"Not sure where to begin." Michael flopped down in a weathered recliner in the corner of the room.

Ziri was sitting at a cheap plywood desk across from him. The Tuareg boy was eating a cheeseburger, tossing fries into his mouth like popcorn.

"You can start with Anaba Raines."

"You got the documents I uploaded?"

"How does a dead soldier go from being a person of interest in a multiple homicide to being a member of the investigative team?"

"The government makes mistakes, EJ. Soldiers marked as KIA, coming home to their families. Happens all the time." Michael perched his elbows on his knees and swallowed the lie, burying his face in one hand. "Just run those documents up the flagpole to Rathan for me, will you?"

"Are you trying to get me killed? Who are these people, Mike?"

"Top professionals in their fields. Their expertise is going to crack this case wide open."

"A mortician, a doctor, a soldier, a priest, and a dead woman who kicked your ass? Sounds like a bad joke, Mike."

Michael closed his eyes. "Are you in the office?"

"No, I'm in my bed watching *Human Centipede* for the fifteenth time because I love torturing myself when you're not around to do it for me!"

"Meet me at the office." Michael glanced at his watch. It was almost five in the morning.

"Caramel latte, extra caramel, and whipped cream," Elijah said. "Make it a large."

"What?"

"My Starbucks order, Mr Trebek. And I want a hot sausage sandwich from that little corner store your mom likes. With an extra hash brown. Don't forget salt and ketchup."

Michael shook his head and laughed. "See you in a bit." With a prolonged sigh, he sat back in the oversized chair and propped his feet up.

"You going to eat that?" Ziri asked, eyeing the extra burger.

"Take it, kid. Somebody should enjoy it." Michael rested his head on the back of the recliner. Sleep was only a few deep breaths away, but he resisted the temptation. "Where's Anaba?"

"Wherever Anaba wants to be," Ziri replied with a shrug.

"Ziri, I need to make a judgment call. I don't think it's a good idea for either of you to go back to Belmont right now. Father Paige said it was okay for you to stay here at the church." Michael shuffled toward the door. "Both of you should try and get some rest."

"Anaba does not sleep." He stared at his food. "The restless spirits call out to her with their *toru.*"

"Their what?"

"Black magic."

"The kel essuf?"

"Yes, the ones she has killed in her old life and the new ones. They spill into this world through her dreams." Ziri reached for the silver cross beneath his shirt and stroked the flared corners of the talisman. "You are a part of those dreams now."

Michael sensed a hint of jealousy in the boy. "I know it was you who wrote that Tuareg blessing on the wall at Belmont." He hesitated in the doorway. "You were trying to protect me. Thank you."

"What I wish for myself, I wish for you." Ziri crossed his hand over his heart in a gesture of sincerity. "May you not be abandoned."

Michael nodded and shut the door behind him. Leaning against the faded black and red Art-Deco wallpaper in the hall, he closed his eyes and took a deep breath. He was overwhelmed, exhaustion exasperating his sense of helplessness. But he had to keep going. The only light in the corridor came from the kitchen. Reluctantly, he followed it.

"It must have been quite the initiation with the Horsemen," Father Paige said, coaxing a dark brew from an antiquated coffee machine. "Here, take this." The priest handed him a steaming cup of coffee. "You must be running on fumes."

Michael sipped cautiously at the rim of the mug, breathing in the pungent aroma. It was delicious and started to revive him. "Samiel said you were there for the Battle of Mount Victus."

"I fought in all three wars: the Battle of the Celestial Throne, the Battle of Mahorela, and the Battle of Mount Victus." He poured himself a cup of coffee and stared into the steam. "It was at Mount Victus that the Morningstar nearly prevailed. Though we had the superior numbers, our forces were overmatched. Until your father led a handful of mounted lancers against Lucifer and turned the tide."

Michael imagined his father, dressed in burnished plate armor, leading a hard charge while carrying the war lance Ah-Azarim Aziagiar against the enemy lines.

"Did you think you came to jousting by accident? Your father was unrivaled. He rode a Haala, a celestial horse. There were so few of them left after the first war. By the final battle, they were extinct. The last to fall was the stallion Nanqueel."

"As in the Crest of Nanqueel?"

"In Enochian, the name literally means power. He died shielding your father. I don't think Mikha'el's heart was truly in the fight until that moment." Father Paige looked away, his lips pursed in thought.

"I need to get back to the office," Michael said, changing the subject. "Have you seen Anaba?"

"She's sulking in the garden." The priest chuckled at the doleful expression on Michael's face. "Anaba's kept to the shadows for a long time. Distrust has helped her survive. Don't expect her to change her behavior so soon. If at all."

"Ziri says she can hear spirits."

"She's a Nightmare, of course she hears them." Father Paige wiped his hands on a dish-rag and tossed it onto the pocked, olive-green counter. "Anaba is what she has always been – an apex predator. A soldier who believes the cavalry is never coming for her."

Michael resented the priest's curt dismissal of the Marine. "She's more than that, Father. At least to me. I can't understand how someone like Anaba was sent to Hell, any more than the innocent Nephilim. She was an exemplary soldier, following orders until she went dark in Syria. Something happened to her. Do you know what?"

"I don't know the ledger of her soul or what sins brought her to this final judgment, but her pernicious nature made her soul irresistible to the Fallen." He took the coffee mug, poured the contents into a styrofoam cup, and handed it to Michael. "For the road. I think you're going to need it."

Michael took the coffee gratefully and nodded. "Thanks, Father. See you this afternoon at the press conference."

"I'll be there."

A solitary lamppost cast its glow across the quaint garden between the parsonage and the rear of the church. It flickered erratically, besieged by moths, offering little illumination. Other than the dull, intermittent hum of the failing bulb, the night was still.

Michael sat down on a wrought-iron bench in front of a koi pond. The warm weather had broken the spell of winter torpor, but the exotic fish were leery, huddling together in the warmer waters at the bottom. Michael stuck his finger into the pond and concentrated on raising the temperature. To his surprise, it worked. Five grateful dorsal fins broke the smooth surface. Unblinking, the koi peered up at him from the water with thankful black eyes.

"Expecting trouble, gunny?" he asked the air.

"Always." Anaba stepped away from the shadows of the fence line. Hands in her pockets, she sat down beside him.

The night skies were blunted by the approach of dawn. It was difficult to look up at the stars with any sense of wonder after riding the Vestibule Road with the Horsemen of the Apocalypse.

Anaba tossed her dreadlocks over her shoulders and crossed her legs. "Isn't quite the same when you come back, is it?"

"Not exactly. How long were you in Hell?"

"Twenty years. Give or take."

Michael stared at her. "Your file says you were listed KIA three years ago."

"Time moves differently in Hell."

"Why is that?"

"How the fuck would I know! God has a sick sense of humor? Go ask Him. You're a Horseman now," she said, irritation in her voice.

"Sorry, dumb question." Michael spread his arms across the metal backrest of the bench. "What was it like when you first came back?"

"Spent three months in Northern Africa, living with the Tuareg, retracing my steps just trying to figure out what happened. The Sahara is beautiful, but not much changes there, so I came home. Sat in Central Park for like nine hours, taking in the sights like some pathetic tourist. Shit, even breathing in taxicab exhaust felt like a privilege."

"Now that's what I call true appreciation."

"After watching the sunset over Manhattan, I went and had myself an ice-cold beer." She turned to him with those discerning eyes that missed very little. "You were only in Hell for a few hours, but you have the thousand-yard stare of a soldier who's been in the shit for a full tour. But this is no time to be shell-shocked, Special Agent Childs. Don't get a god-complex either. You might be the Horseman Famine, but you're mortal, and so am I. Remember that."

"Fair enough," he replied. "Do you mind keeping watch here until the press conference? Anything out of order, I need to know."

Anaba hesitated, as if mulling over her compliance. "Copy that."

"How do I – how do we – stay in touch?"

"A cellphone works," she said with a slight smile. "Pass me your phone and I'll put my number in your contacts. Ziri's, too." Michael handed it to her without question. As she keyed in the information on his phone, it played a bar of the Moonlight Sonata indicating an incoming message. Inadvertently reading the text, Anaba frowned and handed it back.

Michael, we need to talk. –Mom

"Shit." Michael tucked the phone into his pocket.

Anaba snorted. "What are you going to tell her?"

"The plan is to avoid her for at least twenty-four hours," he replied, reaching for his keys. "Hold down the fort. I'll see you at the Javits Federal Building downtown."

CHAPTER 13

Lowering his face into the sink in the office restroom, Michael splashed cold water over his cheeks. The noise of the running faucet soothed his tension but did not eliminate it. If only for a moment, he wanted to feel numb to restore some sense of objectivity and balance. When he reached into the water again, the temperature was much colder. His breath generated a thin fog as the conflicting temperatures clashed in the porcelain basin.

He felt a chill but his body was too fatigued to shiver. Leaning on the counter, Michael stared at his reflection in the mirror. Behind him, he saw a field of purple, waist-deep grass with the shambling hulk of a Titan rising from the pitch beneath a blood-red sky. He closed his eyes and shook the image from his mind. When he dared to look up again, he saw the true reflection of the men's room.

No time for you to be shell-shocked. Anaba's words rang with truth.

Michael rested his hands on the basin and stared down at his injuries. Despite awakening as a Horseman, the burns from the qeres were still inflamed, and he wondered if there would be any permanent damage. The wound from the Titan's blood was even worse – while no bigger than a dime, it resembled a plague boil. He dried his hands carefully so as not to burst it and put a band-aid over the injury to conceal it.

The familiar melody of the Moonlight Sonata played from his pocket sounding the arrival of a message. He reluctantly retrieved his phone and read the text: *Michael?*

Avoidance was never a winning tactic when it came to his mother. *Now's not a good time,* he texted. *Watch CNN at noon. I'm making my TV debut.* Michael imagined her laughter while reading the last line.

Straightening his tie, he went back to his desk.

"Got *da bots*?" Elijah asked around a mouthful of hash browns. His feet were propped up on Michael's cluttered desk. It was difficult to discern if his tone was genuine concern or sarcasm. "That's Southern for diarrhea."

Michael ran a hand through his short unruly locs in bafflement. "And you call me weird."

Elijah cupped the caramel latte in both hands. "My grandmama spent a time or two in a graveyard after dark to pray, but your mom was actually digging up the corpses. If being weird was a contest, you win, Sir Lancelot."

"Whatever. Rathan in yet?" It was early, even for their field office. They looked to be the only agents on the floor. Michael cast his eyes in the direction of the executive suites.

"Rolled in five minutes ago. I was glad you were in the bathroom. He didn't have any reason to stop and hurl insults."

Michael's stomach rumbled. "You plan on sharing that other hash brown?"

"Nope." Grinning at his partner, Elijah bit off a large chunk and chewed loudly with his mouth open before swallowing it. "One hash brown for each asscheek. It's only fair."

"This is why you're still single." Michael noticed a manila envelope on his desk. Without bothering to read the label on the front of it, he reached into it. "What's this?"

"Toxicology report. Lab got a confirmation on that oily shit we keep finding at the crime scenes. And I asked for the small sample to be returned."

Recoiling as if bitten by a rattlesnake, Michael withdrew his hand and leaped away from his desk. He stumbled over the back of his chair and knocked it to the floor.

Startled, Elijah sat back too far and fell out of his chair, rolling under his desk with the urgency of a soldier dodging a grenade. His caramel latte splashed to the floor. "What the fuck, Mike?"

"It's called qeres." Michael examined his hand for signs of the unctuous oil. Though lightheaded, he realized the symptom was a result of holding his breath, not the effects of exposure to the angelic poison.

"So why the fuck are you acting like it's Saran gas?" Elijah crawled from beneath his desk and stared at the remains of his latte soaking into the carpet. "Look at this shit!" He grabbed the envelope and threw the sealed evidence bag on Michael's desk. "You act like the lab sent us an airborne derivative of herpes. Get a grip, son."

"My mom warned me that a small percentage of people are allergic to that shit." Michael leaned over his desk and buried his face in his hands. "All our victims were; it's what killed them. And so am I."

"That's what caused the anaphylaxis?" Elijah said pointing to the bag. "So that bandage on your hand? It's from an allergic reaction to this stuff?"

Michael held his hand up to show the blisters. "Yeah."

Elijah picked up the evidence bag with two fingers and dropped it into a side drawer. Grabbing a bottle of hand sanitizer, he poured half of the solution into his hands and rubbed until his fingers dripped. "Need some?" He offered the half empty container to Michael.

"I'm good. Just need to be careful."

"This is huge, Mike. Why didn't you tell me?"

"There's so much going on right now, EJ." Michael smoothed the edges of the band-aid against his skin. "My adverse reaction to an embalming oil was not at the top of the list."

"I meant about the vics, partner. This is another solid lead. If we can make a connection between this allergic reaction and the victims, we might get the clues we need to break this case."

Elijah rubbed a hand across his chin. "What about these new team members you've brought on board? Isn't one of them a doctor? Where'd you find these experts."

"My mom recommended them," Michael said, looking away as he uttered the lie.

Elijah picked up and flipped through the dossier files from his desk. "Here it is: a doctor from the World Health Organization. She studies contagions; didn't realize homicide could be identified as a disease."

"It's fatal."

Elijah shrugged. "And the mortician?"

"Has ties to the AG's office in DC," Michael said. "Might need the clout to sell this to the Assistant Director."

"And the Marine Corps full-bird colonel?"

Michael braced himself. His partner was as relentless as a polygraph machine. "Why wouldn't the military take an interest? One of the vics was a Marine training in cyberterrorism and intelligence."

Elijah stared at the half-eaten hash brown. Having lost his appetite, he threw it in the trash. "And the not-so-dead Marine who kicked your ass?"

"Raines?"

"Stop playing, Mike. I know your mom's got means, but how in the hell did she pull this off?"

Maneuvering to change the topic, Michael asked, "Did you see the rookie they assigned us from Quantico? What's her name?"

"Rachel Rollins."

"Let Rollins go fishing for those federal court orders to review hospital records. She can start digging into those missing hospital records. Tell her to keep her eyes open for anything on the data breaches." Michael smiled at the slender Black woman dressed in a gray skirt suit approaching their cubicle. "Morning, Chelsea."

"Morning, Special Agent Childs and Special Agent Pope," she replied with a South African accent. "Assistant Director Rathan is ready to see you in his office."

"What's the temperature, Chels?" Elijah asked.

"You don't need a serial killer to get murdered in the press or the court of public opinion, boys." She clasped her hands together. "Tread carefully."

"Hear that, Mike? That's the sound of my ass crying as we go back in for round two. Rathan hates when you think outside of his box." Elijah snatched his coat from the back of the chair. "You owe me another caramel latte."

Michael prided himself on his looks, even when he was covered from head to toe in stone dust and saddle oil. There was an allure to being dressed in armor, riding on the back of a horse, while cheering admirers waved pennants to show their support for his colors at the Renaissance Challenge. But whenever he stood in Assistant Director Rathan's presence, he felt remarkably inadequate. There was something ancient about the man's stoic, brown eyes and his irises that were so dark they could not be seen, even in direct sunlight.

"Special Agent Childs, welcome back."

"Assistant Director?"

"You went uncharacteristically dark. Gave your partner quite the fright. I'm surprised Special Agent Pope didn't call in CIRG." Rathan scrolled across a report on an electronic tablet on his desk. "But I see from this paperwork he didn't need to call in a Critical Incident Response Group, because *you* did. Two Marines, a priest, a coroner, and a doctor. Sounds like the makings of a bad joke."

"See?" Elijah said. "I'm not the only one."

Rathan frowned. "I can't wait to hear the punchline, gentlemen."

"Assistant Director–"

"Save it, Special Agent Childs. I want a full report. Before I approve your request for a press conference, I want to be certain you won't make a fool of the FBI, the City of New York, and most importantly, *me*."

Elijah cleared his throat. "Our serial killer–"

"*Suspect,* Agent Pope," Rathan interrupted. "Words like serial killer tend to alarm the public. Not to mention, the press, who take special delight in playing the naming game. Harbinger has quite the ring to it, don't you agree?"

"The suspect," Michael said, "is showing a pattern of ritualistic, occult behavior, sir. Even with my extensive background in Archaeology, I'm chasing ghosts."

"Thus, the priest." Rathan bowed his head, a smile in the corners of his mouth.

"Father Paige is more than an academic, Director Rathan. He's a familiar face. His presence on the investigative team will reassure the community."

"You seem strangely confident of that." Rathan reared his head back. He reminded Michael of a cobra flattening its neck before striking. "What's changed?"

"You're always talking about initiative, so I took your advice, sir. When my partner and I hit a wall, I went looking for the people who could get us over, under, or around it."

"Clever words, but that's all they are. You can't expect me to go in front of the press with a toxicology report on embalming oils and your good intentions."

"I wasn't expecting you to run the press conference. I should be the one running it," Michael stated. "These experts will give us new insight into the investigation, while reassuring the public the FBI is on the case in earnest."

Rathan folded his hands in front of his chin and looked to Elijah with a bemused expression. "And your take on this?"

"It's solid, sir. Fresh eyes on the evidence. Showcasing our resources. Keeping the community calm. It all goes a long way."

Rathan was silent for a moment. "I don't share your convictions, gentlemen. I'm cancelling the press conference. The matter's not up for discussion." He taunted Michael with a smug grin.

The door to the office cracked open. "Assistant Director Rathan?" Chelsea called.

"Chelsea, I asked not to be disturbed."

"I know, Assistant Director, but there's a Dr Amanda Wyrmwood here. She claims it's a matter of urgency." Chelsea struggled to keep the door closed, but a pair of perfectly manicured fingers pushed through her.

"Never mind! Here they are." Wyrmwood paraded into the office in a pair of six-inch Miu Miu stilettos as if strutting down an exclusive designer's catwalk. With an attitude as vibrant as her crimson lipstick, she was dressed for a night at the opera in a sleeveless, black Gucci dress.

"Michael, darling!" Pestilence embraced him with a kiss on each cheek. "What a dreary flight! Twenty-three hours, even in first class. Downright torture! Who would have thought Africa was so far away."

"Ma'am, you can't–" The frustrated administrative assistant was distracted by another shadow lurking outside the door. "Sir! You can't just walk in there."

"I'm expected," a gravelly voice sounded. Dressed in a somber black business suit, Samiel removed the wide-brimmed hat from his head and walked into the office. With his brown curls slicked back, Death took a black handkerchief from his pocket and dabbed at his forehead.

"Dr Samiel!" Wyrmwood flashed her best smile. "Feels like only yesterday. You haven't aged a bit. What's your secret?"

"Embalming fluid and a decent make-up kit," he replied. "Dr Wyrmwood, you are radiant as ever." He bowed at the waist and kissed her hand.

"I'm so sorry, sir," Chelsea said, flustered. "I did try to–"

"It's quite alright, Chelsea," the Assistant Director replied with slight irritation. "Should I be expecting anyone else?"

"Ah, yes sir," Chelsea replied miserably, stepping aside in defeat. She pulled open the door and invited the remaining visitors through. "Thank you for waiting patiently, Colonel Raijin, Gunnery Sergeant Raines. Please, go in. Everyone else has."

Hearing Anaba's name, Michael held his breath. Raijin walked into the crowded suite dressed in an olive green uniform with a breast full of ribbons. Anaba followed, stern-faced and taciturn, maintaining a respectful distance. She wore the regulation dress uniform of the United States Marine Corps: a midnight blue blouse and slacks, white gloves, and the distinctive white service cap that made the Marines stand out from all other military personnel. The brim of the cap sat low over her brow, pushed forward by the tight coil of dreadlocks wound into a bun at the back of her head.

Carrying his cap under his left arm and a riding crop in his hand, Raijin nodded to the Assistant Director and the other professionals in the room. "Hope I'm not late to the party."

"Just in time, Colonel," Michael said, offering his hand for a firm handshake.

Assistant Director Rathan stood up and buttoned his coat. Lips pursed into a thin, reproving line, he appeared unfazed by the chaos evolving in his office. "Dr Wyrmwood, Dr Samiel, Colonel Raijin, while I can appreciate your willingness to assist the FBI in this investigation, I'm sorry to tell you that I must cancel the press conference today for lack of definitive evidence."

"The hell you will!" a voice boomed as Mayor Leonard Watersworth barged into the office, ignoring Chelsea's pleas to wait and be properly announced. Dressed in a beige tweed jacket and khakis, the city's top politician adjusted the tartan plaid beanie on his bald, white head. Seeing Wyrmwood, his stark, political veneer was replaced with a kinder, more affable expression only seen at election time. "Mandy, my beautiful nightingale! Saving Africa one immunization at a time!"

"Lenny, you got my call!" Wyrmwood kissed the air on both sides of his face as he turned his head to accept the greeting.

"Still single?"

"Still looking for the right one, Lenny, since you're not on the market."

"A man can dream, right?" He smiled showing all of his perfectly-white teeth before remembering his true purpose, and glaring at the FBI Assistant Director. "What's this about canceling the press conference? I won't have it, Rathan. Press conferences are so much BS anyway. Theatrics to make people feel good." He grinned again at Wyrmwood. "People are scared. Our job is to make them feel safe again."

"Oh, Lenny," Wyrmwood said. "I love your take-charge voice."

"As they say on Broadway," the politician said, "the show will go on."

Except for the flaring of his nostrils, Rathan showed little reaction to being overruled. "Mr Mayor?"

"Not another word." Watersworth scanned the room and rigorously shook hands with Raijin and then Samiel. "One hell of a team! Ah, Special Agent Childs!" he said, squinting through his wire spectacles and firmly shaking Michael's hand. "You certainly have your mother's gift for networking."

"You know my mother?" Michael flaccidly returned the handshake. The mayor didn't seem to notice his lack of vigor.

"She appraised a set of 15th-century Turkish armor and put the damn suit together for my collection. Wife hates it, but my grandchildren can't get enough." The mayor then shook Elijah's hand. "Special Agent Pope, you're going places." He slapped him on the shoulder. "What's the hold up? The wolves are at the door, and I have a one o'clock tee-time. Shake a leg, people."

"Mr Mayor," Michael said, "we're waiting on Father Paige from St. Joseph's."

"A doctor, a mortician, two Marines, and a Catholic priest –

sounds like a bad joke," Watersworth said with a chuckle. "Sadly, these horrible murders are no laughing matter. The people of the five boroughs are lucky to have you all."

At that moment, Chelsea came back through the office door, struggling to maintain her composure after being overrun. "Special Agent Childs, Father Paige is waiting downstairs." She paused to look over Michael's shoulder to Rathan. "Sir, the press have been waiting for over an hour. They're getting impatient."

"Bloody piranhas," Watersworth said under his breath. "Shall we feed them?" He threw his arm out for Dr Wyrmwood.

"Lenny, you say the funniest things." As she took the mayor's arm, Wyrmwood pulled Elijah along by his tie. She winked and blew kisses at him while the mayor, oblivious to her antics, walked her to the door.

"Coming, Assistant Director?" Michael asked.

"Well played, Mr Childs." Glaring at him, Rathan sat down at his desk. "As you said, this is *your* press conference. Benediximus."

CHAPTER 14

"Unofficially dubbed 'The Harbinger', an alleged serial killer has New York City and its citizens on edge tonight. According to an NYPD source that requested to remain anonymous, the killer has committed three brutal homicides." A female reporter wearing a white blouse and red blazer stepped off screen as the camera zoomed in on the Jacob K. Javits Federal Building behind her. The footage from the press conference was playing across the widescreen television in the darkened FBI conference room.

"Mayor Leonard Watersworth," the reporter's voice continued, "and Special Agent Michael Childs of the Federal Bureau of Investigation held a joint press conference earlier today to address public concern. Surrounded by members of a newly appointed FBI task force, the mayor asked that anyone with information contact his office immediately. A substantial reward of a hundred thousand dollars is being offered for any tips leading to an arrest."

The tall brunette came back into frame with the microphone in both hands. "The press conference ended with a prayer led by Father Patrick Paige from St. Joseph of the Merciful Heart Catholic Church. The well-respected priest appealed to the guilty party to turn themselves in and bring peace to the victims' families. This is Lisa Walker with WCNB News."

Sitting in the back of the conference room, Assistant Director Rathan pressed the remote control to pause the recording. The cool glow of the overhead lights winked on, but with the dimmer switch set to its lowest level, there was more shadow than illumination.

Police Commissioner Roy Cobb ran a hand across his mouth and chin. "The Four Horsemen of the Apocalypse broadcast openly in the news and these naked apes are too ignorant to realize it." He yanked on the hem of his uniform to stretch the material over his ample stomach. "It was a mistake to give them free will. They deserve enslavement, if only to save them from themselves."

The Assistant District Attorney, Sieara Kirstein, pursed her lips into a fine line. Her thinning blond hair was pinned back from her elongated face and the style made her look gaunt, as if her skin were stretched too thinly over her anorexic frame. "They didn't even bother to hide their names."

"This changes nothing," Cobb said. "Our Enochian wards permit us to infiltrate human society and shield our presence, even from our brethren. The Horsemen don't know who we are, which means we can continue with our objective unimpeded."

"With the Horsemen breathing down our necks?" City Councilman Hunter Wern protested.

"You always were such a coward," Cobb jeered, crossing his forearms over his ample chest.

"There's a difference between picking your battles when you know you can win them and losing everything because you weren't adequately prepared, brother!" Wern shot back.

"Is that Pagiel?" Kirstein asked. "Masquerading as a priest? Can't believe that traitor would dare show himself so publicly." Kirstein's face became angular and cruel. "Samiel must be having a good laugh at all this."

"Pagiel will be rewarded for his treachery," Cobb said calmly. "I'll slice his throat and carve my name into his skin.

He must be hiding the Nephilim in his church. Now that we know where they might be, it's only a matter of finding and exterminating them." The Police Commissioner looked to the head of the table. "Rathaniel," he said, using the archangel's given name, "what of this Nephilim agent of yours, Michael Childs? He needs to be eliminated as well."

Wern gasped. "Have you forgotten who his father is?"

"Rathaniel?" Kirstein stared at the silent Assistant Director, ignoring Wern's dramatics. "This isn't just our mess. It's yours. Say something."

"Defeatists, every one of you. No better than the flawed clay we are forced to walk among." Rathan leaned into the edge of the oak table that he shared with his fellow Grigori commanders. "Have we not used the Son of Mikha'el to our advantage to flush out others like him?" He took a moment to stare at each of them. "Did we not agree that when his usefulness waned, he would also face the Ritual of Descarbia?"

"But he's a Horseman now!" Kirstein slammed her hands against the table. "Raising your blade against a Herald is like raising it against the Lord God, Himself."

"He's a fulfillment of the prophecy. The Qaaun," Wern said, supporting her. "You all remember the sacrifices made to eliminate the last emissary the Father sent to mankind."

"Killing Childs will be no different." Rathan folded his hands, intertwining his fingers, and sat back in his chair. "Pagiel's prayer was to restore public faith to the community."

"So?" Wern challenged.

"We must undermine that faith by destroying any peace of mind at its core, so that we might continue our work without scrutiny."

"And the Horsemen?" Cobb asked. "They're calling us out. They want us to know they're here."

"Who is the woman with them? The one in uniform?" Cobb asked. "One of Raijin's fanatical minions?"

Rathaniel hit the remote, rewinding the footage, and

zoomed in on the Marine standing at Michael's side. "She's a Nightmare."

"Impossible!" Wern said. "She's human. The only Nightmare capable of maintaining its human form was the first. Are you saying there's another?"

"Yes," a voice whispered from the corner of the room. Dressed in a black suitcoat and pants, the Grigori soldier approached the table. "She's the one, Fifth Commander. The Nightmare who saved Childs in the alley."

"Nuriel," Cobb said, his face lined with concern, "are you certain of this?"

"I watched her slaughter one of my brothers." Nuriel pointed her finger at the television screen. "That's her."

"You were aware of this?" Wern accused, glaring at Rathan.

Rathan smiled smugly, ignoring the high emotions of his fellow commanders. "Her presence changes nothing."

"She changes everything. Getting close enough to kill the Son of Mikha'el will be even more difficult now." Kirstein scowled, shaking her head. "We must assume the beast will always be nearby."

"Which is why I'm bringing in an expert." Rathan stared at the image on the screen. He quietly tapped his fingertips together in contemplation.

"What are you up to, Rathaniel?" Kirstein demanded. "Nothing is done without the unanimous approval of this council."

"Do you remember the Archangel Caim Seere?"

"The Cherubim who fell for his foolish indecision?" Cobb fidgeted with the brim of his cap. "What of him?"

"He may be willing to assist us." Rathan looked up to meet the hardened eyes of his fellow commanders. "He has accepted my invitation and is on his way."

"What stake does Caim Seere have in this?" Kirstein brushed a hair from her face. "He's damned already. He has nothing to lose and nothing to gain, either."

"Caim allegedly forged this Nightmare and may yet exercise some control over her," Rathan replied. "More importantly, he's an outsider with no connections in Hell. The Horsemen will not be expecting any treachery from him until it's too late."

"An unusual strategy, Rathaniel," Cobb said. "And a very unorthodox ally. We need time to plan."

"We'll have plenty." Rathan stood up, buttoning his coat. Nuriel hurried to open the door for him. "I've arranged a homecoming party for the Horseman Famine. A little test to see if he can get his house in order... or die trying."

"Meaning?" Wern sneered.

Rathan nodded to each of them solemnly. "We will shake the Horsemen off our scent by giving them other pressing matters to consider."

Kirstein leaned forward with interest. "How do you propose to do that?"

"By putting a wrinkle in the investigations," Rathan replied. "We will orchestrate another ritual. Only this time, the chosen Nephilim will survive, and a human will die."

CHAPTER 15

Industrial ventilation shafts pumped sterilized air into the spacious subbasement beneath the Jacob K. Javits Federal Building, circulating a frigid current throughout the state-of-the-art morgue and the main examination room. The drone of the aging HVAC system competed with the rattle of the central refrigeration unit. Designed to house forty bodies in separate compartments, the stainless steel cube of metal drawers appeared to be more modern art than mausoleum. Four of the cold drawers were opened, their occupants draped beneath white sheets. Opaque and hazy, their vacant, glassy eyes stared into the dropped ceiling.

"Vincent Blake, forty-three, accountant, father of three. He was the first victim." Michael's voice sounded hollow as he read the report to Samiel and Raijin. "Lance Corporal Braeden Harris, nineteen, murdered while visiting family in Harlem. From the defensive wounds on his hands and arms, he clearly put up a fight. Mary Klinedinst, thirty-six, engaged, elementary school teacher. She was the third victim, or so I thought. Nathan Ponds, the final victim, was unofficially housed in the basement of St. Joseph's until a few hours ago."

Michael closed the file and laid it on the examination table behind him. "All four were born with twelve fingers and twelve toes. Blake had his additional digits surgically amputated shortly after birth. Harris' parents had the sixth fingers removed, but left the toes, and Mr Ponds and Miss Klinedinst were fully intact."

"This is horrific, even for the Grigori." Raijin stared down his nose at the indelible glyphs carved into Harris' face. "I've not seen the Ritual of Descarbia since the Battle of the Celestial Throne, where it was first employed by Lucifer's despicable corps."

"I had my own doubts until now." Samiel examined the wounds on Mary Klinedinst's face. "The Enochian is flawless. Mankind is rarely capable of such perfection, at least, not without divine intervention."

"Why would God allow this?" Michael asked.

"The Ritual of Descarbia was a practice so offensive to the Father that He damned any angel who practiced it," Samiel explained. "The Grigori have fallen farther than I feared."

"This is a declaration of war against the Nephilim and a warning to other angels not to interfere." Raijin removed his cap and slapped it against his thigh in disgust. "Revolting, but it's a proven stratagem. If your hand proves heavy enough against your enemies, there is no need to fear retribution. We were right to get involved in this, Samiel."

Michael slid a hand down his face and chin. "That could be me laying in that drawer."

"You are the only Son of Mikha'el," Samiel said. "Killing you might have attracted the attention of your father." He covered up the mutilated face of the schoolteacher and pushed the tray back into the cold drawer.

"And yet they've made two attempts on his life," Raijin countered. "Perhaps they're testing the waters? I'd have done no less."

"Exactly. So where is he? My esteemed father." Michael clenched his jaw. "Missing, as usual."

"You didn't need your father when they attacked, Michael. You had his grace and his training." Samiel covered up the remaining bodies and pushed them back into the drawers with quiet veneration. "And you had Anaba. These people had no one."

"The Nephilim have ties to angels through a distant lineage," Raijin said, "but their blood has become so diluted over the generations. Their grace barely manifests itself. Not like yours."

Michael turned to the Horseman of War for an explanation. "Grace?"

"Your accountant-victim ran an extremely successful business. He had a gift for numbers. That was no coincidence." Samiel discarded his latex gloves into a bin and then perused the file reports. "Miss Klinedinst was a nationally recognized teacher with a talent for working with difficult children."

"Though his records were classified, Harris displayed a gift for counterintelligence." Raijin grinned proudly. "Distant parentage or no, that's the classic trademark of a Cherubim, the warrior class. I should know."

Michael raised his chin, almost in defiance. "What is *my* grace?"

"Considering your lineage?" Samiel replied. "Governance."

"What does that even mean, Samiel?"

"Military authority, my boy," Raijin answered. "You were born to the role of command and leadership, not unlike your father."

Michael closed his eyes, chafed by the compliment. If leadership was his grace, it would explain a great deal about his life: how others looked to him in times of chaos, relied on him for answers, and sought his counsel. It would also explain, given the state of the nature of the turbulent relationship with his father, why he took every opportunity he could to buck authority.

"If God was so angry, why rescind the order to exterminate the Nephilim?" Michael asked, desperate to move the topic of conversation away from himself.

"Initially, He sent the Grigori to slay only the worst of the Nephilim, the monstrosities that threatened the Creation,"

Samiel explained, "but His rage led him to declare a death sentence on them all."

"So destroying them was personal? An affront to His power?" Michael murmured, meeting Samiel's gaze. "Until, of course, He realized that He needed something from them. What was it? What did he need?"

"In war there is only one munition that counts." Raijin forced a chuckle. "*Allies*. After surviving three devastating wars, Heaven is now depleted and divided, while Hell is brimming with the Fallen. A fourth battle is brewing."

"Allies? How many Nephilim can there possibly be?" Michael asked.

"Don't need a vast army," Raijin said. "Just a good one. Leonidas and his Spartans proved that to be true. With a little strategic advice from yours truly." He made a small, self-congratulatory bow.

"Right, OK. But if Heaven will lose without the Nephilim fighting with them, why are the Grigori still killing them?"

Raijin took a deep breath and sighed. "The Grigori do not fear defeat so much as they fear imperfection. They'd rather see Heaven fall than be defiled."

The door to the examination room burst open. "We've got problems," Wyrmwood announced, making her way into the morgue. Her heels clacked noisily against the tile. Anaba followed her like a shadow, pausing at the door to see if they were tailed. The Marine was unusually tense, her body language suggesting she was ready for a fight.

"All is not well within our borders," Wyrmwood explained. "We need to return to DrunGer, and I mean now."

"What's DrunGer?" Michael asked.

"DrunGer is the collective name for our estates." Wyrmwood glanced at a scrap of paper in her hand. Michael recognized the handwriting scrawled on it. Before she could tuck it between the cleft of her breasts, he snatched it out of her fingers.

"Is that EJ's phone number?"

"Maybe..." she said coyly, grinning at him. Her tongue peeked out from the corner of her mouth as she snatched the note back.

"Wyrmwood! He's my *partner*, and he has no idea who you are. Where is he?"

"With Pagiel," Anaba said, brushing by him, removing her cap, and tucking it under her arm. "He's cross-referencing that missing-persons list with the roster of people hiding in the church. He's safe." The Marine glanced at Wyrmwood warily. "For now."

"What's the trouble in DrunGer this time, Wyrmwood?" Raijin asked. "Did one of your mischievous Sylphs pick a fight with my Ifrits again?"

"Our estates are under attack, Raijin. My Nightmare Kali reached out to Anaba." Wyrmwood's Gucci ensemble faded, replaced with the pristine, white archer leathers of her office.

The potent stench of sulfur preceded the arrival of the Nightmares. In a cloud of brimstone that could not be recycled or filtered, they emerged together from a portal of darkness and trotted into the examination room. Transformed within a smaller pocket of depthless night and molten flecks, Anaba stood apart from them, saddled and bridled in her Nightmare form.

"Anaba, what are they telling you?" Samiel said. His business suit dissolved away into the black, hooded robe of the Angel of Death.

Malis says that DrunGer has been overrun, Anaba replied.

"That's a grim assessment!" Raijin's olive uniform had faded into the crimson, multi-plated samurai armor.

"In Hell?" Michael questioned.

"Yes. DrunGer is sovereign land. The name means *the heart within,*" Samiel said. "Think of it as a divine embassy in enemy territory. The boundaries of our estates protect its borders."

A familiar weight settled across Michael's shoulders. His suit was replaced with an olive-green gambeson beneath a full shirt of golden maille. The intricate links caught the harsh light in the morgue and cast golden halos of green and gold across his face. A pleated green skirt of fabric and maille covered his leather leggings and the tops of his tall boots.

Bitter Harvest, his father's war lance, was sheathed at his saddle. Michael yanked it free. The wicked, black tip glistened as if coated in venom. He stood in awe of the lance and the war horse. "Anaba, seeing you like this will never get old."

Anaba bowed her head to him and chewed lightly at the bit in her mouth. *You sound like a fangirl. Shut up and climb on.*

CHAPTER 16

The nexus of spectral byways, switchbacks, and hidden crossroads made traversing the Vestibule Road nearly impossible without a Nightmare to navigate the treacherous pass. In the company of the Horsemen, Michael galloped down the gravel path at a breakneck pace. Riding two abreast, the Nightmares and their Riders took up the width of the road. The conflagration of flame generated by the Nightmares' hooves sent a warning ahead of them and left a trail of fire in their wake.

"By God's Will! Do you feel that, Son of Mikha'el?" Raijin's black wings rose and fell from his shoulders in excitement. "When we ride together as four, there is no greater force to be found in Heaven or Hell!"

"Our power is diminished when any Horseman falls," Wyrmwood interjected. She leaned over the pommel of her saddle and gave her Nightmare a tap on the flank with her bow. Her gray wings fanned out to capture the wind.

Michael swallowed his envy. Despite his lack of wings, their power – *his* power – was intoxicating. "And the Four shall be separate, but as One."

"Yes, Michael." Samiel's black wings were larger than the other two combined. Interspersed with gold feathers, they encircled Death beneath a macabre halo as they rode. "Your powers have not truly awakened yet. Imagine the force we shall be when that day comes."

"So who would have the balls to attack the home of the Four Horsemen?" Michael asked.

"One of us fell, leaving the borders of DrunGer vulnerable. But we shall quickly rectify that!" Raijin beat a fist against his chest. "An attack on one Horseman is an attack on them all. There will be dire consequences."

Michael loosened the reins, adjusting the excess bight across Anaba's mane and withers. "Why do I feel strangely responsible for this attack?"

"You shouldn't," Samiel replied. "The death of your predecessor some centuries ago has led to no end of opportunists seeking to test our resolve."

Raijin's Nightmare veered off the Vestibule Road onto a narrow trail, forcing the Horsemen to ride in a single-file line. The path led into an overgrown fen of wild sedge grass. Pools of murky water lined with cypress trees. The marshy conditions would have bogged down ordinary mounts, but with the Touch of Zephyr the Nightmares maneuvered through the swamps without incident, leaping hedge brushes and cantering across bogs.

Farther in, the verdant foliage turned pale and sallow. Wilted plant life languished in the throes of a devastating malaise that threatened the entire ecosystem. "This is *my* estate?" Michael asked, his disappointment evident.

"These lands have been without a master for some time," Samiel replied. "But I have never seen it like this. I sense the life here… waning."

Michael reined Anaba to a stop beside a sickly tree. A silver liquid dripped from its deteriorating foliage. "What's this?" He allowed the substance to drain from one damaged leaf to another.

"By the look of it – quicksilver. Mercury is the name given by modernity. The element is deadly to mortals and celestials."

Raijin cast a stern look of caution to his fellow Horseman. "Given your nature, Son of Mikha'el, I would give it a wide berth."

"Given the extent of this contamination, we're all in danger," Samiel said. "Mercury sickness produces a malaise that brings pain, even madness. Prolonged exposure can mean an agonizing death of the soul."

"Most angelic weapons are mercurial at their cores," Wyrmwood added. "That's why human weapons are ineffective against angels."

"Can't blame Azazel for refusing to share *all* of his weaponsmithing secrets with man," Raijin said. "Still, it does not explain how quicksilver got to DrunGer. The element's only found in the Cabeiri Pools of Cocytus."

Wyrmwood inspected the marsh grass on the edge of a culvert clogged with the metal. "Someone or something deliberately brought it here. We must find the source before it spreads to the other estates."

Michael spotted a glint of the heavy metal in the water. "Is there a river nearby?" Without waiting for an answer, he galloped up the hillside through the dying trees, the Horsemen following. From the top of the ridge above a shallow vale, Michael saw two narrow rivers snaking across the marsh. Waves of heat undulated and rolled above the farthest tributary. Its crimson waters ran thick like congealing blood along its banks, shooting gouts of flame into the air. The second tributary was brown, its waters flowing with the stink of untreated sewage.

"Now this is more like the Hell my professors talked about," Michael said, his eyes watering. "Where do these rivers lead?"

"To Momao Abai'Vonin," Samiel said.

"Crown of the Dragons?"

"Your Enochian is improving. The Momao Abai'Vonin is the source of the Eridanus, the River of Guilt. Teeming with the tears of the damned, the filth of fallen angels and man, the Eridanus is fed by five great tributaries." Samiel leaned forward and caressed his Nightmare's muscular neck. "The Acheron, River of Woe and the Styx, River of Hate, as you see there. Beyond these waters are the Phlegethon, River of Fire; the Lethe, the River of Oblivion; and finally, Cocytus, River of Wailing."

"A critical source of a Horseman's power is his estate. A strong house means a strong Horseman. We must act swiftly to neutralize this mercury contamination in the water," Raijin said, "or the lad will have no estate to claim, and nor will we."

The sounds of fighting reverberated between a dense cluster of discolored trees below them. Spread out across a mottled glen, men and women with luminous blue-green skin rose from ambush positions in the swamp grass. They wore armor made of leather and cured plant material beneath layers of hardened wood. The sharpened prongs of their tridents and barbed spears flashed with fire, capturing the crimson light of the skies overhead.

"Who are they?" Michael asked.

"The Fossegrim are the vassals who guard your estate," Samiel explained. "They have long awaited a lord who would treat them with the honor and dignity they deserve."

Small, flexible fins protected the subtly placed gill slits along their graceful necks. Flattened noses gave a unique, almost exotic, appearance to their faces, which were weary and haggard from battle. Scores of hairless, mange-covered Yeth Hounds threw themselves at the outnumbered defenders. Ripping claws and teeth pressed the attack, forcing the meager militia into a reluctant retreat near the shores of the Acheron.

"And there you see my vassals," Samiel said, a measure of pride in his voice. "My Black Dogs."

Among the Fossegrim, a dozen dogs the size of dire wolves fought within the ranks of the overrun soldiers. They raised their great heads and howled in an orchestrated arrangement. Their mournful baying caused the Yeth to cower, allowing the Fossegrim and their other allies to rally against the onslaught.

Hovering above the faltering line, agitated vortexes of air produced volatile chains of lightning that rained down on the Yeth Hounds. The charged bolts struck with precision, splitting skulls and severing limbs. Between deadly flashes, Michael saw human forms moving within rapidly spiraling funnels hovering in the air.

Small in stature, resembling very young children with elongated limbs and dragonfly wings, the mischievous fey were clad in gossamer chainmail. Based on the ancient manuscripts of Paracelsus, a sixteenth-century Swiss alchemist and theologian, they were known as Sylphs.

And, lastly, as if marching off the walls of a mural of a lost tribal shrine in the Sahara Desert, a unit of Ifrits moved across the land and water without the benefit of legs, gliding over the marsh on concentrated tongues of fire. Stepping forward from the routed line of defenders to engage the Yeth, six ruddy-faced warriors slashed at the hounds in a synchronized kata. Shrouded in flames, they wielded great scimitars and heavy maces in each of their four hands. In a harmonic chorus, the djinn sang a spirited cadence in baritone voices to measure the rhythm of their attacks.

"There's the source of the contamination!" Wyrmwood shouted, drawing her bow. "The Yeth Hounds. They're covered in it."

Scores of Yeth Hounds blanketed in festering sores threw themselves at the defenders. Blots of mercury smoked and sizzled, scorching holes in their mangy fur. The element left deep wounds that burned into deeper muscle and flesh and surrounding tissue. The scent of burning meat permeated the air. Rabid with pain, the hounds wailed in anguish, blindly attacking despite the danger to themselves.

Anaba snorted a cloud of brimstone from her muzzle and pawed at the ground, igniting the vapor. Her legs erupted into green flames, which engulfed her mane and tail. The other Nightmares followed her lead and the Four Horsemen stood at the crown of the hillock, ringed in fire.

"Huntsman's Formation!" Raijin drew the great katana from its scabbard and galloped down the hill. Nocking two arrows, Wyrmwood allowed him a good lead and fell in line behind him.

"Raijin!" Michael called after him in exasperation. Turning to Death, he drew the war lance out of the sheath beneath his leg and couched it under his arm. "What's the plan here? He didn't exactly leave me with a playbook!"

"Raijin enjoys leading the charge in this formation. Wyrmwood will provide direct cover for him. Our task is to protect them. Kill any stragglers left behind and make certain nothing flanks them." Samiel pulled the black hood over his head, bringing forth the horror of his grinning skull. "The creatures here are tortured souls that exist solely to maim, kill and devour. Not necessarily in that order. Being mortal, you may prove especially tempting to them." He spurred his Nightmare down the hill after their companions.

With a guttural battle cry, Raijin galloped into the swarm. Leaning precariously from his saddle, he dragged the katana across the marsh floor. Enveloped in blue flame, the blade scorched the earth, blackening it and reducing any Hound within three feet to smoke and ash.

The dangerous maneuver left him exposed, but nothing could get close to him. In multiple volleys of three and five, arrowheads gouged the air, felling the Yeth Hounds in great numbers. He rode within a corridor of twitching corpses. A cheer rose from the faltering defenders as the two Horsemen broke through the line of Yeth.

Drawing on all of his joust training, Michael laid the war lance against Anaba's neck to steady it. He dropped the reins, trusting her, and braced himself in the saddle. Leading with a blast of fiery brimstone, the Nightmare charged into the melee.

The war lance punctured a hound's chest, running it through. Michael shouldered the weight of the wriggling corpse, and Anaba slid to a halt, abruptly pirouetting. The sudden reversal threw the corpse to the ground. Anaba then dispersed the crowd around them with a few well-placed kicks, before looking to their next target.

Michael swung the lance across the back of his shoulders to the opposite hand. Using it like a sword, he slashed at another hound and severed its front legs. A vicious headbutt from Anaba then sent it flying through the air.

Overrun by the hairless dogs, Samiel's Nightmare reared and struck out. With a squeal the warhorse's umber flames intensified, devouring the attackers. Some of the creatures fought through the fire, clambering over the blackened corpses of their companions, and leaped at Death.

"Anaba!" Michael shouted.

I see him! Before she could get within two strides of the harried Horseman, ten of the hounds cut them off.

"They're trying to separate us!"

"To their peril!" Samiel yelled. "A cornered Horseman is the worst kind, especially when mounted on their Nightmare!"

Ears pinned flat, Anaba backed her hindquarters up to a small pond to prevent any possibility of being flanked. Taking a deep breath, she exhaled a cloud of black and green vapor. The spores billowing from her nostrils quickly increased and anchored themselves in the exposed sores covering the Yeth. On contact, a powdery brown mold spread across their skin. The infected hounds dropped to the ground in whimpering convulsions. They writhed and shriveled up, completely consumed by the mold.

"What the hell was that?" Michael asked.

"It's Wither on the Vine – a breath weapon," Wyrmwood replied, firing arrows from her bow. She stapled the nearest hounds to the marsh floor. "Once bound by the Crest of Nanqueel, a Nightmare incorporates some of their Rider's powers into their own." Pestilence drove an arrow through another hound's eye with her hand. "See for yourself."

As Samiel cut through a pack of Yeth with his scythe, his

Nightmare blew a dense, brown cloud from his nostrils, coating the enemy in a thin layer of wet earth. On contact, their flesh spontaneously decomposed, reduced to clods of damp soil and maggots.

"Interment of Worms is Malis' breath weapon," Wyrmwood explained. "Each Nightmare has their own, based on their Rider's office."

"We've broken their ranks!" Raijin shouted triumphantly. "Finish them while they are routed."

"Michael, our forces are making a stand at the river." Wyrmwood fired her bow and skewered two retreating Yeth Hounds with one arrow.

"Let's make sure it is not their *last* stand!" Michael said.

The boggy waters of the Acheron churned and frothed behind him, bubbling over the grassy shore. Four black tendrils shot up from the marsh and grabbed the fleeing Yeth by their legs and snouts and tails. The flailing, watery arms pummeled the hounds into the dirt with such force that Michael felt the impact in his stirrups.

"Fall in! Fall in, you fiery bastards!" Raijin bellowed to the Ifrits from the river's edge. His Nightmare reared in protest as he jerked at the reins. The four djinn who had survived the assault formed a detail around the Horseman.

"My beautiful Fey, come to me!" Wyrmwood held the bow over her head to signal them. Eight glowing orbs flew to her call and hovered above. In his peripheral vision, Michael saw the winged Sylphs hidden within their glamours.

"Come around." At the sound of Samiel's quiet voice, ten black heads popped above the tall marsh grass. Renowned in lore as the shadowy protectors of graveyards, the Black Dogs loped toward him and took up defensive positions at his Nightmare's feet.

The remaining nine Fossegrim warriors looked to each other and then Michael for direction. Pale gray eyes stared from beneath tangled locks of braided hair, which covered their elegant, pointed ears and the chiseled slope of their cheekbones. Webbed fingers clenched anxiously at the hafts of their weapons as they waited for Michael to speak.

"Uhm – stand with me?" Michael asked.

They fell into ranks around him. Wide, intelligent eyes stole glimpses of him, but turned demurely away when he met their gazes. With the exception of one. It was difficult to ascertain an age by anything more than the warrior's manner, which betrayed the reckless characteristic of youth. Unlike the others, his hair was white with streaks of blue blending in with the longer length hanging over his muscular shoulders.

The Fossegrim warrior carried a yari spear with an extended blade of barbs. Reluctantly, he bowed his head. "Your orders, enai?"

Michael beckoned the young Fossegrim to Anaba's shoulder. "Is this place your home?"

The soldier looked up at him, perplexed. "Of course, *enai,* I was born here," he replied adamantly.

"Then help me defend it," Michael said.

Smiling, the soldier turned to the other Fossegrim. "You have heard your Lord. No mercy."

CHAPTER 17

The Yeth were in full retreat.

Resting the war lance against the pommel of his saddle, Michael stared out across the battlefield as the last stragglers fled. He was exhausted, his thighs burning from his efforts to stay in the saddle. Anaba was covered in a light lather. He felt her breathing hard. He had lost count of the number of Yeth killed between them.

A blackened patch of ground marked an Ifrit's last stand. Overcome by rabid Yeth Hounds, the soldier combusted, devouring them in the flames of his demise. On the edge of the blast radius, the corpses of four Black Dogs laid in the scorched grass. Their teeth were still locked in the flesh of their enemies. A trio of glowing orbs hovered above the carnage looking for survivors. Finding none, the iridescent Sylphs moved off, the humming of their wings breaking the silence.

"Will-o'-wisps get such a bad rap in folklore," Michael said. His words were slurred, symptoms of fatigue and shock.

"Don't let Wyrmwood hear you call them that," Samiel warned. "She'd likely put an arrow in you. The Fey are mischievous, fractious even, but make exemplary spies. She's quite protective of them."

"What about Raijin's Ifrits? They're pretty badass." He absently wound his fingers through Anaba's mane.

"They are arrogant. A trait Raijin encourages in their ranks. They are superb fighters. A fiercely loyal and fiery retinue."

"And your Black Dogs?"

Samiel turned to him with a smile. "I find their form quite pleasing. They make excellent cemetery guardians and... are very difficult to kill." He raised his fingers to his lips and whistled.

The fallen dogs jumped to their feet to answer their master's call. They shook vigorously from nose to tail, hurling dirt from their rugged coats. Tongues lolling from their mouths, they sat down at the feet of his Nightmare. The largest among them stood up and put its paws on the warhorse's shoulder. Samiel reached down to give it an affectionate scratch on the head.

"Samiel! Michael!" Wyrmwood raced across the field and slid to a halt. "According to my siatris, the attacks are not confined to this estate. There have been casualties across DrunGer."

"Siatris?" Michael asked.

"A caretaker of sorts. The Horsemen spend a great deal of time away from our estates," Samiel replied. "A siatris is usually a most-trusted soldier, who sees to the day-to-day running of your affairs and the defense of your borders."

"My Ifrits confirm the worst," Raijin said, breaking from his minions. "My apologies, lad, but I must see to my own lands. I leave you with four of my finest house guard. They will answer to you just as they answer to me." He laid the reins across his Nightmare's neck and urged the destrier away from its companions. "Come, Gyaku, find a road home."

"The Sylphs who defended your estate will also stay." Wyrmwood's anxious face was streaked with soot. "I will be back as soon as I can. Solara," she called to her siatris, "come, we need to get home."

A glowing orb broke off from the rest of the fey and tucked itself inside the quiver on her back. Pestilence guided her Nightmare toward an open field and galloped away. They disappeared into a portal that led onto the Vestibule Road.

Michael sighed. "I'm guessing you need to leave, too?" he asked Samiel.

"As the longest-surviving member of the Four, my estate is fortified and well attended. Until we have some answers about this attack, I will remain with you. To that end, we must find your siatris and get a report." Samiel turned to the contingent of Fossegrim. "Your master, Famine, is newly risen."

The eight survivors fell to their knees in the grass with bowed heads.

Michael shifted uncomfortably in the saddle. "Is that really necessary?"

"Their prior lord was somewhat heavy-handed with them," Samiel said. He turned back to the Fossegrim. "Where is your siatris?"

"Our siatris was killed in the first attack," said the young Fosse with white hair.

"What's your name?" Michael asked.

"Gideon, enai."

Remembering Samiel's first words when they met on the Vestibule Road, Michael looked down at his soldier and asked, "Will you walk with me?" He glanced over his shoulder at his mentor and saw Samiel's approving nod. Balancing the war lance over Anaba's withers, he agilely brought his right leg over the pommel of the saddle and dismounted. When the anxious Fossegrim dared to look at him, Michael smiled and gestured with his head. "Come on."

They walked along the banks of the Acheron, away from the rest of the Fossegrim. Gideon followed hesitantly, careful not to set the pace. This put him within awkward proximity of the Nightmare. Anaba remained a stride behind, her ears alert for any sign of trouble.

Michael took a deep breath. "I keep expecting to wake up from a bad dream and roll over in my bed." He perched his foot on a stone at the river's edge.

"The burden of leadership is great." Worried about a reprimand for the bold statement, Gideon added, "I–I am not suggesting that you are unworthy, enai."

"Please, call me Michael."

"Enai is your rightful title."

"My Enochian's pretty bad, Gideon. If we must–"

"We must, if only for propriety, enai."

A trained interrogator, Michael felt their sense of rapport slipping. He was determined to get it back with a bit of strategic psychology. "My mother used to read fairytales to me before bed. I remember the story of a Fossegrim who lured people to water with enchanted music, only to drown them." Michael pulled a reed from the sluggish river. "Any truth to it?"

"A regretful legacy bestowed on us by a man named Narcissus," Gideon replied, his nostrils flaring. "It was not his reflection on the water that Narcissus fell in love with, but a Fossegrim who refused his offers of love. Rather than face rejection, he drowned himself in the pool, uttering a slanderous curse on his dying breath. One that forever marks the Fossegrim as monsters to be feared. Since that time, my people have been blamed for anyone who drowns unexpectedly near a lake or river." Gideon squared his shoulders and firmly set his jaw. "We were forced into hiding. Forced to never again play our music or sing openly for fear of accusation that we were luring humans to their deaths." He gazed into Michael's eyes. "Do you have reason to question the loyalty of the Fossegrim, enai?"

"I don't, Gideon. If I gave you that impression, I apologize. Sincerely." Michael tossed the reed into the murky water and watched it float away on the current. "What can you tell me about the last siatris?"

"My father was a courageous soldier," Gideon said, raising his voice.

"Your father? I'm sorry for your loss."

"He died a warrior's death."

Oo-rah, Anaba whispered. The eavesdropping Nightmare pretended to be rummaging through the tall grass with her muzzle.

"And how would your father assess the current situation?"

"Your house is fallen, enai. The land is tainted. The people are without defense: in hiding, praying for a new master – no matter how harsh – to come and save them. Less than twenty of the house guard remain to defend the wellspring, and they stand without a leader."

"Siatris is Enochian for scorpion, right?" Michael said.

"Your Enochian is not as bad as you say." Gideon smiled briefly, a row of pointed teeth showing behind his thin lips.

"Gideon, if we have any chance of surviving this, *you* better start acting like a scorpion."

The Fossegrim's smile faded. "My father has said the same. On many occasions."

"What would he do?"

"It is the Momao Abai'Vonin that the Yeth want. They are mad with quicksilver and seek to bathe in the wellspring's waters. They will spread a plague across DrunGer if we cannot stop them. Those who can stand will fight to the last breath." Gideon tapped the shaft of his spear against his boot. "My father would secure the wellspring at all costs, sending the strongest of us to defend it. Then he would dispatch forces in incremental lines so that the enemy would be forced to fight their way through us, decimating their own numbers."

I like him, Anaba said in a curt snort.

Michael laughed, bringing the war lance over his shoulder. "My partner approves of your plan. And you."

"Your Nightmare, enai?" Gideon stared at Anaba, who stared back. "She advises you?"

"All the damn time." Michael fought to keep his balance as Anaba gave him a hard shove with her muzzle. Sensing the Fosse's uncertainty, he put a hand on his shoulder. "What is it, Gideon?"

"This is unexpected." The Fossegrim looked up sheepishly. "You, enai, are unexpected."

Samiel walked toward them through the marsh grass, leading his Nightmare by the reins. What remained of their ragtag army of Fossegrim, Sylph and Ifrits followed at a distance. "Have you chosen?"

"I'm going with Anaba's judgment," Michael replied, jerking his thumb at Gideon. "I like him too."

"Enai?" Gideon said, his voice tremulous. "There is no rite of succession for siatris. You may find that there are others more experienced than me."

"Decision's been made. You'll be my new siatris. Or..." Michael threw his hands up defensively. "Would you rather explain to *her* why you're not taking the job?"

Anaba pinned her ears and chomped aggressively on the curb bit in her mouth.

"No, enai!" The Nightmare blew a cloud of brimstone in his direction, and Gideon panicked, stumbling over his words. "I mean to say yes!" He bowed his head to Michael and then Anaba as the molten flecks fluttered around his face. "Is your Nightmare to hold a title and position?"

"She's very opinionated. *That's* her position." Michael clapped him on the back. "What she holds are grudges. So don't give her a reason. Nothing holds a grudge longer than a woman... *or* a Marine." He glanced back at the Nightmare.

Anaba swished her tail across Michael's shoulders. The coarse hair rang as it swept across his maille armor. *Might serve you well to remember that.*

"I-I accept, enai," Gideon stammered. "It would be my honor to be your siatris, if that is what you wish."

"Good. Because we're going with your plan to defend the wellspring. So go and explain it to the rest of them." Michael pointed to the motley assembly of defenders, who were walking at a distance behind them.

It was as if all of Hell held its breath. Nothing moved, not even the wind. The Fossegrim swallowed anxiously, reminding Michael of his first day on the job as an FBI agent. Slack-jawed Gideon whispered, "*Me*, enai?"

"Yes. *You*." Trying not to laugh at the young warrior's awkwardness, Michael took him by the shoulder and led him back to their troops.

"Sylphs, we need your cunning and your stealth," Gideon said. Standing above the assembled soldiers, he addressed them from a moss-covered rock, flanked by Famine and Death and their Nightmares. "Our numbers are too few for mistakes. We will rely on you for first warning."

With a buzzing noise of bumblebees harvesting pollen, the eight glowing orbs dimmed. Nearly imperceptible, they sped off into the skies in separate directions.

"Ifrits, fall back to defend the Momao Abai'Vonin. Our remaining house guard will join you. You two will remain with me to defend our enai."

"No," Michael said, "I don't need an escort." He waited for his newly appointed siatris' protests to stop. "Gideon, you said it yourself. The strongest of us will be needed to defend the wellspring. Anaba, you're going with him."

Like hell I am.

"That wasn't a request, gunny." Michael pointed to Samiel and his Black Dogs. "I've got plenty of back-up if anything happens."

So did Lincoln and Kennedy. Do we need to discuss the historical consequences?

"There needs to be a military eye on this. Who better than a Marine?"

You can be a real asshole sometimes. Ears pinned in resistance, the Nightmare raised her tail like a heraldic flag and trotted after the battle-weary defenders.

"This is a thin line of defense, Michael," Samiel sighed.

"You think?" he replied sarcastically.

"We turned the tide with all Four Horsemen. When the Yeth attack again, two will not be sufficient. We must determine who is deliberately marking the beasts and setting them loose within our borders."

Michael knew who was responsible. It didn't take FBI training to put the Grigori at the top of the suspect list. He stooped at the edge of the river and used a branch to stir the edges of the waterbed. Beads of mercury rolled beneath the tip and separated into smaller globules.

"Water is the domain of the Horseman Famine," he said. "What happens if it becomes contaminated?"

"The source of your powers will be greatly diminished, leaving you vulnerable," Samiel said.

"Is that a risk the Grigori are willing to take?"

"To weaken the Horsemen and prevent the awakening of the Qaaun? Yes. Cŵn, come and introduce yourself." The largest of the Black Dogs took a seated position at Death's heel, looking up attentively at his master.

"This is *your* siatris?" Michael asked.

"My oldest and most loyal servant," Samiel replied. He ran a hand over Cŵn's broad head, brushing a handful of loose earth into his palm, and then threw the dirt into the River of Woe.

The soil floated on the surface and defiantly resisted the current. It clumped together across the width of the river and expanded like a sponge, extending downward to the bottom of the waterbed creating a porous dam. While the water continued on its course, the heavier mercury was captured in the webbing.

"A dam? That's only a temporary fix, Samiel," Michael said. "There are four other rivers and more than a dozen smaller streams. We can't protect them all."

Samiel threw the reins over his Nightmare's head. "But we can slow the spread until a permanent solution is found. I will ride to build temporary dams on the main waterways. Cŵn," he said, turning to his soldier, "you and the others are not to leave Famine's side." With barks of confirmation, the Black Dogs pressed their muscular bodies against Michael's legs. "I will accept no excuse for any harm that comes to him."

"I've got a bad feeling about this," Michael mumbled, tightening his grip on the war lance. His knuckles cracked audibly in the stillness.

"Malis, niis!" Samiel raised a foot to his stirrup and mounted his Nightmare. One of the Black Dogs leaped onto the warhorse's flanks. "This attack has been carefully orchestrated," Samiel said, turning his mount toward the open marsh. "Go to the wellspring, Michael. This is far from over."

CHAPTER 18

The five great waters of Hell snaked across the boundaries of DrunGer. Converging in the wetlands at the Momao Abai'Vonin through a network of canals, the powerful currents were funneled into a hub of underground tunnels. Forced upward under pressure, the river waters were jettisoned through the mouths of five 50-foot pillars that resembled the arcing necks of dragons. The various draconic heads were sculpted in different colors and textures to reflect the specific river spewing from their mouths. They created a crown above the mouth of the wellspring.

Smooth, interconnecting scales covered the neck of the black-headed dragon. An inky, putrid-smelling water poured from its mouth and into the basin below. Beside it, a horned crimson head with hooked scales spewed fiery blood that could only be extinguished in the rush of the other waters. Fragments of ice and slush fell from the mouth of a gray head, leaving icicles on the dragon's chin. Ragged, uneven scales covered the brown head, which shot a foul, cascade of sewage into the well. And finally, the aquamarine dragon head sprayed lucid blue water into the chaotic currents.

The frothing waters created a colossal whirlpool, and Michael feared the churning waters would overflow the basin, which was a mere hundred and fifty feet in diameter. But as rapidly as the rivers gushed into the reservoir, they were drawn down into the bowels of Hell just as quickly to form the River of Guilt.

Anchoring himself against one of the dragons, Michael stared down into the watery eye of the maelstrom. "Hate to say this," he whispered, "but I wish you were here, Mom." He marveled at the craftsmanship of the towering sculpture, expecting the undulating neck to which he clung to come to life beneath his fingertips.

"These scales almost feel real!" he shouted at Gideon, who was only a few feet away. The roar from the wellspring was deafening, reminiscent of a horde of dragons feasting.

"They are real, *enai,*" the Fosse replied. "These fossilized heads are all that remain of Tiamat after the Everlasting King had her slain."

Michael stared up at the towering necks of the legendary Babylonian Queen of Dragons. Five heavy chains, with links the size of his Jeep, hung from the necks of them. They were anchored to a featureless stone tablet floating in the center of the vortex. "What's that supposed to be?"

"The Altar of Cain. It sank into the mouth of the Momao Abai'Vonin when he betrayed and murdered his brother. It bears the weight of his guilt, a guilt so heavy it binds Tiamat to this place, preventing her from regenerating her body."

Michael gestured for them to move away from the basin. The constant roar was causing his head to ache, and his throat was raw from shouting. Scattered through the marsh, debris from a fortified edifice encircled the wellspring. Michael paused to survey the ruined landscape as dusk settled over the wetlands.

Cŵn brushed his whiskered muzzle against Michael's hand. The other Black Dogs kept watch in the sedge grass surrounding them.

"What happened here, Gideon? Was there a battle?"

"No battle, *enai.*" Gideon walked beside him, using the *yari* spear as a staff to part the leafy grass. "These are the remains of Master Eligoriel's estate."

"Eligoriel?"

"The old Famine, your predecessor. His tower stood over these lands and protected the Momao Abai'Vonin. When he fell, the tower fell."

"His death caused all this damage?" Michael asked. He climbed onto a collapsed bulwark.

"It has happened before, enai. You are the fourth lord to oversee these lands. When the tower fell, most of the village survived." Gideon looked away with a sorrowful expression. "But without a lord, scavengers came and tore down what was left. They killed anyone who resisted."

"Where were the other three Horsemen?"

"Attending to their own estates. This is Hell, enai. DrunGer has never known peace. These borders are always under siege."

"What can you tell me about Eligoriel? I'm getting the impression he was... difficult?"

Gideon averted his eyes. "It is never wise to speak ill of the dead, enai. Such talk is often what brings them back."

Failing to hide his growing exasperation, Michael sighed, hands on his hips, and stared into the grass. A tremendous sense of guilt and responsibility weighed heavily on his shoulders. "I don't know what I'm doing here, Gideon. There's no FBI procedural protocol for this kind of thing."

"The mantle of a Horseman is difficult to bear," the Fosse said. "I have no counsel, but I know you are a kind and righteous lord."

"You just met me, Gideon," Michael said evenly. "How can you know anything about me?"

"Because you are a Nephilim," Gideon replied. "You know what it is to be without a home."

Away from the noise of the wellspring, Michael heard the distinct melody of a violin. The unusually rich resonation lured him to the makeshift Fossegrim encampment on the outskirts of the wellspring.

"Is that a hardanger fiddle?"

"You've got an ear, enai."

"My mother restored one for the National Gallery in Norway. Eight strings instead of four, right?"

Michael made his way through the camp, mindful that he did not disturb the Fossegrim who had gathered to listen to the music. A lanky Fosse dressed in a white tunic played the fiddle beneath a cascading waterfall. The chords rose in pitch and volume, enhanced by the flow of the water across the bow and strings. As he listened, his chest tightened with unspeakable sorrow. "What's happening?" he whispered.

"This is an iviahe, a song for the dead." Gideon led him closer to the gathering. "Until now, there's been no time to properly mourn them."

The Fossegrim passed a silver goblet between them. Gripping the cup in both hands, the mourners bowed their heads in remembrance and drank from it. The sense of loss among them was palpable.

Feeling that his presence was an intrusion, Michael turned his back on the ritual and blinked back the sting of tears.

"If the music displeases you, enai, I will make them stop. Our former master forbade us from ever playing or even singing, except for funerals."

Michael sat down on a rickety stool. "Tell them to play whenever they want, Gideon. And not just at funerals. I never want the music to stop."

The company of Black Dogs stood up, the hackles on their backs raised. In a chorus of low growling, they paced circles around Michael.

"Cŵn?" Michael followed the pack leader's eyes to a swarm of familiar orbs speeding toward them from the marsh. The fairy lights changed color in a pattern that repeated a deliberate cycle as they grew closer to the camp.

"They're coming!" Gideon shouted. "To arms!"

The funeral ceremony ended with a discordant screech of

the fiddle as the musician secured the hardanger in an alcove of debris left over from the tower and reached for his spear. Running through the camp to collect their weapons, the other Fossegrim hurried to assume defensive positions around the perimeter of the Momao Abai'Vonin.

"There's too many of them. Hundreds this time," Gideon said, still reading the Sylphen warning. "If only there were some means to burn the quicksilver out of the canals."

"Liquid mercury doesn't burn."

"This is Hell, enai. All things burn here, even water, if the master of these lands commands it. All you need is a spark hot enough to ignite it."

"Like a very pissed off Nightmare?" Michael sprinted to the nearest canal and stared down into the murky, brown waters of the Acheron. "Anaba, niis!"

The air pressure changed abruptly as a condensed cloud of brimstone blasted through a wall of flame and shadow. For a moment, Michael could see the gnarled trees that arched above the Vestibule Road. He shoved Gideon to the side as Anaba galloped through the portal.

Somebody call for the Marines?

Michael leaped to her back and guided her to the edge of the canal wall. "The Yeth are back. We're out of time." He kicked her, pressing the Nightmare down into the channel.

Are we going skinny dipping? Because I didn't bring a hazmat suit. She leaped the marble railing and landed, the Touch of Zephyr keeping her suspended above the water's surface. Beneath her hooves, metallic balls of mercury rolled with the undercurrent. *What's the mission?*

"Mercury evaporates, even at room temperature. We're going to speed up the process by turning up the heat. The hotter, the better, gunny."

I live for this shit! Lowering her head, Anaba blew a condensed cloud of brimstone over the river's surface. Deliberately driving the tip of her hoof beneath the water, she raked it across the murky surface of the Acheron. *Fire in the hole!*

The brimstone ignited in a concussive blast that traveled the width of the canal and thirty yards up the river. Flames erupted in a wave that caused a secondary explosion when the methane rising from the surface caught fire. The infernal blaze burned blue with an unusual intensity. The river waters boiled over and steamed in resistance to the coerced evaporation.

Like the legs of a gigantic tarantula, smoking black tendrils shot out of the water. The grotesquely-shaped appendages stood twenty feet in the air. Half as wide as they were tall, the sheer measure of their girth pressed against the sides of the canal's marble walls.

Are you doing that? Anaba jumped backward to avoid being struck.

"No. It must be a weird chemical reaction," Michael said.

A chemical reaction that moves like a spider? The Nightmare ducked as one of the hairy aberrations tried to sweep her legs out from under her.

A trio of Fossegrim soldiers who stood on the edge of the canal were knocked into the river. The chittering tendrils forced them beneath the surface and drowned them. Anaba struck at the base of the appendage, savagely kicking at the inky arm. Scorched and lacerated from the Nightmare's hooves, it broke into pieces like charcoal and crumbled back into the water.

Cŵn howled mournfully to the crimson skies. His cry was taken up by the other Black Dogs.

"What's he doing?" Michael asked.

Calling for reinforcements.

A column of mud broke through the sedge grass to the right of the canal. Eight-feet tall and nearly as wide, with arms and legs the size of tree trunks, the earth golem lumbered toward the besieged canal. As new sprouts of the inky growths shot up to ensnare it, the golem slammed both fists into them, shattering the base of the transformed mercury.

"Now that's what I call backup." Michael held tight as Anaba dodged malignant growths and jumped out of the channel. "We need to set fire to the other four rivers."

More fire might mean more of those things coming out of the water.

"We can use that to our advantage when the Yeth Hounds come. Gideon, fall back to the wellspring. If we need to hold the line, it'll be there. Cŵn, go with him." Michael grabbed a handful of Anaba's fiery mane and braced himself as she weaved erratically to dodge the tendrils of mercury rising from the flames.

Michael snatched the war lance from its sheath and swept the blade down across one of the misshapen limbs. His fingers went numb from the impact. Securing his grip, he ripped it free and, using Anaba's momentum, cut the tendril in half.

"Time to bring the pain with a little Nightmare napalm," he said.

Oo-fucking-rah! And with an excited buck, she raced toward the next river.

CHAPTER 19

As night descended over DrunGer, a wave of flames rolled down the length of the River Styx like a storm surge. Caught in the fiery tempest, scores of Yeth Hounds were trapped in the current, never reaching the opposite shore. The crimson skies glowed with a violet tinge as two of the five great waters of Hell burned.

Black tendrils slithered from the water and suffocated any stragglers in the pack who strayed too close to the canal. Their corpses were dragged into the river and incinerated. Routed by the fiery barrier, the Hounds ran parallel along the bank, encroaching on the Momao Abai'Vonin.

The wellspring was close enough that Michael could hear the roar of the churning waters. The landscape near the basin was littered with hounds and debris from the ill-fated tower, a perilous obstacle course with moving targets. Anaba cantered along a stony ledge above the canal and jumped from the edge into the sedge grass.

Startling a pack of Yeth Hounds, she lashed at them savagely with her tail and ensnared two. The coarse, fiery hair caught in their mangled fur and torched their emaciated bodies. Not interested in a fight with the Nightmare, the rest gave her a wide berth.

As the rivers converged toward the wellspring, the distance

from one to the other grew shorter, less than a quarter mile. Unrelenting, Anaba galloped urgently between them, intent on reaching the next destination: the River of Wailing. Michael rubbed a hand across her sweaty hide. The Nightmare's exertions were showing as a sooty lather on her neck beneath the reins. Grunting with the effort, she lengthened her stride and leaped down into the canal that contained the Cocytus.

It was an unexpectedly sharp descent. Michael braced his hand against the crest of her neck for balance. As the Nightmare slid into the channel, the surrounding temperature dropped thirty degrees, nearly extinguishing the warhorse's natural fire. She landed on the icy waters in a cloud of smoke and frost and brimstone.

"Light it up, gunny," Michael said.

Anaba struck the frozen water, setting off an inferno across the surface. The infernal ice was initially unaffected by her flames, but as she infused the blaze with a steady stream of brimstone, the flames burned pale blue. The river then combusted in a violent upheaval of steam that enveloped them.

Michael threw his arm up to shield his face from the scalding vapor that washed back and over him. Surging toward him like a turbulent spray from a geyser, the searing mist thoroughly coated his armor, as well as any exposed skin. He lowered his arm, expecting significant burns, but found himself unharmed, protected within a cooler diffusion of gaseous water and Anaba's volatile flames.

"Is it me or is it getting hot in here?" he joked, nervously scratching her withers. The mix of stifling heat and humidity made it difficult to breathe.

She pinned her ears. *Keep your clothes on, Agent Childs, I'm busy. Even the* smallest *distraction could ruin my concentration.*

Michael pressed his tongue against the inside of his cheek and chuckled at the insult. "It's not all about the size, gunny."

Suffering two untenable temperature extremes, the canal

betrayed signs of distress. Pressurized steam burst through cracks in the marble, causing additional fractures along the aqueduct. In defiance of the natural law, fire and water trickled through the fissures, spilled onto the marsh floor, and ignited wildfires.

Michael risked a quick glance over his shoulder. The fires in the other waterways had reached the Momao Abai'Vonin. A column of black vapor rose from the edge of the basin as three of the dragon goddess' heads spilled fiery liquid from their mouths. Despite the obvious danger, the Yeth Hounds never diverted their course.

With swords and spears, the Fossegrim met them, backed up by the Ifrits and Samiel's Black Dogs. Three of the lumbering earth golems joined together to create a massive wall, but the numbers were too great. Despite the black tendrils attacking both sides, hundreds of the hounds still broke through the lines.

"It's no use, Anaba. We need to take the fight to the wellspring." Michael pulled on the rein as the Nightmare jumped out of the fiery channel. Refusing to yield to him, Anaba grabbed the bit in her teeth and took off at a gallop toward the next river.

"Anaba, there's too many of them. Gideon and Cŵn can't fight this alone! Setting fire to the last two canals won't do any good! We need to get to the basin now." Michael pulled harder on the reins. But the Nightmare set her jaw and refused to change course.

Michael propped his feet in the stirrups. Using all of his upper body as leverage, he pulled until his fingers went numb. "*Anaba, niis!*"

The iron curb bit raked across her gums, cutting into the corners of her mouth. Michael heard the metal grating against her molars. Unable to evade the pressure on her jaw, the Nightmare gagged and slid to a halt. With a strangled squeal, she threw her head, narrowly missing his face. She then reared straight up on her hind legs before frantically running backwards with her nose tucked in against her chest.

"We don't have time for this!"

Bruised by the bit, the Nightmare's tongue lolled from the side of her mouth. Bloody flecks of foam gathered on her lips. Ears pressed back in agitation, she stood at attention, her sides heaving.

"That's better." Michael put a spur to her side. She whirled around his leg, moving erratically and with exaggerated strides. Fearing she might bolt again, he did not ease up on the reins. Mad with the quicksilver contaminating their skin, the Yeth Hounds ran around them, ignoring the pair, as they raced toward their singular destination: the wellspring.

Michael watched helplessly as hundreds of them leaped into the Momao Abai'Vonin. There was a senseless despair in the act. *Stop thinking ethically,* he told himself. *Whoever is behind this plot never intended for the Yeth to survive. They were simply a means to an end.* The end being the contamination of the Momao Abai'Vonin. And their plan was working.

"Burning the mercury out of the rivers won't be enough," Michael said. "Anaba, there's an altar in the center of the wellspring. Can you get me to it?"

Ears pinned flat against her head, she did not reply.

Michael gave her a hard kick in the ribs, digging his spurs into her flanks. "You can be pissed when this is over."

You haven't begun to see me pissed off!

"Anaba, trust me! You're going to like where this is headed." He loosened the reins.

The Nightmare half reared, her haunches dropping to the ground. She leaped forward at a gallop, easily outdistancing the Yeth in a few reckless strides. At the edge of the wellspring, she leaped into the maelstrom of fire.

Stomach fluttering in his throat, Michael sat back in the saddle and held his breath during the drop. They landed, as if on solid ground, and galloped across the liquefied flames.

Anaba repelled the fiery discharge falling from Tiamat's mouths by intensifying her fire shield to protect them.

Slowing to a trot, she jumped onto the stone altar, grabbed the bit in her teeth, and snatched the reins out of his hands. *Now what?*

"How long can you maintain your immolation field?"

All night long.

"Anaba, be reasonable. It's taken a toll on you. We have to burn the mercury out of *all* the water. Here at its source."

She lowered her neck to avoid the touch of his hand. *I don't mean to be a princess, but that's a tall order.*

"You know what's at stake. I can't do this without you!"

US Army Survival Guide. Page one. Rule one. Call the Marines. The Nightmare shifted from side to side and took a long, deep breath. She exhaled a dense cloud of brimstone, vacating every breath in her lungs. The vapor ignited in a roar that temporarily muffled the thunder of the wellspring and disrupted the flow of the water. A circle of white-blue fire manifested around her and the altar. With subsequent deep breaths, she intensified the flames until the inner walls of the basin radiated with a blue aura.

Michael lowered the war lance until the sharpened, metallic butt struck the humble, stone altar where the eldest son of Adam had made sacrifices to an indifferent God. He concentrated on the River of Guilt below.

A ring of water emerged from the wellspring. Revolving around the altar, the band swelled at Michael's bidding. As it moved through the Nightmare's immolation field, wisps of black vapor evacuated the burning mercury. Before the reaction could spawn any limbs, the bristly tendrils were reduced to ash in the potent immolation. Commanding the waters to rise, Michael summoned more rings to be purged in the Nightmare's flames.

Initially, the weight of the river was negligible, but as more water was brought from the depths, the burden to hold the mightiest river in Hell and the taint of guilt in its current grew exponentially. Struggling to maintain control, Michael concentrated on compacting the rings. He forced them upward through the tongues of blue fire, while Anaba fed brimstone to the tumultuous conflagration.

Converted into a gigantic kiln, visible waves of heat rebounded from the gorge's marble walls. Blue fire erupted from the evolving waterspout at random intervals and rose up the length of it. Legs shaking, the Nightmare fought to keep the infernal fire stoked. Her black hide was slick with sweat. The musky lather dripped from her belly and pooled at her feet.

Silence.

The thunderous roar of Momao Abai'Vonin ceased. All five of Tiamat's heads ran dry as the entirety of the River of Guilt rotated in an undulating funnel above their majestic heads. Michael lost sight of the apex as it pierced the cloud cover above DrunGer.

Seeking death over suffering, the Yeth Hounds continued to leap into the void. Burned to cinders in Anaba's immolation field, their ashes fell like sooty snow into the abyss.

Black vapor continued to pour from the watery funnel like smoke from an industrial chimney stack. The residual vapor spread across the low-lying skies. Lightning struck the miasma. The collision of elements left an eerie blue-green nebula in the sky, a celestial scar that vividly clashed with the crimson firmament.

Michael felt faint. He couldn't breathe. The volume of the water was too heavy to hold. Drenched in sweat, he struggled beneath the weight, fearing it would crush him and Anaba, or worse, break the chains securing the Altar of Cain and send them plunging to their deaths.

Michael?

The sight of the skies above him was magnificent. Michael wanted to withdraw to a peaceful place to rest and observe the perverse beauty. The black clouds arcing from the water spout reminded him of Anaba, wild, unpredictable, and unrestrained.

"Beautiful," he muttered, falling from the saddle. "So beautiful."

Michael!

CHAPTER 20

Slumped in a pew in the rear of St. Joseph's church, Ziri tapped the news alert on his phone. The Weather Channel was reporting a massive waterspout a few miles off the Jersey Shore. He tapped the notification to enlarge the image. The record-breaking anomaly reminded him of the powerful dust devils that swept across the Sahara. Such disturbances were the acts of spirits asserting their presence to man.

Sliding the image offscreen, he reopened his text messages for the third time. Anaba had not checked in. While she was not known for replying in a timely fashion, a response was well overdue.

"Fighting with your girlfriend?"

Startled, Ziri looked up into a pair of brown eyes. "I don't have a girlfriend." He winced at the awkwardness in his voice.

"Could have fooled me." The girl's skin was mahogany, only a shade darker than his own. She was his age, curvaceous in cropped jeans and pink Converse. Her nose and lips were wide, and a fresh coat of fingernail polish matched the sneakers and the headband in her curly black hair. "Maybe her cell phone battery died." She was also brash, her gregarious demeanor reminding him of the Tuareg women in his tribe.

Ziri shoved the phone into his pocket. "I don't think she gets reception where she is anyway."

"How long have you been going out?"

"She's not my girlfriend. I told you. I don't have a girlfriend."

"Just making sure." The girl shuffled past his knees in the narrow pew and sat down, offering her hand. "Name's Jesse Parker."

"Ziri Ag Wararni."

She cocked her head to the side. "Are you a terrorist?"

He glared at her, withdrawing his hand. "No, I'm Tuareg."

"Don't get an attitude. You never know these days." Jesse crossed her arms over a weathered jean jacket. It was covered with pins bearing Japanese kanji and anime characters. "At least you know your real name. My people lost theirs during the Middle Passage on the slave ships coming from Africa. My first name is Mbali. It means beautiful girl in Xhosa."

Ziri suffered a twinge of guilt. Names were important among the Tuareg, the marker of one's value and identity. "May I call you Mbali?"

"No. Only my mom called me Mbali. When she was alive, she did." She stared into her lap, fidgeting with the holes in her jeans. "Does Ziri have a meaning?"

"Moonlight."

"That's a pretty name for a guy!" she gushed. "Really pretty. Like your eyes."

The awkward silence that ensued was interrupted by a toddler. Bundled up in a scarf and coat, she waddled into the pew and climbed into Jesse's lap. The wooden beads at the end of her braids clattered noisily as she pointed insistently toward the front of the sanctuary.

"Is it time?" Jesse grinned at the exuberant two year-old. She playfully pinched her chubby cheeks. "Father Paige lets her feed the koi every night before going to bed. Keisha, say hi to Ziri."

The toddler regarded him with curious eyes, as if noticing him for the first time. She squealed, laughing hysterically, and buried her face in Jesse's shoulder. With one eye opened and the other squeezed shut, she waved her hand.

"Hi, Keisha," Ziri said with a grin. He waved back. "Is she your tamăḍrayt? Sister?"

"Nah. She's in emergency foster care with some lady, a teacher. She dropped Keisha off a few days ago and never came back, so I've been drafted for the job. Everybody here has a sad story. What's yours?"

"How do you know my story's sad?" His smile faded.

Jesse pursed her lips and shrugged. "Your eyes are pretty, Ziri, but you can't hide the sadness in them."

Ziri sighed in agreement. "My mother died when I was a baby. My father and grandfather raised me, until they were murdered by Malian soldiers... *real* terrorists," he growled. "They wiped out my entire tribe."

"Hey," she said, reaching for his hand, "we orphans have to stick together." Intertwining her fingers between his, she rubbed her thumb across the back of his hand. "Wow, you've got really strong hands."

"I'm a jockey."

"Seriously?" she asked with skepticism.

"Don't have my license yet, but that's a technicality. I start my apprenticeship next month when I'm sixteen."

"*Frishes*!" Keisha squealed.

"That's right, Keisha, fishes." Jesse turned back to Ziri. "Wanna come?"

"Never fed a fish before. Is it dangerous?" he joked. He stood up, reluctantly releasing Jesse's hand, and extended his hand to Keisha. The giggling toddler grabbed his fingers.

"Not as dangerous as riding a crazy-ass horse. Or babysitting a fish-happy two year-old."

As Keisha hopped up and down between them, they walked the overeager toddler to the exit in the rear of the church. Her squeals and their laughter echoed in the sanctuary's high ceilings.

* * *

Jesse knocked on the parsonage screen door, deliberately modeling for the younger child. Sucking her thumb, Keisha watched intently and then rapped on the glass frame, too. The toddler stepped back behind Ziri's leg, startled, when the inner door suddenly opened.

"Jesse? Ziri? What a surprise! And who's this?" Father Paige grinned down at the younger child. "Is that little Keisha come to feed my fish?"

"*Frishes*!" Keisha clapped her hands.

Father Paige retrieved a bottle of fish food from a shelf near the door. "Remember, not too much, or they'll get a tummy ache." He handed the bottle to Keisha. The toddler held it in both hands, shaking the contents of the aluminum container.

"Hey, kid!" Elijah called from the coffee table in the living room. "What's your name again? Zachari?"

"It's Ziri, tezz." He rolled his eyes.

"Whatever. Have you heard from your friend?"

"Nothing. What about your partner?"

"Same. You don't think she killed him, do you?"

"If she did, he gave her a good reason." Ziri stepped away from the door. Though he held no personal malice toward the agent, he distrusted all government officials and resented the disruption they had brought into his life.

"Who's that man?" Jesse whispered, walking away from the residence.

"He's with the FBI."

"Here? Guess I shouldn't be surprised. There's been a lot of crazy shit going on the last few weeks. Keisha, stop!" She grabbed the little girl's arm to keep her from wading into the pond.

The tenacious toddler pulled like Samson in the pillars. She splayed her tiny fingers in an attempt to reach the elusive koi beneath the water's surface.

"I keep asking Father Paige if I can get her some goldfish," Jesse grumbled, "but he says it's not safe to leave the church grounds."

"Where would you get them?"

"There's a carnival a few blocks over. Look." She pointed to the dark skies above them where a trio of spotlights cut through the night.

"Let's go," Ziri said.

Jesse stared at him. "But Father Paige said–"

"I wasn't planning on asking permission."

"The gate's locked. Father Paige has the only key."

"We'll go out the front."

Jesse shook her head. "Father Marcus or Sister Christine are always in there watching."

"Then we pick the lock." Ziri glanced back at the parsonage. The door was partially closed. Elijah and Father Paige were preoccupied, comparing notes at the coffee table. "Mind if I borrow one of your pins?"

"So you're a jockey *and* a lock pick?" Jesse removed a Duran Duran pin from the flap of her front pocket and handed it to him.

"I've got an unusual skill set. Makes me a catch."

"It really does." Jesse kissed him on the cheek before he could pull away.

Ziri stooped to work the tumblers inside the simple padlock. It was difficult to concentrate until the heat of her lips dissipated from his skin. Eyes closed, he felt the shank release with a metallic click. "Immînda."

"Is that like voila–"

She cowered in terror when a raven croaked from the elm branches above the fence. Almost hidden by its blue-black plumage, the bird watched them from the shadows. A partial hood of white feathers stood out on the back of its neck.

"That's one ugly pigeon," Jesse whispered, taking his hand.

"That's not a pigeon. He's an aɣrut – pied crow – a white-necked raven. My people believe they carry messages from the spirits. I've never seen one in this country."

"Think it's hurt?" Jesse picked Keisha up and cradled the

toddler protectively against her hip. "What do you think it's doing here?"

Ziri put a hand over his chest and caressed the Tuareg cross beneath his shirt. He hesitated in the gate, "Giving us his blessing... or sending us a warning."

The carnival rides and attractions went dark at midnight, bringing the evening's festivities to a close. As the spotlights faded, the night skies above the park were delivered back to the shadows.

While the night had not been as exciting as galloping an eleven-hundred-pound Thoroughbred around the track at forty miles per hour, Ziri was sad to see it end.

"Is Ziri Ag Wararni your whole name?" Jesse asked. "Is Ag like a middle name?"

Carrying a large, pink teddy bear under his arm, Ziri shifted a plastic bag to his other hand and held onto Keisha's with the other. The toddler giggled loudly as the school of goldfish inside darted in circles.

"Ag means *the son of*. Wararni is my father's name. It means unconquerable."

"Unconquerable moonlight? Damn that's sexy!" Jesse pulled the collar of her jacket against her neck and shivered. Ziri blushed in full view of her, shuffling from side to side to hide it.

"Keisha, hold this for me." He handed the bear to the toddler and the goldfish to Jesse.

"What are you doing?"

"The gentlemanly thing. Don't tell anyone. It would ruin my rep." Ziri peeled off his jacket and tucked it between his knees. Shrugging out of his flannel shirt, he handed it to her.

"What's that?" Jesse asked. Her fingers traced the outline of the silver talisman beneath his threadbare t-shirt.

"My father's Tuareg cross. He gave it to me on my seventh birthday. To protect me."

"Protect you from what?" She took off her jacket and gratefully slipped into the flannel shirt.

"The kel essuf – spirits." Expecting her to mock him, Ziri bowed his head to avoid her eyes. "My grandfather was a friend to the kel essuf."

"Like a holy man?"

He was caught off guard by her interest. "Yes, a healer. When I was younger, he used to take me into the desert to teach me the ways of the kel essuf. He wanted me to follow in his footsteps."

"That's some serious mojo shit, Ziri. Did you listen to him?"

Ziri straightened the collar of the flannel shirt beneath her jacket and frowned. "I never saw the importance of it until I was older, and by then, it was too late. There's no one left to teach me the old ways now."

"That's how our people lose their history," Jesse scolded. "When we choose not to learn, we choose to forget who we are." She kissed him on the lips.

"I haven't forgotten," Ziri whispered. He twisted his hip to show her a leather satchel at his hip. "This was my grandfather's gris-gris – a prayer bag. I know the purpose of everything in it. How it works, and the chants. I just need more guidance."

"That's what the internet's for, silly." Jesse lifted the silver cross from behind the fabric. "Where there's a wi-fi signal, there's a way."

"Sorry to spoil your moment," said the grizzled lady at the funnel cake camper beside them, "but your kid's getting away."

"Keisha!" Ziri called. He saw her running for the avenue of trees lining the exit of the park. The two year-old was hard to miss carrying a teddy bear that was as big as she was.

Jesse rolled her eyes. "That girl!" She attempted to pursue the toddler, but was abruptly cut off by two white men in gray trench coats. "Sorry, mister," she said sarcastically, bumping into one of them. As she tried to sidestep him, he grabbed her.

Lifted off her feet by the throat, Jesse dropped the plastic bag. It split open, scattering water and goldfish over the pavement.

"Jesse! Let go of her!" Ziri changed direction and charged the stranger, but the man's companion intervened, punching him in the chest. Fingers blistered and smoking from contact with the silver cross, the man recoiled in pain. "Grigori!" Ziri exclaimed.

"You a pedophile or something?" An elderly man stepped in front of his worried wife and confronted the attacker. "Put that little girl down."

Still strangling Jesse, the stranger reached out and snapped the old man's neck like a brittle twig. "Do not interfere," he said, addressing the frightened onlookers.

Ziri unsheathed a knife from the scabbard hidden in the small of his back. Carved from the skull of a jackal, he held the relic in a reverse grip. Crouched low, as Anaba had taught him, he feinted a punch and lunged at the second Grigori, cutting across the angel's wrist. Blood spilled across the hem of the gray coat and the pavement.

The angel retaliated with a spinning wheel kick. Ziri blocked it with his left arm, but the impact knocked him to the ground. Though his hand and arm went numb, he raised the dagger to defend himself.

"Don't kill him," the first angel said. "He's human. Bring him with the Nephilim."

Talons fully extended, a raven with a band of white feathers around its neck descended from the night skies. It croaked a protest and flew into the Grigori's face, raking its claws across his cheeks and chin. The horn of its beak glistened as it pecked at his eyes. Buffeting him with its black wings, the bird pushed off and took flight before the Grigori could retaliate.

Ziri retrieved one of the feathers left by the bird. While a stabbing pain shot through his arm and his fingers, he managed to fumble clumsily in the gris-gris bag and retrieved a bundle of tobacco. He lit it and blew furiously over the embers to hasten the flames. Holding the raven feather against the silver cross, he prayed in Tamasheq: *"Great spirits, see me through this holy veil."*

A profuse smoke rolled from the burning tobacco. Defying the breeze, it fanned out into a circle around the Tuareg boy. The bloody Grigori wiped at his ravaged face and tried to grab Ziri but could not penetrate the sacred cloud enveloping him.

Ziri nearly wept in relief and continued his ritual: *"Grant me your protection so that I may know only peace always."* He waved the tobacco in the four sacred directions, his consciousness waning.

Jesse kicked at the Grigori's legs and scratched at his hand, but was unable to free herself. "Ziri!" she gasped.

"I have a friend in the storm, seeking shelter," he whispered, fighting to finish the prayer. Amid screaming spectators and vendors calling for help, Ziri collapsed on the sidewalk with the dying goldfish. *"I pray to you. May she not be abandoned."*

CHAPTER 21

Michael was alone, lost on the Vestibule Road. There were no signs or markers. No discernible landmarks, except the trees arching over the gravel path. That was the least of his worries. He couldn't remember how he got there. "Hello?" No response.

He retrieved his tactical flashlight from his pocket, but the shadows swallowed the beam. Hearing a noise behind him, he snatched his Glock 19M from its holster and swung around to face whatever caused it. He swallowed hard, terror rising in the back of his throat.

Glazed over by the light, fixed, lidless eyes gawked at him from sunken sockets. There were too many to count; their haunted faces were covered in scars, hurling accusations at him. Michael recognized the Enochian glyphs. The grotesque profanities were meant to denigrate their angelic heritage. *His heritage.*

The Nephilim swarmed him. Michael fired, point-blank. The hollow points shot into them but passed harmlessly through their mutilated bodies. As a mob, the wraiths tackled him and forced him to the ground. Smelling of ash and excrement, their clawed fingers forced his mouth open.

Michael gagged, choking on the thick liquid they poured into his mouth. Qeres! He recognized the funerary oil by its musky scent and tried to spit it out. Failing in that endeavor, he tried to call out, but could not find the necessary breath. He was drowning in it, suffocating in his own fluids as his body went into shock from the toxin.

"Anaba!" Michael's strangled cry dissipated into the air as he awoke.

Swells of water cascaded from decorative waterfalls sculpted into the chamber walls. They splashed down over a series of elaborate stone carvings and gathered in marble crevasses around the room. Arrangements of water lilies, marsh marigolds, and red cardinals grew from the shallow pools. The fragrant scent of the wetland flowers and sedge grass freshened the cool, moist air.

Unsettled by the fever-induced dream, Michael sat up, finding himself in a large canopy bed. Crafted in a dark metal streaked with silver, the twisted frame above him reminded him of the trees on the Vestibule Road, only these branches opened up to offer an unfettered view of the vaulted, crystallized ceiling.

Samiel cleared his throat, crossing his legs beneath a woolen throw. He was sitting casually at Michael's bedside in a padded, wingback chair. An ancient tome sat opened across his lap. While there was worry in the Horseman's brown eyes, a puckish grin betrayed his relief. "In all my days, I never imagined seeing a time when the rivers of Hell would run dry… even the frozen depths of the Cocytus. Do you have any idea of the mischief you've unleashed?"

Suffering from vertigo, Michael fell back into sweat-soaked sheets. "Anaba?"

"She's safe. A surprise, considering the feat the two of you pulled off at the wellspring last night. You gave her quite a fright. I've never heard such profanity. At least, not from a Nightmare." Samiel closed the grimoire and set it aside on a table beside a steaming kettle of tea. "I must caution you, Michael. You're mortal. Channeling too much power like that could kill you. Thankfully, you were in the only position that could assure your survival."

"On my Nightmare?" Michael closed his eyes. He remembered summoning the entirety of the River of Guilt and how the weight of it had nearly crushed him. "I just had the weirdest dream. I was on the Vestibule Road, but Anaba wasn't with me."

But… how could that happen? he thought. *Unless I was… Dead?*

Michael turned to the Horseman, his throat constricting in fear. "What happened in the wellspring – that was the second test, wasn't it?"

"The Trial of Endowment." Samiel nodded, pursing his lips into a thin line. "An exhibition of your mastery over your domain. Rejoice, Son of Mikha'el, you passed. Barely."

"The Yeth?"

"Routed, but not defeated, I'm afraid."

Michael rubbed vigorously at his eyes and groaned. His joints ached, bruised as if he'd been unhorsed in the jousting lists and hit the ground full speed in platemail. "How long have I been out?"

"I'd estimate three days."

"Three days!" Michael propped himself up on an elbow, struggling to sit up.

"You needn't fret." Samiel gazed up through the glass ceiling, squinting to see beyond the exaggerated refractions of the water. "You've been absent from the living world less than a day."

"How are you able to track time? My watch has been useless since I got here." Michael twisted his head and neck to follow the Horseman's line of sight. By his unspoken will, the waters cleared, magnifying his vision like a telescope. He saw a definite pinpoint of light in the lower right quadrant of Hell's crimson skies. "Is that the North Star? Sirius? How's that even possible here in Hell?"

"It was a fallen Grigori named Tamiel who taught man how to read the skies and tell the time by the rotation of certain stars."

"And he was cast out of Heaven for that? Why?"

"It was information the Father never intended to divulge to mankind." Samiel took a deep breath, pursing his lips and scratching at his long nose. "What you see there is a star unlike any you would know. It is all that remains of Kronos. His head."

"King of the Titans? The God of Time?"

Samiel nodded. "Another of the Father's vanquished rivals."

"My graduate professors would lose their shit." Bewildered, Michael ran a hand through his tangled locs and laid back to stare at the celestial flicker in awe. "Samiel, I'm sorry if I've caused you any trouble."

"Hardly," Samiel said, his mouth twisted between a frown and a smile. "Fortunately, your manor house was nearby and your siatris could get you to safety, where you could rest and recover your strength."

"*My* manor house?" Michael winced as the sore muscles in his stomach clenched. "There were no buildings on this land. Everything was in ruins."

"No longer. You are the master of this estate, the Third Herald, and you proved it last night." Death poured a cup of tea from the stone kettle and offered it to Michael.

Ignoring the Horseman's gesture, Michael threw off the bed covers. Dressed in simple linen pants and a loose-fitting tunic, he took one faltering stride from the bed and fell. Samiel caught him by the waist.

Michael stared down through the glass floor, intrigued by currents of water and sand sifting in rivulets like a constantly shifting puzzle. As the light in the chamber shifted, he looked into the surrounding bed chamber that was majestically baroque, furnished with a plethora of floor pillows, bamboo divans, and high-backed chairs arranged near a fireplace that was as large as an industrial furnace.

"I built this?"

"The great waters of Hell rained down and flooded the marshes," Samiel said, helping Michael to his feet. "When the waters receded into their proper shores, this house emerged. It was quite the spectacle."

"And the Fossegrim? Where are they?"

"Most are rebuilding their homes. Singing songs about the benevolence of their new lord. Others are here, fortifying your manor and the grounds of your estate." Samiel opened his mouth and then just as quickly shut it.

"What?" Michael asked, rubbing his hand across his feverish forehead. "This isn't over yet, is it?" Faltering every second or third step, Michael pushed through the bedroom doors into a narrow corridor lined with smaller posterns on each side of the hall. As his strength and balance returned, he continued through an archway into a wetland garden decorated with fountains and a wading pool.

"Michael, I think you've gone far enough from your bed for one day."

Michael shrugged free, ignoring the Horseman's pleas. "I have to defend the wellspring, or none of this even matters." At the opposite end of the garden, he studied a set of immense silver doors. The ornate images of cascading water did little to sooth him or his curiosity. Sweating profusely, he pushed through into a chamber that rivaled the grandeur of the Colosseum.

The nearest staircase led eighty-feet down into a six-acre concourse. Michael walked down the cool, tiled steps in bare feet, descending to a spacious landing above the chamber floor, where he paused to listen to the roar of Momao Abai'Vonin. The five stoic heads of Tiamat rose from the center of an elaborate mosaic floor beneath a domed, glass ceiling that was suspended two hundred feet above the wellspring. Terrifying and yet alluring at the same time, the incessant noise from the churning waters reminded him of an F5 tornado.

"I did all of this?" Michael felt lightheaded. The roar of the wellspring came and went in his ears as his consciousness ebbed like the tide.

Samiel grabbed him under the shoulder and sat him down on a landing. "Some wine, please?" he asked of a passing servant. A wide-nosed Fossegrim woman returned with a silver goblet on a tray. "Drink this. Slowly."

With his fingers trembling in shock, Michael held the goblet in both hands for fear of dropping it. The rich aroma summoned his thirst, and he gulped it down in three swallows. He wiped at the corner of his mouth with his sleeve. "Did I break anything?"

"The rivers are flowing, unhindered and uncontaminated. The Momao Abai'Vonin is intact. The sky, however," Samiel said with a chuckle, "that will take some time to restore to its natural color."

"The sky?" Michael strained to peer through the ceiling above the wellspring's basin. The glass shimmered with the evanescence of running water, magnifying and distorting the images beyond it. Despite the peculiar effects, he could see the blue-green taint of mercury vapor hanging below the cloud cover in sharp contrast to the red skies of Hell.

"You've conquered the impossible, but have a care, Michael," Samiel said, his expression stern. "As a Horseman of the Apocalypse, your emotions, *your thoughts,* can be given shape in Hell as well as in the living world."

Michael propped his elbows on his knees. Pressing the cool, metallic goblet to his sweaty forehead, he groaned. "I'll try and remember that." He took a slow deep breath, trying to calm his still-jittery hands. "Where's Wyrmwood? And Raijin? Are they OK?"

"Busy defending three estates between the two of them. The Yeth Hounds have not ceased their incursions into DrunGer."

Michael rubbed his hands vigorously over his face until sensation returned to his cheeks. "And Anaba? Can't imagine she's not here cussing me out right now. I could have gotten us both killed."

"She is with your siatris, rallying what remains of your House Guard."

"You can take the Marine out of the fight, but never the fight out of the Marine." Michael walked along the tiered floor above the basin to a set of smaller silver doors.

Samiel cautiously followed him into the spacious corridor. "Michael, you should return to bed and rest."

Michael turned into a gallery away from the wellspring chamber. He wasn't certain where he was going, but trusted his instincts to lead him to where he wanted to be. With Anaba. "I'm not going to sit on my ass while two Horsemen defend three estates. And a single Nightmare with a handful of soldiers fights to protect another."

The determined slap of his bare feet echoed in the corridor.

As Michael passed them, Fossegrim servants stopped arranging furniture, hanging tapestries, or decorating the palatial house with wetland flora to bow respectfully to their new lord. Michael returned their courtesies, feeling awkward, and continued toward the front of the house. In the midst of moving marble columns into the manor, a trio of Fossegrim guards set down their burden and threw open the main house doors.

From the sallow, dying wilds of the marshland and its fallen tower, the landscape was vastly transformed: it had become verdant and prolific with life. Structured in the fashion of a Roman villa, the grounds of the manor house were divided into gardens. Manicured wedge grass framed the sections and had been trimmed into artistic patterns of waves and spirals.

Out in the courtyard, Michael got his first clear glimpse of the hole in the sky above the Momao Abai'Vonin. The blue-green vapor filled the void like the event horizon of a black hole. He sighed, slumping his shoulders. "Something tells me a bit of paint and plaster won't fix that."

"As aesthetics go," Samiel said wryly, "I think it's an interesting look."

A black Nightmare galloped into the courtyard at full speed, sending Fossegrim tending the gardens to scuttle to the side. With her ears pricked forward, Anaba leaped into the air and bucked, launching all four legs off the ground. She landed and came to a sliding halt in the loose rock. The glint in her eyes and the bounce in her stride made it clear she was pleased to see him.

Michael was no less elated, until he saw the sores in the corners of her mouth. Swollen from where the iron bit had grabbed her, the fleshy folds of her lips were scabbed over. The barbed curb chain had chafed the Nightmare, leaving dried blood where the skin was rubbed raw on the underside of her chin.

"Oh, Anaba, I didn't mean to–"

It's nothing. I got carried away and got quarterdecked. That's all.

Michael laid his forehead against hers and caressed her nose. "I'm sorry, gunny."

Aw, do you need a tissue, Childs? Get a grip. We don't have time for this shit, the Nightmare said. *That little trick you pulled at the wellspring bought us some time to regroup, but the Yeth are back. And we're getting our asses handed to us out there.* She raised her head and stared down her long nose at him. *Are you planning to lollygag in your skivvies all day?*

Grabbing a handful of her mane, Michael jumped onto the Nightmare bareback. "Samiel, care to go for a ride?"

CHAPTER 22

Hunched over Anaba's withers, Michael took slow, deep breaths to alleviate the burning in his lungs. The war lance Ah-Azarim Aziagiar was unusually heavy in his grip. With a slow twist, he extricated the blade-head from a Yeth Hound and disembowelled it. Ambushed by a rabid pack of the curs, he had been forced to summon the lance as well as his armor to defend himself against them. In his weakened state, the weight of the maille left him exhausted. The stench of their charred, smoking corpses made it even more difficult to breathe.

"You shouldn't be out here." Spinning his scythe in a tight arc, Samiel shook the blood and gore from his curved blade. "You've barely recovered from last night. Anaba, take your master back to the manor."

Anaba pinned her ears and flicked her tail dismissively across her flank. *I don't answer to you.*

The Nightmare had always shown a general indifference toward the other Horsemen. But there seemed to be an escalating tension between her and the Angel of Death. Michael gave her a slap on the neck to divert her aggression.

"I'm not going back without Gideon and the others." Through an amber haze that hung in the morning air, Michael saw a tower rising on the horizon. Obscured by distance, the structure had no distinguishing features. Rubbing his eyes, he blinked back his weariness. "I thought God had a thing against towers."

"Balzizras is the reason the Tower of Babel was destroyed," Samiel replied.

"The Citadel of Judgment?" Michael said, interpreting the Enochian name.

"After the crucifixion, the true Son of God walked among the damned on the Vestibule Road. He journeyed across DrunGer for three days until he reached the heart within and came to the tower. Every soul descends into Hell, Michael, but not all of them remain. The chosen Sons and Daughters of Adam take the same journey before making their final ascent to the Eternal Throne."

With her ears pricked toward a rustling in the grasses, Anaba stiffened. *Incoming*!

Four Yeth Hounds scurried over the bluff. The stink of burning meat proceeded them as their hides smoked visibly from the mercury contamination. Before the rabid curs could attack, they were taken down by a trio of Black Dogs led by Cŵn. The fourth was skewered by a hooked yari spear.

"Gideon!" Michael shouted.

"Enai, you are awake!" Gideon buried the barbed spear in the hound's chest and pierced its heart. Yanking the yari free from the carcass, the Fosse moved cautiously to Anaba's side. He signaled the other soldiers behind him to fall back to his position. "Forgive me for being so forward, enai, but it is not safe here."

"If I'm not safe on my estate, Gideon, I'm not safe anywhere."

"A man's home is his castle, but not every man is a king!" Raijin shouted. The Angel of War galloped up to the group on his chestnut Nightmare with Wyrmwood cantering beside him. Both Horsemen looked haggard, their faces streaked with soot from their Nightmare's flames.

"How are we faring, Raijin?" Samiel asked.

"There are hundreds of them. All converging here on Michael's estate. We kill ten and fifty more take their place."

"They're wearing us down." Wyrmwood ran her finger along the curved limb of her bow.

Michael cantered to the top of the bluff and looked down as the next wave loped toward them. The grass was too tall to see the hounds, but he could hear them panting and yowling as their padded feet splashed through the marsh. "The odds aren't looking good!" he shouted.

"Our best recourse is a strategic retreat to the manor house to prepare for a siege. Follow me!" Raijin galloped away in the direction of Michael's estate. Samiel and Wyrmwood followed, trailed by a pack of Black Dogs.

"Gideon, take the others and go back to the house," Michael said.

"I know what you are thinking, enai, but I will not leave your side." He signaled the other members of the house guard to form a defensive line.

"This may not end well," Michael warned, picking up the reins.

"My father died fighting for a master he had no faith in. He taught me to be better than he was." Gideon raised the yari spear in salute and then sank back into an offensive strike position. "If I die today, I will have succeeded."

"Anaba, last chance to convince me this is a bad idea." Michael shifted his weight in the stirrups.

We either take this hill, or they bury us on it. The Nightmare pawed so vehemently at the ground that a blue flame leaped from the brimstone cloud in a flash and ignited. It enveloped her in a field of immolation fire. Rearing, she leaped from the hilltop and charged.

Michael swung the lance across the front of the invading pack like a guillotine suspended on a rope. Anaba's fire incinerated the living and the dead, reducing severed heads and limbs to ash. What the pair did not kill, the Fossegrim finished off with spears.

The Yeth Hounds, however, adapted quickly. They leaped above the flames and threw themselves at the Nightmare and her Rider. Anaba smothered them in a blast of fiery brimstone, trampling many beneath her feet. In a frenzy, the Nightmare tore out blackened throats with her teeth and tossed the corpses into her fire.

Michael's fingers prickled with a piercing itch, as if waking from sleep with a numb arm. An intense thrumming swept through the haft of the war lance. Beads of water bled profusely from the iron tip, but instead of falling away, the droplets converged in a spiral that swirled around the blade-head.

Michael stared into the tiny maelstrom atop his lance. A weight settled over his chest, the pressure quickly escalating as if he were descending into an abyss of water and drowning. His lungs burned, nearly bursting for lack of air. Frightened, he gasped, forcing himself to exhale through his mouth.

Six murky tendrils of bog water answered his call. They rose from the quagmire between the roots of a cypress tree. Twitching violently in the air like the tentacles of an enraged kraken, the watery appendages snatched the wailing hounds by their legs and slammed them against the ground or flung them into the air.

Eight Black Dogs returned to the fight, thrashing back through the sedge grass. With a collective howling, they summoned an earth golem. The construct shook itself free from the swamp mud, covered in roots and moss. It snatched two Yeth from the edge of a creek and smashed their skulls together. It then caught a third by the leg and dashed its brains out against the tree.

Scythe flashing with finality, Samiel galloped alongside Michael and cleaved through three Yeth in one blow. "I'll give you this, Son of Mikha'el. You are as tenacious as your sire." His voice was a hiss from the skull beneath his hood.

"There is no victory here!" Raijin bellowed, galloping up to his side. "You have undone us, Famine!" Brandishing his great katana, Raijin sent a wall of crimson flame roaring across the field. The fiery tide scorched the land as Wyrmwood's arrows rained down on the Yeth. Their efforts did little to cut the swelling numbers.

"Night and day, wind and storm, tide and earthquake, impeded man no longer," Michael said. *"He had harnessed Leviathan."*

Famous last words? Anaba asked.

"It's from a book by E.M. Forster." Michael pulled at the gorget around his neck. "When I was a kid, my mother used to make me rewrite whole sections of the book in longhand as punishment."

This isn't the time for reminiscing, Michael! Call the play!

"This *is* my play, Anaba, and it's a big one." Remembering Samiel's warning about the power of a Horseman's thoughts, Michael stared and concentrated on a memory, willing it into existence. Water trickled from his armor, escaping through the maille, and flowed across his right shoulder, down his arm to the war lance.

Michael, stand down! Anaba cried. *The last time you pulled this shit you nearly got us killed!*

His throat was parched, and he swallowed with great difficulty as he pressed the boundaries of his mortality. Drained by the effort, he pointed the lance toward the ground, his arm trembling to hold the weight of it. Three cloudy droplets collected at the tip of the blade-head and splashed to the ground.

Legends told of an earthquake that precipitated the death of Christ. Michael held his breath as a similar, violent quake shook DrunGer. It grew in magnitude and ferocity as each filmy droplet landed. The marshlands heaved and bucked in the throes of the trembler, causing the bogs to froth and overflow.

Though suspended above the ground by the Touch of Zephyr, the Nightmares struggled to keep their balance. The Fosse stumbled to their knees in the sedge grass with the Black Dogs.

Jagged fissures cracked the surface of the wetlands, expelling plumes of putrid swamp gasses from these unnatural vents. In droves, the Yeth fell inside the crevasses and were impaled on serrated spikes that jutted from the pitch.

"Michael, what have you done?" Samiel signaled his Black Dogs to retreat to his side.

"A Horseman's thoughts can be given shape in Hell." Michael watched nervously. "You said that. I'm just putting the theory to the test."

Hundreds of black tentacles broke out over the land and ensnared the Yeth Hounds, dragging them beneath the surface. A colossal serpent surfaced with a mouth that could only be measured in miles. Rows of jagged, backward-curved fangs glistened in its maw and gill slits. Sparing none, it swallowed the Yeth whole by the hundreds, while crushing others to death beneath its powerful coils.

"Gah, the stench!" Raijin fought at the reins to control his spooked Nightmare. "The whole of Hell could not smell worse."

"It actually worked!" Michael laughed, wiping tears from his eyes. He pulled the collar of his gambeson over his face to shield himself from the cadaverous scent exuding from the beast.

With a grotesque roar, the Leviathan shot upward a hundred feet into the air, the majority of its body hidden beneath the pitch. Arcing back over its squamous form, the creature regarded Michael with one massive eye. Its head was the size of a small moon, its eyes the size of an aircraft carrier. Unblinking, the beast looked to all four of the Horsemen.

Michael pointed his lance toward the retreating Yeth Hounds. Slithering effortlessly through the pitch, the creature sank back beneath the swamps and gave chase. Its scaly coils occasionally broke the surface, spraying pitch and bog mud into the air as it hunted, feeding on the curs.

"I may have soiled myself," Raijin said, glaring at Michael.

"You've summoned the last remaining Leviathan." Wyrmwood watched the Yeth retreating toward the boundaries of DrunGer. She tucked her bow in the quiver on her back.

"Only one being in all of time can make that claim. The Father, Himself."

"There were more of those things?" Michael asked.

"Only two. A male and a female," Samiel said. "God created them, but then realized his mistake. If they had propagated, as living things do, they would have destroyed the Creation. So He sent the Horseman War to slay the female to prevent that from happening."

"Having lost its mate, the male went mad with grief," Raijin explained. "It made a bid for Heaven to get revenge. It failed, obviously, but my predecessor was killed in the attempt."

"The Leviathan attacked Heaven? And killed a Horseman?" Michael asked skeptically.

"The beast is nearly a hundred leagues long!" Raijin pointed to the coils and barbed spines rising and falling across the marsh floor. "The stench alone would have brought down the halls of Heaven."

Wyrmwood laughed, caressing her Nightmare's neck to soothe the warhorse. "Raijin is a bit sensitive about how he came to our ranks. He's the third apocalypse angel to serve in the capacity of War. His office was tied with the most deaths until Eligoriel fell."

"A lapse in judgment – my legion commander's, not mine – resulted in a temporary fall from grace." Raijin elevated his chin in feigned arrogance, ignoring her taunts.

"You're *still* here," Wyrmwood jeered. "Becoming a Horseman isn't temporary. It's a life sentence, I'm afraid."

"What happened to the last Leviathan?" Michael asked, smirking at their antics. "How did it get here?"

"God could not bring himself to order the death of the creature, not after killing its mate." Samiel leaned over his stirrup to console Cŵn with a pat on the head. "To prevent the destruction of His Paradise, the Father cast the Leviathan into the one place He knew could contain such a monstrosity. Now, it would seem the beast has found a new master." Samiel saluted Michael with his scythe. "And the Horsemen have gained a powerful ally."

Michael tried to breathe beneath the weight of this revelation.

"The Leviathan? As a guardian of DrunGer?" Raijin rolled his eyes. "A reckless endeavor, Samiel."

"And yet effective. It's time we return to the living world to begin our investigation in earnest," Samiel said. "A test of our strength was given by the Grigori, and it has been answered accordingly. Let us show them that the Four are not to be trifled with."

CHAPTER 23

The street in front of Covenant Hospital was impassable, thoroughly congested with news vans, satellite trucks, and the press crews that served them. Overeager cameramen and reporters blocked the hospital's Emergency Department entrance as beleaguered security officers fought to keep the mob at bay. NYPD cruisers sat stationed in the driveway to prevent unauthorized vehicles from accessing the emergency lane. Leading the Horsemen, Michael forced his way through the media frenzy.

"Agent Childs!"

Above the calamity of press, Michael heard his name. But he couldn't be sure where the voice came from or who had called out to him in the chaos. He ushered his team of experts through a narrow channel behind the police line.

"Special Agent Childs!"

Hearing his name a second time, Michael honed in on the voice. He recognized the fresh face of Rachel Rollins from her personnel file. "The rookie from Quantico? Welcome to the funhouse." With a wry grin, he offered his hand and gave hers a firm shake. "Want to bring me up to speed?"

"Yes, sir. A nasty dustup at the local carnival. Witnesses at the scene report two Caucasian males assaulted a juvenile male and female." Maroon lipstick accentuated her full lips as she spoke. Her hair was tied back in a stylish wrap. "When the kids fought back, things got ugly. An elderly man stepped in and got his neck broken for his troubles."

"The victims?"

"Jesse Parker, fifteen, and Keisha Griffin, two, were abducted from the scene. I have a BOLO out on them and initiated an Amber Alert. Ziri Ag Wararni, fifteen, took a nasty beating, but they left him behind." Rachel glanced at her phone.

"Ziri?" Ignoring the police escort, Anaba pushed ahead of their group. Her dress blues uniform had more of an impact than any badge on the premises. She made no attempt at courtesy. Shoving her way through the mob, she knife-handed a reporter who tried to intercept her at the door. The result caused a ripple effect, sending the mob of reporters back in a cautious wave. NYPD officers capitalized on the moment to retake the perimeter.

"Can we keep her?" Rachel watched with a sly grin.

"If you agree to do the paperwork to register her as a lethal weapon." Michael hurried to the entrance to catch up to the Marine. "What's the status on the kid?"

"Broken arm. Might need surgery. But he won't cooperate with the doctors. When he's not mumbling in some foreign language, he's asking for someone named Anaba. I sent a language sample to HQ. It's Tamasheq. They're sending an interpreter from the state department."

"Cancel that call."

"Sir?"

"That's Anaba Raines." Michael pointed to the Marine storming through the hospital doors. "Rollins, keep the vultures back. I wasn't kidding about Raines, specifically the *lethal* part."

"I'm on it, Agent Childs." She waded back into the fray of press, shouting orders to further cordon off the area.

Michael rushed through a labyrinth of security as doctors and nurses tried to maintain a semblance of order.

"Michael!" Elijah shouted.

"EJ, have you seen Raines?"

"Never mind her. Where the hell have you been?"

"Getting my house in order." Across the hall, Michael saw Samiel and the other Horsemen conversing with Father Paige. The priest's face was lined with worry and agitation. "What's the situation?"

"Forensics is still working on the CCTV footage to corroborate what happened. They're not hopeful. Bad time of day. Shitty camera angles. Then there's the only witness... who ain't talking." Elijah threw his hands up in resignation. "Can't get a word out of the kid in English."

"Ma'am, you can't go in there!" In the rear of the medical annex, a nurse ran from behind the charge desk, chasing Anaba across the hall.

Two police officers standing guard at the door stepped in to intercept her. Anaba's shoulders were hunched forward, head down, a combative posture that made it clear she was prepared to engage them.

"FBI! Let her through." Michael flashed his badge. "She's the boy's guardian." He caught up to her as she opened the door. A pungent plume of tobacco smoke wafted from the room.

"Oh my God!" the nurse cried, putting her hand over her mouth. "Someone call Dr Kellen. Stat!" She tried to push past the Marine.

Anaba restrained her with an outstretched arm across the threshold. "Get the fuck back!"

"Excuse me, Miss. I'll take it from here," Michael said as he closed the door and walked into the room behind Anaba. Ziri was sitting shirtless on the floor in the center of the dark room, his chest and torso glistening with sweat. His long hair was slick with perspiration. He trembled, almost convulsively, and mumbled unintelligible words between ragged bouts of sobbing.

Using a bone knife, the Tuareg boy cut lines into the flesh of his left arm near the shoulder. Blood flowed from the wounds, staining the sling cradling his arm. He used the blood to complete the circle around him. A small mirror was sitting on the floor in front of him, covered with a handful of cowrie shells.

"Ogăẓ-kăy Măssinăɣ," he whispered, while gripping the silver Tuareg cross in his hand. On the verge of collapse, he waved the tobacco in the air to circulate the smoke.

"What's he saying?" Michael asked.

"He's asking for God's protection, but not for himself. He's asking God to make his enemies disappear." Anaba stood outside of the circle, looking down on the distraught boy. "Bărăd," she said softly. "You're safe now, Ziri. I'm here." She sat down across from him and put her hand on his as he reached for the cowrie shells. "What happened?"

"Išenǵa." Slowly emerging from his fugue, the traumatized boy recognized her. "Anna?" he sobbed uncontrollably. Head bowed, he crawled into her lap, mumbling in Tamasheq between ragged breaths.

"Grigori?" Michael asked. The fury in Anaba's eyes was all he required for translation.

"They took the girls. He couldn't stop them."

Michael laid his hand on the boy's shoulder. "Ziri, it's not your fault, buddy." The door opened behind them. A doctor, flanked by security guards and cops, turned on the interior light.

Anaba took the knife from Ziri's hand and slipped it into her sleeve. She kissed his forehead and embraced him. "Bani – peace, little brother."

A pair of orderlies lifted Ziri to his feet and sat him in a wheelchair. He did not resist, his eyes locked on Anaba's intense gaze. They hurried him down the corridor to the imaging department. A guard stopped Anaba at the badge-only access doors. Forbidden to enter the restricted area, she bristled, pacing the corridor like a newly separated mare searching for her foal.

The corridor lights flickered erratically in the emergency annex. Staff and patients looked anxiously around the ward for signs of trouble. Unaware of the real peril. Fidgeting with the wide-brim of his hat, Samiel whispered over Michael's shoulder, gesturing to the lights. "You had better settle her."

"Anaba's causing this?"

"You've seen the damage a Nightmare can do." Samiel scanned the crowded suite. "These people have not."

"Anaba?" Michael reached for her arm.

"Don't!" She met his eyes with a ferocity that he had never seen, not even in her Nightmare form. White-gloved hands balled into fists, she marched down the hall out of sight.

Ignoring the disgruntled looks of the staff, Michael followed her down the hall and went into the women's bathroom. He hung the CLOSED FOR CLEANING sign on the door and pressed it shut as one of the overhead bulbs burst. The fluorescent tube shattered, scattering glass shards across the tile floor. "Anaba?"

She leaned over the sink, staring into the mirror. Her white cover sat on the counter with her gloves neatly placed on the brim. Falling free, her dreadlocks hung loosely over her shoulders and hid one side of her face in shadow.

The reflection staring back at her was not that of the soldier peering into the glass, but the Nightmare she was in reality. An intense heat emanated from the reflection as a corona of green flames swept across the crest of her neck. Wisps of black smoke roiled off the top of the mirror, creeping up the wall, and across the ceiling. The busted light fixture and the remaining bulbs grew black from the heat and resulting pressure.

"You're going to set off the fire alarm," Michael said as calmly as possible. "Not exactly what we need right now."

Anaba took a deep, audible breath and exhaled. The heat diminished but did not entirely fade. The reflection of her true form remained in the mirror, nostrils flared and ears pinned flat. "I should have been here. I shouldn't have left him alone."

"I was the one who suggested leaving him at the church, remember?" He put his hand on her shoulder and squeezed.

Her pain was his, and the burden of it was stifling. She leaned heavily over her hands and bowed her head, but made no attempt to throw him off. "Anaba, we don't have the option of you going nuclear. Not here."

"Mike!" Elijah burst through the door. He retreated a step back into the corridor to escape the intense heat and the stench of brimstone. "What the fuck?"

"Not now, EJ!" Michael tried to close the door on him.

"You're going to want to hear this, partner. A lady out walking her dog found the missing girls. One's on the way to the ER. The other..." Elijah clenched his teeth and leaned into the doorframe. "It's the little girl, Mike. The bastard carved her up and laid her out like the others."

"Son of–" Michael pressed his fingertips into his forehead until his skull ached. "Damn it!"

Anaba wound her dreadlocks into a bun at the nape of her neck, tucked her hat under her arm, and picked up her gloves.

Elijah stared at her, the ruined lights overhead, and the shattered glass crunching beneath Michael's shoes. "You all right, man? This wasn't round two, was it?"

Michael shook his head. "Give us a minute, will you?" Elijah retreated as Michael closed the door.

"Spread a little thin, aren't we?" Anaba said.

"Yeah," he replied, rubbing his hand along her arm to comfort her. "Come on, let's get out of here. Bad things seem to happen after I've been standing in the ladies' room with you." His attempt at levity was rewarded with a smile.

Back in the hallway, Agent Rollins met Michael's gaze and held up her notebook. Michael turned to Anaba. "I've got to check in with my partners. You mind staying with Ziri?"

"Copy that." Slapping her gloves against the palm of her hand, Anaba proceeded down the corridor toward the isolation room.

"What do we know?" Michael asked.

"Check this shit out." Elijah gestured for Rachel to begin. "There's a reason this one graduated top of her class."

"Once the federal court order was approved, I started examining medical records," Rachel said. "Three of the city's largest hospitals claimed their information servers had been scrubbed."

"What?"

"Wiped squeaky clean."

Michael looked over the list of hospitals in her notebook. "That's the equivalent to wiping out the Library of Congress. Why didn't anyone report this?"

"Because all of the data's been restored, except for any patients who were born with polydactyly disorder."

Michael stared at her skeptically. It wasn't unusual for a rookie to jump to conclusions to impress their peers in the field. "If the data was scrubbed and then retrieved intact, Rollins, how do you know any files are missing?"

"Because of the Monks," she replied with a grin. "It's a gaming club. A bunch of hackers led by my little brother. I ran a few questions by him, and he sniffed it out immediately."

Michael wiped a hand over his mouth to cover a subtle smile. "You broke protocol? On your first day?"

"I just took a leap of faith." She held up her phone to share the document with them. "My brother was able to retrieve the lost data from this hospital, recovering hundreds of files of patients born with this disorder."

"Hundreds?" Michael asked.

"Too small a number to be missed," Rachel said. "Polydactyly is a relatively common birth defect. Covenant Hospital reported fewer than two hundred occurrences at this facility last year. But this is *one* hospital of how many in the greater metropolitan area?"

"Gives our killer a ripe playing field with plenty of targets."

"My little brother assembled the files into a database, and he assures me that someone's been making a list and checking it twice."

"So I did a little cross-referencing with NYPD's missing

persons list," Elijah said. "Four familiar names popped out: Vincent Blake, Braeden Harris, Mary Klinedinst, and the stiff you brought in, Nathan Ponds. They were all born at this hospital."

"Special Agent Childs?" Samiel interrupted, bowing his head to all of them. Wyrmwood and Raijin stood on either side of him in a show of solidarity. "We've been brought here for a purpose. What can we do?"

Michael sighed, a sense of urgency replacing his misgivings. "Agent Pope, take Dr Wyrmwood with you to the crime scene. Dr Samiel can prep for the autopsy here at Covenant."

"Shotgun!" Wyrmwood winked at Elijah and wrapped herself around his arm. She dragged him into an adjoining corridor to the exit.

"I'll have a full report prepared for your review." Samiel pushed the black hat down on his head and trailed behind them.

"This killer might try to finish what he started," Rachel said. "Jesse and Ziri are going to need a security detail."

"Where there is a Marine, there is a way." Raijin snapped to attention and saluted Rollins with his crop. "I will leave Gunnery Sergeant Raines here at your disposal, Agent Rollins. Until your detail arrives."

"Trust me, you won't find better," Michael said. "That covers the boy."

"Thank you, Colonel." Rachel smiled and returned Raijin's salute. "Until the Bureau sends someone, I'll put a call in to my girlfriend for backup."

"Girlfriend?" Michael asked.

"Yeah, she's the SWAT team commander." Rachel grinned, tilting her head to the side. "She's also a professional cage fighter with like three black belts, including Brazilian Jiu Jitsu, but who's counting. Trust me, nobody's getting in here to hurt these kids."

"I don't doubt it," Michael said, turning to leave. "Um...

Elijah had high hopes for scoring a date with you. Let him down easy, all right?"

"Better me than Althea. She'd just dislocate his fingers."

CHAPTER 24

Eight hours after returning to the living world, Michael found himself not among the living, but the dead. Specially prepared for the investigative team, a section of the hospital's coroner's office and suite had been restricted to authorized FBI personnel. Though the examination room was smaller, less state-of-the-art than the facility utilized by the Chief Medical Examiner, it was no less macabre. Especially with the body of a two year-old girl laying on the cold drawer slab.

Keisha Griffin's lidless eyes stared into oblivion. Her pallid gray skin had been scrubbed clean, but the antiseptic could not erase the Enochian profanities carved into the tiny canvas of her face.

Father Paige straightened her tangled braids, rolling the wooden beads between his fingers. "This is not what the Father intended, Samiel. The Grigori were gathered from every tier of Heaven to protect mankind and to fight the Father's enemies." He caressed her mutilated face. "This child was no one's enemy. She's not even a Nephilim."

"Someone's trying to throw us off the scent." Samiel threw his latex gloves into a trash can and discarded his lab coat into a laundry bin. "This time the Nephilim was spared and a human was murdered using the forbidden rite."

"Spared? You call what they did to Jesse a mercy? Simply

because they let her live?" Father Paige shook his head insistently.

"They meant to take the boy, but he fought back," Raijin countered.

"Ziri?" Michael massaged his temples. "Christ, don't let Anaba hear that."

"Anaba's no fool." Father Paige folded his arms across his chest. "If she meant to retaliate, she'd have caught their scent and been on the hunt by now."

"She can sniff out Grigori?" Michael asked.

"The refuse of Hell is comprised of humans and angels. Nightmares hunt both indiscriminately. But through the use of sigils, our natures can be suppressed to avoid detection, even from Nightmares," Samiel said. "We must assume the Grigori are here, and like Pagiel, living in plain sight among the levithmong."

"Levithmong?"

"Forgive me, Michael. It is a derogatory term for mankind," Samiel said in remorse. "I only use it out of turn to prove a point."

Michael's phone vibrated with an incoming barrage of messages from Rollins. "Wyrmwood's report." He scrolled through a dozen texts and images of Jesse Parker's injuries. From the angle and the depth of the wounds, the suspect who killed Keisha Griffin and mutilated Jesse was the same responsible for the other four murders. "I don't recognize some of these glyphs."

Samiel scrutinized the preliminary report. "The profanities on the girl's face mark her as ababalond."

"Unclean?"

"A whore," Raijin corrected. "It's a judgment and a warning. Frankly, I'm not inclined to be lectured. Not by a bunch of halfwit weeping angels holding a grudge against their kin. No offense, Pagiel."

"None taken."

"Wyrmwood says she's thinks the killer used a Vaoan Dagger?" Michael double-checked the spelling. "A Dagger of Truth?"

"Wyrmwood is a Virtue from the Second Sphere of Angels, her expertise in such matters surpasses mine. There's no refuting–" Samiel held his hand up for silence. "We have an interloper," he whispered and summoned his scythe from the ether, hiding in the shadows by the morgue entrance.

Wielding his great katana, Raijin took a position on the opposite side. He signaled for Michael and Father Paige to remain as they were.

A figure moved hesitantly toward the examination room. Beyond the opaque windows, the shadow pitched to and fro with uncertainty. Elongated arms reached for the handles and parted the swinging doors, allowing the intruder to peer inside.

Samiel grabbed the trespasser by the neck, slammed him against the wall, and pressed the curved blade of the scythe against his throat. Raijin charged in to assist, holding the blade parallel to the ground. The whetted point came a hairsbreadth from the tip of the stranger's angular nose.

The intruder squirmed in pain as Raijin carefully poked him. A wisp of smoke rose from the slight contact between the katana and his skin. "Do you mind, Raijin? I rather like my nose."

"You are far, far from any familiar shore, Marcuriel!" Samiel stepped back cautiously and nodded for Raijin to do the same. Both Horsemen kept their weapons poised over the man's head. "State your purpose."

Marcuriel held up empty hands in surrender. "Arezodi, Samiel, Son of God. I bid you peace with no intention of malice or mischief. I come at the behest of my master, Prince Lucifer." He took a silk handkerchief from his breast pocket and dabbed at his forehead and then his nose, wiping away a smear of soot.

He was dressed in a gray morning coat with white, leather spats, a vest, and a silver pocket watch and its chain. His hair was long and thin, slicked back into a pigtail at the nape of his neck, much in the style of colonial America.

"Did you not hear Samiel?" Raijin demanded. "Speak quickly. I have a mind to take your tongue as a trophy."

Closing his eyes, Marcuriel drew in a deep breath to compose himself. Briefly regarding the tiny corpse laying on the slab, he said, "My master has had no involvement with this tawdry affair, if that concerns you. Nor does he have any business with *you* directly." His astute eyes turned to Michael. "My business is with him, and him alone." Marcuriel gasped in horror as Raijin lunged at him and dragged the non-edged side of the katana across the folds of his neck. "Samiel, if there is any modicum of decorum left in you, call off your dog!"

"Raijin only wants your tongue, Marcuriel. I, however, am more inclined to take your head," Samiel said. "What business does your master have with Famine?"

Marcuriel dramatically straightened his rumpled coat and the waistcoat beneath, then grinned and took a bold step toward Michael. He was promptly intercepted again by Raijin.

"What harm can I pose to one Horseman with two others standing in the room?" Marcuriel waited until the way was clear before approaching Michael again. With a low bow and a flourishing of his arms, he announced, "To the newest Horseman Famine, Son of Mikha'el, Son of God, allow me to introduce myself. I am Marcuriel, diplomatic envoy of Baal, attaché to Beezelbub, seneschal of Belial–"

Michael pulled the Glock 19M out of its holster and took aim. "Right now, all you are is an enemy blip on my radar."

"Anaba's temperament has been good for the lad," Raijin said with a chuckle. "Still, a bullet won't kill him, Michael."

"No, but it'll hurt." Michael leveled the semi-automatic at Marcuriel's face. "Speak your peace. I'm a little busy right now."

"How irascibly charming, not unlike Eligoriel. But then, you're only a Nephilim. Your appalling manners will fit in perfectly with this lot," Marcuriel complained, weighing his words. "I am an emissary representing Lucifer Morningstar."

Michael shrugged. "I have no business with the Devil."

"But my lord does have business with you." Marcuriel reached into his interior breast pocket, prompting Michael to place his finger on the trigger. The Glock clicked obediently.

"He may be the newest Horseman, but he is not to be trifled with, Marcuriel," Father Paige warned.

Marcuriel frowned, his face bearing the expression of someone smelling a repugnant odor. "Pagiel, looking well I see. Despite slumming it with the levithmong. Clearly it suits you." Returning his attention to Michael, he bowed his head with over-rehearsed courtesy. "I am fully aware of Famine's prowess, despite the taint of his humanity. Summoning the Leviathan was no small feat for a half-breed."

"Is that why your master has sent you?" Samiel asked. "Some complaint about the Leviathan? I remind you that DrunGer is sovereign territory. Your master holds no sway there."

"The Leviathan is but one of many hot topics of conversation among Hell's aristocracy. The discoloration of the sky. The massacre of Yeth Hounds. The discoloration of the sky. The great rivers running dry. Oh, did I mention the discoloration of the sky?" Marcuriel frowned, tutting with his tongue. "But before broaching sensitive, diplomatic matters, my master believes formal entertainment is required. Thus, he has sent me with an invitation." He held out a heavy bonded envelope crafted from black parchment paper.

Michael holstered the 9mm and warily took the envelope from Marcuriel's gloved hand. Breaking the waxy red seal on the back, he removed the ivory-colored invitation inside:

Lucifer Morningstar requests the pleasure of your company
for an evening of music and dancing.

You are invited to a silent auction and fundraiser for
My Brother's Keeper Global Food Initiative
Saturday, February 14th
Reception at 7:00pm
Dinner at 8:00pm
Metropolitan Museum of Art
1000 Fifth Avenue at 82nd Street
New York, New York
Full evening attire requested.

Raijin slammed the katana home into its scabbard. "Please tell me it's a declaration of war."

"It comes close." Samiel peered over Michael's shoulder. "Lucifer means to welcome the newest Horseman in style... and in person." He pointed to a subtle glyph pressed into the corner of the parchment. "See here, the seal of Raziel, the sigil of forbidden knowledge. While the parchment may be of this world, the writing is not. It's Enochian."

Michael looked at the invitation again. The Latin letters shifted into Enochian glyphs and merged to create a different message:

Prince Lucifer Morningstar,
Son of Perdition, Ruler of Eternal Darkness, Lawless One,
requests the pleasure of your company for an evening of
music and dancing.
You are cordially invited to a coming-out gala
in honor of the newest Horseman of the Apocalypse,
Famine

"You needn't worry about being a wilting wallflower in a party of one." With the grace of a street magician, Marcuriel produced four more invitations from thin air. "Can't have a proper coming out ball for a Horseman without your companions present. No one has been excluded."

Wary of the scythe, the fallen angel stretched his arm out to deliver three of the invitations to Samiel. "I trust you'll ensure Pestilence gets hers." With a dramatic bow, he turned back to Michael. "And last but not least, a special invite for the ever-so-proud parent."

"My father?"

"Heavens, no! Esteemed dignitaries only! I'm afraid your father is not on the guest list. The invite is for your mother." With a scowl, he glared at Father Paige. "You're not invited either, Pagiel. But there might be a need for an extra bar-back, if you're interested."

"Are we even considering this?" Michael turned to Samiel in a panic.

"Everyone who's anyone will be there," Marcuriel said cheerfully, working his way back to the morgue doors. "So... *be there,*" he added with menace before vanishing into the corridor.

"Weaselly little bastard. I'd rather enjoy plucking his feathers out one handful at a time." Raijin retrieved his invitation from Samiel and read it. "Lucifer's pulling out all the stops. Insufferable braggart."

Michael stared at the extra invitation in his hand. It was addressed in perfect cursive – Dr Serra Childs. "Doesn't this represent some conflict of interest?"

"I'm afraid we're in no position to refuse," Samiel said. "While we may serve the one true God, we must never forget whose domain it is in which we live. Our duties include making nice with our hellish neighbors from time to time. To keep the peace."

"You call those attacks on DrunGer peaceful?" Michael asked. "If the Leviathan swallows any more mercury we're going to discover if Hell really is bottomless."

"This could work to our advantage, Michael. Lucifer may

have answers for us. If we stroke his colossal ego, he may provide them or put us on the path to finding our own."

"Full evening dress?" Michael grumbled, staring at the invitation.

"A white-tie affair," Raijin said. "Wyrmwood will be utterly delighted. She rarely gets to dress up."

"Says here I can bring a guest. What about Anaba?"

"If she's going to be by your side, dress blues simply won't do," Raijin stated. "And a .50 caliber Desert Eagle will not go well with a ball gown."

"Who's going to explain that to her?" Michael felt his mouth go dry.

"They call them Nightmares for a reason." Raijin clapped him on the shoulder. "Good luck with that."

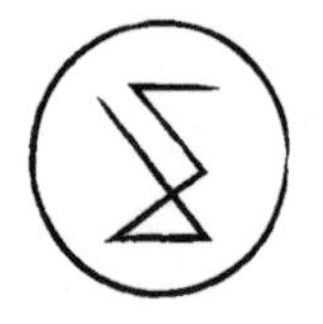  

CHAPTER 25

Rain drenched the sidewalks in front of the Javits Federal Building. Anyone walking outside without an umbrella would have been soaked. Caim Seere not only had an umbrella but also an assistant to hold it over him to protect his Armani suit. The inclement weather was a precursor to the welcome awaiting him inside the FBI's Manhattan field office. While he was not necessarily in enemy territory, he was not among friends.

Are these potential allies? He hadn't had an ally in a very long time. Not since the Fall.

Before ascending to the rank of archangel, he was a Domination of the Second Sphere, charged with bringing guidance to heads of state and government officials. When it came to minions, he had connections firmly entrenched in the most influential organizations: NSA, CIA, DIA. They had not forgotten his counsel and welcomed him back with open arms.

While he admired how the Grigori had infiltrated the FBI to pursue their schemes, his personal bias always leaned toward the Central Intelligence Agency. When it came to getting a job done, few were as well equipped or as morally bankrupt.

"Thank you for coming on short notice. I'm Special Agent Kobey McKabe." There was an irritating smugness in the agent's voice. After a brief exchange of credentials among their retainers, Caim followed him through the lower atrium.

Without revealing their true nature, the celestial beings in the building made their sentiment known: a disparaging glance, a disdainful frown, a challenging glare. Unaware of him as anything but a high-profile visitor, the humans barely acknowledged his presence, a sign that the sigils he was using to suppress his nature were working.

McKabe opened the door to the executive suite and held it as Caim stepped across the threshold. He closed the door, leaving him alone with a familiar presence.

"You look well, Caim Seere, considering the circumstances," Rathan said, leaning back in his chair. "I trust your journey was uneventful?"

"Don't patronize me, Rathaniel. It's beneath you." Caim straightened his suit coat and walked to the front of the desk. He surveyed the small library of books, art work, and other furnishings about him. "I must admit, the last thing I ever expected was a request for an audience from a Watcher."

"I have a proposition that will serve to elevate our separate causes. Please have a seat." The Grigori wasted no time getting to the heart of the matter. "Is it still your wish to wear the mantle of a Horseman? If it is, I may be in a position to assist you."

Caim sat down, crossing one leg over the other, and rested his hands on his thigh to mask his excitement. "An intriguing offer, Rathaniel. I'm anxious to hear the details."

"It is my mission to remove a blight from the Creation." Rathan licked his lips. Rising from his chair, he walked around the desk and sat down on the corner. "But in doing so, I risk making powerful enemies."

"You speak of Samiel and the other Afflictions?"

"I'm speaking of your Nightmare." Leaning over Caim, Rathaniel pointed an accusing finger at him. "I'm surprised you let such a creature slip from your grasp."

Caim stiffened, having no retort. "It was… unfortunate."

Rathan shrugged his shoulders. "She could still be yours."

"Impossible! The compact has been sealed." Caim got up from the chair and paced the room, folding his arms across his chest.

"If her Rider fell, it could just as easily be unsealed." Rathan stood up, blocking Caim's agitated march. "She would be yours to claim. None could oppose your rise to the office of Famine, not even the other Horsemen."

It was dangerous talk. Caim felt the collar of his shirt constricting his throat. He tugged at it with a finger. The Grigori commander was plotting to kill the Son of Mikha'el. The Qaaun. Two thousand years ago, they had plotted and successfully assassinated the previous divine emissary on a cross. "What are you proposing?"

Rathan returned to his chair, folding his hands on the polished top of his desk. "Separate them and keep them separated, and I will make certain that the current Famine falls."

"The Rider and the Nightmare are bound," Caim said. "No matter where he is, he can summon her to his side."

"He can't summon her if he's dead."

Caim frowned to avoid presenting an obsequious smile. Leaning his head into one hand, he said, "There will be repercussions for his death."

"Once you are a Horseman, I will go about my responsibilities unchallenged. There will be no repercussions."

A sharp knock interrupted them. The office door opened, and Agent McKabe stepped into the room, closing it behind him. "Agent Childs is reporting in," he said with a smirk. "He's holding on line one."

Rathan sat up in his chair with a coy grin and cued the speaker. "Special Agent Childs. It would seem prayers and hope were not enough to keep Manhattan safe from a killer. Now there's a dead two year-old lying in the morgue. What other *good* news do you have for me?"

A light static played from the opposite end of the line. "Sir, my team's been on the case for less than twenty-four hours. Barely enough time to read through the paperwork."

"I'm not sure the mayor would appreciate that excuse. Not while his constituents are being murdered." Rathaniel stared at McKabe, who shifted uneasily in his gaze. "What can you tell me about the two witnesses?"

"Agent Rollins is overseeing the protective detail for the female witness. I've taken the boy into my custody. I'm taking him to my mother's farm. He should be safe there for a few days."

"Sounds promising, Agent Childs. Keep me updated."

"Yes, sir."

The telltale click terminated the call. Rathan grinned, rubbing his fingers over his hands. "Opportunity presents itself."

"What guarantee do I have that your soldiers won't kill the Nightmare?"

"None," Rathan said, flicking his hands dismissively. "If she becomes a problem, we will do what we must." He offered his hand across the desk. "Do we have an accord?"

"Noib. We do." Caim buttoned his coat and accepted Rathan's hand to seal the agreement.

"Agent McKabe will show you back to your vehicle. Good hunting, Caim Seere."

Caim trotted down the concrete staircase with a bounce in his stride. His exuberance forced his escort to hasten their steps. A smile curled in the corners of his mouth as he approached the black SUV waiting at the curb. He signaled the front-seat passenger to remain in the vehicle and opened the back door to let himself inside.

"You look like the cat that got the mouse, the goose, *and* the family dog," Paul Steiner said, sitting on the far side of the backseat. He was a handsome man, middle-aged, with dark, closely cropped hair and piercing blue eyes.

"This meeting was unexpectedly fruitful," Caim replied. "You, on the other hand, look as if you've seen the Devil himself."

Steiner shuffled through a packet of glossy eight by ten pictures. "When you said Warlander was alive, I didn't believe it. *Still* can't believe it." He pointed to the CCTV surveillance on a tablet, which showed Anaba Raines and Michael Childs walking together on the sidewalk outside of Javits Center after the press conference. "I was sure I'd never see her again."

"You sound as if you regret betraying her?"

"My bank account in the Caymans says differently." Steiner shoved the photos into an envelope and tossed them on the floor. "Call it professional envy. Raines was the best damn asset I ever had. I mean, she was lethal by herself, but with her wife beside her?" He snorted and shook his head. "Those girls did the job a hundred Stinger missiles couldn't accomplish."

"Professional envy and bank accounts aside, why do you sound so concerned?"

Steiner tugged at the collar of his shirt. "Does Raines know what you did to her wife?"

"Does it matter?" Caim adjusted his tie to tighten the half-Windsor knot as their SUV convoy pulled into traffic.

"You may not give a shit, but being on the wrong side of a master sniper's scope could be problematic for me. Does Raines know I was involved?"

"Have I ever let you down in the past? No? Then stop pining about it." Caim tapped the back of the driver's seat. "Jaeger, isn't it?"

"Yes, sir," came the reply.

"Take me to one of those Italian restaurants. A fancy one." Caim snapped his fingers impatiently. "What was the one you were talking about in the office? Della Voce?"

The driver looked back in the rearview mirror. "You need a reservation, Mr Seere."

"Mr Jaeger, you're an agency man. We don't take no for an answer, and we don't make reservations."

"It's alright, Alec," Steiner said. "I'll make the necessary calls."

Glancing at the Rolex on his wrist, Caim pulled down the cuff of his shirt and sat back with a grin. "I'm going to need a full team. And some place quiet with the proper wards in place to contain her."

"A team? For what?"

"I want her back," Caim replied, smoothing the fine fabric of his pants. "Anaba belongs to me, and I need to make that clear to her."

Steiner frowned, his gestures and expressions slowed by calculating thoughts. "I'll make the necessary arrangements."

"See to the incantations yourself," Caim said. "I want no mistakes. We must ensure Anaba doesn't escape again." He glanced at Steiner. "Because if she does, she will know of your involvement. We can't have that, can we?"

Steiner glared at the fallen angel and then looked away in disgust. "No, we can't."

CHAPTER 26

Michael turned off State Route 27 into a private driveway. Despite a persistent drizzle, the rain had finally ended. He let the Jeep idle in front of a pair of royal blue utility gates, headlights lighting up a narrow lane and a stone pillar beyond them. The brick light post had a bronze sign bolted into it: *Talveh Farm.*

"Are you sure Ziri will be safe here?" Anaba asked, unbuckling her seat belt.

"This is the safest place I know." The gates opened and Michael drove down the path between the familiar five-rail fence. He stared through the branches of the aged oak trees lining the driveway and was reminded of the Vestibule Road. Unlike in Hell, he could see the telltale twinkling of the stars.

He pulled into the yard and parked in front of the house. It was three hundred years old, raised to the frame in colonial times. The property had served as a dairy farm, a vineyard, and finally a Thoroughbred racing stable, formerly owned by a family tracing their roots back to the founding fathers. Every exterior light across the property was on, illuminating the wraparound porch, the driveway, and the riding arena beyond the barn.

A familiar figure waited on the porch, wringing her hands in her apron. "Michael?" Draped in a woolen shawl, Serra

Childs descended the stone stairs and hugged him. She stood on tiptoe to wrap her arms about his neck. He returned her embrace with far less enthusiasm.

"You look exhausted." Serra straightened her slender frame and ran her thumbs along his cheeks.

"It's been a long day," Michael sighed and waited for Anaba to step out of the car. "Mom, this is Anaba Raines."

Serra glanced at the Marine and then back to her son. "Is she the one who rearranged your face?"

"I can assure you he deserved it, Mrs Childs," Anaba said, helping Ziri out of the backseat.

"I like her." Winking at Michael, Serra extended her hand to Anaba in welcome. "Michael can have that effect on people. Believe me; he wasn't raised that way." She grasped Anaba's hand in both of hers and shook it vigorously. "Please, call me Serra."

Eyeing the cast on Ziri's arm, Serra's demeanor took on the sympathetic expression only a mother could muster. "A Tuareg cross? May I?" With his permission, she curled her fingers beneath the silver talisman. "Ăssălam ăɣlekum. M-isem-năk?"

"Ăɣlekum ăssălam," he said out of habit before he gasped, "You speak Tamasheq?" He jumped when Anaba kicked him in the ankle. "Ziri!" he responded to her question. "My name is Ziri Ag Wararni." Flustered, he looked away to avoid any disrespect and stared at his feet.

"I know enough Tamasheq to get myself in trouble. Maybe you can help me learn more?" Serra brushed the hair from the boy's forehead and laid her fingers against his feverish skin. When he did not reply, she raised his chin. "I saw the blessing you left for my son, Ziri. I thank you." Serra put her hand over her heart. "What I wish for myself, I wish for you."

"Mom," Michael said, interrupting them, "I was wondering if Anaba and Ziri could maybe–"

"Of course, they can stay." Serra put her arm around Ziri's shoulders and led him toward the house. "Ziri can have your old room. I'm guessing Anaba and you will want the spare?"

Anaba shoved her hands into her pockets. "I'd rather sleep in the driveway."

"That won't be necessary, Anaba. I was just checking." Serra squeezed her shoulder and grinned. "Michael doesn't often bring beautiful young women home to meet his mother."

The sound of neighing caught Ziri's attention. He turned toward a stone path leading to a bank barn situated forty yards from the house. "There are horses here?" he asked, excitement raising the pitch in his voice.

"Michael keeps his jousting mounts here in the offseason. His older brother is doing a night check. Want to go down and have a peek?" Serra took a few steps toward the barn, cupped her hands around her mouth, and shouted, "Noah, Michael's brought guests! They're coming down to see the horses!"

"There's another one of you running around?" Anaba whispered while Serra was distracted.

Michael frowned and shook his head. "Noah was adopted before I was born."

Anaba glanced over her shoulder to where Serra stood, embracing Ziri in her arms. "Need me to stick around?"

"Appreciate it, gunny." Michael put his hand on her shoulder. "But it just puts off the inevitable conversation. Head on down to the barn with Ziri. He could use a little hippotherapy."

Hugging herself beneath her shawl, Serra returned to where Michael stood and watched as Anaba and Ziri made their way to the barn. "How much do they know?"

He bit his lip. "Everything."

"Michael–"

"I broke my promise, Mom," he confessed, seizing control

before she could outmaneuver him and dominate the conversation. "I touched the qeres."

"You what?" Serra dragged him by the arm into the porch light as if he were still only five years old. "Michael, how could you!" She ripped off the band-aid, taking hair and skin with the adhesive, and examined the burn left by the Titan's blood during Michael's first battle in Hell. Confused by the injury, she unwrapped the gauze on his other hand and scrutinized the blisters on the heel of his palm. "Was it worth risking your life?" she whispered, her voice cracking.

A drenching rain suddenly fell from the skies. With the rain came the wind. But not one drop landed on them. Serra stared at the dry asphalt beneath her feet and then at the scattered raindrops splashing to the ground, soaking into the driveway around them. "Michael?"

"Mom, qeres is the least of my worries." Michael held his hand out. A dozen cold drops collected in his palm. He poured the rain into her hand. "I've galloped across the fields of DrunGer. Seen the summit of Mount Victus. Ridden on the Vestibule Road." He reached into his pocket and pulled out a petrified scale. "This is from the dragon goddess Tiamat. Her severed heads form the crown of a wellspring above the Eridanus River of Guilt."

"Momao Abai'Vonin." Serra closed her fingers over the petrified dragon scale and let the water run between her fingers. Her breathing was labored. "It's all come to pass as your father predicted."

"Mom," Michael gasped. "You've known about all of this? And you never mentioned–"

"What was I supposed to say to you, Michael?" she pleaded, pressing her hand over her heart, fingers trembling. "What was I to tell you that would not have compromised our safety? *Your* safety?"

The candor in her voice frightened him, but the sting of betrayal weighed heavily on him and, he took a step away from her.

The hurt and alarm in Serra's eyes was authentic. She glanced over her shoulder to the stables. "Who is Anaba? Does she have something to do with what's happened?"

"She's a Nightmare. *My* Nightmare." His throat tightened in regret for upsetting her. "I'm still breathing because of her."

Serra took a deep breath and exhaled. "You are a descendant of Enoch, who begat Methuselah, who begat Lamech, who begat Noah–"

"Mom, this isn't the time for a lecture. We're a little beyond the whole two-by-two into the ark story–" The abrupt slap across his face halted any further sarcasm. Michael stretched his jaw to alleviate the sting.

"*You,* Michael Jered Childs, are a *direct* descendant of Enoch, a man who walked with God so long he was transformed, and the Father took him to become Metatron the Exalted, Prince of the Archangels, the Scribe of God. Enoch was my father. Your grandfather. Your father is the Archangel Mikha'el, who vanquished Lucifer the Morningstar and his corps of rebellious angels."

Michael felt the heat of her slap intensifying with the flush of shame. "Noah?" He looked down toward the barn.

"Named after my favorite great nephew. He has no blood ties to this family." She swallowed hard, her lips and chin quivering with emotion. "My relationship with your father was an act of disobedience. It was overlooked because of my father's importance to God."

"How did you survive the Flood?"

"I should have perished with the others. God was so angry. Even my father's presence could not soothe Him. Mikha'el sent Uriel to take me away and guard me until it was over." She took Michael's hand and held it tightly against her cheek. "Your father knew I wanted to bear his child. We resisted for millennia. There was no way to determine if the child we brought into the world would become another Minotaur or a Plato. Despite his fear, we consummated our love for the first time twenty-eight years ago and brought a beautiful little boy into this world. You are a perfect reflection of your father's goodness."

Michael bowed his head and struggled to catch his breath. "Does Noah know all of this?" He exhaled slowly when she nodded affirmation. He turned his back on her, leaning against the Jeep for support. "Damn it, Mom! You should have told me. Why keep me in the dark?"

"It was too dangerous for you to know your true heritage."

A loud crashing came from the direction of the stable. It was the harsh noise of heavyweights exchanging body blows. The entire foundation of the barn shook under the stress, and the muffled cries of horses pierced the night air.

"What in the world?" Serra asked.

Michael sprinted down the path to the barn. Through the open Dutch doors on the side of the building, he saw frightened horses pacing frantically from side to side in their stalls. In human form, Anaba went flying upside down through the center aisle. The sound of her body crashing into the wall echoed beneath the eaves.

The green flash and roar of Nightmare flame sounded, and Michael ran faster, holding onto the lamppost to whip himself through the front door of the tack room.

Wearing a leather jacket and jeans, a Black man was kneeling on the concrete floor in the wash rack. A pair of large gray wings were partially unfurled at his shoulders. Ziri was pinned facedown beneath his knee. The boy was sweating, gasping in pain between ragged breaths. His broken arm was trapped beneath him and his other arm was twisted in a painful lock.

"You have no right!" In dusty jeans and a flannel shirt, Noah threatened the angel with a pitchfork in his hands.

Down the broad center aisle, Anaba was savaging a second angel. She grabbed a tangle of long blond hair in her teeth and shook him viciously. Her intense flames rolled over the angel, singeing his flesh.

Squinting in pain, the angel looked up at Michael with a smile. "Hiya, Mike."

"Uncle Gabe?" Michael then stared down the opposite aisle at the angel restraining Ziri. "Uncle Raph?" Despite not seeing them in more than a decade, he recognized the two most prominent men of his childhood. Feeling the fool in a joke where he alone was the patsy, Michael's jaw slackened. *Gabriel. Raphael.* His father's brothers. *Archangels.* "Uncle Raphael, please get off Ziri."

"No can do, Michael," Raphael replied, his voice a smooth baritone. "He's with the beast. He'll have to be put down as soon as Gabriel deals with the unclean creature." The archangel peered around Michael to Gabriel. "How goes it, brother?"

"Nothing like roasting marshmallows," Gabriel gasped. "Unless you're the marshmallow."

"I'm not going to say it again, Raphael. Get off the boy!" Noah demanded. Flustered, he turned to Michael. "One minute we're talking horses and feeding treats. The next, these two jump us."

"Michael, your father charged us with protecting you and your mother," Gabriel grunted. "Raphael only took down the boy when he tried to interfere!" He buffeted the Nightmare with his wings. Readjusting her hold, she trampled him, crushing his sensitive pinions beneath her fiery feet.

"A little late for that, Uncle Gabe." Michael extended his hand, and the war lance Bitter Harvest materialized in his grip. Water flowed from the blade-head, spilling up his arm and across his chest. The armor of his office coalesced over his body with the current to form the golden-green chainmail shirt.

"You're one of *them,*" Raphael said. "You're an Affliction!"

"Enough of this!" Serra shouted, running through the tack room door and into the aisle. "Raphael, get off that child. Can't you see he's hurt?"

"I didn't harm him," Raphael complained.

"I'm not accusing you," Serra said. "I'm asking you to do something about it."

Effortlessly lifting Ziri by the belt, Raphael stood up. "Mind yourself, boy." The archangel removed the sling and soft cast, working his fingers against the arm while Ziri stood stiffly, observing him.

The boy flexed his fingers and cautiously rotated his arm. "It's… it's not broken anymore?"

"I believe the words you're looking for are *thank you,*" Raphael mumbled.

"It was an iblis like you who broke it, so I guess we're even." Ziri glared up at the angel.

"Neutral corners, all of you!" Hands balled into fists, Serra closed her eyes and shook her head. "Anaba, please?"

The Nightmare blasted Gabriel's face with brimstone and retreated. Choking on the noxious fumes, the angel crawled to the opposite side of the barn aisle.

"Noah, take Anaba and Ziri to the kitchen. There's hot chocolate and sandwiches on the counter. Help yourselves. Anaba… while you're a sight to behold, two legs not four in the house, if you please."

Anaba trotted past her, snorting a challenge at Raphael. Ears pinned flat against her head, she put herself between the angel and the Tuareg boy. Herding Ziri at her side, she followed Noah out of the barn.

"Raphael and Gabriel, my study. I don't care if my own father calls to you. Do not leave from there until I come for you."

Raphael ducked beneath Gabriel's shoulder, raised him to his feet, and helped him limp down the aisle. "Thought you said you could take down the beast," he muttered.

"Next time, *you* fight the Nightmare, and *I'll* sit on the human child."

"Michael," Serra said, "go to your father's dojo garden. We need to talk."

"Mom?"

She clasped her hands together in front of her, her shoulders firmly set. "Do as I ask. I'm going to settle these horses. I'll be there shortly."

He sighed in defeat. Just like that, she was back in charge.

"Michael."

"I'm going." Michael's eyes traced the rooftops of his father's dojo against the darkness. Frustrated, he walked out of the barn and into the rain.

CHAPTER 27

Michael paced the footpaths in the meditation garden outside his father's dojo. The narrow geometric lines were unmistakable, leading to no particular destination. Their purpose was to evoke a sense of peace. "*We must be still and still moving,*" he whispered, a quote from the poet T.S. Eliot. It was one of his father's favorite mantras.

Nothing but time had touched the garden or the surrounding buildings. The walkways needed to be swept, the weeds pulled, the sand raked, and the rocks realigned. Feral rose bushes had encroached on the paths from overgrown beds. Still, the dojo courtyard possessed an undiminished symmetry.

Michael made his way onto the porch and approached the dojo doors, his heart pounding in his chest. Time shifted, and he was a little boy again, breathless from running all the way from the barn to spend the afternoon sword training with his father. The anticipation left him holding his breath. As he pushed the sliding doors aside, he was greeted by the reality of dust and darkness and silence.

Hearing the splash of footsteps on the stone path behind him, he watched his mother running through the storm, a shawl covering her head. Michael tapped the metal butt of the lance quietly on the wooden veranda and suspended the rain.

In a waltz of wonder, Serra maneuvered between the raindrops. She touched a drop with the tip of her finger. It burst in slow motion and splashed across her nail. Draping the damp shawl across her shoulders, she smiled up at him. Her eyes twinkled in the dim lights shining from beneath the eaves. "Michael, that's amazing."

He heard the pride in her voice and couldn't help but smile. "Just a bit of rain. When Moses parted the Red Sea? *That* was amazing."

"Moses was a Nephilim, so it should come as no surprise." She held his hand, steadying herself as she walked up the wet stairs. Brushing away cobwebs from the recessed lights built into the canopy, Serra slipped out of her damp sandals and stepped inside the dojo. "Your father loved Japanese culture, especially those aspects pertaining to the samurai and their bushido."

Michael kicked off his boots to follow her to the back corner of the training room beside a display stand cradling an antique Kamakura katana. Nearly seven hundred years old, the blade was sheathed in a polished scabbard made from mulberry wood imported from the Izu Islands of Japan.

"Mikha'el loved everything about humanity. Everything that was noble and good. That's why he named the farm Talveh. Family." With her left hand, she clasped the hilt of the sword.

The wall behind the sword rumbled and shifted, pushing outward from an imperceptible seam in the wooden facade and sliding to the side. Lights winked on behind the panel and revealed a hidden study. Arranged in a septogram, the seven walls of the room were bordered with desks and bookshelves lined with scrolls and ancient tomes. An alchemy set was neatly arrayed on a lab table beside a mortar and pestle, as well as other apothecary tools.

Michael turned in a slow circle. "I know this room. I used to play here." Seven distinct sigils were prominently carved into each wall of the chamber at a height of ten feet. "Uncle Raph? Angel of the East. Uncle Gabe, Angel of the West." He exhaled deliberately through his mouth to calm his breathing. "Samiel, Angel of Death." Across from his father's sigil, he recognized the familiar logo for the family farm. The two were nearly indistinguishable.

"This is a safe room. Your father built it to protect us from his enemies. Among all the angelic signatures, these are the most powerful that can be invoked." Serra laid her hands on his shoulders. "When written in blood, they become even more potent. Enochian talismans of power and protection or terrible curses of death and destruction."

Michael chuckled nervously, feeling unhinged as his memories of childhood struggled to catch up, integrating themselves with his new reality. He leaned against his father's desk. On the blotter was a splotched, watercolor picture of an angel, a portrait as only a child could render, with smeared gray streaks for wings. The sigil for Talveh was crudely written as the artist's signature in the bottom corner. "I always thought you and Dad were speaking some made up pidgin to keep me in the dark. You were actually speaking Enochian."

"And what's that supposed to mean?" she asked defensively.

"Mom, you translated *Deadpool* into Klingon at Dragon Con last year. You're the only person I know that can watch Lord of the Rings without *any* subtitles. Tell me that's normal."

Serra laughed, jabbing him in the ribs. "Is that such a bad thing?"

"Not at all. It's why I got into linguistics. I was jealous and wanted to be just like you."

"Michael," she whispered, caressing his cheek, "maybe your father and I didn't say it enough… but we're both very proud of you."

"If dad's so proud, why isn't he here?" Swallowing his disappointment and resentment, Michael fled from the chamber. Outside on the porch, he closed his eyes and breathed in the scent of the rain. It did little to comfort him. Jamming his feet into his boots, he sat staring at the ground beneath them. His mother lingered at the door before coming to sit beside him.

"Back at the restaurant," he croaked in a strained voice, "you were trying to warn me about the Grigori."

"I didn't want to alarm you," Serra replied, shaking her head. "I wasn't certain it was them until you sent those crime scene photos. I wanted to be wrong."

"What can you tell me about them?"

"Nothing good. They're relentless, driven, and ruthless. They were named by God as Watchers for a reason. There were once twelve garrisons, some more militant than others. To think they're using qeres like dictators use biological weapons. Utterly reprehensible!" Serra laid her head on his shoulder. "Michael, I'm so frightened."

"When you know what has to be done, there's no room for fear," Michael said. "You taught me that."

She tilted her head in confusion. "Yes, I did. But I'm not sure what you mean–"

"I've been invited to a ball at the Met to celebrate my coming out as a Horseman."

Eyebrows raised, Serra pursed her lips in a reproving line. "Stepping up in the world, are we?"

"Mom, the ball is being held by Lucifer Morningstar. Talk about bad blood!" Michael snorted, chewing at the inside corner of his lip. "This could make the Hatfields and the McCoys look like playground bullies."

"No, Michael. Promise me you won't go!" she said, distraught. "You can't go. What I know of Lucifer comes from your father's accounts of him. This is a showdown of sorts. He's taking a measure of you, seeking retribution–"

"Samiel says I don't have a choice."

"Samiel?" Serra's eyes widened in shock. The color left her face, leaving a gray pallor over her features.

"You know him?" Michael snorted.

"The Angel of Death? No," Serra said, shaking her head emphatically. "It's just you mention him so casually, like he's a colleague from the office."

"He's a Horseman, Mom. *I'm* a Horseman now. We *are* colleagues."

Serra turned away from him, burying her face in her hands. She steadied herself by propping her elbows on her thighs.

"Mom?" Michael wrapped his arm around her and kissed the top of her head.

"I'm sorry, Michael. It's just a lot to take in."

"I know. It's a lot for me too." He paused briefly, feeling the weight of her in his arms. "Lucifer invited you, too." He retrieved the invitation from inside his gambeson and handed it to her.

Serra opened the black envelope in her trembling hands and read the parchment inside. With a shuddering, deep breath, she pushed the invitation back inside. "I wonder if Versace is having a sale?"

"Don't bother. You're not going."

"A coming out ball for my son? At the Metropolitan Museum of Art?" Serra said. "You'd need a Nightmare to keep me away."

"I can arrange that."

Serra smiled at his retort. "Michael, this isn't your decision to make. Your father may not be here, but I am. I'm no archangel, but Lucifer Morningstar will learn that I am not afraid of him!" Angry tears began brimming in her eyes. She held a hand against her stomach as if a cramp troubled her and leaned back against the steps.

"I won't be alone. The other Horsemen are coming." In an awkward reversal of their roles, he stroked her hair as she had done for him when he was upset as a child. "More importantly, I'll have Anaba."

"I know so little about the Nightmare," Serra said, trying

to compose herself. "She would have killed Gabriel tonight."

"Uncle Gabe attacked her!"

"Why are you defending her?" Serra looked up at him with desperate eyes. "Is there something between you two?"

"Mom!" Michael pulled away from her, refusing to answer the question. "I can't believe you. Anaba was forged to serve a Horseman. She's got my back, and I've got hers. I trust her with my life... and so should you."

"If she keeps you safe from the Grigori... *and* Lucifer," Serra said with a deliberately inscrutable smile, "I'll write her into my will."

Michael stood up, helping his mother to her feet. "I've had my fill of haunted places for the evening." He closed the dojo doors and wrapped his arm around Serra's waist.

"We still have a great deal to talk about." Serra cupped his chin in her palm, affectionately stroking his cheek with her thumb.

"What more is there to say?" Michael was not in the mood to be lectured, especially if the topic was his father.

"Michael, your father's not here to explain–"

"And he hasn't been here for ten years, mom," Michael interrupted her. "*Ten years,* we've been on our own. He's the cause of this!" His resentment of his father swelled into his throat, accentuating each word with accusation. "There's not much more that needs to be said."

Eyes narrow with indignation, Serra glared at him. "While you may wield that lance with the same mastery as your father did, do not force me to remind you how well I wield a switch."

The fact that he was a grown man did not matter. The insinuation of the threat was real. Michael took a respectful step back and away from her, bowing his head. "Yes, ma'am."

"Now go to the study and have a word with your uncles. I'm sure they have questions," Serra said, usurping the final word. "I'll take Anaba and Ziri to their rooms and get them settled. I'll meet you shortly."

CHAPTER 28

There was no underestimating the comfort of a long, hot shower to wash away fatigue and the grime of the world. Michael could not remember the last time he had the opportunity to simply enjoy the pleasure without having to dash to a meeting or a crime scene. His newly acquired talents to control water density, temperature, and directional proximity only heightened the experience.

The tantalizing smells of bacon, coffee, and scrambled eggs filtered in through the cracked window above the bathroom door. Before his mother could chastise him for using up all the hot water in the house, he turned off the faucet and stepped into the swirling steam. While drying his hair, he overheard a raised voice outside in the hall.

"What do you mean the goddamn horse is lame? An entire show season and on the most important day, the thing's three-legged?"

Michael recognized his brother's voice but not the helpless frustration in it. Putting on a clean pair of boxers and jeans, he cracked the bathroom door and listened, eavesdropping over the low murmur of the ceiling fan.

"Staci, I'm not blaming you. I know the horse had good care. I paid for most of it, remember? Bullshit! Of course, I know how important this is to her. To all of us! How much time do I have? I'll be in touch. Bye." Noah paced the corridor at the base of the stairs.

Instead of retreating into the bathroom, Michael slouched against the doorway, letting the towel wrapped about his head fall to his muscular shoulders. He coughed to get his brother's attention.

"Mike?" Noah pressed his knuckles against his temples and rubbed vigorously at his receding hairline. "Guess you heard that. When it rains it pours, right?"

"How's Bryana feeling? In all the excitement last night, I didn't even think to ask about her."

"She's dying, Mike." Eyes filled with tears, Noah cleared his throat. "My little girl's only twelve years old, been chronically ill all her life, and – oh – her mom and I are splitting up. How's she supposed to feel?"

His brother and his wife Stacia were former heroin addicts. An overdose caused the premature birth of their only daughter Bryana, leaving her deaf and afflicted with Waardenburg Syndrome. Though the condition was a fault of genetics, they blamed the heroin and each other. Twelve years clean and sober and they were still using the girl's fragile health as a weapon of their guilt. Every new condition or symptom was grounds for another battle.

"The heart thing?" Michael asked, devastated by the news.

"Fucking hypertrophic cardiomyopathy, and it's getting worse."

"Why didn't anyone tell me?"

"Because you're busy, Michael. You're always busy," Noah replied, resuming his pacing.

But this is family. Nothing's more important, he wanted to say, but the words failed him.

"Did you know she qualified for the equitation finals at Bridgehampton?"

Michael nodded somberly. "I got Mom's text message."

"Noah, what did Staci want?" Serra walked into the corridor

from the kitchen, wiping her hands on a dish rag. "Ah, you're up. Morning, Michael." She kissed him on the cheek. But the cool reception from them roused her suspicions. "What's wrong?"

Noah bowed his head without answering. Michael averted his gaze. It wasn't his story to tell.

"Boys, you're frightening me. Has something happened to Bryana?"

"Bryana's horse is lame." Noah snatched the ballcap from his back pocket and jammed it onto his head. He exhaled forcefully through his mouth, causing his cheeks to inflate from the pressure.

"But the championship's this afternoon," Serra said.

"Noah, there's a dozen horses living on this farm." Michael grabbed a white polo from the banister and shrugged into it. "We'll hook up the truck and trailer and bring her another one."

"They're too old, Mike," Noah protested. "Most of these horses haven't been off the farm in years."

"Knockout's only five, and he was in New Jersey two weekends ago."

"Knockout was at Medieval Times for jousting, not a rated hunter show in the Hamptons. No eighteen-hand Budweiser reject's gonna win the Classic against those fancy, imported warmbloods." He rubbed his fingers across his furrowed brow. "This is so fucked up." He looked at Serra. "Sorry, mom."

"Bryana got this horse through the Make-A-Wish Foundation," Serra explained, caressing Noah's back and shoulders to comfort him. "When she *could* ride, she spent the better part of the year competing for points to qualify for the Classic in her age division."

Noah pressed the back of his hand against his mouth. "This might be her last chance."

"Mom," Michael begged, "you have to know someone from the university hospital?"

"Bryana's been seen by the best physicians in the country. Experts in their fields. They're confounded that she's lasted this long."

"Uncle Gabe? Uncle Ralph?"

"Not even in the equation." Noah laughed, but it was a bitter, defeated sound. "A busted arm. A deep cut. No problem. But when it comes to actually saving a life, our *uncles* get real particular. Something about interfering with the original design."

"Noah, that's not fair," Serra scolded. "Archangels possess limited abilities beyond their spheres." She looked up at Michael with sorrow in her eyes. "This is no longer about preserving Bryana's life, but ensuring the quality of the time she has left."

"Anaba worked at Belmont track." Michael followed his mother into the kitchen. "I bet she knows someone who has a nice track pony we can borrow."

"Finding a horse of this quality to compete at this level? At Belmont? I doubt it." Noah propped his arms on the counter and shook his head. "Besides, there's no way we'd get a horse from Belmont to the Hampton show grounds in time."

"Then we lease a horse for the day!"

"I don't have that kind of money, Mike! And no, don't tell me I can borrow from you or Mom." Noah avoided making any eye contact with either of them. "This is my burden."

"Don't need to find a horse." Ziri walked into the kitchen, his eyes buried in a leather tome. The book was heavy enough to require both hands to hold it. "Anaba can do it."

"Ziri? Your bed wasn't slept in last night." Serra stared at him, concern in her eyes. "Have you been awake in the study all night?"

"Whatever the iblis did to my arm cured my fatigue, too. I spent the time reading and studying the Tuareg relics in your collection. You wrote a book about the friends of kel essuf, the shamans, and their contract rituals. That is how you know my language." Ziri looked up from the tome. "My grandfather can no longer teach me the old ways, will you?"

"I would be honored to share what I know with you, Ziri, but first you must stop referring to Raphael and Gabriel as iblis. The term is quite offensive to angels." She glared at him as she served up a steaming plate of sausage and eggs. The admonishment needed no further discussion. "Now come eat your food and drink your tea before it gets cold."

Michael leaned over the breakfast nook and laid his arms across the page Ziri was reading. "What do you mean 'Anaba can do it'? Last time I checked, the United States Equestrian Federation didn't recognize Nightmares as an established breed. Could be wrong, but I think the brimstone and fire might be an issue, not to mention her temperament."

"In 1281 BCE, Pharaoh Ramesses the Great ordered his clerics to slaughter his entire stable of black horses. He feared a Nightmare was living among them. All twenty of his prized chariot horses were killed and buried in a mass grave."

"So?"

"So, Ramesses was right. There *was* a Nightmare among them."

"How do you know that?"

"Because it got away." Ziri pointed to a tomb mural depicting a herd of galloping black horses. The fresco portrayed their grisly slaughter by the pharaoh's priests and the subsequent burial. In the background, a single black horse watched from the dunes. Its mane and legs were engulfed in green flames.

Michael snorted, carefully scrutinizing the book for authenticity. As part of his mother's collection, the tome and the mural were irrefutable evidence. "Well, damn. Where is Anaba?"

Ziri pushed Michael's arms off the book. "I overheard the iblis–" he paused, peering at Serra before correcting himself "–your uncles talking about testing her worthiness. They went out to the dojo together."

"They *what*?" Michael hurried to the sink and stared out the kitchen window overlooking the meditation garden. "How long have they been out there?"

Never looking up from the book, Ziri yawned and sipped his tea. Not finding it to his taste, he added three tablespoons of sugar.

"Ziri!"

The Tuareg boy glanced at him. "Long enough to piss her off."

CHAPTER 29

Throwing the screen door aside, Michael leaped the porch steps and sprinted into the garden, closely followed by Noah. He arrived in time to see Gabriel's body flipping through the dojo doors. The archangel landed hard, bounced like a rag doll, and skidded through a row of rose bushes. Laid out among stripped petals, crushed branches, and cracked thorns, he groaned, still conscious.

"Anaba almost took your head off last night!" Michael yelled. "You seriously asked for an encore?!"

The winded archangel struggled to his feet. Bent over his knees, he panted, "Rank… absolutely rank." Gabriel gripped the collar of his breastplate with both hands. It was badly dented from the impact of two hooves. "If there is an Enochian word for evil… it's Anaba."

"Gabriel!" Serra said, hurrying to catch up with her sons. "What were you thinking?"

Retrieving his longsword from the ground, the angel leaned on it. "For the record, this wasn't my idea." Gabriel took a deep breath, laboring to catch his wind. "Being that Michael's an apocalypse angel and all, Raphael wanted to know if she was good enough to protect you." He took a faltering step backwards. Noah steadied him before the angel collapsed. "She gets top marks in my book."

Black smoke billowed from the top of the dojo's door, accompanied by the stench of brimstone, which drifted through the garden. Discarding his shoes, Michael rushed inside. His hasty entrance was met by a whirlwind of wings, hooves, flashing steel, and fire. He stepped back outside and caught his mother by the shoulders before she could walk into the maelstrom.

Orchestrating a backflip into the center of the dojo floor, Raphael stood poised on the balls of his feet. He wielded a pair of kalis blades in his gauntleted hands: one in a traditional manner and the other in an underhand grip. Enochian glyphs illuminated the fuller of each sword. The whetted edges of the wavy blades caught the light from the open door. The archangel extended his wings to their full ten-foot span and spun in tight circles to fend off the fury of the attacking Nightmare.

Anaba was undaunted by the display and charged him. Crouched over her forelegs like a jaguar about to leap into a tree, she ducked beneath his wings. From this position, the Nightmare reared up and struck Raphael in the chin with her knees.

The archangel swung the underhanded kalis and hit her in the face with the weighted hilt. She retaliated with a headbutt that left the archangel reeling. Striking at his hands, the Nightmare sent both blades flying to the floor. She pivoted on her forelegs and delivered a double-barreled kick to the chest that launched Raphael across the room.

He hit the wall and fractured the wood, crashing to the floor in a heap amid the shattered remnants of a weapons rack. Fumbling for a weapon, he picked up a broken ranseur. The section with the blade-head was beyond his reach, so he grabbed the remaining shaft of the polearm to use as a makeshift spear.

As blood and brimstone trickled from her nostrils, Anaba reared and hooked the crude spear behind her knee. She yanked it away from Raphael, knocked the unbalanced angel to the floor, and straddled him as flames reignited along her legs.

"Your belly is exposed!" Raphael cried out.

So is your face! She lunged at him with bared teeth.

"Anaba, niis!" Michael cried. "Knock it off, both of you, before someone gets hurt!"

The Nightmare rolled her eye back to look at him, the whites showing contempt for his interference. Aggressively pinning her ears, she retreated, but not without blasting Raphael with brimstone. The assault left a layer of soot across the choking angel's face.

"Are you satisfied?" Michael glared at his uncle. "Or does she have to kill one of you?"

"I was convinced last night." Gabriel winced, stretching his aching back and shoulders. "Raphael wanted to see for himself."

"She fights with all the ardor of the Haala," Raphael said, grimacing as he got to his feet. "She is a suitable mount for you, as Nanqueel was for your father."

Tell me you didn't come out here to break up a little playground scuffle? Anaba raised her head to prevent Michael from examining the cut on her nose.

"Not just that," Michael replied. "I need to ask a favor."

If it involves adding another feather to this damned crest, I'm in! She glared at Raphael, swishing her tail to fan the flames on her legs.

"Mike, wait," Noah said, removing his ballcap and shoes. "I should be the one to ask."

Ask me what?

Before either man could speak, Ziri walked barefoot onto the dojo's tatami floor. "Anaba, ărdăɣ." He knelt down and reached into his gris-gris bag. Placing the mirror on the mat, he showered it with cowrie shells. The boy spoke in a low voice. In the absence of a drum, he rapped his knuckles rhythmically against the floor.

"Boys, we should leave this to Ziri," Serra said, waving them all back to the dojo doors.

"What's he saying?" Michael asked.

"What is good, that I love," Serra translated the Tamasheq, her eyes tearing up. "He's explaining to her the importance of these words and why she must listen. He's making an offering to her, only the prayer is not for himself, but for Bryana."

Taking the bone knife from its sheath, Ziri cut his hand, made a fist, and let the blood flow over the mirror and the shells.

Raphael stirred restlessly at the door. "I don't believe the Father would approve of this."

"God's not here," Noah growled, glaring at him. "Anaba is."

Nostrils flared, the Nightmare sniffed at the bloody offering, flicking her lips across the cowrie shells as if to rearrange them and predict the future. Ears pricked forward, she turned to look at Michael.

"Anaba?" he whispered.

Closing her eyes, she took a deep breath. Every tongue of fire was extinguished, retreating into her glistening, black hide. Thick, natural hair fell from her neck and dock, replacing spectral wisps of night and shadow. The taint of brimstone in her nostrils thinned, then vanished from her breath. She stepped tentatively backward, legs unsteady beneath her as her hooves touched the floor. The wood creaked under her weight.

"Teknâ tihussay hullen," Ziri whispered with a grin. Running his fingers through Anaba's forelock, he glanced at Michael. "She is very beautiful!"

"Something's not right." Michael ran his hand along the length of the Nightmare's neck. "Anaba?"

When she opened her eyes, a small tongue of green flame erupted from her forelock. Shaking her head, Anaba closed her eyes again, and with a groan, the flame went out.

"You don't have to do this," Michael whispered, kneeling

beside her. "I know you want to help, but this might be going too far."

She rubbed her eye on his shoulder. Ears splayed, the Nightmare showed every sign of true submission. *H- h- hard.*

"Sure, maintaining this form has to be hard."

Headed.

"Hard headed?" Michael asked, the sting of tears in his eyes. He laid his head against her withers and stroked her face. "Yes, you are."

Oo-rah.

"Noah, get the truck and trailer. Back the whole rig right into the garden. I'm not sure how long Anaba can keep this up." Michael chuckled, turning to his mother in the doorway. "Guess we're going see what those fancy warmbloods can do against a Nightmare."

Sitting in the back of an SUV in a shaded culvert, Caim Seere stared out the window at the five-post fence that marked the boundaries of Talveh Farm. He was unusually anxious, but the peaceful landscape soothed him, countering the turmoil within his mind. It would not do well to show impatience among his human subordinates. "Any word, Mr Steiner?"

"They've left the farm," Steiner replied, covering the receiver of his phone. "Childs is in the front passenger side of the vehicle. His brother is driving. The older woman riding in the backseat must be their mother. There's also an unidentified juvenile male."

"The Nightmare?"

"Riding in a horse trailer. The boy is in the back with her. All too easy." Steiner scrolled through the numbers on his cell phone's directory. "I'll have the state police pick them up and detain them."

"Because the boy is riding in the trailer? A minor traffic violation," Caim protested. "The most they'll do is ticket the driver. That is, if Childs doesn't flash his FBI badge to quash the matter. Stick with the plan." He rubbed his fingers across his white knuckles. "Is the safe house prepared?"

"A private hangar near La Guardia. Everything's been arranged to your specifications." Steiner glanced across the array of surveillance cameras positioned on the property. "Are you sure those binding wards will hold her? I warned you she was a tough son of a bitch."

"The wards will hold. You need to adopt a similar attitude of faith." Caim took a deep breath and closed his eyes. "I'm hungry. What's on the menu for lunch?"

CHAPTER 30

"This is the first call for the final four riders in the Gretchen V. Blakey Memorial Cup. Riders, please check in with the ring steward for jump order."

The female announcer's voice echoed across the manicured grounds of the Bridgehampton Show Grounds. Above the feedback of the PA system, Michael heard the familiar noises of cantering hooves, neighing horses, and trainers giving last-minute instructions to clients. The clatter of Anaba's hooves as she stepped down the trailer ramp brought him back to the moment.

He unbuckled the show blanket draped over Anaba's shoulders and swept it back across her flanks. Adjusting a twisted braid, he ran a brush over the meticulously groomed Nightmare. Though Anaba would never admit it, she had enjoyed the soapy bath and thorough primping for the show before being loaded into the trailer. Her polished hide gleamed despite the overcast skies.

"Mr Childs?" said a young woman in a business suit.

"Which one?" Noah asked. "There's two of us."

The secretary smiled and held a tablet out to him. "I need the owner of the horse and a bit more information before your rider can go in the ring."

"That'll be my brother." Noah pointed to Michael. "He's the handsome one."

"Mr Childs?"

"Michael Childs." Michael handed the lead rope to Ziri and took the tablet.

"I'm Shelly DeVance, the horse show secretary. Your signature here…" She waited until he had signed the digital form. "…and here." Glancing at Anaba with admiration, DeVance smiled. "She's beautiful. Imported?"

"You might say that," he replied with a smirk.

"It's nice your rider could find a replacement on such short notice." DeVance took the tablet back to confirm the signature. "I transferred all the important documents for the USEF. Just need a show name for the registration papers."

"My friggin nightmare," Noah muttered under his breath, ducking beneath the gooseneck of the trailer.

Eyebrows raised in judgment, DeVance typed the name into the tablet. "Is that all one word? I know the Jockey Club allows–"

"That's not her name," Michael glared at his brother. Following Noah's gaze, he saw the indignant figure of Stacia, his soon-to-be ex-wife, marching toward them from the parking lot. "He wasn't talking about the horse."

"Her name is Safiyya," Ziri said, playing along with the ruse. "It means pure."

"I hope that proves to be the case." DeVance tucked the tablet under her arm. "I also noted your request for a sign-language interpreter. Our judge, Dr Wade Wisner has a daughter who is Deaf. He's a favorite among the community because he's fluent in ASL. Good luck." The secretary smiled sympathetically and left.

Like a kid sentenced to recess detention, Noah sat on the rear bumper of the truck. Stacia wagged her finger at him, hissing under her breath in a mix of Spanish and English to avoid attracting too much attention.

Dressed in a black riding coat and canary breeches, Bryana stood helplessly on the macadam watching them. Despite being born Deaf, her hearing had been partially restored through surgery. The oversized profile of her riding helmet hid the cochlear aids, but could not hide the despair in her face as she overheard the undercurrent of angry voices. Her eyes, one brown and the other blue, were big and brimming with tears.

"Michael, do something," Serra whispered.

Michael walked over to his brother and his wife. "Would you two please act like something else in your life mattered besides tearing each other apart." He turned his back on them and stared down at Bryana. "Miss, I was sent to coach a future Olympic show jumper," he signed. "Could you tell me where I might find her?"

"Uncle Michael!"

"C'mere and give me a kiss." He opened his arms wide to greet her.

Bryana jumped into his arms, embracing his neck. "Did you hear about Shamrock," she signed. "He's lame."

"Grandma put an urgent call into the FBI, and here I am. My badge, my gun, and my new horse." Michael led her to the back of the trailer. "Bryana, this is Ana–" He bit his tongue and forced his fingers through the correct sequence of letters. "Safiyya."

"Is she a jousting horse?" Bryana tentatively stroked Anaba's shoulder, giggling when the mare regarded her with a warm eye. "She's beautiful, Uncle Michael."

"She's a real live war horse, and you… will be the first to ride her in competition." He tugged on one of her braids, noting the streak of gray caused by the Waardenburg Syndrome.

"You are not putting my daughter on some nag you and your brother pulled out of a kill pen!" Stacia shouted.

Michael glared at her. "Says the junkie who wouldn't know a show horse from a plow horse."

Nag? Anaba hissed under her breath. The Nightmare pinned her ears. *Bitch called me a nag?!*

"Settle down." Michael shoved a hand in Anaba's face, diverting the Nightmare's bared teeth.

"Mommy, don't call Safiyya a nag," Bryana signed furiously.

"I'm sorry, honey. I didn't mean it. Mommy just doesn't think this is a good idea."

Michael took the bridle from Ziri's hand. Rubbing his fingers across the corners of Anaba's mouth, he regarded the healing sores with remorse. "I trust this mare with my life." He briefly looked into Anaba's eyes.

A piercing alarm sounded. Flustered, Stacia reached into her purse and retrieved the electronic device. The shrill noise grew louder outside of the bag, attracting annoyed glares from spectators.

"What's that?" Michael asked.

"Bryana's heart monitor. It gives off an alert if her heart goes into arrhythmia. Damn thing's been going off all day with error messages." She reset the device and looked at Bryana. "You feeling all right, baby?"

Bryana laid her head on Anaba's shoulder. "Better now that Uncle Michael's here with Safiyya and that cute boy." She winked at Ziri. "I'd feel even better if you'd stop yelling at Daddy. This isn't his fault."

"Mommy's just a little stressed out, Bry. No more yelling." Stacia scowled at Noah. "Scout's honor."

"Let's go have a look at the course." Michael picked Bryana up and sat her in the saddle, bringing the reins over Anaba's head. "Safiyya needs to see the course, too." He brushed the Nightmare's face as they walked to the bulletin board beside the in-gate.

"Need to move this along, folks. A storm's coming in," the ring steward said. He took the ballcap from his graying head and wiped the sweat from his brow. "Fences are currently at 3'6. Do we need them lowered?"

"She only started jumping three feet a month ago," Stacia said. "Lower them."

"Leave the fences where they are." Michael straightened Bryana's number. "You scared to jump big fences?"

"No, Uncle Mike."

"Do you trust me?"

"Yes."

"Then trust her," Michael signed, affectionately pulling at Anaba's ears. "Let me hear you say oo-rah!"

"Oo-rah!"

"Louder. Safiyya didn't hear you."

"Oo-rah!" Bryana gestured with enthusiasm.

"Let me hear you say good to go?"

"Good to go!"

"Next in the ring is number 151," the announcer said. "Bryana Childs-DeJesus aboard Safiyya."

"I can't watch this." Stacia hid her face in her hands. "Michael, I swear to God if my daughter gets hurt…"

"She's got this," Michael said, speaking of the Nightmare, not of the child. He watched the pair trot to the far end of the oval arena. On cue, Anaba picked up a canter and headed into the first fence, a white gate with brush beneath it.

The casual conversations around the ring ceased as trainers and spectators paused to observe the pair riding from line to line without missing a beat. After the pair galloped the final fence, the spectators gave a genuine round of applause.

Winded but grinning from ear to ear, Bryana came out of the ring and threw her arms around Anaba's neck. "Querida," she squealed, signing frantically at the same time. "I love her, Uncle Mike. Can I keep her? Please, please, please."

Michael scratched between Anaba's ears. "Get in line, kid. She's one of kind."

"Will the following riders please return to the ring for a performance test," the announcer said. "Number 138 E. Avery Jackson on Babylon, 125 Ellen Geduldig on Rihanna, 300 Erica Businо on Heritage KM Rose, and 151 Bryana Childs-DeJesus on Safiyya."

"Fourth place?" Noah spat, leaning on the fence. "On a horse she's never ridden! Come on, judge, that round was flawless."

"Are you trying to get her disqualified?" Stacia hissed. "Lower your voice. This isn't your red-neck hockey league."

Michael tickled Bryana's chin. "Ignore them. How you feeling, squirt?"

Bryana grinned, her chin shrinking demurely into her neck. "Feels like I'm riding in the Olympics."

The steward pushed the gate open as the other competitors returned to the ring. He chuckled, having overheard the conversation. "Put in another round like that, Miss," he signed crudely, "and you'll bring home the gold."

The four riders walked to the center of the ring and lined up. Tucking a clipboard under his arm, a man dressed in a business suit climbed down from the observation box and into the ring. A surge of wind swept across the grounds forcing him to shield his eyes.

Ground pegs and sod went flying through the air as a powerful storm gust inflated the canopy of the spectators' tent near the main ring. Lifted by the sudden squall, it flipped over and landed on its roof like a deflated zeppelin, scattering horses, riders, and spectators in its wake.

Frightened by the pandemonium outside the ring, the black gelding Babylon reared, unseating Avery Jackson. She landed on her feet and ran after her spooked mount. They were followed at a clipped trot by a heavy, dark bay mare, whose rider managed to keep her seat, if not her stirrups. Then the spotted white mare carrying Erica bolted, retreating to the in-gate, only to find it closed. She spun in circles as Erica struggled to regain control.

Standing alone in the center of the ring, Anaba looked at the collapsed canopy and watched the bedlam of trainers and grooms racing to collect frightened horses and fallen riders. Stretching her neck, the Nightmare closed her eyes and yawned lethargically. The judge hurried to grab the reins to prevent her from running off. Rubbing her foamy mouth on his sleeve, she yawned a second time.

"Lovely horse, Miss Childs," Dr Wisner signed. "I think you passed the performance test. Just not the one I had in mind. Congratulations." He waved to the steward. "Pin the class in order. Move the number 4 horse into first."

Stacia held her hands to her face. "What just happened?"

"Bryana just won the class," Michael replied with a proud grin. "The class is judged fifty percent on the rider's equitation. And fifty percent on the horse's manners, performance, and suitability for the rider." He crossed his arms over his chest. "Still think she's a nag?"

"Ladies and gentlemen," said the frazzled announcer, "in light of the weather, we will be taking a break and resuming with the Ladies Side-Saddle competition after lunch in the indoor arena. Our grand champion and winner of the Gretchen V. Blakey Memorial Cup is number 151 Bryana Childs-DeJesus aboard Safiyya. In second place…"

"So this is why you need a team of grooms at these horse shows," Noah said. "To carry all the damn loot." He shifted the heavy, silver trophy in his hands. "Can you drink out of this thing like the Stanley Cup?"

"Gross, Daddy." Waving her tri-color ribbon, Bryana shook free of the stirrups and hopped down to the ground. She adjusted the royal blue championship cooler draped over Anaba and pulled the reins over the Nightmare's head.

As the family walked back to the parking lot, Michael stared down at the sample print from the show photographer. It was the first time they had posed together for a family picture in ten years.

"Michael," Serra scolded, taking his arm. "This is supposed to be a happy moment. Smile."

"You're right mom. Hey, Noah, did you see this swag bag?"

Michael held up the boutique satchel. "Dibs on the Ralph Lauren limited edition sunglasses." He put them on his face and tried to look serious. "I'm an FBI agent. I need these for work."

"Uncle Michael!" Bryana signed.

"I *did* bring the horse! Pay up, kid!"

"Mommy has the check I won."

"Oh no," Stacia said, "this $500 is going right into your college fund."

"Bryana, take Safiyya back to the trailer. We have a long drive. She's probably exhausted." Michael gave Ziri a telling glance, expressing his concern for the Nightmare, who had been unusually quiet.

"Come on, Ziri." Bryana skipped ahead, causing Anaba to jog along beside her. "Safiyya, looks pretty in her champion's cooler, don't you think?" She spoke slowly annunciating her words while signing, but left no time for Ziri to answer. "She did a good job, didn't she? Do you have a girlfriend?"

"Bryana Zsajhira DeJesus-Childs!" Stacia rolled her eyes. "The only boyfriend you're allowed to have is a horse."

"Leave her be," Noah said.

"She's twelve years old!" Abruptly, the heart monitor went off in her purse. The piercing noise spooked a nearby horse. "I'm so sick and tired of this thing–"

Serra stared down at the device. "That's not an error message."

Bryana turned back to stare at them, her eyes wide with terror. "*Mommy*?" She clutched at her chest, eyes rolling up into her head, and collapsed to the ground at Anaba's feet.

"Call the medics!" Michael shouted. The world shifted into slow motion as he ran to Bryana. He loosened the collar of her shirt, helpless as the struggling child gasped for air.

The Nightmare stood over them with one ear pinned defensively and the other sharply attuned to the distressed girl. Stationed near the warm-up ring, the ambulance crew hesitated to approach until Ziri led Anaba a few steps away.

"Bryana!" Stacia cried. "No, let me go!" She struggled in Noah's arms.

"Let them do their jobs!" Noah pleaded. She relented and wept on his shoulder as Serra embraced the two of them.

"FBI." Michael showed his credentials to a show official who tried to shoo him away. "She's my niece." He picked up the championship ribbon that had fallen from Bryana's hand and gave it back to soothe her, but the girl was not reaching for it. She was reaching for Anaba.

Yanking hard at the reins, Anaba dragged Ziri to the side of the gurney and pressed her nose into Bryana's trembling fingers. She followed the nervous paramedics as they wheeled the child to the back of the ambulance.

Confirming with the medical team, Michael said, "Staci, only one of you can go with her."

Tears streaming down her face, Stacia hurried into the cabin with the paramedics.

"Mom, take Noah to the truck. We can follow along behind them. Ziri, pull that tack off and get Safiyya back on the trailer."

Michael slammed the door of the ambulance and stared at the back of the vehicle as it sped toward the main highway. In shock, he stooped to pick up the fallen show ribbon. *How could such a wonderful day end so horribly?*

CHAPTER 31

Michael paced the empty foyer of the Stony Brook Southampton Hospital. In a state of heightened agitation, he chewed the inside corner of his lip until he tasted blood. Wincing in pain, he clenched his jaw. Helplessness was a kind of chaos, and he resented being out of control.

"Michael?"

He turned to the welcome sound of Anaba's voice. Ziri followed close behind. While the family had rushed into the hospital, the Tuareg boy had driven the truck and trailer to the outskirts of the parking lot and waited there until sundown before risking the Nightmare's transformation.

Michael laid his head on her shoulder as they briefly embraced. "You good?" he croaked.

"Never mind me. Some nachos and a cold beer, and I'll be cherry. Where's your mom?"

"Cafeteria, getting coffee for everyone."

"Ziri, find Mrs Childs and see what you can do to help out." She waited until Ziri hurried away down the corridor. "How's Bryana?"

"Her heart's failing." He looked away, but not before a tear spilled over his cheek. Being vulnerable in front of her should have been humiliating, but he was oddly comforted by her presence. "Those error messages her monitor was receiving all morning? They weren't errors. The primary pediatrician was talking about airlifting her back to the city, but he's afraid she wouldn't survive the trip. Anaba, to look at her, you wouldn't think anything was wrong. She's laughing, talking, joking."

"So what are the doctors doing?"

Michael pursed his lips tightly together, his jaw aching. "Waiting." He closed his eyes and propped his hands on his hips. "I think Noah sees the writing on the wall, but Staci?" He shook his head. "I don't know. I overheard them talking about getting back together and living at the farm again."

Anaba rolled her eyes. "Never understood why it takes a tragedy to bring clarity to our lives."

Michael straightened his muscular frame and moistened his lips. "I want to thank you for what you did today. That wasn't easy, though I know you'd never admit it." He brushed a stray dreadlock over her shoulder.

"I serve at your pleasure."

He resented the insinuation. "You're not my slave. You're my partner."

"I'm a Marine, Michael. It's all I've ever been. All I've ever known. When I signed my name on that dotted line, I committed to serve."

"But you didn't sign up for *this*, Anaba. We stepped into this together."

"It was step up or die," she said, leaning into his face aggressively. "I knew what I was getting into, you didn't. Don't mistake my willingness to *serve* as your Nightmare as submission. *I* chose this."

"You're not anything like the other Nightmares."

"No," she replied, not backing down, "I'm not."

"Is that why you and Samiel are always at each other's throats?

"Let's just say we've had our disagreements when it comes to you and your well-being."

"Michael, I can't reach our neighbors – the Dennisons. I've been trying to call for the last hour, but no one's answering." Serra walked down the hallway with a laden tray of coffee cups. She gasped, losing her grip on the unbalanced load. Ziri caught the sliding cups and carried the tray for her. "Ziri, please take these to Noah and Staci in the ICU."

"I'll take care of it, Mom." Michael retrieved his phone to call the owner of the Thoroughbred farm bordering his mother's property. He could feel Anaba's eyes boring through him. The line rang twice and then went to voicemail.

"Noah was supposed to stop by the old storage barn and pick up some hay. Mr Dennison offered to do it, but his back–"

"I said I'd take care of it, Mom," Michael growled, electing not to leave a message.

Silenced by his tone, Serra stared at him and then Anaba. "Are the two of you fighting?" Her usually benevolent face was lined with fatigue and worry.

Anaba shook her head. "It's nothing, Mrs Childs."

"Oh, Anaba, what you did for our family today," she whispered, embracing the Marine. "I'm so glad you're here with us. Bryana's been asking for you."

"Me?" Anaba stepped back.

Handing a coffee to Michael, Serra took her by the arm. "She knows it was you this morning."

"But how?" Anaba glared at Michael.

"Anaba, I didn't say a word!" Unjustly accused, Michael threw his hands up, accidentally spilling the hot coffee. His first instinct was to flinch to avoid being scalded. In response to his distress, the steaming drops of water rolled harmlessly across his fingers and trickled back into the cup.

"He didn't have to, Anaba," Serra said in Michael's defense. "My father once told me that the closer one is to death, the clearer their sight. I never understood what he meant until much later in my life. Please, Anaba, will you go to her?"

Anaba looked to Michael, but he walked away. "Mr Dennison isn't answering. I'll head home to feed the horses." Reaching into his pocket for the truck keys, he tapped the fob against the heel of his hand. "Be back before you know it." He glanced over his shoulder to see Anaba and his mother headed down the hallway. Bowing his head in resignation, he retreated to the parking lot through the security doors.

When it came to cuisine in the Hamptons, there were few establishments better known than the Stone Creek Inn. Opened later than usual for the influx of tourists and exhibitors brought to town for the horse show, the upscale restaurant was crowded. Reservations were impossible on a weeknight, especially after 8pm, but fortunately, Caim's CIA connections had the necessary influence.

He took the cloth napkin from the meticulously set table and spread it across his lap. The waitress brought out his meal: a side order of duck meatballs steamed in a thick sauce beside a platter of grilled venison with cabbage, crispy pancetta, and mushrooms. The sights and scents were transcendent. To complete the gourmet feast, a bottle of champagne rosé sat in a chill bucket beside his table.

The fallen angel took up his utensils in both hands and sighed. He was eagerly anticipating the first, hot morsel, when a shadow fell across his plate.

"Steiner," Caim said, "you had better have good news. I won't tolerate anything spoiling this delectable culinary masterpiece."

The CIA officer sat down across from him. With the couth of a cutpurse, he helped himself to a meatball. "Looks like you're just getting started." He sat back in the comfortable chair, contemplating the meatball before eating it in one mouthful. "Would you like a little dessert *before* your dinner?"

Steiner licked his fingers. "Operation Final Anthem is ready to initiate."

Caim stopped chewing a morsel of venison. "They've been separated?"

"Special Agent Childs left the Southhampton Hospital twenty minutes ago. He was *alone* in his mother's pickup truck, hauling an *empty* horse trailer. He's headed in the direction of the family farm."

"Anaba?"

"Surveillance puts her at the hospital," Steiner said with a smug grin.

Caim braced himself. "I sense a caveat?"

"The prognosis for the little girl isn't good." He leaned forward and took a string bean from Caim's plate. "It's a shame. If my people hadn't hacked that heart monitor, the kid might have gotten the help she needed in time." He fell silent when the waitress reappeared and set down a clean glass in front of him. Waving his hand at her, Steiner declined the offer of a drink. "My friend's going to need a few boxes, honey. This meal is now designated to-go."

Caim set down his silverware and pulled the cellphone from his breast pocket. "Mr McKabe? Tell me you have a team in place near the Hamptons?"

"Did your people plant the device on the vehicle?" McKabe's voice crackled through the phone.

With a nod from Steiner, Caim replied, "Yes, the truck can be shut down at any time. Your problem is knowing *when* and *where* to do it. If you make a move outside of the warded area, he will summon her, and our efforts will be for naught."

"We'll deal with Childs. You keep the Nightmare out of our way." The line went dead.

"Are we a go?" Steiner asked.

Caim stood up, unable to contain the smile on his face. "We're a go, old friend."

"Sir," the waitress said, handing him the bill, "was everything to your liking?" The anguish and confusion in her face was evident as she quickly set to packing the steaming meal into boxes.

Caim handed her three crisp hundred dollar bills. "Yes, Kimberly," he said, reading her nametag for the first time. "I'm certain it will prove delicious as leftovers. Keep the change."

CHAPTER 32

Anaba disliked hospitals. The pungent antiseptic scent was not much different from the sterile scent of a funeral home. She reluctantly slipped through the sliding glass door into the private ICU room across from the nurse's station.

Expecting to find Bryana hooked to machines via IV lines, she was surprised to find the precocious girl sitting cross-legged in pink pajama bottoms and a hospital gown. Her dark brown hair was interspersed with streaks of gray. Still braided in pigtails laced with ribbons from the horse show, they hung across her slender shoulders.

Bryana sat up as she entered. Sorting through a collage of pictures scattered on her bed, the girl held up an eight by ten glossy image. "Safiyya," she signed the individual letters. The picture showed Bryana perched on a black horse, jumping a 3′6″ oxer in perfect style.

Anaba did not reply. The CIA had taught her that when your cover was possibly blown, it always best to remain silent.

"*This* is you." Bryana's gestures faltered, awkwardly, as she scratched at the electrode pads on her chest. "*You* are her."

"It's really late," the Marine signed with deliberate care, never acknowledging the child's assertion. "Shouldn't you be sleeping?"

"You know how to sign?" Bryana gestured excitedly, her eyes wide with delight.

"A soldier I worked with taught me ASL," Anaba replied. She stayed close to the door, hoping for a quick retreat. "Why did you ask for me?"

"I know that my Uncle Michael asked you to help me. I wanted to thank you, Anaba." Bryana gasped abruptly and coughed into her hands. Her face twisted into a mask of anguish as the harsh, rattling cough forced her to wheeze through her mouth, desperate for breath.

Anaba turned toward the door. "I'll get a nurse."

"No!" Bryana said aloud and forcefully, catching her breath. "They're nice ladies, but they're running out of kind things to say."

"Are you in pain?"

"Coughing makes my chest hurt really bad. Gets hard to breathe, too. But I'm used to it." Bryana drew in a slow, deliberate breath. "This belongs to you," she signed, holding out the championship ribbon. The rosette was five inches wide with a metal medallion in the center. Three strands of blue, red, and yellow satin streamed away from it.

"You earned that ribbon," Anaba insisted.

"We won it together. But I want you to have it before I go."

"The docs are letting you go home?"

"No." Bryana stared at Anaba with the wisdom of a soul much older than her twelve years. "That's why you're here. Grandma said you'd be taking me to Heaven."

Anaba's jaw slackened. She shook her head. "I think your grandma–"

"Have you ever been to Egypt?"

Anaba's eyes narrowed at the randomness of the question. "When I was in the military."

"Have you ever seen the Great Pyramids?"

"From a distance. Bryana, your grandma–"

"Grandma used to tell me stories about the ancient Egyptians. Are the pyramids truly beautiful?"

"Never had the time to go sight-seeing, kid. Too worried about getting shot or blown up."

Bryana sat up on her knees. "I always wanted to visit. Bet they look magical when the sun comes up."

Anaba took a deep breath and exhaled. She walked to the window separating the hospital room from the ICU annex. Serra was standing at the nurse's station, staring at her. She folded her hands to plead her case.

Bryana collected her pictures and carefully put them back into an oversized envelope. "Anaba, why do you look so sad?"

"I always look this way before I go on a mission."

"A mission?"

Anaba pulled the chain to close the blinds and checked the time on her watch. "You want to see those pyramids by sun up, don't you?"

"Seriously?" Bryana's eyes watered in response to the acrid scent of brimstone inundating the small hospital room. She put her hand over her nostrils to stifle the smell. Noticing the green flames licking up the Nightmare's legs, Bryana shrank back. "This is what you really look like? I thought I was dreaming."

The fire won't hurt you. Anaba stretched her head out to her, encouraging the wide-eyed girl to caress her muzzle.

"You're so beautiful!" Bryana threw her arms around the Nightmare's neck.

Wheels up, kid. Our mission clock is ticking.

Bryana balanced tiptoe on the end of her bed, clinging to the pommel, and scrambled into the saddle on Anaba's back. "What's this?" She wrapped her hand around the war lance sheathed in a sling beneath the stirrup leather.

Hands off. That belongs to your uncle. I keep it safe in case he needs it.

Anaba manipulated the veil of shadows, calling them to coalesce at her command. The darkness defied the light and the room grew dark. Colorful instrument panels flashed and sputtered as a spiraling portal of brimstone swallowed a corner of the room.

Sensing no hesitation in the child, Anaba cantered into it and onto the Vestibule Road.

* * *

Accuracy was always an issue with shadow portals, even for a Nightmare. While working with the CIA, Anaba had been to Cairo on a few reconnaissance operations to acquire intel, even mingled with the locals in the various street markets. It had been years since she was in Egypt or its sprawling capital. Her home away from home had been in the desert, and that is where the Vestibule Road led her.

Undulating ridges of sand were etched into the dunes for miles like textured glass. The night air in the sandy basin was cool, a reprieve from the desert's oppressive heat. She wasn't far off course. If she needed confirmation, she had only to look at the stepped pyramid jutting two hundred feet into the night and the ruined temple hidden in its moonlit shadow.

"Is that it?" Bryana covered her eyes to see into the distance, gracious disappointment in her tone. "I thought there were three pyramids?"

This is Saqqara. It's only half the size of the ones at Giza. Trust me, we're close.

A recent storm had blown the sand into an oceanic floor of perfect, knife-edge waves and treacherous dunes. Flames licking from her legs, Anaba galloped headlong into the desert. There was no time for discretion if they were to reach Giza before sunrise.

Nightmares rarely left any evidence of their presence. The slight hint of brimstone on the air. A lingering shadow that defied light before dissipating. But if in a hurry, the telltale imprint of their hooves could also be found due to the contact of their flames with the ground. Sizzling sand melted to glass beneath the fiery tips of Anaba's hooves, leaving the barest of footprints on the ridges. Before any pronounced trace could be left as evidence, the dunes shifted in the wind and buried the tracks.

"Faster, Anaba!" Bryana pointed to the purple horizon as

the first rays of dawn pierced the skyline. "We're going to miss it."

Not if I can help it.

The Nightmare raced the horizon in defiance of all nature. Molten clods of sand and glass scattered behind her. She propped her hind legs beneath her and slid down into a deep basin. At a canter, she charged up the steep embankment on the other side in three explosive strides and leaped to the top of it.

"There!" Bryana shouted.

Bathing the dunes in orange light, the sun broke over the skyline. The tips of the two highest pyramids came into view, jutting four hundred feet above the desert floor. As the Nightmare galloped closer, the third structure emerged from the fading veil of night. Anaba slowed to a trot and stopped on a sandy ridge overlooking the complex.

Bryana put a hand over her heart, eyes wide in appreciation of the magnificence of the ancient structures in the dawn. "They're more beautiful than I imagined." She took a long, deep breath and exhaled dramatically. "You really can smell the Nile. It's like the rain. Thank you, Anaba."

Anaba watched the shadows retreat as the sun rose over Giza. *My pleasure, kid.*

Resting her head on Anaba's neck, Bryana twirled her fingers in the roots of the Nightmare's mane. "My Mommy and Daddy are going to be sad." She rubbed her fingers across the Crest of Nanqueel, smoothing the hairs over the brand. "Will you tell them I was happy and that I love them both very much."

Anaba clenched her teeth. A death notification. It was not an uncommon duty for a Marine, but still a burden she did not want to carry. *Sure.*

Bryana sighed and sat up. "Then I'm ready to go to Heaven now."

Yeah… about that… The Nightmare stood rigid, keeping her

head down. The flames about her legs grew muffled and were extinguished in a single puff of smoke that was dissipated in the desert wind. *Heaven's not exactly a place where someone like me is welcomed.*

"You know the way, don't you?" Bryana clung to the pommel, leaning precariously over the side of the saddle to look into Anaba's face.

Getting there isn't the problem. It's the getting in that worries me.

"Grandma says we're expected."

Expected, huh? Hope that means a welcome mat and not a noose around my neck. Anaba cantered down the steep angle of the dune crest and jumped into the darkness of a shadow portal at the bottom.

CHAPTER 33

Every soul had a particular scent to it. The more unpleasant the scent, the more unpleasant the soul, and the life it left behind. The filth of sin was the cause of the stench that permeated Hell. Anaba associated the smell with the bittersweet scent of roses withering on the vine. While the musk was enticing to the damned, there was another essence capable of driving them mad. Innocence.

"Are we in Hell again?"

This is the real thing, kid. Not a side road. Now keep quiet.

Anaba had briefly utilized the spectral path to find a portal to Cairo. Traveling to Heaven required a journey on a much longer, harder path. As a Nightmare, she was in her element. Bryana was not. The only difference between a soul destined for Hell and another destined for Heaven was an angelic escort, usually for the latter. Unescorted souls were fodder for the damned – sustenance. With this in mind, Anaba broke into a trot and then galloped down the road in haste, looking for a nexus to DrunGer.

The restless souls that walked the Vestibule Road usually kept to the shadows, but the scent of Bryana's soul drew them from the gray obscurity of their miserable existence. A throng pressed in from the edges of the treeline. A blast of brimstone was enough to deter them initially, but Bryana's scent was too alluring. They crowded the road ahead.

"Who are they?" The compassion in Bryana's voice goaded the wraiths, urging them to risk the ire of a Nightmare to come closer.

No one, Anaba replied, *not anymore.*

Anaba pawed at the road, striking the fire that would engulf her legs. Her mane and tail combusted into a shield around Bryana. Despite the undulating wave of flame, the lost souls continued to press toward her. In retaliation, Anaba summoned the most volatile of her flames. The fire turned a dull violet and then went blue as the effects of immolation spread from her in a circular pattern.

Souls were eternal, but not invulnerable. Any wraith that ventured into the field was incinerated. Their ashes would rematerialize in agony back at the Gate of Hell. The damned wisely fell away and crowded at the perimeter of the blue fire.

There were few things for a Nightmare to fear on the Vestibule Road. A fact that made them prized mounts for the Fallen. But the Vestibule Road was not without peril, mostly the revenants of those desperate beings never born of woman and never fated to die – angels. Choosing neutrality over war, these unclassified damned were cast from Heaven for their imperfections and rejected by Hell for their disloyalty.

Summoned by the furor on the road, three Apostates moved out of the ravening crowd. The angels were almost indiscernible from the damned; they were covered in grime except for their moldering, filth-encrusted wings.

Anaba wheeled on her hind legs and bolted in the opposite direction. The blue flames of her immolation fluttered intermittently. She struggled to maintain the concentration necessary to keep it active. The blistering flames cleared a path through the overeager dead, but another pair of angels dropped in from the crimson skies to cut off her path.

She blasted them with a snort of brimstone that temporarily blinded them and leaped over the pair, delivering a savage kick to the backs of their heads. Landing beyond, she took one stride, pivoted her weight on one front leg and leaped off the Vestibule Road into a covert.

The by-road brought her into an ancient forest of black-leaved trees. Crowded on top of each other, the tall, languid trees grew at peculiar angles in a haphazard pattern that gave a new definition to chaos. Bryana squealed when a low-lying branch slapped her in the face. A thicker limb then dislodged her, dragging the frightened girl over the back of the saddle.

Anaba slid to a stop before she was completely unseated. This was not the place to be separated. *Keep your head down and stop screaming.*

Scrambling across the Nightmare's hindquarters, Bryana slid back into the saddle and tucked her head down beside Anaba's withers. "Where are we, Anaba?"

The Wood of the Suicides.

Anaba shook her neck, manipulating the flames of her mane to burn off low-hanging branches that might ensnare Bryana. Above the hiss of hungry flames and popping sap, the anguished cries of multiple voices rose in a discordant rhythm. The macabre chorus reverberated between the trees.

"I hear people crying, but I don't see anyone," Bryana said.

You're looking too hard. There are souls all around you. The forest floor was treacherous with gnarled roots, forcing Anaba to slow to a walk.

"The trees?" Bryana inadvertently raised her head. A charred branch slapped her in the face, scratching her skin. Clasping her cheek, she ducked down low again and clung to the Nightmare's neck. "This is a terrible place, Anaba."

That's kind of the idea, kiddo.

Bypassing a deep depression in the ground where the roots of the trees slithered like copulating serpents, Anaba leaped the pit and landed on the narrow path beyond it.

"Will they follow us?"

Not worried about them. Anaba distantly heard a violent crashing coming through the trees behind them. She stepped into a cautious canter and proceeded through a shadowy copse of trees to gain some distance from their pursuers. *There are worse things than fallen angels in this forest.*

"Like what?"

Harpies.

Graced with the faces of beautiful women and the full breasts to match those seductive visages, the harpies were a grotesque irony. Flying on leathery wings scaled with sordid feathers, they lured unsuspecting souls into the forest with their sultry voices and then attacked them. The curved, black hooks of their talons were designed to render flesh from the bone. They were fiercely territorial too, using the branches of the trees as spiders used their webs to detect prey. Anaba heard their shrill, furious shrieks as they intercepted the angels who had dared to enter their forest.

"What reeks?" Bryana pressed her nose against Anaba's hide.

Anaba hurried her steps, saying nothing that might panic the child. While a harpy's claws were a formidable weapon, they were also a warning. Covered in decomposing flesh and the excrement that harpies enjoyed throwing at their victims, the putrid scent of their presence always gave them away. Even through the scent of brimstone, Anaba could smell the hideous creatures long before she saw three of them descending from the trees to chase her.

Hang on, kid! Anaba galloped into a blind thicket made from older, fallen trunks. She tucked her front legs and leaped over the rotted wood. Before her hind legs could touch the ground, she jumped again, bouncing over a bunch of felled trees as the sounds of pursuit grew louder.

Harpies hunted in packs, as Nightmares did. The forest was their preferred habitat and they were even more dangerous in numbers. Blindsided, Anaba was struck from the side and driven bodily into a trio of gnarled trees. They splintered under the impact.

Bryana grunted as she fought to stay secure in the saddle. She screamed when a grinning harpy landed on Anaba and dug its talons into the Nightmare's flesh.

Hook your right leg over the pommel! Go side saddle!

Anaba waited for the child to draw up her leg and then slammed herself into a tree, smashing the harpy between her and the trunk. She gritted her teeth as hooked talons reflexively contracted and bit deeper into her ribcage. Snatching the harpy by the face with her teeth, the Nightmare knocked it senseless against the tree, threw it to the ground, and trampled it, leaving the creature to writhe in the potent flames of her immolation.

"Anaba?"

Sit tight. They're more interested in me than you. The only thing harpies like better than maiming souls is horseflesh.

"They eat Nightmares?"

We're not staying for dinner.

With the sounds of pursuit drawing nearer, Anaba cantered toward a loosely packed group of trees. Summoning a portal between the scarred trunks, she increased her pace with a powerful surge of flame and leaped into it.

CHAPTER 34

Three miles off Route 27, there were no streetlights. Except for a few exterior lamps on a private greenhouse and its outbuildings, there was no light at all.

"Mom, I'll be a little late getting back to the hospital," Michael said into his phone. "The truck broke down. I'm about a quarter mile from the hay barn. Don't worry. Call me when you get this message."

He hung up. Being alone in the dark didn't bother him. He knew Barringer Lane intimately from a childhood spent riding horses up and down the farm road by day and night.

Staring into the night sky, he marveled at the stars and resumed his walk. Despite the circumstances, he was looking forward to taking the offroad four-wheeler out and traveling the back trail to the boundaries of the family property. The adventure would certainly take his mind off Bryana's plight and Anaba's troubling words.

"I knew what I was getting into, you didn't... I chose this," the Marine had said.

She was right, as usual, but Michael had also made a choice, and now he was left to wonder what the collateral damage would be for making it. Would his family be targeted by the Grigori, even though they were not Nephilim?

"Let's just say we've had our disagreements when it comes to you and your well-being." Anaba had also said when Michael questioned her about the growing tension between her and Samiel.

What the fuck was that supposed to mean? At the time, he didn't have the courage to ask her.

A pair of headlights lanced the darkness. A Ford Explorer rambled down the road behind him. While he was inclined to ask for a ride, he was wary of strangers traveling the old farm road at night. They were usually lost tourists from the horsey set or delinquent teenagers looking for a secluded spot to get high. As the vehicle rolled up, he was ready with his badge to frighten them off.

"Is that your rig back a ways?" a gruff male voice asked from the passenger side. "Broke down?"

Surprised by the maturity in the voice, Michael stopped. In the darkness, it was difficult to discern the two faces in the front seat. "Yeah, it's been that kind of day."

A flicker of light caught Michael's eye. Glancing over his shoulder, he saw a set of headlights wink on from the parking area near the greenhouse. When a car door slammed shut from that direction, he skipped his badge and went for his gun. "Federal agent–"

A sharp blow to the back of his head cut him off. He dropped to his knees in the grass. Garbled sound inundated his ears from a distant, hollow place, disorienting him. The contrast of shadows and multiple headlights contorted his blurry vision and brought on a wave of nausea. A subsequent blow to the face cut through the distortion, ringing with the perfect clarity of pain.

A rough hand grabbed Michael by his hair and dragged him off the road. Unnaturally powerful fingers tightened about his neck and lifted him from the ground. He struggled to break free of the strangling hold, but his fingers were slippery with blood.

"I say we carve him up ourselves. Leave him on display like the others. Why should Kokabiel always get the honor?"

Infuriated by the callous tone, Michael suppressed a swelling surge of fear and panic. There was little doubt in his mind that they meant to kill him. Either here or after delivering him to this Kokabiel. Rushing his assailant, he delivered a quick knee strike to the angel's groin. This did little more than aggravate the assailant. The Grigori tightened his grip, wrapping his other hand around Michael's throat, and shook him violently.

Consciousness waning, Michael held his hand to the side. His lance materialized in his grip. Rotating it into position, he drove the eight-inch blade-head into the angel's leg, nearly severing the limb at the ankle. The angel dropped Michael back on his feet and he swept the war lance upwards, across the angel's throat. Before the corpse could fall, a second angel grabbed him by the shoulder.

Kakeukr. The Enochian word trickled through his mind in a whisper, underscored by the gentle bubbling of water over algae-covered river stones. Kakeukr. He saw the same creek bed reduced to sand, the plant life diminished to dust in a relentless sweltering sun.

"Wither," Michael rasped the translation. He imagined a vine shriveling in the swelter of the sun.

Dressed in blue mechanic's overalls, the angel clutched at his arm. The entire length of it went limp. A greenish-brown dust fell from the loose sleeve. Michael spun the war lance over the back of his hand and slashed at the angel's undefended torso. The angel stumbled back as innards spilled through the surgically precise wound.

A third Grigori punched Michael in the back of the head with a weapon similar to a cestus. With the pealing of a bell resounding in his head, Michael fell to the soggy ground and suffered another blow to the face from the weighted glove.

Adrenaline kicked in to protect him from a third hit. Slashing at the angel's face, Michael then rolled onto his back. He threw up his arms, wielding the lance in both hands just in time to block a sword attack from a fourth Grigori. Michael kicked out the third angel's knee, causing her to hobble temporarily. The maneuver knocked her out of an offensive position so Michael was able to roll up and swing the war lance at her legs. She went down screaming. Her severed feet and ankles were still firmly planted on the road in boots, but the rest of her body lay writhing in the mud.

"Anaba, niis!" Michael looked to the shadows for back-up, but there was no answer to his summons. Deflecting a sword sweep at his back, he took off at a run toward the greenhouse.

It was hard to gauge their numbers in the dark and he was injured, bleeding badly. The bells ringing in his ears were an ominous sign, even before his limbs grew cold and insufferably heavy. Without Anaba, the conclusion seemed evident.

Michael set his jaw. He wasn't going down without a fight. The war lance and his Nightmare were not the only weapons at his disposal. He ran into the fields behind the greenhouse. Illuminated by the headlights from the road and the parking lot, six figures pursued him, two of them in flight.

He tripped in an irrigation ditch, wrenching his ankle. As the muddy water splashed around him, he laughed. *X always marks the spot.* Thoroughly soaking through every layer of clothing, the water converged into scales and rings all over his body and transformed into the maille armor of his office.

The ground shifted with a violent tremor. Hundreds of slender tendrils reared up from the irrigation ditches around him, weaving back and forth like agitated vipers. The embodiment of Famine's domain stabbed and pierced the darkness like rabid, burrowing worms. They bit through the cloth and skin of the oncoming Grigori and buried themselves into vulnerable flesh. Siphoning away fluids, like spiders suck their prey through webbed cocoons, the watery coils flung the drained corpses to the ground.

Forewarned of the danger by the screams, the remaining

Grigori summoned their battle armor. Unable to penetrate the hardened metal, the thin, muddy tendrils looped together into ropes instead, ensnaring arms and legs. They crushed their captives in constricting bands, then haphazardly launched the corpses into the night. The crashing of glass sounded from the greenhouse as three winged figures were tossed like rag dolls into the structure.

Michael stumbled out of the irrigation fields and into a forested area between the properties. Dabbing at the wound behind his left ear, he was alarmed by the amount of blood smeared between his fingers. He needed to staunch the bleeding. Thankfully his mother kept a first aid kit inside the barn for accidents, so he made his way towards it.

Motion-sensor security lights clicked on at the front of the barn and the interior as he made his way inside. As soon as he had thrown the wooden bar across the door to secure it, the frame burst inward. The crack of splintering wood resounded like thunder. Caught in a flying tackle, Michael was knocked off his feet and carried into the utility closet. Wearing leather armor caked with mud, the Grigori headbutted him and slammed his knee into Michael's abdomen. Tossing the semi-conscious agent across the room into a row of pitchforks and other farming tools, he said, "You were marked for death the moment you were born." The angel drew a curved saber from its scabbard and reasserted his grip on the hilt, one finger at a time.

Despite his armor, the blindside assault had been crippling. Struggling to breathe, Michael pressed an arm against his ribs. It was difficult to gauge if they were bruised or broken. Either way, he felt faint. When the angel advanced on him, Michael tried to defend with the lance, but the soldier easily knocked it out of his fumbling hands.

"Anaba, niis," Michael breathed.

"Cease fighting, adrpan." He picked Michael up by the gorget and threw him across the room again where he collided with the tractor. "This is your fate and the fate of all the unclean progeny who infest the Creation."

Adrpan. The word meant cast down. Michael grinned at the irony, as he tried to drag himself across the concrete floor. Bleeding profusely from his mouth and nose, he gritted his teeth in defiance of every nerve firing damage signals to his concussed brain.

"My garrison wants to make an example of you," the Grigori said, "but I am not without mercy. You never asked for this life, so I will end it before your suffering can truly begin."

Michael dipped his finger in his own blood and instinctively traced the iconic crest of the family farm. "Hope you're watching, Dad," he whispered, "because I could really use the back-up."

A blast of wind blew in from the outside. The gale's current slammed the ruined barn door shut, wedging it into the frame. Multiple eddies of dust and hayseed swelled and rotated around the Grigori. The spiraling debris tore at him like the sharpened cogs of an invisible machine, eviscerating him from the outside. As if presenting himself for penance, the angel fell to his knees with arms extended to his sides. His mouth was agape, but no sound escaped it.

"You are granted that which you have been seeking," said a voice. *"Oblivion."*

The barn lights flickered, and then the bulbs shattered, showering glass over the haystacks. A column of piercing, white flame penetrated the top of the Grigori's skull and shot out of his frightened eyes, nostrils and mouth. Snaking beneath his skin like varicose veins, fissures of celestial fire tore minute fissures in the angel's flesh. These eruptions spread across his body and grew so bright that only the negative outline of the Grigori could be seen in the darkness. With a splintering noise reminiscent of firecrackers, the petrified body imploded.

Michael threw himself over a stack of hay bales and shielded his eyes from the staggering radiance until the rain of ossified flesh subsided. Though the body of the Grigori was gone, the white fire remained, licking up the walls of the barn and sealing the door.

"Very clever, Nephilim." Michael recognized the voice of the man who had originally spoken to him from the car. "All you've managed to do is give yourself another hour to live, perhaps less. No one is coming for you. Not your traitorous father, not the Horsemen, and most certainly not your Nightmare. We will break this seal. You are not the only one skilled in the old ways." There was laughter beyond the door. "Call Steiner. Have him send in his team."

Michael reached for his cell phone. In the twenty-first century, there was no need for rituals if you had signal. He stared at the iPhone's shattered, black screen and groaned. "Anaba, where are you?" He closed his eyes and passed out.

CHAPTER 35

Anaba broke from a shambling trot to a walk. Flames extinguished, she stumbled through the purple, waist-deep grass of DrunGer. Lathered and bloody, she was on the verge of collapse.

Recent events had awakened dormant fragments of memory best left buried. The physical weakness and fatigue were secondary symptoms to an impending psychological break. An emerging neurosis lapped at her conscious mind like a relentless storm surge on a beach.

Get a fucking grip, Marine!

They were deep in Hell, surrounded by peril from the elements, the terrain, and innumerable enemies. There was no calling for reinforcements. No hope of extraction. Anaba closed her eyes and tried to take a deep breath, but it hurt. Agreeing to take Bryana to Heaven was a bad idea.

"Where are we, Anaba?"

The girl had not spoken a word since their narrow escape from the Apostates on the Vestibule Road. The ambush run through the Wood of the Suicides had led to another breakneck chase across the frozen lake of Cocytus, dodging cave trolls and ice giants. The child was thoroughly traumatized.

A place called DrunGer.

"When I was seven, I put a horse turd in Dorothy Beck's lunchbox. It was just a joke, but Mommy said I'd pay for it because karma is a bitch. Am I stuck here?"

Anaba snorted. *Don't worry. We're only sight-seeing.*

Bryana jumped down from the saddle and examined the swollen gashes on the Nightmare's ribcage. "That looks like it really hurts."

Sergeant Bill used to say if you're not bleeding, you're probably not working hard enough. Anaba craned her neck about and sniffed at the puckered wounds from the harpy's claws. She could smell the infection setting in. She would need to burn it out before it fully took hold.

Working her way over to the rocky banks of a small brook, Bryana tore a piece of cloth from her hospital gown and reached for the quiet surface of the water. "Is something going to jump out and try to eat me?"

Anaba lowered her head to stretch the tight muscles in her back. *This land belongs to your uncle.*

"My Uncle Mike owns all this?" Astounded, Bryana spun in a slow circle to take in the vastness of the wetlands and its feral beauty. "It's got to be *way* bigger than Grandma Serra's farm."

A little bit, Anaba replied, suppressing her sarcasm.

"Then we're definitely safe here." She dipped the frayed cloth and her hand into the water. Examining the wounds again, Bryana clenched her teeth, hesitated, and then pressed the makeshift compress against Anaba's bloody flank.

See that tower? Anaba asked, trying not to flinch. *It's called Balzizras. That's where we're headed.*

Bryana squinted into the distance. "It seems awfully far away."

Anything worth fighting for usually is. Mount up.

The road to the Citadel of Judgment was, by far, the longest, hardest road in Hell. That distance was meant to discourage the unworthy from attempting the journey. There were no spectral portals or crossroads to shorten the trip. Undaunted by the distance, Anaba galloped faster.

Balzizras rose from a foundation that was three hundred feet in diameter. Casting no shadow, the high tower surpassed any structure known to man. The upper tiers of the alabaster monolith pierced the crimson skies. A steady wind swept across the fields of purple grass surrounding it and created concentric ripples that moved through the foliage like ocean currents.

The only approach was a direct one. Anaba felt her heart quicken. She slowed to a walk and made her way toward the tower. Having never been this close to the structure, she was cautious, acutely aware of the sentinels that stood guard at the base of the citadel.

There were ten of them – all Cherubim. In artistic circles, they were miscast as mischievous children, baby-faced chaos makers shooting arrows into mismatched humans to cause them to fall in love. The reality was a stark contrast. They were the second highest order of angel, an elite corps of warriors, formidable and difficult to kill, even for a Nightmare.

Dressed in burnished silver breastplates, bracers, and greaves, the twelve-foot tall sentinels knelt at the base of the tower on one knee. Their backs were pressed against the tower as if to support it. They clasped claymores in their gauntleted hands. The tips pointed down, penetrating the ground at their armored feet. Nine feet long from hilt to blade tip, the swords flashed with an ethereal light, which came from no discernible source. They were blinding to look upon, as if forged from lightning.

Sculpted, silver helmets were raised with central crests and plumes of white horsehair that cast shadows over their serene faces. Their wings were poised in midair, partially unfurled above their shoulders as if they might abruptly leap up and take flight.

Disturbed from their reverie by the Nightmare's intrusion, the Cherubim lifted their heads from peaceful repose and opened their eyes in unison. Massive clods of earth the size of oil barrels were ripped from the ground and flung into the air as they swept up their swords into a defensive, 45-degree position.

Their stance reminded Anaba of a Czech hedgehog, a crude but effective anti-tank obstacle. It was an unmistakable warning. But twelve grueling weeks of boot camp on the infamous Parris Island had rewired her fight or flight instinct. Ears pinned against her head, she took another step toward them. There was no flight left in her.

In a second synchronized maneuver, the Cherubim raised the flats of their blades to their faces in a unanimous salute. First one and then another drove their blades back into the earth until all of them were leaning forward, their wings fully unfurled across their backs. A stone doorway slid open, revealing a passageway into the tower.

"Grandma did say we were expected," Bryana said. "What happens now, Anaba?"

Anaba took a few more cautious steps toward the citadel. When the Cherubim did not react aggressively, she halted and lowered her head to the closest sentinel. *Not exactly sure how these backstage passes work, kid.*

The surrounding wind intensified, channeling into the interior of the tower. It tugged insistently at the Nightmare's mane and tail. As the winds gathered within the confines of the citadel's walls, it created a conduit of energy that vibrated with the rush of a thousand flapping wings.

Ears twitching, Anaba ignited her flames. The emerald green fire swept across her shoulders and ignited her mane and tail. There was no sense hiding what she was. With clouds of brimstone spewing from her nose, she ducked her head beneath the stone archway and trotted inside.

CHAPTER 36

The vortex of wind dissipated, leaving Anaba and Bryana in the uppermost level of the citadel. The chamber was nondescript, not much different from the one at the base of the structure, including one apparent exit. An aura of light prevented Anaba from seeing what lay beyond the room or what might be awaiting them outside. As the cacophony of wings faded with the current that had carried them, she looked down into an unobstructed view of the abyss beneath her. Needing no further prompting, the Nightmare trotted out of the tower.

She emerged onto a bustling thoroughfare. As an agnostic, Anaba's knowledge of Heaven came from a Baptist grandmother, who related tales of pearly gates and streets paved with gold. What she saw beyond the alabaster structure defied religious logic.

Custom-painted horse trailers were parked in rows in a grassy field. Beige and green tents served as temporary stabling for horses and ponies arriving on the grounds. Hanging from canvas wall displays or truck windows, ribbons of all sizes and colors fluttered in a cool, morning breeze. Horses were being bathed at water stations, cantered on lunge lines, or warmed up in various arenas across the show venue.

"Anaba!" Bryana leaned over the Nightmare's neck, ecstatically signing, "Is this Heaven?"

A stillness slowly filled the crowded spaces. Every activity ground to a halt. There was cause for concern among the denizens of Heaven. A creature from the infernal underworld stood in their tranquil midst.

Anaba lowered her head in a sign of submission. Tiny tongues of flame curled around her fetlocks as she walked obsequiously on the gravel path, weaving between stunned spectators and mounted competitors.

"You dare defile this sacred ground!" A Hispanic man dressed in a gray, three-piece suit stepped down from the judge's gazebo. Silver, plated armor shimmered across his body, replacing the illusion of the summer suit. He drew a longsword from a sheath between his wings. With malicious intent in every stride, he moved to engage her. Three other angels drew their swords and converged from the opposite side, flanking the Nightmare between them.

"Don't you hurt her!" Bryana's demand went unheeded. With a violent flourishing of the blade, the angel brought it down toward Anaba's neck.

"Stop! If that blow lands, it will be your last!" The authority in the speaker's voice was potent, rising from an indelible confidence. He was used to being obeyed.

Resigning herself to fate, Anaba stood motionless, uncompromising and undaunted. Marines didn't flinch or beg. While there was no white flag to wave, she would not be the aggressor here.

She felt the rush of wind behind her ears, caused by the abrupt arresting of the sword. The blow was intended to sever her spine and would have been immediately fatal.

"This creature is an abomination. Here on blessed soil! Allow me to kill it where it stands," the angel said.

"Do you presume to know better than Heaven? If the Father had not wanted the Nightmare here, do you think she would be standing there before you now?" A thick mane of dreadlocks hung across the speaker's shoulders and down the middle of his back. Bound with silver rings, they were twisted and looped in intricate designs that framed his noble black face.

"But General," the angel replied. "The beast carries your war lance. Ah-Azarim Aziagiar."

"Stand down, Arethiel. The only abomination here is your lack of manners. Return to your posts. This is a family matter." The lines of his high brow and jaw were uncannily familiar.

"Grandpa?" Bryana signed. She slid from Anaba's back and leaped into his arms, showering his face with kisses. "I've missed you! Where have you been?"

"Watching over you, little one," he replied.

Anaba took a wary step away from him, recognizing the brown eyes. They were Michael's eyes, but this was not him.

"Going so soon?"

Not exactly feeling welcomed. The Nightmare glared at the angelic soldiers still flanking her.

"Forgive us any offense, Anaba." There was a peculiar, soothing quality in his voice that negated her suspicion. "My given name is Mikha'el. In the name of the Father, I bid you welcome." Despite a natural inclination toward caution, Anaba felt at ease and lowered her guard. "Bryana, you're going to miss your first class." Mikha'el took the reins of a chestnut pony from a groom.

No more than fourteen-hands tall, the gelding fumbled in the archangel's pockets for a treat. He was rewarded with a stolen peppermint. Crunching noisily, he nickered at Bryana.

"Georgie, is that you?" Bryana's hospital smock dematerialized, replaced by tan riding breeches, tall boots, and a black show coat with the number nine tied about her waist.

"Will competitor number nine, Bryana Childs-DeJesus and Prince George please report to the in-gate." The announcement rang out across the show grounds.

Bryana ran back to Anaba and hugged the Nightmare's neck with a ferocity born of gratitude. "Thank you, Anaba." The grinning girl stepped back and stroked her face. "Take care of my Uncle Michael. Mommy and Daddy have each other.

Grandma has everyone. He needs someone like you to protect him." She kissed Anaba's nose and returned to the waiting arms of her grandfather for a leg up. The beaming girl picked up her reins and trotted to the in-gate.

"This is the day Bryana won her first championship," Mikha'el said. "Later that night she collapsed in her bedroom while hanging the ribbon on the wall. The next morning, her parents learned she had a heart condition that would cut her life short."

You could have spared her. Anaba let the accusation roll with no filter.

"Spare her from what?" The archangel spread his arms out to indicate the show grounds. "This paradise?" He reached out to stroke the Nightmare's shoulder, running his fingers across the Crest of Nanqueel.

Anaba pinned her ears and shied away from him. But not before the archangel had traced the raised outline of one specific feather.

"Velendriel was a cherished friend who believed in sacrifice for the greater good."

Seeing an opportunity to get the jump on the Nightmare, one of the angels flanking her ignored the orders to cease and desist and suddenly charged her. He struck her injured ribcage, knocking the wind out of the Nightmare and bringing her to her knees. The unexpected violence of the broadside assault was an attempt to drop and roll her with the impact. But Anaba's greater body mass saved her from being forced into a vulnerable position on her back.

The attacking angel wore silver maille and wielded a shortsword as well as a dagger in an underhanded grip. He was fast and sliced at her neck, missing by inches.

Anaba propped herself onto a shoulder, twisted her hindquarters, and retaliated with a kick to the head. The blow shattered his nose and sent blood splattering across his face. She drew back and kicked again, striking him in the throat. He collapsed to his knees, grasping at his neck.

The Nightmare reared up and lunged at the wounded angel. Buffeted by his wings, she blasted him with brimstone and ignited the vapor. Blinded and unable to breathe, he fell backwards, choking on blood and black smoke.

"Anaba!" Mikha'el shouted.

The authority in the archangel's voice was familiar, but she ignored him. There was no iron bit to stop her. She latched on to one of the bleeding angel's wings with her teeth and shook him until she felt the tendons pop under the stress.

"The forging of a nightmare begins in shadow and in fear. A billowing blast of cruelty to produce the blackest tear."

The words of the incantation sent a cold shock through Anaba as effectively as a hollow point to her skull. Mikha'el's voice resonated through her memories, echoing across a labyrinth of recollections from the forging process.

Releasing the injured angel, the Nightmare fled backwards. Desperate to escape the binding magic, she crashed through a wooden fence into an empty paddock. The whites of her eyes showed as she flung her head up like a ballast and struggled to stay up on her feet. Flames extinguished, she collapsed in the grass as if hobbled by iron chains.

Mikha'el stared down at her. His eyes solemn with resolve. "A modicum of desperation will bring about a sweat. With just a dash of devilment, bleed the soul and leave it wet."

You fucking bastard! Anaba recognized the voice that had long haunted her from the shadows. *Caim didn't forge me – you did! You're supposed to be one of the fucking* good *guys! Guess the Bible got that wrong, too.*

Mikha'el's expression shifted, his stoic features betraying a profound, inner remorse. "The greatest plague the Father ever unleashed onto the world were His angels." He gestured to his subordinates to give the incapacitated Nightmare a wide berth. "I'm not asking for your forgiveness, Anaba. Only that you fulfill the destiny I have set before you."

How is this possible? I'm bound to Michael.

"Michael completed the rite properly, as I knew he would, but *I* forged you. There will forever be a connection between us."

I should kill you.

"You've certainly become powerful enough to do so." The archangel pointed to indicate the distinct pinwheel of three feathers on her left shoulder.

Then release me and give me the title shot! Anaba squealed in fury, fighting for control of her body. All she could manage was a series of harmless spasms.

"I am sorry, Anaba, for all the pain I have caused you: Caim's deception, the cruelty to your wife… the forging, but I needed you to protect my son." Mikha'el knelt down beside her and ran his fingers over the branded outline of the apothecary scales with interest. "I am determined that Michael will not face his terrible destiny alone."

He's in danger because of you! Anaba hurled the accusation. Gritting her teeth, she strained to break free of the spell, but the power of the forging incantation was irrefutable. *What about Serra? Did you ever really love her? Or was she just a pawn?*

"I loved Serra enough to break with the Father's will and give her the child she so desperately wanted. I harbor no regrets. There is a design in place that is not mine to question, Anaba." Mikha'el looked away, his face stricken with sorrow.

So this is God's *plan? Or just another cover for a celestial fuck up?*

"As a fellow soldier, you should understand."

She hated him, hated everything about the archangel, in the same way she detested officers who knew nothing about what it was like to live or die in the field. But in that moment she understood. Too many times, orders were handed down – not to be understood but to be executed.

Did you ever *think about what would happen to* him?

"That is why I chose you!" The archangel risked the danger of coming within striking distance of her legs to caress her forehead. "My actions have set in motion a chain of consequences that are not only mine to suffer."

Serra? Michael?

"A person's worth is not a true measure of who they really are because some have more to give than others," Mikha'el said. "Our true worth is determined by *what* we are prepared to sacrifice."

And what would you sacrifice?

"Everything. Michael is the Qaaun foretold in prophecy. The one who will lead the Nephilim to their rightful place. Though he has not fully awakened, he is a danger to the Grigori, and they *will* kill him."

Then fucking do something to stop them. Don't just stand on the sidelines. She felt a weight lifted from her. Feinting a kick, she lunged to her feet and backed away, flames reigniting across her body.

"Free will is the privilege of man. I have broken every law in Heaven to protect my son, but I am bound by a vow of obedience I cannot break again. Forgive me, Anaba. I can only pray that in time, you will understand why I tricked Caim into taking your soul. Why I allowed him to think I would help in his bid to become a Horseman. Why I forged you and set you on this path as a Nightmare." With each confession, his handsome face became distorted by shadows.

The illusion about him shifted, and she saw the archangel in his true form. An ornate, silver cuirass covered his torso. It was banded at the ribs by leather straps. Maille hung over the waist. His wings were gray and so large that they could have embraced Anaba's entire body. An elegant scabbard with moonstones and sapphires hung from his sword belt.

He stepped forward, and she spooked at his approach. "Steady," he said, palms open. He tugged at a decorative chain at his right shoulder and tugged his pauldron loose from the armor. It glowed and transformed, elongating and thickening into a peytral. He fastened the plate collar around Anaba's neck and secured it with a sturdy buckle and chain, before adjusting it across her chest. "This breastplate is inscribed with the Seal of Enoch the Exalted, Michael's grandfather. My mount Nanqueel wore it until the day he fell at the hand of Lucifer. Now it is yours."

The Seal of Enoch?

Mikha'el stood back to admire her. "This sigil will protect you from most Enochian magic by negating the effects of any spells or wards taken from the *Keys of Solomon*. Any attempt to bind you will fail. There is no sigil that can break the power of the signature of Metatron, the Scribe of God, save the Word of the Father himself."

"General!" Arethiel cried out. "Your war lance!" He pointed to the sheath at Anaba's shoulder as the weapon faded into the ether, called to the hand of its master, and disappeared.

Mikha'el held his hand up for silence. "Ah-Azarim Aziagiar is no longer mine to claim."

"*Anaba, niis...*" The Crest of Nanqueel burned at Anaba's shoulder, an indication of Michael's summons. His voice was distant and strained, a tinge of fear underlying the fatigued utterance of the command.

Wheeling on her hind legs, Anaba spun around toward the sound of his voice. *Michael!* Agitated, she cantered a stride and then slid to a stop, frantically scanning the faces of the people around her for some sign of him. Finding none, she flattened her ears and lunged at his father. *Where is he? What have you done?*

"Michael needs you. Go to him and let nothing born of Heaven or in Hell deter you."

Anaba galloped across the length of the ring and jumped the fence near the parking lot. Charging headlong toward a shadow portal, she leaped into the horizontal tear before it had fully formed at the mouth of a maintenance road. The blue flames of immolation roiled across her black hide as she tucked her knees beneath her chin and vanished into the darkness.

Mikha'el knelt down to examine the fiery footprints left in the wake of the Nightmare's retreat. Cupping his hand around the smoking soil, he scooped it up and made a fist around it. The heat did not dissipate, and burned against his skin. The archangel did not flinch.

He breathed into his closed hand to feed the fiery embers. "Well done," he whispered, "well done, thou good and faithful servant."

CHAPTER 37

"Anaba!" Michael sat up, reaching for his duty pistol. Instead of the Glock 19M he got a handful of sweaty sheets. He was lying in a twin-sized bed on a flimsy mattress that smelled like stale bread. The cheap decor and threadbare drapes made it obvious that he was in a hotel on the wrong side of the city.

The ACE bandage supporting his bruised ribs offered little relief from the stabbing ache that intensified with every frantic breath. Unable to piece together the events that brought him there, he panicked, until his eyes landed on Anaba.

She was sitting in a chair near the only window, the curtains drawn. Dressed in jeans and a bloody gray Henley, the Marine sat with her hand poised over a glass of bourbon. A half empty bottle of Jim Beam sat on a pockmarked plywood table beside her within arm's reach.

"I was calling for you."

Anaba threw back the bourbon. "Better late than never."

"And where the fuck were you?! Anaba, I needed you–" He gasped, sucking air between his teeth as the bruised ribs pulled, squeezed against his tense abdominal muscles. "I needed backup. And you were nowhere to be found. The Grigori were trying to kill me."

"But they didn't. You finally put your big boy pants on and handled your own business."

"Where are we?"

"Seedy little dive in Harlem. I like to call it home when I'm not in the mood for the world's bullshit." Anaba shrugged. "I thought about going for a five-star downtown, but you weren't looking so good."

"How are the bad guys looking?"

She gave him a wry smile. "You killed four angels all by yourself. I'm all kinds of impressed."

Michael swung his legs over the side of the bed. "There were seven of them, I think."

"*Were* being the operative word."

"You killed the other three?"

"Didn't exactly have a choice, Agent Childs. Foul language wasn't working." Anaba poured herself another shot. "Imagine my surprise when they all turned out to be human. Thought they went down a little too easy," she whispered as an aside and slammed the shot. "They were so busy trying to break into that barn to kill you, they didn't know what hit them. Could have used that little tactic back in Syria."

Michael buried his face in his hand. "Jesus. I'd just left a message for my mom."

"Everyone's back at the farm, including that bitch who called me a nag."

"They left Bryana at the hospital alone?"

Anaba refilled the glass and drank it. "Bryana's dead, Michael." She reached for a clean glass, filled it halfway with bourbon, and shoved it across the table. "She died shortly after you left the hospital."

Michael stood up, one hand perched on his ribs for support, the other on the nightstand for balance. "How did Noah take it? My mom?"

She shook her head, staring intently into her glass. "Not sure how you expect me to answer that. She was just a kid. She's dead now. It doesn't seem fair. And it's not. *That's* how they feel. They're coping."

Numbed by the news of Bryana's death, Michael took a faltering step to test his balance and nearly fell. He leaned against the wall for support.

"Maybe you should lie back down." Anaba glanced up at him and poured herself another drink. "One of your ribs might be busted. I wouldn't play grab ass with any angels for a bit."

"I'll be fine." He swallowed hard and pushed himself away from the cheap paneling. "Are you hurt?"

"Took a few good lumps." She looked down at the bloody side of her shirt. "Better off than you, though. *You* were out cold with a nasty bump on the head." Anaba shoved a chair toward him with her foot. "Come have a drink." She raised her glass. "To our fallen."

Michael brushed aside the dreadlocks covering the left side of her face. No longer hidden, the half-inch gash above her eye was held together with suture tape. Her eye was discolored with speckled reddening, and the skin surrounding it was purple, dark, against her brown skin.

He noticed a bloody serum seeping through the thick fabric of her shirt at the left shoulder. "What's this?" he asked. He undid the first button, just enough to reveal the curve of her breasts. Taking her silence as permission, he unfastened the other two. She was wearing a peculiar metal pendant around her neck that he had not noticed before. Dismissing it, he pulled the collar of the Henley over her shoulder. Beneath the damp fabric, he saw the freshly branded feather etched into her flesh above her shoulder blade.

"Velendriel. Briathos. And now Eyoniel."

Anaba drew back when he touched the inflamed area. Goose bumps raised across her skin as she shrugged back into her shirt.

Running a hand through the cottony texture of her dreadlocks, Michael traced the curve of her jaw with his fingers. He felt the warmth of her breath on his palm.

Anaba stiffened involuntarily, her jaw tensing. "What are you doing?"

Michael sank to a knee in front of her and laid his hands on her thighs. "Something I should have done when I first met you. Maybe then you wouldn't have kicked my ass."

The Marine sat back in the chair, crossing her arms over her chest. "And what's that?"

"When God presented Adam to the Elohim, the first among them to kneel was my father."

Anaba looked away, avoiding his eyes, but not his touch. "Following in your old man's footsteps?"

"With one exception." Leaning between her legs, he waited for her to look at him and then kissed her.

She responded with an audible sigh and then, without warning, put a boot in his chest. Missing his injured ribs, she sent him careening across the room.

"Don't ever fucking do that again!" Anaba snatched her oilskin duster from a hanger on the back of the door and threw it over her shoulders. Leaving the door hanging open, she stormed out of the room.

Michael crawled up the side of the mattress to get back to his feet. While it was not the reaction he had expected, her violent response was excessive. She was hiding something from him, he could sense it. Grabbing a hoodie from the flimsy corkboard closet, he chased her into the night.

A blue moon canvased the sky, illuminating the empty parking lot with a brilliance powerful enough to eclipse the stars. Michael glanced at his watch. It was just a few minutes after midnight on Valentine's Day. He rushed down the steps from the third tier balcony, catching up with Anaba. "What the hell, Anaba? Was I out of line? That was a little dramatic. Even for you."

Anaba paced the sidewalk in front of an ice-box with an "Out of Order" sign taped to the door. She punched the unit, leaving a dent and a bloody smear on the lid. She looked down at her hand where she held a pair of battered dog tags and a silver wedding band looped on a ball chain.

"You're married?" he asked, feeling the fool. "Didn't take you for the marrying type. Who's the lucky guy?"

Anaba glared at him. "Why must pair bonding always come down to an equation that includes a penis?"

"Lucky... girl?" Feeling awkward, Michael shoved his hands into his pockets and stared at the cracked concrete. His heart ached more than his ribcage. "Where'd you meet her?"

"Aleppo, Syria"

"She a Marine?"

"Army," Anaba replied, closing her fingers over the dog tags. "I was with an expeditionary force when some insurgents decided to introduce themselves with a grenade launcher. Natalia–" Anaba stopped abruptly and closed her eyes. "Natalia got separated from her unit. She was in trouble, so I went to help. We ended up in a sewage ditch fighting for our lives."

"Sounds crazy."

"It was, but we survived. Thirteen hours. In shit. Literally. When we got back to base, all that stress and frustration just came out while we were together in quarantine. I thought it was a fluke. War nerves." Anaba shook the dog tags clasped in her hand. "It was my first time being with a woman. But it was the last time I would be with anyone else. We got married, quietly, a month later."

"Military didn't approve?"

"It was more than that. The only thing more dangerous than a Marine is a disobedient one. After that clusterfuck in Aleppo, I refused to work with anyone but her." Anaba rolled her eyes. "The Marine Corps sent me stateside for a mental eval. That's when the CIA came calling."

Michael shivered and blew warm air into his hands. "That's why your file was so heavily redacted."

"They needed a blooded sniper. My one and only request was that Natalia be my spotter." Shoulders slumped in defeat, Anaba leaned against the ice box. "We did five back-to-back tours in Syria and loved every minute of it. Because we were together. Then one night, Caim Seere showed up."

"The archangel that turned you into a Nightmare?"

Anaba's eyes narrowed as the corners of her mouth were drawn into a frown. "We thought he was a meddling Company man checking in on the assets. But he was there for much more. Next thing I know, Natalia and I are engaged in a rolling hit-and-run skirmish in the heart of Bādiyat al-Shām." She noted his confused expression. "It's a desert. A big one."

"He betrayed your position."

"Bastard led those insurgents right to us." Anaba wrapped the ball chain between her fingers. "An IED took out our vehicle. We called ourselves lucky to be alive. Until a grenade rolled down the dune where we'd taken cover. Next thing I know, Natalia was on top of it."

Michael bowed his head. "Christ, Anaba. I'm sorry."

"Not as sorry as I was. Mistakes were made. Mistakes that can't ever be rectified."

He stared at her in confusion. "I don't follow you."

"Natalia didn't die, Michael." Anaba stared into the skies above them. "That's when Caim revealed himself as one of the Fallen."

"You sold your soul to save her."

"You're damn right, and I'd do it again." Despite her affinity with the shadows, the darkness could not hide the sorrow in her face. "The forging of a nightmare begins in shadow and in fear," she said, her voice strained with emotion. "A billowing blast of cruelty to produce the blackest tear. A modicum of desperation will bring about a sweat. With just a dash of devilment, bleed the soul and leave it wet. Blast it in an open flame; burn humanity from its eyes. Clap its mouth and feet in iron, then bid the bloody beast to rise."

"What is that? Some kind of invocation?" Michael asked, curious about the verse.

"That's part of the incantation he used. Repeating it over

and over again." Anaba looked at him, her eyes betraying her pain. "Should've been me on top of that fucking grenade. He made me relive that moment until it broke me. After I escaped, I learned the truth."

"What truth?"

"Bastard had honored the contract. Natalia's alive. If you call being a legless torso, breathing on a ventilator living."

"That's why you came back to New York." Michael rubbed a cold hand against his face in horror. He laid his hand on her shoulder as Anaba leaned over the broken ice-box. "What hospital did you say she was in?"

"I didn't say." She glared at him over her shoulder. "Fuck you, Michael. I didn't spill my guts so you could drag me to her bedside. I tried to go see her, but I couldn't bear it. This is all my fucking fault."

Risking her ire, Michael took her arm. "You held up your end of the contract. Caim didn't. Now that you're with me, he'll keep Natalia alive, suffering like that, to punish you. Find us a road."

"Michael?" She bowed her head, staring at the ground at her feet.

"This isn't up for discussion, gunny. Find us a road." It was not in him to compel her but, as her Rider, he would be obeyed.

Reluctantly moving between buildings, Anaba was engulfed in a cloud of brimstone and shadows. The acrid scent of sulfur tickled the insides of Michael's nostrils. Crestfallen, she reemerged as a Nightmare, her noble head hanging submissively above the ground.

Michael tugged at the reins to pull her head up. She resisted, pressing her forehead against his chest to avoid making eye contact. "We need to make this right," he whispered, caressing her neck. "You know that."

Vaulting to her back, it took no prompting to move her forward. She cantered into a veil of shadows.

CHAPTER 38

Michael held onto the pommel of his saddle as Anaba trotted off the gravel surface of the Vestibule Road. The shadowy, dogleg trail brought them into a darkened corridor on the eighth floor of the New York Harbor VA Hospital. Despite the stench of brimstone, he recognized the pungent, antiseptic in the air.

"All right, you two!" said a voice, startling them. "Come out of that portal."

Wearing a black pencil skirt that rode her hips and narrowed seductively over her thighs, the Horseman Pestilence waded into the vortex of shadow and flames as it dissipated. Arms crossed over her buxom chest, she pushed a pair of ruby, tortoiseshell glasses up the bridge of her nose and glared at Michael.

"Wyrmwood?" He promptly dismounted.

"That's *Doctor* Wyrmwood to you."

"What are you doing here?"

"Samiel tasked me with keeping an eye on you. So I had my Nightmare, Kali, keep an eye on her." She pointed to Anaba as the taciturn Marine resumed human form. "Good thing, too. You're about to make an epic, rookie mistake."

"Rookie mis–"

"Did the two of you think you could walk among the dying

and not make a spectacle of yourselves? Without the proper sigils, the near-dead can see us for what we are. We're called Heralds for a reason, newbie." She batted her long lashes at him.

"Samiel sent *you* to babysit me?"

"He has reasonable cause for concern. That little reception near your mother's farm? A bit too close for comfort. Filthy Grigori! Trying to take out a Horseman? They've truly gone to the dark side, but," she said, wagging a finger at him, "they're not acting alone."

Anaba raised her head with interest. "Meaning?"

"EJ found surveillance gear hidden in your mother's truck. Some confounding gadget capable of killing the electrical systems." She handed her phone to Michael, swiping through the images.

"So it was an ambush?" Michael's jawbone cracked under the strain of clenched teeth. He showed the images of the equipment to Anaba.

"That's some serious, high-end spookware." Anaba enlarged the pictures and scrutinized the components. "CIA issue."

"EJ certainly believes they're involved," Wyrmwood said. "Did you ever notice he gets this sexy little eye twitch whenever his heart rate goes up?" She squeezed her eyes shut and grinned with the pure glee of a child on Christmas morning. "He's so delicious."

Michael rolled his eyes, shaking his head, and followed her to a small office behind the nurses' station. "Was there anything else found at the scene?"

"Besides the corpses and angel ash? Yes!" With an unapologetic blush in her cheeks, she adjusted the glasses on her nose. "Samiel discovered Enochian glyphs spread out over a mile-long radius. Potent sigils specifically designed to prevent the summoning of a Nightmare."

"That's why Anaba didn't answer when I called for her?" Michael sat down in a chair across from the Horseman.

"This could have used a stitch or two." She fretted over the cut behind his left ear and the bruises along his jawline. Blowing into a pair of latex gloves, she slipped them on and reached for a bottle of antiseptic. "How Anaba ever managed to find you is a mystery. If there's one thing Samiel despises, it's an enigma *he* cannot unravel."

"I followed his scent when he didn't check in." Anaba shoved her hands into her pockets. She stared intently down a corridor designated as intensive care.

It was a lie, but Michael kept quiet. There was no arrangement between them to check in.

"Hmm, that infallible Nightmare sense of smell. Makes perfect sense," Wyrmwood said, tapping her nails against the counter. "What doesn't make sense, though, is what the two of you are doing here."

"Anaba's wife is here," Michael replied. "Thanks to Caim Seere. They got into a tight spot while on duty overseas. Anaba sold her soul to save Natalia, but Caim tricked her."

"Her wife?" The jovial, sarcastic expression that was Wyrmwood's usual demeanor faded. Wyrmwood turned to the soldier. "Are you sure she's here Anaba?"

The Nightmare tapped her nose and pointed down the corridor.

"No need to go about this haphazardly, upsetting these poor wretches. Let me find her." Wyrmwood frowned, glancing at the digital wall clock. "Clara will be back any minute."

"Who's Clara?" Michael asked.

"Night charge nurse. I sent her on a Starbucks run when Kali confirmed you were coming." Wyrmwood swung the office chair around to a computer terminal. "Last name?"

"Alfaro-Raines," Anaba said.

"Sergeant First-Class Natalia Alfaro-Raines. They took her off a ventilator a week ago, expecting the worse, but she's hanging in there. Caim's doing?" Wyrmwood rolled her eyes. "He may forge the finest Nightmares in Hell, but welching on a contract? Despicable, even for a fallen angel! She's in 860. A private room at the end of the ICU hallway. Left side."

Anaba conveyed her unspoken thanks with a subtle nod. With tears shining in her eyes, she turned toward the dimly lit hall with the conviction of a condemned prisoner on the way to the death chamber.

"Anaba, wait," Michael called after her, but fell silent with a tugging on his sleeve.

Wyrmwood held a finger over her lips to indicate quiet before prodding him to follow Anaba into the corridor.

Trailing the emotionally staggered Marine through the specialized ICU annex, Michael followed her into the assigned room. It was small and austere, crowded with blinking monitors. Multiple IV machines and oxygen tanks formed a hub around a sole hospital bed. A wall of long, plastic strips stretched from ceiling to floor to create a sterile, inner chamber. Transparent, the misty cocoon left little privacy for the patient within.

Troubled by an ominous odor, Michael wrinkled his nose in dismay. "What's that smell?"

"Overdue death." Ignoring infection protocols, Anaba pushed into the chamber and stared down at the scarred, hairless near-corpse lying in the bed. "Natalia?"

Natalia opened her one remaining eye. It widened in horror. The heart monitor at her bedside captured the potency of that fear, which her ruined face could no longer express. To give a voice to her terror, a piercing alarm went off.

"Ssh, mami, it's me." Anaba held up the battered dog tags and the wedding ring. She pressed them into Natalia's scarred palm. "Semper fi, baby. My wedding vow, remember?"

The clatter of the dog tags cut through the shroud of confusion and fright. Natalia wrapped her fingers around Anaba's hand and the relics of their old life. Badly damaged from the grenade blast, her own wedding ring had been cut away, leaving an obvious indentation in the flesh below the knuckle.

A single tear fell from her eye, navigating a labyrinth of scar tissue along her cheek. "Anaba?"

Anaba kissed her forehead and then her hand. "I've missed you so much." She closed her eyes as Natalia's fingers weakly fluttered across her face. "Nat, this is Michael. He's a friend."

Reluctant to join Anaba at Natalia's bedside, Michael hesitated beyond the plastic barrier. "Natalia," he whispered, stepping into Anaba's shadow.

Arm trembling with the effort, she reached out to him. As their fingers met, lucid flashes of her memories passed over to him, overwhelming his senses. Hot days making love in the backseat of a derelict pickup truck. Tender nights sweating beneath a desert sky. A stolen kiss as AK-47 rounds rained overhead.

Michael suffered an ardent pang of jealousy. It all ended with a blinding, white shock of indescribable pain. A deafening blast lifted his body on a powerful, explosive wave that suspended him on a column of heat and flame. The scent of burning metal and flesh assailed his nostrils until the sinus passages were stripped away and clogged with blood. As his consciousness waned, he called out for Anaba, but it was not his voice that he heard. It was Natalia.

You love her.

"Wh-what–" Michael stuttered, confused. He stood shivering at Natalia's bedside with his hands grasping at his lower torso.

"Don't be afraid, Michael," Wyrmwood said from the doorway. "If you can hear her, you're experiencing one of the vested powers of an apocalypse angel: the Last Confession."

Looking down at her, Michael gently squeezed her hand. "I'm listening."

She won't move on as long as I'm here. And she can't move on alone. Natalia pressed the dog tags into his hand.

"What's she saying?" Anaba asked.

"She wants–" Michael struggled to get the words out of his mouth. "–me to release her." He clasped the dog tags in his hand until the metal edges bit into his skin.

"Can you do that?" Anaba asked.

"The contract is an infernal binding. Caim's dirty dealings in small print," Wyrmwood explained. "But you are the Third Horseman – Famine. No mere minion of Hell has the power to stand against your will."

"I- I'm not sure what to do." He looked at Anaba's despondent face and felt helpless.

"Yes, you do," Wyrmwood said kindly. "Water is the essence of all life. Samiel may be the Angel of Death, but we each have the power to severe the ties of the living."

"Are you sure?" Michael held Natalia's scarred hand. He knew the terrible consequences of his abilities to call forth and weaponize the element of water, even beyond the borders of Hell.

Love exists without boundaries. Not even death. When you decide you can't live without her, say these words to her. Anaba will know.

Before he was cognizant of his thoughts, the decree slipped from his lips. "Wither."

The results were immediate and more violent than he intended. Water rapidly drained from Natalia's broken body and seeped into the mattress. The machines surrounding her bed announced the impending death with alarms. In the red glow of their instrumentation panels, Natalia's body convulsed in fitful spasms. Her soul offered no resistance, straining to be released, but a malevolent presence held her to this world to suffer.

Anaba climbed into the narrow bed and embraced her wife. "What's happening?"

"There's a sigil of restraint – the seal of Caim." Michael nicked himself with a paperclip and rubbed his bloody thumb across the infernal glyph glowing on Natalia's forehead. Recalling a prayer of banishment from his brief studies with an exorcist at Oxford University, he whispered, "I rebuke you, Caim Seere, Son of No One, and I invoke you, Mikha'el, Archangel of God, Defender of Innocents." He traced his father's sigil over Natalia's feverish skin.

Natalia's emancipated body fell still. Closing her remaining eye, she slumped against Anaba's chest. Anaba laid her back into the pillows, and, with a final, peaceful sigh, she was gone. Her body disintegrated to a fine dust that shed out in layers on the damp sheets of the hospital bed.

Trembling in shock, Michael stumbled out of the sterile chamber. Staring at the dog tags and the wedding ring in his hand. He propped himself against the nearest wall.

"Did she say anything else?" Anaba asked. Her hands were covered in the ash of her dead wife.

Michael shook his head, incapable of uttering the lie. He put the dog tags and the ring into her hand and closed her fingers around them. "You good, gunny?"

"No." Her eyes were vacant, red, and glassy.

Michael wrapped his arms around her. He held her close, his chest tightening, and wondered if he had the fortitude necessary to be an apocalypse angel. If Anaba had escaped Hell, could she help them both escape destiny?

"I owe you." Anaba laid her head on his shoulder.

"After everything you've done for me? I'm not keeping score." Michael wiped a tear from her eye with his thumb. He turned to the doorway, but Anaba lingered in the room.

"Go on before the charge nurse gets back. I'll take care of her," Wyrmwood said, caressing the distraught Marine's arm. "Proper and with dignity. You have my word."

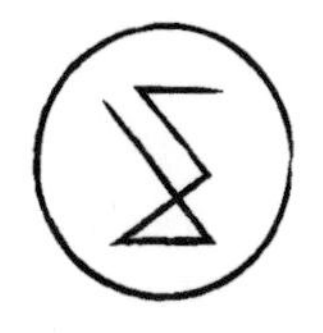  

CHAPTER 39

Four black SUVs pulled up to the curb in front of the Jacob K. Javits Federal Building. The surrounding traffic yielded to the ominous vehicles and gave them a wide berth. They came to a simultaneous halt, their tires chirping on the wet asphalt. Attentive figures in black business suits quickly exited the doors.

Six CIA officers took positions near the vehicles, while another eight assumed defensive positions around Caim Seere and Paul Steiner. Escorting their assets from the middle vehicle, the team made their way up the stairs to the front doors and proceeded into the foyer.

"Stop right there," Agent McKabe said. He held his hand up, flanked by a tactical team.

Agitated, Caim tugged at his coat sleeves, adjusting his cuff links. "I don't deal with subordinates. I'm here to see Rathaniel. Considering the botched op from last night, I'm not sure you're even qualified to be a messenger boy." He glanced at Steiner, who was on his cell phone, speaking in a muffled voice.

"Wait for it," Steiner said with a sinister smile, ending the call. "Four, three, two, one."

McKabe retrieved the vibrating phone from his coat. "Yes, Director Rathan, I'll bring them along directly." Scowling, the Grigori bowed his head. "Gentlemen, this way."

The lead CIA officers fell in line behind McKabe. The other four sandwiched Caim and Steiner between them. Caim smiled. For humans, they possessed a sharp acumen: fiercely attentive to detail and unflinchingly lethal when provoked. They reminded him of better days, before Lucifer's rebellion, when he held a respected place among his brethren as a commander. However, the memory of past glory did little for his dismal mood.

McKabe opened the door to Rathan's office, head held high, his eyes defiant. Caim met his gaze with mutual vitriol and walked into the room with Steiner. Their armed escort stood guard in the outer office. Coming into the room behind them, McKabe closed the door.

"What's the human doing here?" Rathan asked from behind his desk, glaring at Steiner.

"Mr Steiner is here because, unlike *your* minions, he knows how to get things done," Caim replied.

"Mind your tone, Caim Seere!" McKabe hissed.

"My tone is sufficiently appropriate considering the situation. It's your incompetence that is out of bounds. You had *one* simple task, Kokabiel: kill the Nephilim. My people put everything in place: the surveillance, the logistics, the hardware, and the footwork. I drew the wards and sigils myself."

"Two of your people were killed."

"Only after *yours* called them in! My people were not tactically prepared for the situation. They were killed, not by a Nephilim, but by the Nightmare who crashed the scene."

Rathan stood up, rapping his knuckles across the polished top of his desk. "If your wards and circles were so effective, they should have prevented the beast from being summoned."

"You needed time to kill him. I bought you that time, and it was squandered. How many Grigori does it take to kill one half-breed?" Caim asked, shrugging his shoulders in feigned confusion. "I held up my end, Rathaniel."

"How did Childs manage to circumvent the sigils?"

Caim held out his hand to Steiner, who slipped him an envelope. "By a seal of protection drawn in blood." He tossed the photos onto Rathan's desk.

"The Sigil of Mikha'el." Rathan sat back down, staring at the familiar signature. "Impossible. No infernal beast can be summoned in the name of an angel."

"He called to his father, and the Nightmare answered." Caim ran a hand over his silk tie. "Clearly, you have underestimated the reach of the Father's most revered general."

"Perhaps what was underestimated was your resolve, adrpan." McKabe muttered the slur under his breath.

"Did you say something, Kokabiel?" Caim turned to confront the disgruntled angel. "I didn't hear you, not with your clipped wings and manufactured authority. I'm no Nephilim. Why don't you try carving your profanities into *my* flesh?"

McKabe pulled a small, straight-blade dagger from a sheath hidden in his coat. "You deserve nothing less than a Nephilim."

"Not a good idea," Steiner warned, snatching a Glock 23 from its holster. "Rethink it before it's too late."

McKabe laughed at him. "After I deal with you," he said to Caim, "I'm going to permanently muzzle your pet." Raising the Vaoan Dagger, he rushed the fallen angel.

The gunshot rang loud, reverberating through the office. McKabe was thrown backwards into a bookshelf. Hit in the shoulder, he collapsed to the floor, holding his hand over the wound as blood poured between his fingers.

Alerted by the shot, half the CIA security contingent barged in from the reception area to check on their superiors. The others fended off armed FBI agents in the crowded suite. Rathan nodded an "All Clear" to restore the peace.

"Go back to your posts," Caim ordered of his men. When the door closed, he pulled the silk handkerchief from his breast pocket and threw it on McKabe's heaving chest. "Hurts, doesn't it? While angels need fear no human weapons, the bullets from that gun were not made by human hands."

Rathan knelt down beside his second. Picking up the dagger from the carpet, he positioned the tip of the blade above the wound. At McKabe's nod, he cut into him to retrieve the bullet. He examined the spent round, scrutinizing the signet on the munition to confirm its maker. "The Sigil of Hephaestus – Azazel's handiwork." The Assistant Director stood up, holding the bullet in his bloody fingers like an accusation. "You dare to consort with traitors?"

"Says the Grigori Fifth Commander who requested the aide of a fallen one to capture a Nightmare!" Caim straightened his lapel and grinned smugly. "Hypocrite."

"Rathaniel, this is my fault." McKabe whispered, shuddering in pain. "I should have been there to kill Childs myself."

"A lapse of judgment that I cannot defend, brother." Rathan offered him an arm, helping McKabe to his feet, and then into a nearby chair. "I'm listening, Caim." He turned to face the fallen angel and his human companion.

"We need to come at this from a different angle," Caim said. "This time, I will make the first move. I will apprehend the Nightmare and isolate her in a controlled environment where she cannot be summoned." He gestured for Steiner to meet him at the door. "Without her to interfere, the Nephilim will be vulnerable. Perhaps then you can get the job done."

"Keep me apprised of your operation." Rathan adjusted the blood-soaked handkerchief under McKabe's fingers. "When the time comes, I will see to the demise of Michael Childs myself."

With a grin, Steiner returned the semi-automatic to its holster. Retrieving a business card, he flung it in McKabe's face. "You've got heart, Feeb. Might have a job for you if your boss lets you go. We're short-staffed on janitors at Langley." He laughed and followed Caim Seere out of the office door.

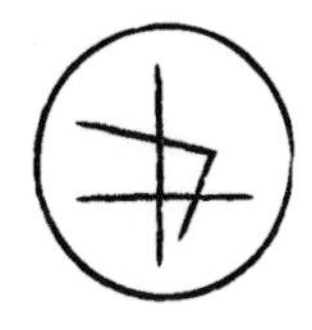

CHAPTER 40

"They're late." Michael paced the red-carpet outside the Metropolitan Museum of Art. Clad in full evening dress, he flipped the tails of his coat in agitation and tugged at the white bow tie. Samiel had knotted it too tightly for his personal taste. Rolling up the back of his glove, he checked his watch.

"Michael Childs," Samiel grumbled. "Where is your sense of propriety?" He held Michael by the arm, unlatched his wristwatch, and removed it. "Raijin, your spare?"

Raijin handed him an exquisite white-gold timepiece on a diamond chain. "Careful with that, Son of Mikha'el. Winston Churchill presented it to me after the successful evacuation of Dunkirk."

"Evacuation, old boy? Wasn't that a retreat?" Samiel grinned as he attached the pocket watch to Michael's vest.

War rolled his eyes. "A retreat is nothing more than a strategic attack from a different position."

"Speaking of retreat. A word of caution, Michael." Samiel adjusted the watch chain. "Despite the pomp and circumstance you see here, nothing is what it seems."

Raijin brushed a bit of lint from Michael's lapel. "Especially when it comes to the Prince of Hell."

"You two sound like my mother." Michael pushed by his mentors and stood at the curb, staring into the slow-moving traffic on 5th Avenue. Glancing at the elegant pocket watch, he whispered, "Something's wrong. They're really, really late."

"Isn't tardiness the feminine prerogative?" Samiel asked.

"Nonsense, Samiel, we're about to go to war." Raijin straightened the wool blouse of his military dress uniform. "No such thing as being late to a war. Unless you plan to surrender."

"Don't send up that white flag yet." Samiel straightened his tails and gloves. "Our reinforcements have arrived."

"It's about time." Michael hurried to meet the white stretch limousine as it pulled up to the curb.

A grinning valet sidestepped the anxious FBI agent and opened the limousine's passenger door. He held it open as a second attendant came to assist Wyrmwood out of the backseat. She was dressed in an ivory gown, sleeveless, with a plunging neckline. The skirt was made from heavy lace arranged in layers that tumbled downward like the white-capped waves of an ocean.

"Dr Wyrmwood, you are the epitome of a heavenly figure." Raijin kissed the back of her hand.

Wyrmwood covered the lower half of her face with a decorative bamboo fan to hide a demure smile. "Raijin, you wolf!" She abruptly snap-folded the fan and tapped him on the shoulder as an admonishment. "It's amazing what a mani-pedi can do for a girl!"

Her auburn, spiral curls bounced in a choreographed rhythm around her pale, freckled face. "I thought Anaba was going to kill the nail tech. And getting her in that gown!" Wyrmwood closed her eyes and tapped her forehead with the fan. "I'd rather sow the Black Plague across Europe again than ever take her back to a salon. Might have been easier if Michael had let her come as a Nightmare."

"Thank you." Serra Childs stepped out from the limo, wearing a silk, rose-colored dress that featured a high mandarin neckline. Her graying hair was braided with pearls and strips of kente cloth. A gossamer Watteau train hung from her shoulders.

"Mom?" Michael gawked at her before recovering his senses and offering his arm. "Y–you look great."

"Far too modest a compliment for such resplendent beauty." Samiel interjected himself between mother and son and offered his arm to Serra. "Such splendor requires a proper, dignified escort."

Awkwardly, Serra took Death's arm with a cordial nod to his charming manners. She kissed Michael on the cheek and whispered, "Anaba's not taking this well." She cast an anxious glance back to the limo. "I have to wonder if she's ever worn a dress."

"I don't think they cover that in basic training, Mom." Michael turned to the limousine in time to see the valet being rebuffed. The lanky man withdrew his hand after a slap.

Anaba peered out from the passenger compartment as if surveilling the location for hostiles. When the uniformed attendant insisted on helping her, taking her by the elbow, Anaba glared at him with such lividity he backed away. She stepped out of the vehicle and stood alone on the red carpet.

Her dreadlocks were spun into multiple twists, coiled into an elaborate knot at the top of her head, and bound with a jeweled chain. The sleeveless gown she wore was crimson with an overlay of silver brocade embroidered across the tight-fitting bodice. The full length of the skirt blossomed from her slender waistline into a court train that trailed behind her on the sidewalk.

Like a ritual aesthetic reserved for seasoned warriors, the Crest of Nanqueel stood out from her left shoulder as artistic and tasteful. An elongated silver bib necklace hung just below her prominent collarbones and matched the pair of beaded hoops dangling from her ears.

Realizing that he had been holding his breath, Michael pulled at his starched collar. "Anaba... you... look amazing."

Eyes downcast, the Marine gruffly took his arm. "Quit gawking. You're making me uncomfortable."

"Come along, you two," Samiel whispered. "We're in hostile territory. Time to meet the enemy."

Lucifer Morningstar. For the Devil, he was a remarkably affable host. With a charm bordering on audacity, he welcomed each guest in a receiving line, greeting them by name with a handshake for the men and a kiss on the hand of every woman. He wore a tailcoat of superior stitch, a maroon waistcoat, and a starched shirt with a white bow tie. Loose black hair, closely cropped at the nape and sides, was meticulously swept back in a style that framed a mature, handsome face. The tasteful five o'clock shadow of a beard drew attention to the square, noble lines of his mouth and chin.

A raven-haired woman stood at his side like an iron statue. Scowling in a halfhearted attempt to smile, she was dressed in a scintillating black gown that mirrored her skin.

"Nine o'clock," Anaba whispered, awkwardly clinging to Michael's arm.

A group of three men and three women stood near the receiving line. The stone-faced sentinels wore custom livery, but from no particular country. White riding pants and polished black tall boots were reminiscent of the French Cavalry. They carried sabers sheathed in silver scabbards with black berets perched on their heads and maroon sashes tied beneath their sword belts. They stood at attention, scanning the immediate vicinity and guests.

"Security? Can't say I'm surprised. Tonight's guest list reads like the society page in *The Times*." Michael tapped Wyrmwood on the shoulder. "Who are they?"

"The Black Seraphim," she replied.

"Do I need to be worried?"

"It's not the cobra that kills you, it's the venom," Raijin said. "They serve as Lucifer's personal bodyguard. Mind your footing. They're not to be trifled with."

Realizing that the Horseman was speaking to Anaba and not him, Michael felt her stiffen. "Why are you devil-dogging me?" she demanded. "I've got no issue with them."

"Raijin's caution is appropriate, Anaba. The Black Seraphim ride Nightmares," Wyrmwood said.

"I thought only an apocalypse angel could ride a Nightmare?" Michael said, glancing at the prominent brand on Anaba's shoulder.

"The Fallen use them to hunt and as war mounts. There are thousands of Nightmares roaming Hell," Raijin said, "ranging in quality from the flawed and mediocre to the exceptional." He eyed Anaba with a devious smile.

"Blood has been spilled over the acquisition of a unique Nightmare." Samiel glanced casually over his shoulder. "The danger here will not be just the interest of the Black Seraphim, but their master, Lucifer."

Michael pulled Anaba closer to him. "Why Anaba?"

"Only one Nightmare has ever been capable of maintaining its human form," Samiel explained. "Her name is Lilith, the first woman of Eden."

As a classically trained archaeologist, Michael knew the legend of Lilith. Created from the same clay as Adam, she was to be his equal in all things. But her sexual appetites overwhelmed him. When Adam complained to his Creator, God cast her out of the garden and crafted Eve from Adam's rib to make her subservient.

"In a blasphemy against God, Lucifer forged the first Nightmare from Lilith's soul and made her his consort. There she stands, the first and the most powerful Nightmare in Hell." Samiel looked back at Anaba. "Until now."

Greeted by attendants with trays of champagne, the guests ahead of them were ushered from the receiving line into the museum. The Black Seraphim stirred, no longer concerned with the vulgar throng of humans. They turned their attention to the Horsemen maneuvering into position to greet their host.

"Lucifer Morningstar." Samiel brashly offered his hand before the host could. "It's been a long time."

"Could have gone a bit longer, brother," Lucifer replied, reluctantly accepting the greeting, "depending on your intentions this evening. Business or pleasure?"

"All pleasure. May I introduce Dr Serra Childs, the mother of the guest of honor."

"Serra, darling." With a charming grin, Lucifer kissed the back of her hand. "Powder me green with envy. Always knew Mikha'el had good taste. He did well to hide you from us. Kiss, kiss." He leaned forward and gently kissed her on each cheek. "We're practically family. Morbidly dysfunctional, but still, family."

Serra bowed her head to the Prince of Hell. "Thank you for the invitation."

"Eventide, Lucifer." Pestilence disentangled herself from Raijin and embraced him, much to Lilith's disdain. "Good health to you, brother."

"Wyrmwood," Lucifer gushed. "You wouldn't happen to be wearing that little leather number under all those ruffles, would you?"

"Wouldn't *you* like to know?" She tapped him on the shoulder with her fan.

"Oh, I would," he replied, eyeing her salaciously. "I definitely would."

"But not today." Raijin thrust his arm out to separate them when Morningstar closed in for a kiss.

"Raijin?" Lucifer sighed, his disappointment manifesting in a frown. "As always, ruining the fun."

"A road either to safety or to ruin, depends on how you see it." Raijin clasped forearms with the fallen archangel. "Heard that from the mouth of Sun Tzu himself, while we were drinking rice wine before the Battle of Boju."

Put off by the Horseman's brusque demeanor, Lucifer narrowed his eyes. But his expression changed to immediate elation as he turned to greet Michael. "The man of the hour!" He stepped back to take an appraisal of him. "Michael Childs, my dear nephew, Son of Mikha'el, my not-so-dear brother." He offered his hand in friendship.

"Uncle... Lucifer?" Michael stumbled through his words, awkwardly accepting the handshake.

The Prince of Hell drew back, an astonished grin spread across his lips. "I like him! Such manners! Must run in the family. Enoch's side, anyway."

"Lunch would have been fine. This... really wasn't necessary."

"My only nephew – well, the only one I care to claim – has risen to the ranks of the Four Afflictions." Lucifer raised his chin with unambivalent pride. "A celebration was imperative to commemorate the milestone. We've raised $6 million for the My Brother's Keeper Global Food Initiative in your name. Besides, we've so much to discuss: family dynamics, daddy issues, whatever it is you did to the skies down under, and your new pet... the Leviathan." Lucifer wagged an accusatory finger at him. "I personally love what you've done with the old estate, but the more conservative-minded denizens in the neighborhood have gotten their panties in a knot over it.

"Speaking of panties..." The Prince of Hell turned to his consort, who was glaring at Anaba with such loathing it was palpable. "Say hello, Lilith... or not," he added when she refused to speak. "Is this your plus one? Do tell, nephew, who is this ravishing minx?"

"Anaba Raines," Michael said.

Lucifer bowed and kissed Anaba's hand, his lips lingering on her skin. "Forgive my curiosity, but I must see it – the Crest of Nanqueel." He put his hand up to silence Michael's protests. "All in good fun, nephew. Come now, Anaba, give us a spin." The fallen angel twirled his finger as if giving a command to a faithful dog.

Anaba broke off her stare-down with Lilith. She raised her chin in defiance, staring down her nose at their host, and stood her ground, not moving.

A malevolent smile parted Lucifer's lips. "Indulge me. I could just *make* you."

"And you could get your ass handed to you for trying!" Anaba hissed, her shoulders hunched forward, ready for a fight. Triggered by the Marine's aggressive stance, the Black Seraphim posted by the wall a few yards away moved in to intercept her.

"Such spirit! Such fire!" Lucifer held his arm out to restrain Lilith and used the other hand to signal the Black Seraphim to remain steadfast at their posts. "Tell me, nephew, is she any good in bed?"

Before Anaba's could explode in a fury, Michael wrapped his arm about her waist and pulled her closer to him. "Gunny, we didn't come here for a fight," he whispered in her ear. "Show him your stripes." Rearing back, he looked down at her with a mischievous grin. "No harm done pulling rank, right?"

Michael took Anaba's hand, cradling her against his hip. He rarely had a chance to be this close to her in human form. He slowly rotated her around him in a stiff waltz until her back was facing Lucifer. "Eyes on me," he said quietly. Her eyes softened, and she relaxed in his arms, bowing her head.

"Three feathers! Three vanquished angels." Lucifer clapped his hands together in admiration. "Lilith only has two to her credit. *You*, nephew, will be the envy of every duke in Hell." He waited until Michael had completed the anxious three-step with Anaba and brazenly stepped between them as if cutting in for a dance.

Michael doubted the intrusion would go well. For any of them. He held tightly to Anaba's hand, refusing to let go of her.

"And what's this?" Lucifer ran his perfectly manicured fingers over the bib pendant at Anaba's neck. "A splendid little relic. I know my brother would not have parted with this easily. Did he offer it in exchange for his life? Or did you kill him and pry it from his cold dead hands?" He closed his eyes. "Please tell me it was the latter."

"He gave it to me," Anaba said, animosity in her voice.

Michael turned sharply to Anaba and studied the pendant at her neck. Scrutinizing the relic, he saw his father's sigil inscribed on it within a larger, more complex signature.

"Mikha'el *gave* this to you? Interesting," said Lucifer. A chime rang behind them, resonating beneath the eaves of the building. "That's our cue. We'll speak again, Michael." Taking Lilith's arm, Lucifer moved to lead his entourage of Black Seraphim into the museum.

"Treasured guests," he announced to the assembly, "the night is yours and so am I. Let the debauchery begin!"

CHAPTER 41

The Metropolitan Museum of Art's newest and most controversial exhibit was a condemnation of the African slave trade. It was a memorial to the victims who had suffered and died. To accurately capture the experience, an entire wing had been transformed into the cramped cargo hold of a slave ship, inaptly named *Hope*.

Rough-hewn wooden planks formed multiple tiers that hung from the ceiling on heavy iron chains. These represented the racks where captured Africans were bound together in shackles during the Middle Passage. Their silhouettes laid between the shallow wooden compartments.

Atmospheric lighting made it nearly impossible to see their anguished features, rendering the victims' faces as imperceptible as history had made their names and stories. Built to induce claustrophobia, the low ceiling forced guests to crouch as they moved through narrow, overcrowded stacks to get to the main part of the exhibit.

As recordings of weeping and groaning played from hidden speakers, Michael dragged Anaba by the arm beneath the velvet rope barrier meant to keep guests out of the display and through the macabre labyrinth. At the rear chamber of the exhibit, the slave ship's upper decks were torn away to reveal an open sky at dusk.

The sculpture of an oak tree occupied the entire back section of the hall. Its sprawling canopy stretched across the firmament, where the stars were masterfully painted on the exhibit ceiling. As if sprouting from the ocean floor and through the slave ship, the tree's trunk had five words carved into it within the outline of a heart:

Why have

you

forsaken me?

Thousands of white lights hung from the oak's branches. Each represented a man or woman or child who was murdered in the bloody tide of a uniquely American phenomenon: lynching. The sorrowful voice of Billy Holiday sang *Strange Fruit* as Michael continued to drag Anaba from below deck and shoved her against the tree, trapping her between his outstretched arms. The irony of the exhibit weighed at him, but his fury overbore it.

"You met my father? And didn't tell me!" His indignant voice reverberated into the domed ceiling. He was hurt by her betrayal, as deeply as his father's abandonment. When she tried to turn away from him, he grabbed her by the shoulder and pinned her back against the tree. The fact that she had not laid him out with a kick was a testament to her guilt. "Anaba, answer me!"

"Michael, stop it! This is my fault." Serra tried to restrain him. "Bryana was dying. When Gabriel and Raphael refused to take her to your father, I asked Anaba to do it."

"A Nightmare in Heaven? That must have been a spectacle." Raijin went silent with a glare from Wyrmwood.

"Doesn't excuse the fact that you didn't tell me!" Michael threw himself at Anaba. "So, you saw him?" He got in her face as if intimidating a suspect.

"Yes," she replied and turned her head away from him.

Michael heard his heavy breathing echoed back at him from the bark of the tree. "You spoke to him?"

"Yes."

"Goddamn it, Anaba! What did he say?"

She sank down to the base of the oak and huddled against the trunk as if in shock. The train of her dress settled on the floor like a trail of blood flowing from the roots. "I was with Caim… for so long. I just assumed it was him…"

"Anaba, you're not making any sense." Unsettled by the sight of her in distress, Michael rested his hand on her shoulder, hoping to reassure her, but she recoiled from his touch. "What are you talking about? The forging?"

"It wasn't him. It wasn't Caim. I couldn't be sure because he hid his face," she rambled. "But he couldn't hide his voice." Anaba stared up into the oak's branches. The solid white bulbs winked off, one by one, to signify a death. "He said he was sorry. He needed someone close. To protect his only son."

"Wh–what are you saying?" Michael staggered back, shaking his head in disbelief. "*My* father did this to you?"

She reached over her shoulder and traced the scars of the Crest of Nanqueel. "I remember it now. When he released me from the iron chains, we were to go hunting on the Vestibule Road. His friend Velendriel came to stop him. They argued. I… I killed him, thinking to protect Mikha'el. That was the day he gave me to Caim."

"He… *he* forged you? Did he say anything about me?" Michael winced at the desperation in his voice. Deliberately breathing into his fist, he tried to calm himself.

"He said you were the Qaaun, and that the Grigori would kill you to prevent your awakening."

"Willful Nightmare! What other deceits are you hiding?" Samiel bellowed. He hurried toward her with heavy, aggressive strides. "When were you planning to reveal *this* information to us?

"You want to have a go, Samiel? Don't let the fancy dress stop you." Anaba stood up to face him, her head tilted to one side in defiance. "Word of advice: you might want to summon your scythe. Then when it's over, we can say it was a fair fight." The bib pendant about her neck flashed, emitting an ethereal illumination around her in a circular pattern that shimmered on the floor.

"The Sigil of Enoch!" Raijin said with dismay. "Have a care, Samiel."

"Stop this!" Wyrmwood cried. "We're in enemy territory. The last thing we should be doing is fighting among ourselves."

"Is there a problem?" a voice asked from the back of the chamber. A tall, pale woman with black hair walked into the exhibit hall through an auxiliary door. She was accompanied by four members of the Black Seraphim, who fanned out to surround their guests.

"What is the meaning of this, Cerberus?" Samiel demanded of her as Lucifer's minions flanked their group. "We are here at your master's invitation."

"You're in no danger, Samiel." The fallen angel turned her head to regard Michael and winked. A malevolent grin revealed unusually pointed canines, as three slate-gray irises in each eye appraised the Horsemen. "We were merely curious. If we meant to engage you, we would have."

"You act as if you'd survive the melee." Raijin laughed sardonically, reaching for the hilt of his saber. "Come, do your worse, cur. I'll see to you in your true form and cut off *all* three of your heads, mount them on a pole, and leave them on the Vestibule Road as a warning not to trifle with the Angel of War!"

"For a prize such as her?" A powerfully built man pointed at Anaba. "I'll take that risk." His left eye was blue, the other green. He stood a foot taller than the rest of the Seraphim with the exception of the one standing beside him. His white-blond hair was tied tightly at the nape of his neck.

"Where you lead, brother, I follow," said his identical twin. The only notable difference between them was his right eye was blue and the other green.

"Scylla? Charybdis?" said a voice just outside the ballroom door. "When Lucifer said to go enjoy the hor d'oeuvres, I don't think he had this in mind." The leader of the Black Seraphim, as designated by a gold sash beneath his sword belt, walked into the exhibit hall. "Leave us."

With a look of mild annoyance, he waited for his fellow Black Seraphim to exit the room. "A playful jest, Mighty Heralds. Forgive them. Being outcasts adversely effects the self-esteem." Crossing a hand over his heart, the Seraphim bowed respectfully. "Allow me to introduce myself."

"You need no introductions here, Loki'el," Samiel said.

"Perhaps to you, brother, but I have not yet been formally presented to the latest Horseman. I bid you fair greetings, Michael, Son of Mikha'el, Son of God." Remaining in a bowed position, he looked up, his mischievous eyes focusing on Anaba. He straightened with a grin. "And you, Daughter of Eden's First Queen. *Especially* you. Well met."

"What's this about, Loki'el?"

"It's about punctuality and how much Lucifer hates tardiness." Loki'el stood at parade rest with his hands behind his back. "My master requests your presence for the 'Requiem to the Dawn.'" He gestured with an extended arm toward the auxiliary door and the darkened hallway beyond it.

Michael stared into the adjoining corridor, unable to shake the feeling of being led to his execution. "Someone want to clue me in about this 'Requiem to the Dawn'?"

"It's a dance that recreates the Battle of the Eternal Throne – the First Celestial War – when Lucifer fell from Heaven," Wyrmwood explained. "During the song, couples retire from the dance floor. When the music ends, Lucifer is all that remains... because he was the last to fall."

"Black Seraphim, you are called to order!" Loki'el shouted, standing at attention by the door. Hailing his call, the angels drew their sabers, saluted, and crossed the blades to create an archway into the ballroom.

Serra jumped in terror, steadied only by Samiel's arm. "Why does the story of Damocles suddenly come to mind?"

"If the Apocalypse was coming, my good lady," Samiel said, "you would be among the first to know."

"I lost my temper," Michael whispered. Regretting his cruel treatment of her, he glanced down at Anaba and took her hand. She allowed him to intertwine his fingers between hers. Relieved that she did not pull away, he brought her hand up to his chest and across his heart. "I'm not asking for forgiveness, gunny. I need to earn that." He felt his voice cracking. "I just need to know you're with me."

She held his gaze, almost defiantly, and then relented, bowing her head. Stepping to his left side, she took his arm and whispered, "Oo-rah."

CHAPTER 42

Vying for space beneath a gossamer canopy of silver streamers, a hundred couples maneuvered for a place on the ballroom floor. Even among the rich and powerful, there was an exclusive pecking order that commanded respect. Michael lost sight of his fellow Horsemen and his mother, who were swept away in a sea of black tailcoats and gowns.

"Ladies and gentlemen," said an announcer over the PA system, "it is with great pleasure that I present the evening's guest of honor, Mr Michael J. Childs."

The room went dark. A solitary spotlight pierced the shadows, highlighting Michael and Anaba. Genteel applause, muffled by gloved hands, broke the stillness. Michael bowed stiffly at the unwelcome attention, while Anaba stood immobile at his side. The ballroom lights slowly came back up with a hypnotic ambiance and the whisper of violins.

"Tonight's music for the 'Requiem to the Dawn' will be provided by members of the New York Philharmonic-Symphony orchestra, who will be accompanying Ms. Loren Allred for her rendition of 'Never Enough.'"

The haunting chords of a piano drifted from the orchestra wing. A twinge of panic seized Michael's heart. Every eye in the room was on him and the woman in his arms. Fortunately, his extensive travels had exposed him to a variety of cultural dance traditions. From the Irish Highland Jig to the Scandinavian Waltz. He felt confident even in a crowded field of pampered aristocrats.

"Mind if I take point?" Holding Anaba's right hand in his left, Michael wrapped his arm about her waist.

The strings section produced a resonance in the room, underscoring the lyrics with an unrequited longing. Michael guided Anaba in a slow, graceful circle across the dance floor. Spinning and twirling on his arm, the Marine followed through every step. After the applause ended, they were joined by their fellow dancers.

"You've done this before," Michael said with a grin.

"I was on a diplomatic track at one point," she replied, swaying in his embrace. "Ballroom dancing was a BS-MOS."

"BS-MOS?"

"Bullshit-Military Occupational Specialty."

With each rotation, dozens of couples left the dance floor, falling away like spring blossoms in a wind. A third of the revelers removed themselves with no prompting and stood watching from the perimeter.

Michael saw his mother for the first time, agilely spiraling with the grace of a seasoned dancer in Samiel's arms. She was nodding earnestly to whatever the Horseman was saying, her eyes often falling away from his gaze. "Those two seem awfully chummy. Wonder what they're talking about?"

"If he's making a move on her," Anaba said, "I'll happily take a swing at him."

He chuckled and guided her to the left and then back to the right as the rotation of the dance shifted like a tide. "Think you could beat him?" He glanced down at the bib pendant his father had given her.

"Might want to evacuate these civilians. Throwing down with Death would be a literal clusterfuck of biblical proportions."

"I'm sorry, Anaba," Michael said, breathless, his heart racing within his chest. "I'm so sorry. For a lot of things. I never meant–"

"This isn't the time, Michael."

"There may never be a better time," he persisted, despite her cold stare. "Did he hurt you? During the forging? Did my father hurt you?"

"Michael."

"Anaba, please. I need to know."

"How do you expect me to answer that? I've been shot. Three times. Blown thirty feet by an RPG. Tortured as part of my training. But the forging?" She sighed. "It was like nothing I've ever experienced." Anaba laid her head on his shoulder. "It was like being drowned. Skinned. Incinerated. Starved to death. All at the same time. Is that what you wanted to hear?"

"I honestly don't know what I expected." Resting his chin on her head, Michael tightened his embrace. "This is my fault. All of it."

Anaba squeezed his hand. "Everything happens for a reason. Whether we like it or not. I've been looking for my purpose for a long time. So long that I had forgotten what purpose looked like. What it felt like."

"And now?" Michael swept her backwards and held her just inches above the floor, feeling her relax in his arms.

"I swore an oath to defend my country against all enemies, foreign and domestic. I consider angels to be on that list." The conviction in her eyes was real. She held onto him as he pulled her back to her feet. "My purpose is you, Michael. Protecting you. From them. Whatever it takes."

"Not sure I'm worthy, gunny," he whispered, reveling in the curve of her hip beneath his hand.

"I would have killed you by now if you weren't."

Michael laughed, nearly missing a beat of their waltz. Three couples were all that remained by the crescendo of the song. Inhaling the scent of sweet lavender and vanilla from Anaba's skin, Michael hardly noticed the dwindling ranks. "Do you want to know what Natalia said to me last night?"

Anaba stiffened. "So I'm not the only one keeping secrets?"

Michael leaned over her until his lips touched the folds of her ear. "Love exists without boundaries," he whispered, repeating Natalia's final words. "Not even death."

She went limp in his arms, but he held her firmly. "Natalia's wedding vow."

"I love you, Anaba Raines." He tilted his head and kissed her, reveling in the warmth of her breath on his face. Her eyes softened. Encouraged by the involuntarily arch of her back, he drew her into his passion and kissed her again, finding no resistance in her parted lips.

The world ceased to exist, so did their dance. Michael grinned as Anaba wrapped her arms around his neck and embraced him. His heart ached for her as they stood together, motionless, beneath the spotlight. Cupping her face in his hands, he kissed her forehead and then her lips again. "I could get used to that."

"That makes two of us." She laid her head on his shoulder and melted into his arms.

Every couple had left the dance floor, except for them, Lucifer and his consort. Michael felt the fallen angel's gaze boring into him. "I don't plan on surrendering the high ground, gunny." He looked down into her face, a glint of mischief in his eyes. "My father cast Lucifer from Heaven. I intend to do the same thing on this dance floor. You with me?"

An equally mischievous smile broke across her face. "Oo – fucking – rah."

The last bars of the song faded with the final notes of the singer's voice. The ballroom was silent, with one exception: the forlorn sound of footsteps from their gregarious host. Upstaged by a kiss, Lucifer Morningstar and Lilith begrudgingly retreated from the dance floor.

Michael and Anaba stood alone under the spotlight. The resulting applause was thunderous.

"Ladies and gentlemen, dinner will be served among the majestic treasures of the ancient pharaohs of the Eighteenth

Dynasty," the announcer said. "Please make your way to the Egyptian gallery to be seated."

"What a finale!" Serra cried, kissing Michael and Anaba on the cheek. "I always knew my son could be a gentleman, but a romantic?"

Flanked by his Black Seraphim, Lucifer led Lilith across the ballroom to join them. "Dessert before dinner, nephew?" Though the inscrutable grin masked his bitterness, the fallen angel's voice was thick with sarcasm. "I'm certain we can find you more private accommodation *somewhere* in the museum. Perhaps the cell of the Marquis de Sade? Or the boudoir of Catherine the Great? Do you have a personal preference?"

"Sorry, Uncle," Michael said, taking Anaba's hand. "I got a bit carried away."

"A word before dinner? I'm sure you can wait, you've already had your *appetizer.*" Lucifer gestured to a set of stairs leading up to the second floor.

"Michael?" Serra's smile faded. "I don't think–"

"Sweet Serra, does he really need your signature on a permission slip? It's well past time you cut the apron strings, don't you think?"

"You'll understand her hesitation, Lucifer," Samiel challenged. He laid Serra's hand on his sleeve to comfort her.

"And ours," Wyrmwood added.

Lucifer bowed deeply. Taking Serra's other hand in humility, he kissed the back of it. "How rude of me to forget recent tribulations. If it serves to calm your heart, dear lady, the hellacious Anaba may stand watch."

"It's all right, Mom," Michael said. He turned to Lucifer. "Lead the way."

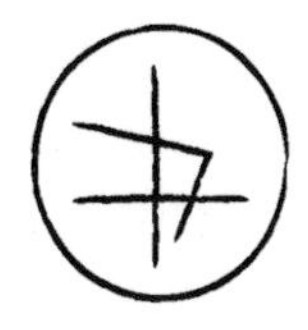

CHAPTER 43

Polished, mahogany banisters framed the ivory staircase leading up from the ballroom floor. Five Black Seraphim escorted the Prince of Hell to the secluded, second-floor overlook.

"Your Nightmare will wait here," Loki'el said to Michael, his gaze intently fixed on Anaba.

The four remaining members of the Black Seraphim approached as Loki'el pulled a crimson velvet rope between Michael and Anaba. They paired off, standing sentinel on opposite sides of the stanchions, effectively separating the Nightmare and her Rider.

"You good?" Michael whispered from the side nearest the stairs.

"Frosty." Undaunted, the Marine locked eyes with Loki'el. "Sound off if you need me."

Straightening his tailcoat, Michael made his way up the stairs to the balcony reserved for VIP guests. The exclusive wing was decorated in beige and gold with matching lounge chairs and tables across the floor. Lucifer sat at the keys of a grand piano and played a melancholy excerpt of the Lacrimosa from Mozart's 'Requiem in D minor'.

"That was quite a stunt you pulled, usurping my dance. I've slaughtered angels for far less." Accepting a glass of champagne from a waiter, Lucifer saluted Michael with a wry grin. "I fancy boldness, Son of Mikha'el, but there's only room for *one* morningstar in this great big universe."

Michael bowed his head. "Considering all the trouble you've gone through to honor me, the last thing I want to offer is any disrespect. I apologize, Uncle."

"Humility?" An astonished Lucifer stared at him. "Not a trait I'm used to in humans. Or angels. But then, you're not quite human *or* angel, are you?" Crossing his legs, he fidgeted in his breast pocket. "Tell me, Nephew, how does it feel to walk between two worlds and not fit in either one?"

"Lonely." Michael glanced back down to the main floor. Anaba was standing where he left her. Loki'el was unsuccessfully attempting to engage her in idle banter.

"My Black Seraphim are under strict orders not to engage the Horsemen nor the sole Nightmare among you." Lucifer held out a silver case of hand-rolled cigarettes. "Smoke?"

Michael shook his head politely. "No, thank you."

"Blunt?" He opened a different compartment in the case. The pungent scent of marijuana wafted into the air. "These are a Jamaican-blend, one of the many perks of this world." He grinned, choosing one for himself.

"I don't smoke," Michael said.

"Pity, you look like you could use a vice… or two." Lucifer tucked the blunt between his teeth. "Anubis, a light please." The Seraphim promptly came forward with a lighter.

"Anubis? Scylla? Cerberus? Loki?" Michael snorted softly. "I'm beginning to wonder if any of the mythology I studied in college is accurate."

"It's the interpretation that can be a bitch. You've heard of *Pride and Prejudice?* The angelic version of the classic is called *Pride and Disobedience.* Every fallen angel in Hell has their own chapter, including the Horsemen." Lucifer inhaled deeply, the tip of the blunt glowing between his fingers, and stared intently at Michael.

Cheeks flushing from the unwarranted attention, Michael

cleared his throat. His scalp itched, as it always did when he felt an urgent sense of anxiety. "Is there a reason you asked me here?"

"Ssh, don't ruin the moment, nephew," Lucifer grinned wantonly. The canines of his teeth were unnaturally long, lending him the appearance of a true predator. "So far, you've proven to be far better company than your predecessor."

Tired of the comparisons, Michael bit his lip and exhaled. "So everyone tells me."

"By our nature, angels are arrogant. Why shouldn't we be? We came first." Lucifer took a long drag and held his breath, savoring the marijuana. "It's living up to that nature that gets us in trouble with the All Mighty."

"For Mankind, the off ramp was free will," Michael said. "Are you saying the exit for angels was pride?"

"Exit? It's the bloody expressway! Paved with nothing but good intentions. But it's never enough, not for the Father." Lucifer's face darkened, the shadows creating irregular, angular shapes across his brows and cheekbones. "And when it comes to power, He doesn't share well, not even with His Elohim."

"Why are you telling me this?"

"So that you will understand the consequences of disobedience. Take Loki'el, for example. He had one simple task: assassinate the pretender Odin. What he did was set in motion a series of events that led to Ragnarok and plunged the universe into chaos."

"Ragnarok was a mistake?"

"Thankfully, there was a reset button." Lucifer's eyes glowed with the aura of the burning embers as he inhaled. "When the Father cast Odin and the rest of that mead-swilling pantheon into Hell, he cast Loki'el down with them. For an angel, there are repercussions for coloring outside the lines. Even a *half*-angel."

"You're talking about the Nephilim?" Michael asked defensively.

"Free will makes you a free agent. You're a wild card. That's why the Grigori want you dead." Lucifer stood up and leaned against the balcony railing.

"And what about you?"

Exhaling smoke into Michael's face, Lucifer grinned malevolently. "The Grigori believe the Nephilim are inferior. I'm not so sure."

Michael took a step through the smoke and stared into the Devil's eyes, just inches from his face. "Not sure if I'm inferior? Or not sure if you want me dead?"

"You have your father's eyes, Son of Mikha'el, and his penchant for being a *total* killjoy." Lucifer's eyes went black with the vitriol in his voice. A chill swept across the room. Clearing his throat, he blinked until the whites of his eyes returned to normal. "Speaking of Heaven's favorite MVP, may I see it? My brother's war lance? I hear you've taken possession."

Michael nervously chewed the inside of his lip. He didn't feel in a position to refuse. He glanced down at the dance floor. Anaba was gazing up at him, as if sensing, implicitly, that the ante was about to be raised.

Holding his right hand out to the side, Michael summoned a Bitter Harvest. The war lance materialized in his grip, and he wrapped his fingers around the shaft. Water dripped from the obsidian blade and rolled across the fabric of his glove, leaving no moisture on the cloth. A small puddle pooled at the base beside Michael's shoe.

"And there it is. After all this time," Lucifer whispered, retreating a step. "It's easy to recognize from this angle." He slowly ran his index finger along the flathead of the blade and across the black feathers fastened below it.

The ominous hiss of steel echoed in the balcony ceiling as Lucifer's bodyguards drew their sabers.

"Edgy bastards those Black Seraphim. Always spoiling for a good fight," Lucifer said, transfixed by the lance. "Handy if you decide to crash a Republican Super-PAC picnic."

"Boss?" Cerberus said, fingering the grip of her sword hilt. The heightened concern in her voice caused the other Seraphim to take note from the floor below. They all reached for their weapons.

"Stay where you are, or I'll clip your wings myself. No reason for worry, or is there, nephew?" Lucifer asked, his eyes narrowed in challenge.

"Not unless you give me one." Michael tightened his grip on the lance. "Let's dispense with all the high society bullshit. Why am I here?"

"Fair enough. I am often referred to as the Prince of Lies. A malignant misnomer," Lucifer said. "If anything, I'm all about the truth, which is what led to my fall. I brought you here because I wanted to see your truth for myself."

"And?" Despite the scent of sandalwood incense, Michael detected the distinct smell of brimstone. He smiled.

"Frankly, I'm underwhelmed. I don't tell you this to be insulting. *I like you,*" Lucifer said, deliberately annunciating his words. "Many wagered you wouldn't make it this far." He nodded to where Anaba was standing on the dance floor in her gown. "They forgot to factor *her* into the odds."

"Is this a pep talk or a threat?"

"Neither. It's a warning, nephew. Allow me to paint a harsh reality for you, just as you painted my sky with mercury vapor. There are forces aligning against you. Powerful forces from within and without. If you are not half the angel your father is," Lucifer chuckled at the irony, "you won't survive what's coming."

Michael's mouth went dry. "Would that disappoint you?"

"Immensely. Consider yourself warned, Son of Mikha'el, Son of God." Lucifer took a champagne flute from a waiter's tray and doused his joint in another. "Enjoy your dinner and cocktails."

* * *

Lucifer watched as Michael descended the staircase in haste to be welcomed back into Anaba's arms. The couple gave one anxious look back up to the balcony. Lucifer saluted them with his champagne glass. "Terrible thing to have an itch you can't scratch, eh, Loki'el?"

"I can see why Caim wants her so badly." Loki'el stared from the overlook to where Michael and Anaba joined Mayor Watersworth and Wyrmwood. "If Michael Childs were anyone else–"

"Careful, brother, you're drooling. It's more likely she'd add another feather and your name to her crest than serve any master but him."

Loki'el frowned, his disappointment evident. "Still, we were right to warn the boy. He has got a quality Caim Seere lacks."

"Conviction!" Lucifer nodded. "I agree."

"The Nephilim will likely thrive under the Son of Mikha'el," Loki'el said. "Maybe even rise against you."

"The best ally is not the one who owes you something, but the *near* ally who *thinks* he does," Lucifer replied.

Loki'el chuckled, straightening the breast lapel of his livery. "How do you want me to respond to Caim Seere's request for an audience?"

"The crops shall be as stone, and the soil like unto dust... for Famine shall consume all the land," Lucifer replied. "This is a family matter, Loki'el. I don't consider Caim family. Tell him he's on his own."

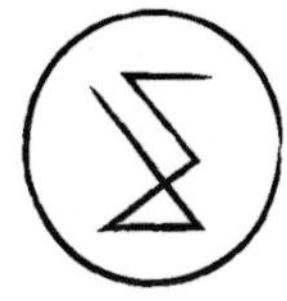

CHAPTER 44

White headstones lined the hallowed grounds of the Calverton National Cemetery. Arranged in meticulous rows, the markers created a solemn memorial to commemorate the sacrifice of fallen soldiers. An emissary of the living, a sole Marine, stood among them, surrounded by the silent, marble sentinels that forever stood at attention.

In full dress blues, Anaba peered down at Natalia's grave, clasping a folded American flag beneath her arm. The flag had been presented to her in tribute by the United States Army, and was a token to acknowledge Natalia's life and military service. The chaplain's solemn words of benediction haunted her. *Remember those who have gone to their glory, but shed no tears… for their deeds will live forever, watered in the blood of honor and valor.*

"Anaba?" Michael whispered. Two funerals over the course of a week had taken a devastating toll on both of them. First Bryana's, and then three days later, Natalia's funeral with full military honors.

"Can you give us a minute?" she asked.

"Stay as long as you like." He ran his hand across her shoulder and left her alone, walking back to the pedestrian path.

In her peripheral vision, Anaba saw Ziri staring off into the horizon. Clutching the ancestral silver cross in his hand, he mumbled Tuareg prayers of safe passage. A few feet away from him in the shade of an elm, Elijah, Wyrmwood, and Rachel talked quietly among themselves as Michael joined them.

Anaba sank down on her haunches to be at eye level with the grave marker, running a white-gloved finger over the name etched into the marble. "Don't give me that look, sarge. I know he's cute, but fuck he can be annoying." She shook her head and chuckled. "You told him your wedding vow?"

The wind shifted, carrying the sharp report of honor guard rifles and the odor of spent gunpowder.

Elbows perched on her thighs, Anaba sighed. "He's got some skills… not like us though. We're in deep shit, mami. But I will make the shore, and I'll drag his ass with me."

She laid the battered dog tags and her wedding ring on top of the gravestone, kissing the cold marble. A tear spilled over her cheek for the first time that day. Wiping it away, she abruptly stood up, took a step back from the headstone, and snapped to attention with a salute. "Semper fi, baby. Over and out."

Michael watched Anaba's farewell, marking the rigor of the Marine's final salute. She then executed an abrupt about-face and slow marched away from the gravestone, never looking back.

As he went to meet her, four black SUVs sped down the access road and pulled up in a line in the parking lot. Several occupants in black suits spilled out of the vehicles. They moved with a chilling, hive-like precision that made the hairs on the back of Michael's neck stand erect. "Heads up," he said, tapping Elijah and Rachel on the shoulder.

"Who the fuck are they?" Elijah watched as they swarmed the most recent gravesite and the only mourner left near it.

"Gunnery Sergeant Anaba Raines," said a man, without identifying himself. "You are under arrest for war crimes committed on foreign soil during military action authorized by the United States government."

"Who the hell are you?" Retrieving his badge, Michael flashed his credentials.

"Stand down, Special Agent Childs. You've got no jurisdiction here."

"Last time I checked the FBI was the home team. The CIA were the visitors," Elijah retorted. "You're out of bounds."

"Witty, Special Agent Pope. I'm CIA Special Agent Paul Steiner out of the Office of Counter-Intelligence. Someday, you and I will be having a little chat about the info you *coaxed* off our servers. But for now, in case you didn't hear me, you're to stand down." He turned to Anaba with a sardonic grin. "It's been a long time, Warlander. You remember your old handler, don't you?"

"If it smells like shit, it's probably shit." Anaba looked at the number of armed men surrounding her. "Running a little heavy, aren't you?"

"Seemed appropriate," Steiner said with a chuckle. "You *were* a heavy hitter. One of my best."

"I always knew the Agency would send somebody one day. Never figured it'd be a spineless rodent like you."

"Ah, that mouth." Steiner put his hands on his hips and grinned. "I've missed you, Raines, but we're about to get reacquainted. Cuff her."

"Sergeant Raines is a federal consultant on a multiple homicide case under FBI jurisdiction!" Michael tried to break through to her. Three officers restrained him, twisting his arms behind his back and taking him to the ground.

"Spooky Ivan, get your fucking hands off my partner!" Elijah yelled. "Or your next burn notice'll be your obituary." He rushed the officer kneeling on Michael's neck and shoved him away.

"This gives me all the jurisdiction I need." Steiner held up a set of papers inside a blue envelope. "I'd share these documents with you, but the intel inside is well above your pay grade."

Anaba remained at attention as her hands were cuffed behind her back. She glared at the ground where one of the arresting CIA officers had discarded the American flag.

Spewing a steady stream of Tuareg profanities, Ziri lunged at one of the CIA agents restraining Michael and punched him in the throat. As the man fell, the boy grabbed his head and slammed his knee into his face. Alarmed by the sight of a colleague down and bleeding, one of the three operatives released Michael and drew a Glock 17. The distinctive sound of a hammer cocking echoed in the stillness of the cemetery, but it wasn't from his weapon.

Rachel jammed the muzzle of her Springfield XD-E into the back of the officer's head, hard enough to make him wince in pain. "Pulling a gun? On a *kid*? You compensating for something? Drop it before I drop you."

"Iv'baato," Wyrmwood whispered the Enochian conjuration for affliction and swatted the last man holding Michael in the head with her purse. He reached for his face as pus trickled from the tear duct of his eye. "Tut-tut. Severe conjunctivitis can cause blindness when not properly treated. You might want to get that checked." The Horseman snatched the gun from his holster and tossed it.

"Everyone stay calm," Steiner said. "We're all just doing our jobs, right? A little inter-agency cooperation goes a long way." He turned to one of his operatives. "Make the call."

"That *cooperation* seems a little one-sided from where I'm standing." Back on his feet, Michael finished off the bloodied officer with a right hook and left him unconscious among the grave markers.

Ziri drew the bone knife from its scabbard, but Michael caught him by the waist and held him back. *"Essesnăn-kăy Măssinaɣ!"*

Anaba laughed, and Steiner turned to her. "What's he saying?"

"Something about God causing you pain. It's the Tuareg version of fuck off and die."

"You're going to get the kid killed, Raines," Steiner warned. He nodded to the half-dozen weapons glinting in the afternoon sun. "Call him off!"

"Ziri, abdad!" Anaba ordered. "This is not the desert. Nor the place to find your soul."

"Wăr ăksodăg wăla!"

"I know you're not afraid of them, but this isn't the path your grandfather saw for you."

Ziri lowered the knife. Wyrmwood pulled the distraught boy into her arms. He held onto her, refusing to break eye contact with Anaba.

"Put the guns away," Steiner said. He gave the thumbs up as one of the officers whispered in his ear. "Special Agent Childs, may I suggest you answer that call?"

"What call?" On cue, his cell phone vibrated insistently. Michael glanced at the caller identification and rolled his eyes at Elijah. "Assistant Director Rathan."

"Oh, shit, this can't be good." Elijah holstered his sidearm, signaling for Rachel to do the same.

"Special Agent Childs, you are interfering with the apprehension of a war criminal. Stand down immediately," Rathan's voice said. "This matter is beyond our authority."

"We're done here." Steiner impishly winked at Michael and gestured to his officers to move out. "Take her to the car. If anyone tries to stop you, shoot them." He followed behind his men as they led Anaba to their vehicles.

Michael turned back to his phone, "Director Rathan–"

"You're being recalled, Agent Childs." Rathan's voice was calm at the other end of the line. "You and Agent Pope are to report to my office immediately for debriefing."

"Recalled?" Michael protested. "What about my team?"

"You no longer have a team. If you hope to salvage what's left of your career in the FBI, get back to Manhattan. Now." Rathan curtly hung up.

"What kind of bullshit is this?" Elijah ran a frustrated hand over the back of his neck. "Spooks show up and we're suddenly demoted to Cub Scouts?"

Michael closed his eyes and massaged the tension over the bridge of his nose. "Rachel, I need you to give Dr Wyrmwood and Ziri a ride back to my mom's place."

"I'm not leaving your side." Wyrmwood stared after the detail of CIA walking away with Anaba handcuffed in their midst. "Especially not now."

Michael handed his key fob to Rachel. "Take Ziri to my mom. Tell her what happened. The address is in the GPS." When the junior agent hesitated, he sighed. "I know you're down with the team, Rachel. It's appreciated, but you need to steer clear of this right now."

"Understood, Agent Childs. Come on, Ziri." Rachel took the agitated boy from Wyrmwood's arms, wiped the tears from his cheeks with her palm, and led him to the parking area.

As the procession of black SUVs prepared to leave, Michael watched Steiner climb into the rear of the vehicle. He recognized the profile of the man sitting across from Anaba in the backseat. "Is that who I think it is?" he muttered, pulling at Wyrmwood's pink blazer. "Son of a bitch!"

"Caim Seere. Why am I not surprised?" Wyrmwood said. "Anaba said he had CIA connections."

"Who the hell is that and how do you know him?" Elijah demanded.

"He's responsible for what happened to Anaba and her wife in Syria. Actions that resulted in Natalia being buried here today." He walked back his emotions, struggling to get control of himself, and headed for Elijah's truck. "If we don't do something, Anaba will be next."

"I'll text Samiel and Raijin to see if they can run some interference," Wyrmwood said.

"If Rathan pulled the plug, their credentials won't get them very far." Elijah held the front passenger door open for her. "Another hour, maybe two, and the carriage turns back into an ordinary pumpkin."

"Trust me, partner," Michael said, slamming the door, "when it comes to those two – there's nothing ordinary about them."

CHAPTER 45

Michael fastened the button of his coat and rushed off the elevator before the doors had fully opened. Elijah and Wyrmwood scrambled after him. It was late evening, and the Manhattan field offices on the 23rd floor of the Jacob K. Javits building were empty, most agents opting for late dinner plans with their partners to review their caseloads.

As they came around the corner into the shared office space, the administrative assistant was waiting for them. "Special Agent Childs," Chelsea said, mustering her best smile. "Special Agent Pope. Dr Wyrmwood. Welcome back. Assistant Director Rathan has been expecting you. This way."

"Hello, Mr Ass, meet Mr Foot," Elijah grumbled under his breath. "I hope the two of you get along because you're going to be working together for the next six months."

"EJ," Michael said, "let this fall on my shoulders."

"Not letting you go down alone, Mike. We're neck deep in this shit together. Don't care how it lands."

Chelsea led them through the adjoining corridor to the executive conference room in the rear of the main office suite. "Good luck, Michael." Her anxious eyes flashed a warning to the agent and his partner. "You're going to need it." Clasping her hands in front of her, Chelsea regarded Wyrmwood with a respectful nod. "Dr Wyrmwood, can I get you some coffee or tea while you wait in the lounge?"

"Neither. I'm going with them, sweetheart," Wyrmwood replied. The tone of her voice refuted any further question.

"Suit yourself." Chelsea cut her eyes back to Michael and knocked on the window. She waited for a moment before opening the door.

Wyrmwood pushed through Elijah and forced her way into the room ahead of them. Like penitents on a pilgrimage, the agents followed.

Assistant Director Rathan was waiting for them, sitting at the head of an oblong conference table. The rest of the expensive Corinthian leather chairs were empty, except for the smug specter of McKabe. The agent's left arm was cradled in a black sling. Both were avidly looking at the graphic images that flashed across the widescreen television in the front of the room.

The current picture showed the remains of three Syrian soldiers. The corpses were blackened, bloated, and grotesque. With the click of a remote, the image shifted, depicting the burned-out hulk of a Ford F-150. Still smoldering from a rocket hit, the husk of a .50 caliber machine gun leaned haphazardly in the remains of the bed.

Close-ups showed a charred, mangled body slumped over the gun. The driver, or what remained of him, was hanging out of the crumpled doorframe. His head was partially caved in. Blown through the windshield, the passenger laid sprawled across the truck's buckled hood. With no tongue, his mandible was frozen open in a silent scream.

"These images are from a classified CIA dossier handed to me earlier this morning," Rathan said.

"What is this?" Michael asked.

"This is the handiwork of Gunnery Sergeant Anaba Raines, aka Warlander, United States Marine Corps, who was under contract with Langley. These images were taken during the three months that Raines went rogue after an unfortunate incident involving her wife, Master Sergeant Natalia Alfaro-Raines, US Army."

He clicked to bring up an image of Natalia in her service uniform. The next picture was the horrific image of what was left of the soldier after the grenade attack in the desert.

"Raines' CIA handlers were fine with her settling the score for her wife, but she went too far when she started taking out their more valuable assets."

The next image was taken inside a small, one-story house. Seven headless occupants sat at a rectangular table. On a white, linen cloth, their untouched meal had been laid out with care, arranged around the bloody centerpieces of their severed heads.

"The Agency issued a burn notice. But the gate was already open, and she was in the wind. A month after this *last supper,* a trio of insurgent leaders turned up dead. They had to use DNA to verify their remains. That's when Raines went dark. She never came out of the desert. The CIA disavowed any knowledge of her, so the Marine Corps declared her dead – killed in action. Until she popped up mysteriously as a member of your task force."

Three months. Michael wondered if that was the time Caim Seere had given the Marine to settle her affairs before taking her to Hell to become a Nightmare. He could not fathom Anaba's anguish after the grenade attack or imagine her rage in the aftermath.

"Sergeant Alfaro-Raines died four days ago, sir. She was buried today at Calverton National Cemetery. One of the men who took Raines into custody at the funeral had something to do with her death." Michael propped his hands on the table and stared at Rathan. "What are they trying to hide?"

"Agent Childs, the FBI has a duty to be model Eagle Scouts. We help little old ladies across the street and save kittens from trees, while taking down domestic terrorists and foreign extremists who threaten our borders. We exist so that Americans can sleep at night." Rathan put the remote down on the table, leaving a close up of the gruesome dinner on the screen. "Our cousins at Langley? *They're* the ones who create the things that go bump in the night."

The Assistant Director was baiting him. Michael had little choice except to follow the trail of breadcrumbs. "That's not an answer. Why is the CIA suddenly so interested in my investigation?

"You brought a war criminal onto an investigative team of so-called experts," he replied, glancing at Wyrmwood, "and harbored her under the banner of the FBI. You've tainted every level of this case and disgraced the reputation of this country's oldest and most beloved institution."

"The only thing tainted here is your conclusion that Anaba Raines is a serial killer," Wyrmwood said.

"Dr Wyrmwood, your presence here is a courtesy. The credentials you're wearing are no longer valid. Please return them before you leave the building." Rathan took a deep, audible breath and exhaled, an inscrutable expression of satisfaction on his face. "Bodies are stacking up in our backyard. The public wants answers. We have failed to provide them. The CIA has claimed jurisdiction of the case."

"Since when?!" Michael demanded.

"Since three hours ago."

"The CIA handles international, not domestic cases. This is *our* territory," Elijah argued. "Unless... you gave them the green light?"

Rathan tapped a pack of documents folded in a blue envelope against the table. "Raines is wanted for international war crimes. Atrocities, which she brought home. Therefore, her apprehension is to be handled by the Agency. She is the CIA's blunder. As a colleague, I am obliged to help them, especially if it makes my problem go away."

Michael was tired of the subtle cat and mouse game of semantics. "Plausible deniability."

"Correct. While the CIA cleans their house, I'm obliged to clean mine." The Assistant Director pivoted in the chair and leaned back against the headrest. "As of right now, Special Agent Childs, you're suspended."

Michael took a step back as if struck. "On what grounds?"

"Incompetence comes to mind. For a start. This homicide investigation has seen one blunder after another," Agent McKabe said with a snicker from the corner. "Oh, and there's the issue of aiding and abetting a war criminal, which the Bureau frowns on."

"I'll need your badge and your gun." Rathan pointed to the top of the conference table with his index finger like an overly strict schoolteacher demanding candy contraband from a student in detention.

Elijah stared, slack jawed. "Suspended? For how long?"

"Given the circumstance – indefinitely, pending a full internal review." Rathan straightened a wrinkle in his suit coat and scrutinized a possible speck of dust.

Indefinitely… it was a death knell. Michael stood paralyzed with the realization that his career was over.

"Are you deaf, Childs?" McKabe asked. "The Assistant Director requested your badge and your gun."

"Mr Childs' delayed response is expected, Agent McKabe. It's simply his way of adjusting to his new reality."

"This is bullshit!" Elijah said.

"Careful, Agent Pope. Your future with the Bureau is nearly as tenuous but I'm prepared to spare your career any public humiliation. Consider it a small token of appreciation, provided your partner goes quietly by the wayside."

"You're blackmailing us!" Elijah lunged at Rathan in fury, but Michael intercepted him with an outstretched arm.

"I suggest you go home before I change my mind." Rathan tugged at his tie. "You'll be briefed on your new assignment in the morning."

"You slippery son of a bitch!"

"Still interested in a career with the FBI, Special Agent Pope? These are not idle threats." Despite the menace of his words, Rathan's expression was one of amusement. "Go pack whatever personal belongings you have at your desk and leave the building or leave your badge and gun on the table."

Michael put a hand on Elijah's arm to stop him as his partner reached for the requested items. "Let this fall on my shoulders, EJ."

"Mike, we're partners! Up to our neck in this shit, remember! Son of a bitch is crazy!" Elijah glared at the Assistant Director, the whites of his eyes showing even in the dim light. He pointed at Rathan. "You're crazy!"

"I'll meet you in the office. Give me a few minutes." Michael took his best friend by the shoulders and turned him toward the door.

With an exasperated sigh, Elijah stormed out of the conference room, slamming the door behind him.

Michael placed his Glock 19M on the table in front of Rathan and pulled his badge and credentials from his waistband before laying them beside the 9mm. "Where are you sending him?"

"Somewhere cold, remote, and very far away."

"Are you done being a vindictive ass?"

"Almost." Rathan folded his hands in his lap and met Michael's defiant eyes with a grin. "Don't bother stopping by your desk. I'll have Chelsea pack your things. She'll call when the box is ready." He yawned, glancing at his watch. "I'd rather not embarrass you further by having you escorted to the door. Be certain to take the good doctor with you."

"You should really get that scratchy throat checked," Wyrmwood said, throwing her badge in Rathan's face. "It's flu season, you know?"

Puzzled, Rathan narrowed his eyes. "I'm not ill."

"Give it a minute." She followed Michael out of the

conference room and slammed the door so hard the glass in the window frame rattled.

Michael stood outside in the hallway. His pragmatic sense of preservation ran through a list of different positions he could take in his field of Archaeology. But there was only one job he wanted, and it required a badge and a gun. Stunned by the suspension, he paced in an abbreviated line, then pivoted in midstride and punched the wall.

The wooden panel splintered. Gold and green maille manifested over his bloody knuckles, glittering like water over his wrist and coat sleeve.

"Michael," Wyrmwood whispered. "Not here."

He took a deep breath. "I'd like nothing more than to go back in there and break Rathan's neck."

"If Raijin were here, he'd go with you." She took his arm and led him down the hallway toward the elevators. "Trust me. Feminine guile and subtlety are far crueler mistresses. Don't forget my specialty at WHO."

"You gave Rathan an STD?"

"A little tickle of oral gonorrhea." Wyrmwood curled her tongue in the corner of her mouth. "When this is over, I'm going to send Kali to visit him with a nasty side order of crotch crickets."

Michael stared at the blood dripping on the floor at his feet. Shoulders slumped in defeat, he took a step towards the office and stopped. His path would take him directly by Elijah. Retreating back in the opposite direction, he made his way through another corridor to the stairs.

"Where are you going?" Wyrmwood asked, trotting after him. The sound of her high heels reverberated in the empty hallway like marbles falling down concrete steps. "Michael?"

"There's a bar down the street." He was overwhelmed, too flustered to look at her.

"You're going out for a drink?" Wyrmwood ran in front of him and blocked the way into the stairwell. "We're in crisis mode."

"I need to get out of here and wrap my mind around this," he said, pushing by her. "For Anaba's sake. And my own."

"And Elijah?"

"You heard Rathan," Michael said. "If I go quietly, EJ keeps his job."

Wyrmwood kicked off her stilettos and trotted down the stairs ahead of him. "Fine. First round's on me."

Agent McKabe stared out of the window before closing the blinds. He locked the conference room door. "We could have killed them. Childs and his pathetic, loose-end of a partner."

"With Pestilence standing between them?"

"Wyrmwood may be a Horseman, but she's not invincible. Virtues are known for their passion, not their battle skills." McKabe leaned against the door, scowling in the shadows.

"You sound overeager, Kokabiel."

"Every breath Childs takes is a reminder of my failure." Taking his arm from the sling, McKabe bundled the cloth into a ball and threw it onto the table.

Rathan nodded. "We may need to temporarily suspend operations in this area, but not before one last ritual."

"Childs? Give me another chance, Rathaniel." McKabe sat on the corner of the table, flexing his injured shoulder. "With the Nightmare out of the way, there will not be a better opportunity for me to redeem myself."

"Your commitment is unrivaled, brother."

"Still, you have doubts?"

Rathan nodded pensively. "Gather your team. Kill Childs." He held up a cautionary finger, tempering the Grigori soldier's enthusiasm. "I don't care about Wyrmwood. She's not your priority."

"What about Rollins?" McKabe stood up, leaning over the table. "Do you mean to truly clean house?"

"Send Nuriel to deal with her."

"And Pope?"

Sitting back in his chair, Rathan rested his elbows on the arms. "Use him as a lure, and then kill him. I can't think of a more fitting reassignment."

CHAPTER 46

It was a toss-up as to what hurt more. Her battered face or the rest of her bruised body. Wrenched joints ached like dental drills boring through enamel. She had been in enough barroom brawls to recognize the damage. Lying face down on concrete, Anaba coaxed her bloated eyelids to open.

Her tongue scraped across the roof of her mouth like sandpaper on tree bark. She managed to cough, sparing herself the indignity of retching at the taste of stale blood. The involuntary reflex exacerbated her pain. She groaned and pressed her feverish forehead into the cold, concrete floor.

Her wrists were bound behind her back. She heard the clinking of the chains attached to the cuffs even before she felt the weight of them. They rattled noisily against the floor. *Iron.* The scent of it sickened her. Friction from the manacles clamped over her woolen uniform had rubbed her wrists raw.

Anaba pulled her torso up and backwards, sitting on her legs. A second set of iron shackles bound her ankles, jabbing into the backs of her thighs. The iron collar padlocked around her neck was the greater insult. Thankfully someone had loosened the high, tight collar of her uniform blouse before securing it.

Three splotches of blood stained the concrete where she had been lying. A split in her lip, caked nostrils, and a cut above her left brow accounted for the blood loss. Closing her eyes, she rubbed her thumbs across her knuckles, disappointed to find them unblemished. Confirmation that the fight had been one sided.

Her last memory was of being handcuffed and herded into the back of an SUV. One operative held a taser on her in case she resisted when the black hood went over her head. But she didn't resist. The hood was protocol, and so was the cocktail injected into her neck to knock her out. However, the beating that followed was unnecessary, given that she was unconscious.

"Bastards." She scowled, spitting bloody phlegm onto the floor.

Iron shackles were not part of the usual CIA tool kit either, at least, not on domestic soil. Neither was Enochian magic. She recognized the containment glyphs surrounding her on the floor. The symbols were incorporated into an intricate network of circles drawn with chalk, salt, and blood.

They were designed to confine her true nature and prevent any possibility of transformation. Without transformation, she was denied access to any powers she possessed in her Nightmare form. It was potent abjuration magic. The iron restraints were a secondary measure, and equally effective.

Anaba let her head fall back onto her shoulders. Her dreadlocks hung loosely down to her waist and dampened the sound of the metal. She feigned disorientation, stretching the kinks in her neck while getting a sense of where she was being held.

The hardened aircraft shelter was eighty by two hundred fifty feet, spacious, partially built underground and reinforced with steel walls and doors. An Agency asset, she had spent time in similar off-grid sites and recognized the spartan furnishings of the temporary safehouse, which was probably somewhere on the outskirts of the city near the airport. A small Cessna jet sat at the far end of the room. A team of fifteen armed men in tactical gear stood guard near the plane and both the exits.

Anaba snorted. *PMOOs*. They were paramilitary operations officers. Homegrown Agency mercenaries. To alleviate the discomfort of the chafing iron collar, she let her head fall forward and rolled her shoulders. The smaller steel door opened and closed behind her.

"Awake at last." Paul Steiner clapped his hands. He walked into the containment circles and, with a savagery all too familiar to Anaba, punched her in the face. "Comfy, old girl?" The CIA operative shook his hand as he stood behind her.

Knocked to the floor by the blow, Anaba spit fresh blood onto the concrete. "You still hit like a bleeding pussy, Steiner."

"And you still have that filthy mouth." Grabbing her by the hair, he slammed his knee into the side of her head. "That's payback for what your brat did to one of my team," he said with a sardonic laugh, exiting the circle. "Just like old times, eh, Raines?"

"That's affirmative, sir," she replied sarcastically. Dazed by the strike, she rapidly blinked her eyes to clear them of stars.

"You were tough to break, Raines. But then I never really did break you, did I?" Steiner rubbed his knuckles. "No, I had to be careful. If I'd taken you too far over the edge, you wouldn't have become the killer I needed." He grinned, pointing a finger at her. "I left a bit of that wildness in you. Paid off, too."

"If I was so good for business, why'd you double-cross me? And Natalia?" The paralyzed expression of fear in his face was all the confirmation she needed. "Yeah, I figured it out, asshole. Had a lot of time to think when I was in Hell. Unlike you, the Fallen know how to throw a beating." She spit blood in his direction, but could not cover the range to hit him. "What did Caim Seere promise you? 'Cause I assure you, it wasn't enough."

"I never liked you, Raines, or your bitch." Steiner raised his chin, staring down his aquiline nose. "A more lucrative offer came my way."

"You're a sorry shit-brick of a man, Steiner. I've got all the blood on my hands, remember that. You just buried the bodies. Bitch work."

"I'll be a hero by tomorrow morning, Raines. You'll be a disgraced soldier who went rogue in the desert, killing friends and allies, before coming home to turn her wrath on innocent civilians. I'm going to parade you around in chains for the American public before sending you back to Hell where you belong." Steiner grinned impishly, placing his hands on his thighs as if talking down to a dog. "Don't look so sad, Warlander. You gave up looking for happily ever after a long time ago."

"The forging of a nightmare begins in shadow and in fear." Caim Seere stepped through the guarded door and strolled across the concrete foundation with a bottle of water in his hands. "A billowing blast of cruelty to produce the blackest tear."

Anaba squeezed her eyes shut and doubled over, tucking her head to her knees. Hands balled into fists, she stared from beneath the heavy mane of dreadlocks. Shoulders shaking, she laughed at him, snickering until she was out of breath. "Does that make you hard, Caim? Can you even *get* hard?" The Marine chuckled uncontrollably, a tear running from her eye. "Because as I remember it, you were the limp dick that couldn't get the job done when it came to forging me."

"I should never have listened to Mikha'el." Moving into the circle, Caim opened the water and set the bottle on the floor in front of her as an offering. "Your forging should have been my pleasure. *My* honor." He took her gently by the chin and examined her injuries. "Is this your handiwork, Mr Steiner?"

"You said keep her gentle," Steiner replied. "So I did."

As Anaba wrested her chin from his hand, Caim regarded her blood on his fingers. "Nightmares can take a great deal of damage, but they can still die. She is one of a rare bloodline. Not much is known about their resilience in human form."

Steiner threw his hands up and shrugged. "Stop with the lecturing. She can handle it."

"I don't plan on dying," Anaba whispered. "Can't say the same about you." She lunged at Caim, but before she could land a blow, Steiner shot her with a taser.

The twin prongs penetrated her right thigh, and the resulting electrical surge incapacitated her. Muscles rigid, she knocked the water bottle over while convulsing on the floor. Steiner released the trigger, stepped into the circle, and kicked her in the face as she gasped to recover.

"You *will* submit to me," Caim said.

Panting for air, Anaba turned her head away as the fallen angel brushed the hair from her face. She groaned, overwhelmed by fatigue and pain.

"I told you we were going to get reacquainted," Steiner said, ripping the taser's prongs out of her flesh. He laughed when she cried out.

Grabbing a handful of dreadlocks, he forced her head off the floor just long enough to wedge an iron muzzle over the lower half of her face. He locked it into the iron collar and threw her back to the ground. The impact sent a shower of sparks across the concrete. "Be a good girl and stay down. You're not exactly at the top of your game."

The room dissolved into a smear of neutral colors as Anaba relaxed her head on the concrete and passed out.

CHAPTER 47

Michael slammed back the last tequila shot. The liquor ravaged the back of his throat and left him comfortably numb. He signaled the waitress to bring another line to their table.

"Free will makes it impossible to assert any authority over mankind." Wyrmwood drank her shot and slammed the glass to the tall table. "You want the perfect remedy to chaos and mayhem?" she asked, her words slightly slurred. "Cultivate a little influenza here. Sow a little pneumonia over there. Stack and rack the hottest STDs and wham! Quarantines. Curfews. Martial law."

"Wyrmwood, that made no sense. You're drunk. I didn't think angels could get drunk."

"Who do you think introduced booze to mankind? Dionysus."

"Dionysus? As in Bacchus, the God of Wine?" He arranged the fresh shot glasses in front of her.

"The very same. Before Eden was destroyed, he lifted the essential ingredients to make all things intoxicating: wheat, barley, hops, grapes, even marijuana."

"God cast him out of Heaven for that?"

"Well, no. Dion also stole a few apples from the Tree of Knowledge. That was the coffin nail." Her phone chimed musically with a rendition of 'Knockin' on Heaven's Door'.

She reached into her ample cleavage to retrieve it. Looking at the screen, she closed her eyes and dramatically collapsed on the edge of the table.

"What is it?"

"Samiel and Raijin followed those CIA goons to a bookstore, but it wasn't really a bookstore. It was a front, and the bastards gave them the slip!" She snorted loudly. "Raijin made a scene, and now he's being detained by police."

Michael threw back another shot. "I can always try summoning her."

"You're a slow learner, Michael. Caim Seere's involved in this." Wyrmwood rolled her eyes. "Remember when the Grigori ambushed you near your mother's farm? You tried to summon Anaba and failed. He would have thought of that and taken steps to prevent her from transforming."

"He can do that?"

"With the right Enochian wards and a bit of iron, yes. Nightmares are powerless against iron. Most infernal things are."

Michael's phone rang. He glanced at the screen with a crooked grin. "EJ! Where the hell are you?"

Wyrmwood grinned salaciously. "Tell tall, dark, and chocolate I said hello."

"Wait, EJ, let me put you on speakerphone." He set his phone on the table between them. "Son, I've been texting you since Rathan handed me my ass and my walking papers."

"Michael," Elijah said, his breathing labored, "listen–"

Nostrils flared, Michael sat up straight on the bar stool, his eyes widening in alarm.

Wyrmwood frowned. "What's wrong?"

"He never calls me Michael." Through a haze of tequila, Michael picked up the phone and increased the volume. "EJ?" He heard scuffling on the other end of the line and the sound of blows. "Elijah!"

The bar patrons looked up at the sharp report of Michael's

voice, but not seeing enough participants for a brawl, they went back to their drinks and idle discussions.

"Special Agent Pope can't come to the phone right now." The voice was muffled and deep, but familiar.

"McKabe?" Michael said. "What the fuck are you doing with EJ's phone?"

"I'm not interested in your levithmong partner, Childs. I want you.

Wyrmwood's eyes widened in alarm. "Did he just use Enochian?"

Michael gripped the edge of the table, coldly sober, as fear lanced through him. "I want to talk to Elijah."

"Then I suggest you get here quickly. Or Special Agent Elijah Pope will be missing his eyelids and tongue by the morning. Just like the others."

"Where?"

"Central Park. Southern end near the carousel. Come alone or don't come. You've got ten minutes." The line went dead.

"Fuck!" Michael ran his hands across his face. "McKabe is one of the Grigori. He must be using FBI resources to find his victims."

"Angels invented hiding in plain sight." Wyrmwood tossed a $50 bill on the table. "What was Lucifer before he was the Devil? An angel. The Devil's greatest trick was convincing mankind he didn't exist. Those are not just pretty words."

"Danger from within and without. Lucifer tried to warn me." He balled his hands into fists until the nails bit into the skin.

"I'm calling Samiel."

"*Don't!* You heard what he said. Come alone." Michael held his hand over her phone. "Wyrmwood, McKabe's got EJ."

"You know it's a trap." The Horseman tempered her words in a whisper. "No telling how many Grigori will be there. Waiting to kill you. Even with Anaba, you wouldn't stand a chance against such odds." Wyrmwood led him by the arm through the doors to the sidewalk outside the bar. "I'm going with you, if only to carve my name into that adrpan's forehead with my cuticle trimmer."

Car keys dangling in his hand, Michael stumbled to the curb, staring into the bottleneck of cars crowded on Broadway. Staggered by the weight of the situation and the tequila, he felt nauseous. He took a deep breath, exhaling forcefully through his mouth. "We're never going to make Central Park in ten minutes. Not in this traffic. Not even with emergency lights."

"Stop thinking like a cop. You're a Horseman." Casting a quick glance around the sidewalk, Wyrmwood pulled him into the street between the buildings. It reeked of decomposing food, stale beer, and urine. "Kali, niis."

The pale Nightmare walked out of the shadows with clouds of brimstone billowing above his ears. Regarding Michael with a slight bowing of his head, the warhorse nickered to his Rider.

Wyrmwood caressed his face. In the glow of molten flecks, the Horseman's crimson blouse and skirt faded into pristine white leather armors. Secured in a quiver at her saddle, the recurve bow effortlessly slid over her shoulders as Wyrmwood stepped into the stirrup and mounted.

"Quit pouting and get up here." Kicking her foot free from the stirrup, she waited for Michael to climb into the saddle behind her.

"Kali, find a road."

CHAPTER 48

A low ceiling of clouds dulled the full moon's brilliance in the skies over Central Park. Hidden in the shadows between the trees, Michael listened to the winter-brittle branches scraping against each other.

He scanned the surrounding area for a familiar silhouette, unable to find where Wyrmwood was hiding. If her Nightmare was manipulating the darkness, locating her would be impossible. He had to trust that the Horseman would keep her word and not interfere unless he needed her.

Using a line of park benches as cover, Michael made his way toward the entrance of the carousel house. The entrance was completely sealed, closed up with a metal security shutter. The adjacent exit door was rolled up. Steel fragments of the broken lock laid scattered on the ground. With his back pressed against the wall of the brick structure, he peered inside.

"Shit!"

In the auxiliary lighting, Michael saw a body slumped over the back of a stationary carousel horse. Michael recognized Elijah's polished brown wingtip shoes and the gray Brooks Brothers suit. As the carousel began to rotate, the horse took the body out of sight. Michael cautiously followed the revolution of the ride until the familiar form came back into view.

Michael jumped onto the carousel and dragged his partner's body from the horse to the wood-lined floor. "Elijah?" He was relieved to find him still breathing. He winced, examining the bloody gash at Elijah's temple. "EJ? You with me, brother?"

Confused from the blow to the head, Elijah responded with a groan. His lids fluttered open, the cloudiness in his eyes fading when he saw Michael's face. He fought to sit up, went temporarily catatonic, and fell back against the carousel horse's front legs.

"What happened?"

"That bitch McKabe. He came out to my desk. Said he had orders to escort me out of the building. Jumped me in the elevator. Next thing I know, I'm waking up here."

"He's the killer–" Michael fell silent as Elijah crammed the cool profile of a Springfield Hellcat into his hand. The three-inch barrel of the 9mm made it the perfect concealment weapon, which was why his partner carried one, hidden in an ankle holster in case of emergencies. Personal weapons were not a violation under Bureau policy so long as they were legal under the firearms code.

Hand shaking, Elijah pointed to the entrance. "Behind you!"

Michael secured his grip on the gun and swung around to cover them. His finger squeezed off a single round, but the 9mm was knocked from his grasp. McKabe executed a back-wrenching hip throw, which launched Michael into the air. He crashed into one of the carousel horses. The impact splintered the wooden legs and dislodged it from the pole.

Before he could regain any sense of balance, Michael was falling backwards off the slow-moving ride with the Grigori on top of him. "McKabe!"

"My given name is Kokabiel, if you please." He pressed down into Michael's neck with his thumbs. Having the advantage of weight and leverage, Kokabiel punched him in the face and grinned, delighted by the smear of blood coating his fingers. "My name will be the last thing you hear before you die."

He drew the Vaoan Dagger from his sleeve and thrust it into Michael's abdomen.

Michael arced his back, attempting to bridge his hips beneath the angel's weight. It was all he could do as the blade penetrated his lower torso, buried to the hilt.

With a sardonic grin, Kokabiel withdrew the six-inch dagger and deliberately thrust it back into him. Eyes glazed with madness, the Grigori leaned back for a third attempt.

Pinned helplessly, there was no escaping the angel's wrath. "Wither," Michael gasped.

The blade of the dagger deteriorated in flaking layers of oxidized rust. As the corrupted metal turned orange, pitted and pocked by decay, the hand at the hilt grew waxy like a corpse in the final stages of decomposition.

Michael's suit dematerialized, replaced by the forest green leather of his Horseman's armor. The gold-tinted maille shirt washed across his chest and shoulders like an ocean surge. Scraping against the concrete beneath him, it caught the tip of the ruined dagger, and the weapon crumbled to dust.

With a strangled cry of shock and pain, Kokabiel fell back into a kneeling position. He gripped the withered remains of his right forearm as his curled, shriveled fingers disintegrated before his eyes. He retreated, narrowly escaping the blade-head of Bitter Harvest when the war lance materialized in Michael's hand.

Michael swung the lance in a wild arc. Though Kokabiel lurched farther away, the tip sliced his cheek. On a return pass, the blade cut a second, deeper gouge above his right brow and diagonally down across his eye. The Grigori soldier fled back into the park.

"What the fuck were you aiming for?" Still unsteady on his feet, Elijah held onto a carousel horse for balance and stepped down from the revolving platform. "You should have shot that bitch in the face."

"He's an angel, EJ," Michael said, keeping his back to his

partner. He applied pressure to the wound bleeding through his chainmail. "Ordinary weapons can't hurt him."

Elijah wiped his eyes and struggled to refocus them. "Why did you come to rescue me dressed like a fucking elf from *Lord of the Rings*? I ain't no damn hobbit, Mike. The only ring I want is from my alarm clock, waking my ass up from this fucking nightmare."

"It's like I was trying to tell you before, EJ," Michael limped to the interior wall near the exit. "McKabe is the serial killer."

"What?"

"The bastard threatened to cut out your tongue and remove your eyelids." Michael opened and closed his eyes rapidly. The wound in his abdomen was deep, and he couldn't control the bleeding. He struggled to take in a deep breath.

"I guess that makes sense…" Elijah confessed, wincing as he touched his bloody temple. "Before leaving the office, I got a message from Rachel. The data breaches in the hospitals were caused by thousands of digital inquiries, all pinging the servers at various times en masse. Hundreds of thousands of inquiries that eventually weakened their firewalls. They all came from one source: inside the Federal Building. Wanna guess whose office?"

"Assistant Director Rathan."

"Whoever tried to cover it up was fucking good, but not good enough to hide their trail from a bunch of Fortnite-playing-no-hair-on-their-nuts hackers."

"We need to warn Rachel." Michael leaned on the war lance. The tip scraped the ground and left grooves in the concrete. "They might try to get to her, too."

"She's probably hanging with her MMA diva and her SWAT team." Wrinkling his nose in disgust, Elijah dabbed at the gash in his head with his tie. He met Michael's surprise with a indignant smirk. "Yeah, I know about the girlfriend *and* her fight record. When I asked her out for coffee, she sent me a promotional poster. I ain't touching that."

Michael laughed. The involuntary spasm pulled at the puncture wound, and he doubled over in pain.

"Is that your blood or mine?" Elijah pulled his hand away from the injury. "Christ, Mike!" He stood up and went to retrieve the gun from the floor. "Imma peel McKabe's cap back. One in the dome and two in the chest, and then he'll be a real angel."

"EJ, that's not going to kill him." Michael slumped against the wall. He felt cold and weak, the armor weighing him down.

"I got you, son!" Elijah ducked beneath his shoulder and helped him walk through the raised exit door.

Gripping the stump of his arm, McKabe/Kokabiel was waiting for them. He glared at Michael with a malevolent, half-crazed grin. "Kill them both."

Six angels landed beside Kokabiel and folded their wings. Carrying scimitars, they unsheathed their blades and charged in a line.

"What the hell am I seeing?" Elijah leveled the 9mm at them and fired. The impacts registered as mild flinches, but did not stop them.

Michael shoved Elijah back into the carousel house. Propping the war lance across the doorway, he deflected the incoming attacks, and then dropped to a knee. He tilted the war lance downward and stabbed one of the angels in the ankle, withdrew the blade, and drove the spiked butt into the closest aggressor's chin.

Whistling as they cut through the night, arrows descended from the skies. The projectiles penetrated armor and clothing, embedding themselves into the Grigori. On contact, the flesh around the injuries swelled into sallow pustules the size of golf balls. The rabid infection of boils spread, causing hair and skin to slough off in uneven clumps. Choking on blood and phlegm, the angels fell to the ground, screaming in agony.

"We're surrounded!" Wyrmwood shouted. "Get back under

cover!" Gray wings unfurled across her shoulders, she leaped from Kali's back as the Nightmare landed in front of the carousel house.

Brimstone spewed from his nostrils as the Nightmare pirouetted on his fiery hind legs, surrounding himself in white flames, to protect her. The warhorse headbutted a Grigori, caving in his skull, and kicked a second angel in the throat, crushing his windpipe. When the others fled into the skies, he launched himself into the air to give chase.

"Since when can Nightmare fly?"

"If they bear the Crest of Nanqueel and the Rider has wings, they can fly." Wyrmwood breathlessly pulled back the string of her bow, but released it without firing. "Get down!" She brought her wings around the two men, creating a pulsating shield with her wings. A hail of incoming daggers fell harmlessly to the ground.

"Dr Wyrmwood?" Elijah stared at her, dumbstruck. "You've got wings. You're an… an angel?"

"An apocalypse angel to be exact. Get inside, handsome." She led them back into the carousel house. "We can't hold them out here."

Elijah stared at the white leather armor, and then turned to Michael. "And you? Are you hiding wings too?"

"I'm a Nephilim." Michael nodded his head. "No wings, partner. I'm only half angel."

"And that – that fucked up looking horse?" Elijah tentatively pointed in the direction of the park.

"Kali is my Nightmare," Wyrmwood replied.

"What the fuck is a Nightmare?"

Candidly, Wyrmwood replied, "Warhorses forged in Hell from damned human souls."

"From damned–" Elijah turned Michael, his eyes wide with suppressed terror. "D-do you have one too?"

"Yeah." Michael winced, pressing a hand against his side to staunch the bleeding. "The CIA have her."

"Wait... Anaba!? But... she's human! Not some freakish, fiery fleabag." Elijah retreated.

Michael chuckled. "You haven't seen her in her *true* form."

"Mike!" Elijah threw his hands into the air in disgust. "This secret keeping shit is going to kill me–"

Wyrmwood grabbed him by the tie and stared wantonly into his eyes. "No time for talking, sexy. If we survive this, Michael will explain everything. Or, if you prefer the explicit-lyrics version, you can hear it from me while we get naked."

A crash of wood and brick sent a deafening shriek through the carousel house. It was accompanied by the explosive chime of shattering glass. Michael peered around the corner in time to see part of the ride's roof collapsing. The framed windows in the back wall imploded as Kali fell into the room. He landed on top of the carousel, leveling the wooden horses beneath him. With a squeal of fury, the Nightmare scrambled to his feet. Flames licked at his legs with such intensity the entire room was lit up in blue fire.

"Kali, no!" Wyrmwood shouted. "Niis."

The Nightmare bowed his head and splayed his legs defensively. Blood trickled from numerous gashes across his muscular body. A few shards of glass jutted from the warhorse's heaving flanks. He sent a blast of brimstone that ignited into blue fire up the wall, blocking a barrage of projectiles that came flying through the ruined casement. The darts were reduced to ash.

Holding his arm up to shield himself from the heat, Michael carefully looked over his hand. "They're airborne," he said, seeing the silhouettes of the Grigori taking to wing in the smoke.

"Not for long," Wyrmwood said with a wily grin. "Can't fly if the wind won't carry you."

A torrent of air enveloped the Horseman. It tugged at her auburn curls and the fringe of her armor. The tempest swelled and moved out of the carousel house into the park. Carrying shards of glass and debris, it grew in power, speed, and violence, flattening grass and splintering the limbs of trees. The clouds dispersed, revealing the full moon. And then, it ceased.

The air became noticeably thinner. Michael watched half a dozen angels fall from the skies. Those who descended from higher elevations did not rise again. Their broken bodies left indentations in the grass, bursting into flame within their shallow graves. Those closest to the ground were left staggered.

"Kali, Caustic Contagion," Wyrmwood whispered.

Kali jumped out of the carousel enclosure and galloped into the shadows to attack the disoriented angels. The Nightmare took a deep breath and exhaled, spreading a putrid, gray vapor over them. Howling in anguish, the angels began convulsing, riddled with disease, and dropped like pus-covered logs of flesh.

"That's not going to deter them for long," Wyrmwood said.

"A little backup would be nice right about now," Michael said. He swallowed with difficulty, pressing his hand harder against the wound to temper the throbbing beneath his fingers. "Where are Samiel and Raijin?"

"Kali called to Gyaku and Malis, but they're not answering." She drew back the bow. Three black arrows appeared in the string. "We're going to have to hold them off and hope they come for us in time." She turned to her Nightmare and called out, "Kali, darkness!"

CHAPTER 49

Marines were trained to believe they had no breaking point. But the body and the mind would always have limits. There was bullheaded stubbornness, and then there was the brink. Anaba teetered on that precipice.

Consciousness returned in fragments of white light and pain. The light came from a trio of heat lamps mounted above her head. The pain was from her shoulders and wrists as she hung from iron shackles, suspended on a hook that held her body a few inches off the floor.

"This is not the way it has to be, Anaba," Caim whispered in her ear. He brushed the dreadlocks from her face, stroking her forehead and neck with his cool fingers.

It was a lover's touch and she resented it. She would have spit in his face, but the muzzle wedged against her mouth and nose hindered any attempt. It was slowly smothering her, reeking of sweat and blood. She tried raising her head, but the weight of the head collar prevented her. "I will never serve you."

Caim frowned. He nodded to Steiner and stepped aside, allowing the CIA operative to drive the prongs of a cattle prod into the back of her thigh.

Suffer patiently... patiently suffer. It was a sniper's motto. Anaba felt a tooth crack as she clenched her teeth. Her body jerked erratically as 5000 volts ripped through her. The scent of burning flesh assailed her nostrils, exacerbating the smell of the iron.

Stalk – The ability to gather intel without being observed. The most important weapon for a sniper wasn't a rifle. The enemy could take your physical weapons, but they could never hijack your training.

"Goddamn this brings back memories." Steiner removed the prod and waited for her to recover. "Ever the fucking bad ass, eh, Raines?"

"Fuck you," she croaked.

He laughed and punched her in the solar plexus, just below the sternum. The blow knocked the wind out of her. "Sitrep, sweetheart. Your boy Childs has been playing for the wrong team and didn't even know it. The Grigori tried to take him out in the Hamptons, but Rathan's people botched the op."

"Rathan?" Anaba opened her eyes.

"He prefers to go by his given name: Rathaniel." Steiner scratched his stubbled chin, leering at her. "I'm surprised you didn't sniff him out."

"The scent of angels isn't much different from human souls, Steiner. They all stink."

"What stinks is your track record." He taunted her with the cattle prod, pretending to jab it at her before abruptly withdrawing it. "Anybody who gets too close to you gets dead. Dead wife. Dead kid–"

"Ziri?" Anaba gasped.

"No, not worth the bullet. I'm talking about the little girl from the horse show. In order to get to you and Childs, I had to get to her. Didn't end well, I hear." He laughed at her. "Don't look so disappointed, Raines. Just another ghost to add to your collection." Steiner jammed the prod into the small of her back above a kidney.

The familiar taint of brimstone burned in Anaba's nostrils. She struggled to breathe, gagging on the caustic fumes. In human form, the vapors singed the sensitive lining of her nostrils and left a painful burning sensation. Enochian sigils carved into the iron restraints glowed fiercely, signaling an imminent transformation. The enchanted metal contracted, hardening its mass to prevent the shift.

Hold – Patience was the hallmark of a good sniper. Knowing when to fire and when to maintain position was the stamp of a great one. Anaba let the pain wash through her and suppressed the metamorphosis.

"Is that supposed to happen?" Steiner said, warily. He propped the three-foot cattle prod over his shoulder and retreated from the protective circle.

"No." Caim splayed his fingers across the muzzle covering the lower half of her face. "The iron must be weakening her more than I anticipated. She's barely breathing!" Detaching the muzzle, he threw it aside and removed the iron neck collar.

Steiner laid his cattle prod on a table of syringes, pliers, and other implements of torture. He watched as Caim removed the leg shackles. "Is that a good idea?" the agent asked, shrugging into his dark suit coat.

Breathe – The war of nerves could be conquered with the right breath. Anaba closed her eyes and let her muscles relax, ignoring the unnatural wrenching of her shoulders. She had the intel she needed and was in position, ready to put her finger on the trigger – no turning back – one shot, one kill.

Like a high-velocity round discharged from a sniper rifle, Anaba was in motion before Caim or Steiner could react. Snapping her knees up to her chest, the Marine wrapped her legs around the fallen angel's neck and used this leverage to hoist herself up and off the suspension cable. Like a lopsided gyroscope, she swung her body down to the floor, bringing the stunned angel to the concrete with her.

Anaba wrapped the chain between the manacles around Caim's neck and dragged him across the floor. Using him as a tactical shield, she yanked the industrial hairpin from her breast pocket and jammed one end into the lock. Made of horn and designed to bear the weight of her dreadlocks, the prong shimmed the locking mechanism and allowed her to slip one cuff and then the other from her wrist.

A cloud of brimstone enveloped her. Caim closed his eyes from the flurry of molten specks. As he fell to the floor, Anaba emerged from a shroud of flame and shadows in Nightmare form. She kicked at the fallen angel, striking him in the head. Her shrill, piercing squeals reverberated throughout the hangar and shattered the fluorescent lights.

A tendril of water spilled from her forelock, down her neck, and over the dock of her tail. Dark green maille barding materialized over her back and flanks, reinforced with bands of leather that harnessed the armor into place.

Ablaze with green flames, the Crest of Nanqueel and its scales shed an infernal aura over the silver breastplate at her chest. The peytral and its sigils cast a halo of light on the floor, blurring the containment's glyphs on the ground around Anaba. Tongues of white flames erupted from the carefully arranged Enochian glyphs. Scorched beyond recognition, the patterns were rendered unrecognizable.

"You said she couldn't transform!" Steiner reached for his sidearm.

"The Sigil of Enoch?" Caim exclaimed, seeing the emblem blaze on her chest. "These wards were useless." Caim held his bloody fingers over the gash in his forehead and dragged himself away from the Nightmare's fiery feet. "She was never bound."

"Oh, she *was* bound," a voice said.

Caim whipped around and saw Samiel cantering from the mouth of a shadow portal.

"That is until you ill-advisedly removed her iron restraints." Samiel smiled. He abruptly reined his Nightmare to a standstill and dismounted. "One must wonder at the arrogance of archangels, eh, Raijin?"

War followed his fellow Horseman through the portal,

a triumphant smile on his face. "Arrogance is for the weak! It has no place on the battlefield." Leaping from his saddle, Raijin drew the great katana from its scabbard. The curved blade burst into flame. "Did you think you could hide your treachery, Caim Seere? You are fallen! You will never have a place amongst the Horsemen!"

"You hid yourself well, but not your ambitions" Samiel said, gripping the snath of his scythe in skeletal hands. "Anaba permitted you to capture her, knowing the Sigil of Enoch would negate your wards, allowing us to find our way to her… and to you."

"Code Nightshade!" Steiner shouted into his comm. "I need immediate tactical support! Hostiles are celestial! I repeat, hostiles are celestial!" Snatching the Glock 23 from its holster, he did not hesitate and fired the .40 caliber at Raijin.

Raijin's head was driven backwards, his neck violently jerked back by the ballistic impact. Staggered by the lethal projectile, the Horseman was thrown against his Nightmare's shoulder. Striking the raised visor of his gusoku helmet, the bullet splintered the thick ornamental crest adorning the crown.

Raijin snatched the damaged helmet from his head and scrutinized the fractured metal. A trickle of blood dripped from his forehead, down and across the bridge of his angular nose. He ran his fingers over the superficial wound and retrieved the flattened hollow point protruding from his skin.

"You pathetic naked ape!" the Horseman of War thundered. "I shall flay every inch of skin off your bones and feed it to you until you choke on your own filth!"

"The Mark of Azazel?" Samiel said, admiring the craftsmanship of the spent round and the sigil etched into the heel of the bullet. "Have a care, brother. These men come prepared to do battle with angels."

Sprinting from the opposite end of the private hangar, twenty mercenaries open fired on the Horsemen with high-capacity pistols. Ten more, heavily armored operatives burst through the terminal door with HK416 assault rifles and laid down cover fire for Caim and Steiner's retreat.

"Yea, though I walk through the valley of the shadow of Death, I will fear no evil; for thou art with me," Samiel said with a chuckle. He tilted his head, pulling the heavy cowl of his robe over his face. "I'm afraid you've walked into the *wrong* valley."

Translucent black wings sprang from his back, unfurling across his shoulders. Vibrating rapidly, they wrapped about him and formed a cocoon to shield him from a barrage of bullets. Deftly maneuvering into the determined gunmen, Samiel spun his blade horizontally and decapitated four shooters. He flipped the snath in his hands and threw the scythe, impaling another who was taking aim at Raijin. Ripping the blade free, Death gutted the soldier from his groin to his neck like a deer. The dying operative collapsed to the floor, struggling to push his intestines back in place.

"You want war!?" Raijin bellowed. "You have found him!" He propped the great katana over his shoulder. Holding up his left hand, he curled his index finger and thumb together to form a sacred mudrā and swept his hand from right to left in a horizontal line. "Turn the tide."

Redirected by War, the bullets racing toward him reversed course and sped back to their points of origin. The deadly rounds hit and sawed through the mercenaries' ballistic vests, tearing through flesh and shredding the muscles to the bones beneath.

Raijin charged the decimated line. With a simple flick of his wrist, he decapitated a shooter and sent the man's head flying twenty feet across the room. *"War is cruelty! The crueler it is, the sooner it will be over*!" he shouted.

He easily impaled another soldier. "Are you familiar with Colonel William Tecumseh Sherman?" he asked.

Gasping for breath, the injured man crawled across the floor, desperately reaching for his weapon with trembling, bloody fingertips.

"No matter. You'll be joining him in the afterlife." Raijin pinned the soldier's neck beneath his boot, cutting his face with the rowel of his spur, and then thrust his katana into his chest with a twist to lacerate the man's heart. Raising the great sword over his head, he gave it a sharp, downward sweep that sprayed blood across the floor between him and the remaining operatives. "None of you is worthy of honorable steel. Gyakusatsu, Terminal Exsanguination! Bleed the rest of them!"

The chestnut Nightmare arced its powerful neck, and with a squeal, he exhaled a red, viscous miasma. It spread through the eight closest members of the tactical team. The mercenaries dropped their guns and clawed at their faces, frightened cries strangled in the backs of their throats. Bleeding out from their mouths and eyes, they collapsed to the concrete floor, contorting in violent convulsions. They died in anguish, hemorrhaging from every orifice.

All three Nightmares herded the soldiers into a kill zone. As Gyaku bled them with his devastating breath weapon, Malis reduced three assailants to nothing more than damp earth and wriggling worms. Using the flames of immolation, Anaba shielded the Horsemen from a hail of bullets.

"This is why they are collectively known as a *misfortune* of Nightmares," Samiel shouted above the noise.

"Run!" Steiner yelled, shoving Caim toward the door. He covered him with the last four operatives. Shaken and pale, they held the line, facing their oncoming death.

"Leave Steiner to Anaba," Samiel called to Raijin. "They have unfinished business."

Still enveloped by an immolation field, Anaba closed in on Steiner. She cut off his escape, kicking the reinforced door shut in front of him and wedging it into the frame. Blue flames surged outward from her like water cascading from a spring and enveloped him.

The CIA officer dropped his gun and crumpled to the ground, hands and fingers blackened in the fierce conflagration. He groped for the remnants of his lower extremities, but the Nightmare's fire had incinerated his feet and ankles already, and continued, devouring his legs. Leaping up his right arm, the rabid inferno burned the limb to ash in a steady, controlled blaze that consumed only the flesh and left the brittle, blackened bone exposed.

Steiner opened his mouth to scream; a weak, hollow gasp escaped his throat with a wisp of gray smoke. His pain was excruciating, but fleeting, as overwhelmed nerve clusters were seared away in sixth-degree burns. The scent of scorched meat overpowered the stench of brimstone. Steiner choked on the rancid odor. His left arm was shriveled up across his chest, useless, but intact. The wedding ring on his finger glowed red, burning into the surrounding skin and flesh. Succumbing to shock, he groped for his gun with blunted stumps as Anaba peered down at him.

Eyes rolling into the back of his head, Steiner opened his mouth to beg for a merciful death, but the Nightmare continued her relentless assault, blowing a fine green mist into his mouth. The texture of his tongue grew unnaturally thick, swelling to twice its normal size. The muscle detached itself, covered in ulcerous sores and mold, and lodged in Steiner's throat, choking him. Unable to roll to one side and vomit, Steiner gagged and swallowed the vile, hardened clump.

Don't worry, Steiner, I'm not going to kill you. I'm going to leave you like Caim left Natalia. She lived in agony for three years, breathing through a ventilator, Anaba said. *But I don't think you'll last that long.*

"Oh, no," Samiel said. "He will live a *long* life. I am Samiel, the Angel of Death, and I grant you my blessing, Paul Robert Steiner. From this day until I call for your judgment, you will find no comfort nor sanctuary from this life. For the wickedness of your deeds, there will be no hope of peace. Beg if you must, but no Affliction will hear your pleas for mercy."

Anaba stared down at Steiner, snorting fiery brimstone into his anguished face. *I'll be seeing you again. You can count on it.* She raised her head as high as her long neck would allow. *Where's Caim?*

"Run off like a coward. What can one expect from the fallen? Gyaku nearly had him, too." Raijin wiped his Nightmare's bloody mouth with the back of his glove.

"Caim's fate can come another day," Samiel said. "But now we must leave. I sense that Wyrmwood and Michael are in trouble. Malis, find a road!"

CHAPTER 50

Elijah clenched his teeth as Wyrmwood used his tie as a tourniquet on his upper arm. "Damn it, woman!"

"Tourniquets are supposed to hurt." She tightened the knot. "Serves you right. I told you to stay down." Yanking the small knife out of his arm, she wrapped the rest of his tie around the injury.

Michael glanced back at them from his guard position in the corridor. "What's wrong?" he asked, noticing Wyrmwood's reaction.

"They're using qeres. I can smell it on the blade." Wyrmwood kicked the bloody knife across the floor.

"Fuckers are trying to embalm me? While I'm still alive?" Elijah held on to one of the carousel horses and stood up.

"Qeres is a poison, EJ." When Elijah's eyes went wide in terror, Michael added, "But it's only effective against angels and half-angels, like me."

"So that's why you freaked out in the office?" Elijah shook his head, his lips pursed in a thin, angry line. "Mike, these secrets–"

"EJ, I'm barely treading water here." He laid his head against the brick wall. "Cut me some slack."

Retrieving his gun from the floor, Elijah jammed it into the waistline at his back. "Well, if I can't shoot the bastards, what can I do?"

Wyrmwood retrieved an elegant, heavy dagger from a scabbard strapped beneath her quiver. "Mind the gut hook," she warned. "Strike for the heart, twist, yank it out. They're not taking prisoners, and neither are we." The Horseman took a defensive position behind a chariot on the carousel platform.

Agitated, Kali pawed the floor, generating a flame that spread up his legs and reignited his mane and tail.

"What's wrong with him?" Elijah leaned away in fear.

Wyrmwood angled her bow in the direction of a clatter above them. "They're on the roof."

The crooked-winged body of an angel fell through the hole left by Kali's crash landing. Flames still licked at his clothing, but were snuffed out by a second body that fell on top of him. The dead angel was moving, but not under her own volition. Hundreds of maggots and worms wriggled through her decomposed flesh. A third corpse rolled across the rooftop and landed among the bodies. It was emaciated and withered by a creeping mold, but still alive.

"War is hell with but one purpose! To be won!" a voice cried from the shadows.

"Raijin!" Wyrmwood called. "Where have you been!" Wyrmwood carefully looked to the rooftop of the carousel house as Gyakusatsu leaped across the hole.

"We had a reprise of Pickett's Charge with the CIA," Raijin said. "Same folly. Same results. We came at the first possible opportunity."

Samiel sat back as Malis jumped down from the roof. "And look who's with us."

Anaba cantered across the top of the carousel house and jumped down. She took one of the dying Grigori angels by the arm with her teeth and hauled him across the shattered glass. Kali leaped out of the chamber and joined in her attack on the semiconscious soldier. They dragged him across the pavement, tearing at him until his guttural cries were silenced.

"Anaba!" Michael crawled over the brick foundation. Slipping on the glass, he lost his footing and fell to a knee.

The Nightmare dropped the dead angel and trotted over to him. *You're hurt?*

"McKabe's – or should I say Kokabiel's – doing," Michael said. He threw his arms around her neck and held on to her, relieved to have the Nightmare back safely. "He's a Grigori."

Steiner already gave up the intel, she replied. *The Grigori have infiltrated the FBI. Rathan's one of them too.*

The effort of hauling himself into the saddle left Michael panting. "We need to know what they're planning. We need to find Kokabiel."

"We'll hunt him down and get to the root of it," Raijin said. "Samiel, feel like a bit of night flying? When the urch realizes the tide's turned, he'll take to wing."

"Nobody's flying anywhere at the moment." Wyrmwood leaped to her Nightmare's back.

"Wyrmwood, you've declared a no-fly zone?" Raijin raised his fists in triumph. "A ground assault it is then. What are we waiting for?"

"Dr Samiel? Colonel Raijin?" From the safety of the carousel house, Elijah stared at them. "And th-that's Anaba? What the fuck?"

"Time to ride, sexy." Wyrmwood shook her foot free of the stirrup and gestured for Elijah to join her.

He took a step back. "Uh-uh, I am not getting on that thing!"

"EJ, now's not the time for clowning." Bent over Anaba's neck, Michael exhaled slowly to control his breathing. "Safest place for you is in the saddle with Wyrmwood."

"And not just to keep me warm," she said, pouting. "I need somebody to watch my back."

"Our quarry is getting away with all this talk." Raijin slapped Gyakusatsu's shoulder with the bight of his reins and galloped away with Samiel riding beside him.

Clinging to Wyrmwood's forearm, Elijah stuck his foot in the stirrup. Unfamiliar with the process, he nearly somersaulted to the opposite side. Kali sharply swung his hindquarters to save him from falling.

Wyrmwood grabbed the mortified agent by the collar and settled him in the saddle behind her. Wrapping his arms about her waist, she gave the Nightmare a kick. "I don't break, handsome. But *you* might, if you don't hold on." They galloped after the other Horsemen, illuminating the darkness with every stride.

Unable to flee into the night skies above Central Park, the Grigori closed ranks beneath the trees. Armed with swords, they spread their wings across each other to create a feathered phalanx.

The night came alive with the shrill whistle of Wyrmwood's arrows. The black shafts found their marks: center mass, an eye socket, the fleshy folds of the neck. Riddled with disease, the front line of defenders fell. The park walkway was lit with the bonfires of angelic corpses.

Bracing in the stirrups, Michael laid the war lance across Anaba's neck. Together, they charged through the survivors. As swords rebounded off her barding, Michael buried the war lance into the nearest Grigori's chest, retrieved the weapon, and drove it into another.

The phalanx was a trap. The Grigori could not fly, but they could fall. Taking advantage of the high ground, they descended from hidden positions in the treetops. Michael braced the butt of the lance on his stirrup, skewering a soldier on the tip. But the momentum of the falling body dragged him from the saddle. He hit the ground at a gallop with the Grigori on top of him. They bounced and rolled in a tangled heap beneath Anaba's feet.

"Mike!" Elijah jumped down from Wyrmwood's Nightmare. Rolling the body off his friend before it burst into flame, he cradled Michael's head in his lap. "I got you, partner."

Standing in her saddle, Wyrmwood balanced herself with a foot in the seat and the other planted on Kali's hindquarters.

"I'm in the mood for a plague!" She drew back the bowstring. Five black arrows materialized, glowing with an ethereal yellow-green illumination. "Who needs a colonic when you can mix a dash of hemorrhagic fever with a virulent strain of Ebola?" She released the arrows. They splintered into separate shafts before shredding through the treetops. Writhing in agony, ten bloody, pus-riddled bodies fell onto the path.

How bad is it? Nostrils flaring, Anaba sniffed at the injury beneath Michael's bloody hands. *I'm gonna gut the bastard.*

Near the end of the path, the trees grew sparse, giving way to grassy fields. The moon highlighted the silhouette of a lone figure sprinting for the low hilltops toward the city. A pair of considerable wings sprang from Kokabiel's back as he ran.

"I thought you said the Grigori couldn't fly?" Elijah said.

"My domain is powerful, but limited. I can feel the wind returning." Wyrmwood drew back the string of her bow and fired on the Grigori soldiers closing on their position. "Kali–Caustic Contagion! Keep them back!"

"We need him, gunny. He's the one who's been carving up Nephilim," Michael said, trying to sit up. He dug the lance's tip into the path to pull himself upright. "Don't let that son of a bitch get away." Coughing up blood, he collapsed back into Elijah's lap, fading into unconsciousness.

Copy that! The Nightmare reared, her neck arced with such tension Michael thought it might snap. She galloped away, blue flames erupting from her legs.

"Can she make it?" Elijah asked.

Wyrmwood looked desperately to the fading treeline. "If that urch makes it to the top of the ridge..." She shook her head, glancing down at Michael, a mixture of disappointment and sorrow in her eyes. "He'll be able to fly again. Anaba won't."

Anaba galloped with such ferocity she left smoking, fiery hoofprints in the gravel. All she could hear was the wind and her breath roaring back with every stride as she raced to close the gap. Brimstone billowed from her nostrils like a locomotive running at full speed.

Kokabiel leaped into the air, testing the wind, and captured a thin current beneath his wings. It lifted him twelve feet into the air above the hard-pressed Nightmare. Embolden by this success, he paused to look down at her with a smirk.

Anaba launched herself like a ballistic missile and jumped into the air on a furious detonation of flames. Legs tucked tightly beneath her, she defied all laws of gravity and caught the Grigori by the ankle in her teeth. She dragged him back to the ground and hurled him over her head, repeatedly slamming him against the turf. His body left deep furrows in the grass.

The Grigori fought back, raking her face with the tips of his wings, forcing her to temporarily release him. In retribution, she kicked him in the back of the head and crow-hopped on his wings in a deliberate attempt to damage the sensitive flight pinions. But simply trampling him was not enough. Baring her teeth, she bit into Kokabiel's wing and shook her head violently.

"She means to kill him! We need to uncover how deep this goes. Can't force any information out of him if he's a corpse!" Raijin shouted. "Michael, recall her!"

"She won't answer." Samiel pulled the black hood from over his face. "Anaba wears the Sigil of Enoch. She cannot be compelled, not even by her Rider." With the Grigori forces dead or in retreat, he dismounted and walked toward the hill, carrying the scythe in his right hand.

"What's he planning to do?" Elijah asked.

"We need him alive. If Samiel cannot convince Anaba to release the Grigori," Raijin sighed, "he'll be forced to kill her."

Wyrmwood knelt down beside Michael. They were nearly face to face, but her voice came from such a distance. "Michael, call to her."

Michael took a shuddering breath, struggling to keep his eyes open.

"Anaba!" Samiel shouted, raising his scythe. "Release him."

Narrowing her eyes, the Nightmare defied him with a curt, dismissive snort. A puff of singed feathers escaped from the corners of her mouth. She threw her head and trotted away with her quarry, dragging the semiconscious angel by his dislocated wing.

"Willful, defiant Nightmare! Drop him!" Samiel demanded. He chased her down, but she cantered up the hill. The Nightmare made no effort to avoid stomping on Kokabiel as she hauled him through the grass beneath her feet.

Michael laughed at her antics. Anaba's defiance was, by itself, a fierce force of nature, and he loved her for it. However, the animosity between her and Samiel was an enigma that needed to be resolved before tragedy struck. Drawing in a deep breath, he called for her, "Ana–" A fit of coughing cut him off. The pain wracking his body made it even more difficult to breathe.

"Michael!" Elijah gently slapped his cheek. "Stay with me!"

Remembering that night at the ball when he kissed her, Michael smiled. The pain was subsiding, but he felt cold without her. "Anaba," he whispered. "Niis."

One black ear pivoted forward at the sound of his voice. The other remained to the side, trained on Samiel. Anaba glared at Death and lowered her head as if she might charge at him.

Abruptly, she spit Kokabiel's wing out of her mouth. Kneeling her weight on his chest, she vigorously rubbed her bloody mouth over him, aggravating his injuries. With an ill-tempered snort, she bared her teeth and snapped at the Grigori's face. *The few, the proud, bitch. Remember that.* She pranced away, gave a playful buck, and galloped back to Michael with her fiery tail streaming in the wind.

With Elijah's help, Michael got to his knees. Lacking any strength, he would have fallen to the ground, but Anaba caught him with her broad head and held him up. Staring into one large eye, he stroked her face and took comfort in the warmth of her breath. "Is he still breathing, Anaba?"

Not for lack of trying, but yeah.

"That's my girl." He laid his forehead against hers and blacked out.

CHAPTER 51

Hands tucked behind his back, Raijin turned away from the grandeur of the Momao Abai'Vonin. The Horseman let out a guttural sigh that was part exhalation, part growl, and stared down at the bloody, broken body of an angel lying on the tiled floor. "There's not much left of him."

Kokabiel rolled to his side and spit a gout of blood at Raijin's feet. "Is this the balance the Horsemen have chosen? The Nephilim? As long as the Grigori exist, we will hunt them down and fulfill the edict." He tried to sit up and failed, crying out when Raijin assisted by grabbing a broken wing. War forced him into a kneeling position.

"Welcome to DrunGer, Kokabiel," Samiel said. "More aptly, welcome to Momao Abai'Vonin in the House of Famine."

The Grigori's eyes glazed over. "The son of Mikha'el lives?"

"He does. It was *you* we were worried about. Your injuries are rather extensive."

"Why am I still alive then?" Kokabiel wiped at his bloody face with the back of his remaining hand. "I will tell you nothing, Samiel."

"You needn't tell *me* anything. But you will tell them *everything*." Samiel pointed to the Nightmares gathered near the wellspring.

Kali, Malis, and Gyaku pawed viciously at the tiled floor. Molten flecks ignited the brimstone between them, and flames leaped from their hooves to their legs. Anaba stood apart, watching with her head lowered in a ring of green fire.

"You remember her from the park, don't you, Kokabiel? She hasn't forgotten you." Raijin lifted a flagon to his lips and drank. "I'm going to rather enjoy this."

Samiel laid a hand on Kokabiel's shoulder. "I give you my blessing, brother, so that you may know every bite and every kick and every lick of flame without any fear of dying."

"No! No!" Kokabiel begged, reaching for Samiel's leg.

"The unjust shall be made to carry empty bushels and suffer in undying hunger, and Famine shall be satisfied." Samiel kicked free of the Grigori and walked away. "He's all yours now, Anaba."

With a squeal that reverberated above the roar of the five rivers pouring from Tiamat's mouths, Anaba charged across the basin floor. The other Nightmares galloped after her. She grabbed McKabe by his ankle and ran with him. Gyaku latched onto a wrist and pulled in the opposite direction. Encouraged by the angel's screams, Malis took a wing; Kali bit into the other, and they ran in alternate directions.

Raijin sat down on a suede divan situated above the chamber floor. "How I miss the days of the gladiatorial games! Are you sure they can't kill him?"

"I'm certain." Samiel helped himself to a handful of grapes and cheese. "The last thing we need is Anaba adding another feather to her crest."

"The number of man is six."

"A number we must avoid, brother."

Raijin winced, spilling his ale. The Nightmares had Kokabiel boxed in a corner and were taking turns crow-hopping on him. "The Creation is in its death throes, Samiel. Why resuscitate it?"

"Michael's not ready. The Nephilim are not ready. We must delay the inevitable." Samiel watched the misfortune of Nightmares racing back across the basin on a tide of blue fire. They dropped their struggling quarry into the center of the immolation and let him burn before resuming their tug of war game with his flesh.

Wyrmwood joined them on the balcony overlooking the wellspring. She leaned over the marble railing and rested her chin on her forearms. "How long are you going to let them play?"

"They've only just started." Samiel propped his feet on a plumed ottoman. "How is he?"

"The bleeding's stopped, and he's stable. He heals faster than most humans, obviously," she replied. "His mind is what worries me."

"What of his companion? The man you brought with you from the living world?"

"Elijah is having his own troubles coping. This is difficult, Samiel. For both of them."

Raijin stared into his goblet. "You're a Virtue, Wyrmwood. Is Michael beyond even your ministrations?"

"I've done what I can. Physically, he'll be fine. He needs her." She watched the black Nightmare savaging Kokabiel with a headbutt. "He needs his Anaba."

"Wait for her at his door," Samiel said. "I will send her shortly."

Alone in his manor bedroom, Michael sat in the shadows, except for the flames roaring from the fireplace beside him. Water trickled from the crown, over the mantel, and streamed backwards into the firebox. Converted into a fine mist, the soothing steam spread outward into the chamber. It did little to comfort him or quell his uncontrolled shivering.

"There's no greater drought than the famine in a man's heart." The words from a Knight Marshal echoed back to him across a decade. It was the eve of the World Jousting Championships when the Knight Marshal spoke to him. The night his father abandoned him.

He was eighteen years old, the undisputed champion. His father had helped him train, accompanied him to every competition, and on the last day of the tournament, left him standing alone at the tilt-rail. He wanted to forfeit, to spite his father, but his mother and the old man in charge of the lists talked him off the ledge.

At least, that was the lie Michael told himself.

He wanted retribution. To vent his wrath on someone, anyone, and since he couldn't get to his father, he went for the next person in line – the European champion, Rutger Klimke.

Their lances were designed to shatter on impact, but the force and fury that Michael brought down on Klimke knocked him unconscious. The Austrian fell from his horse, landing on his head, and broke his neck. The event organizers had to evacuate him from the site in a helicopter. When he awoke from a medically-induced coma six days later, the thirty year-old banker, father of four, was a paraplegic.

The Knight Marshal in the lists declared it a good hit. The judges ruled it a sanctioned pass. Michael won, but the victory had cost his soul. If ever there was a soul deserving damnation, it was his.

Michael buried his face in his hands and coughed until tears rolled from the corners of his eyes. In the throes of a fever, beads of sweat rolled across his forehead and into his eyes. The thin coverlet draped across his shoulders was damp with it and clung to his back and chest like a shroud. A knock from the doorway was a welcomed distraction.

"Remember, he needs to rest," he heard Wyrmwood whisper.

The shadow that approached was familiar. He needed no light to recognize the confidence in her walk.

"Anaba." Sitting up in the ornate chair, Michael tried to stand, but lacked the strength. The movement pulled at his injury, and he flinched, hunching over his knees. He weakly extended his hand to her.

"You look like shit." Anaba dropped down to a knee in front

of him and took his hand. "You should be in bed." She ran her hand through his locs, twisting the thick textured coils around her fingers. "C'mon. I'll even tell you a bedtime story about a boy who became an apocalypse angel and the special-ops Nightmare assigned to protect him." She stood up, but he refused to move. "Michael?"

He pressed his face against her hip and wrapped his arms around her, cocooning her in the sheet against him. "I finally figured out why you and Samiel don't see eye to eye."

"Besides the fact that he's a bossy asshole?"

He laughed, wincing in pain, and held her hand to his lips. Her skin was cool to the touch and soothed his disquieted spirit. "I died tonight, Anaba, didn't I?"

"You're wrecked." Cradling his head against her stomach, Anaba laid her hands on his head and neck. "You need to get some rest."

"Don't deny it, gunny. The last thing I remember is EJ freaking out. And then I woke up... on the Vestibule Road – where the souls of all Nephilim go. But you already knew that. You were there." Haunted by the memory, he swallowed with difficulty. "You herded me away from the other souls. Forced me off the Vestibule Road and brought me back. And it wasn't the first time." He looked up at her, tears rolling down his cheeks. "That night when I summoned the rivers at Momao Abai'Vonin. I died then, too. I thought I was dreaming but I wasn't. That's why you and Samiel can't get along – he's afraid of you."

"When it comes to you, he better be." Anaba leaned down and kissed him, brushing her lips suggestively over his mouth.

Her tenderness invoked a visceral need within him. He felt weak, breathless in her presence. Taking a deep, faltering breath, he laid his forehead against hers. "What if I said I didn't care about the Nephilim?"

"You'd be lying." She kissed the corner of his mouth, her breath quick and eager, as she shrugged out of her duster.

"What if I said I only care about you?" Covering her neck

with feathered kisses, he cradled her in his arms and pressed her down to the floor beneath the weight of his desire.

"Then I'd say to hell and back again." Anaba grinned as he tugged the shirt over her head and ran his fingers across her stomach.

Michael unbuttoned her jeans and worked the black denim over her hips. Leaning back to pull them over her feet, he winced and froze, his injury reminding him of his compromised condition.

"Maybe this isn't such a good idea right now." Anaba ran her fingers across his shoulders. "You might hurt yourself."

He leaned over, wanting to devour her, and kissed her until he was forced to come up for breath. "It would be worth it."

Michael allowed her to roll him onto his back, putting her in a sitting position on top of him. "In that case, given the circumstances, Special Agent Childs, why don't you leave the riding to me."

Michael kissed her fingers. "Oo-rah."

In the corridor outside of Michael's room, the Horsemen gathered in silence.

"Why are you grinning like a Cheshire Cat?" Eyes narrowed in suspicion, Wyrmwood, stared at Death.

"We are seeing something that has never been recorded in the annals of time. Did you blink? Did you miss it?" Samiel asked to taunt her.

"You've lost me," Wyrmwood said.

Raijin frowned. "Speak plainly, old friend."

"It's time, Raijin. Time that the Son of Mikha'el was fully awakened."

"The Trial of Torezodu?" Raijin said. "You said the boy wasn't ready."

"He needn't master his destiny in a day," Samiel said, "but the door must be opened, and he must be forced to step through it."

"What if you're wrong?" Wyrmwood insisted. "You gave your word to Serra that you'd look out for him."

"If I am wrong, then he will die," Samiel said, regarding her sadly. "My promise to Serra was to mentor him, not keep him or her from their inevitable destinies."

"I shall mourn the boy if he dies," Raijin said. "Mostly because I do not envy the task of dealing with his Nightmare."

"Wyrmwood, did you drug him as I asked?" Samiel led the other Horsemen away from the main bedchamber and into the foyer.

"When Michael falls asleep, he will not awaken for some hours."

"Which gives us just enough time to deal with Anaba." Raijin rolled up the sleeves of his kimono. "It's best done while she is in human form."

Wyrmwood sighed audibly. "This feels so wrong."

Samiel frowned, unsettled by the worry in her face. "Do you doubt him?"

"Do you?" she challenged, meeting his gaze.

"No," Death replied. "I haven't been this excited since David slew Goliath. See to it that all is made ready. We will not get a better chance." He turned to his companions. "May the Four be separate, but as One."

CHAPTER 52

Michael awoke from blissful dreams with a shameless grin on his face. Beneath an olive comforter, he reached for Anaba, but grasped empty sheets. Her side of the bed was still warm and smelled like coconut from the oil she used in her hair. He rolled over onto her pillow and breathed it in. "Anaba?"

There was a chill in the air, so he wrapped the comforter around his shoulders and scooted to the edge of the bed. Her clothes were gone.

Slipping into a pair of leather pants, Michael walked across the room to the fireplace and its dying embers. Before fastening the belt, he peeled back the bandages around his torso to examine his wound. "Would you look at that!" He ran his fingers over what was now a small scar and the purple discoloration surrounding it. "Anaba? You here?"

He grabbed his clothes and was tucking in his green tunic, when a soft knock came from the door. Donning a pair of boots, Michael quickly buckled the straps and hurried to answer it. "Anaba, where did you go?" Poorly masking his disappointment, he took a step back. "Oh, Wyrmwood."

"Samiel has called for us at the wellspring." The Horseman curtly turned on her heel and walked into the hallway.

Michael frowned. "What's wrong?"

"Nothing," she replied.

"Where's Anaba?" Leaving the door to his bedroom opened, he followed her into the antechamber.

"She was awake when I came to get you. I asked her not to disturb you until Samiel was ready."

A rigid semblance of apprehension heightened the syllables in her words. "Is EJ okay?"

His partner's name brought a smile to Wyrmwood's face and a sparkle to her eyes, but it was fleeting. "He's fine."

"Wyrmwood, where's Anaba?" he asked, more directly.

When suspects evaded questions during an interview, they were usually hiding the facts. The Horseman's refusal to answer his query left Michael with a knot tightening in his stomach. In human form, Anaba was vulnerable.

That was when he heard her – not the usual sarcastic crack – but the desperate, enraged squeals of a Nightmare.

"Anaba!"

Her screams reverberated across the basin floor, seeming to come from all angles of the chamber. Michael hurried down the main staircase to the mosaic-tiled floor and found her, locked in chains. An iron head collar was latched around her throat. The slatted muzzle jutting from it covered her mouth and nose.

Violently throwing her head, the lathered Nightmare frantically sat back on her haunches and pulled at the manacles hobbling her legs. Her pasterns were slick with blood from trying to break free. *It's an ambush!*

"An ambush?" Michael jumped the last few stairs and sprinted toward her. A wall of fire reared up like a hellish tsunami and cut him off. The roar of the conflagration was deafening and drowned out the sound of the wellspring and Anaba's high-pitched cries. Michael retreated, shielding his face from the intensity of the flames. He turned to the Horseman War, who stood at the bottom of the staircase. "Raijin?"

Raijin solemnly drew the great katana from its scabbard. White flames erupted from the exquisite sword. Uttering a guttural battlecry, he lunged decisively at Michael's chest.

Michael dropped to a knee and rolled, dodging him. "What are you doing?!"

War spun on the balls of his feet and performed a sweeping strike. The blade whistled in its passage, but missed again with a blow meant to separate Michael's head from his shoulders.

Answering his desperate call, a Bitter Harvest materialized in Michael's hands. Golden-green maille spilled across his body and manifested in time to deflect the biting edge of the katana. While the sword did not penetrate the armor, the intense heat shot through the rings. Michael gritted his teeth against the searing burn and blocked a subsequent blow with his war lance.

Remembering a movement his father taught him, he crouched and swung the shaft of the lance at the Horseman's foot. When Raijin lifted his right foot to avoid the maneuver, Michael feinted and swept the other leg. Raijin fell to the floor in a clatter of rattling armor and roaring flame.

Your six!

Narrowly avoiding the curve of Samiel's scythe, Michael threw himself to the ground and rolled. The sickle cleaved the air with a menacing hiss and obliterated the floor tiles, digging a foot-deep trench in the floor. He considered himself a long shot against one Horseman, but doubted he was a match for two. In a desperate bid to even the odds, Michael parried Samiel's retaliatory strike then jumped and tucked, retreating beneath Raijin's sword in a desperate bid to reach Anaba.

He heard the distinct whistle of incoming projectiles before he saw them. Six bristling arrows arced in the air and landed with the explosive might of mortars. The floor quaked. Shattered mosaic tiles became shrapnel, designating the area between Anaba and him as no man's land. Michael took a defensive position on the ground and covered his head.

Anaba reared against the chains. The iron shackles groaned under the stress until the manacle binding her right foreleg broke. She pawed aggressively and summoned the blistering blue fires of immolation. Wisps of blue-black smoke roiled from the iron bindings. But still, the chains held fast.

"Calm your Nightmare before she breaks her neck!" Samiel shouted.

"Before she breaks *her* neck or yours?" Michael replied.

Samiel spun the scythe over his hand and set the snath on the floor with the authority of a judge slamming a gavel. "Kill her if she breaks free," he shouted to Raijin.

"What?" Michael cried. The Horsemen's betrayal cut as deeply as any Grigori dagger. "Samiel, what's going on? What did I do wrong?"

"Question is, Son of Mikha'el, what have you done *right?*"

Michael maneuvered into position behind Death's flowing black robes. Using Samiel as a distraction and a shield, he thrust the war lance at Raijin and pierced the Horseman's gauntlet. Before he could recover, Michael brought the war lance's blade across his hand a second time, hooked the katana's guard, and ripped the sword from his grasp.

As the stunned Horseman swore under his breath, Michael delivered a spinning elbow to his face and shoved Raijin backwards out of the melee. He caught the falling katana with his right hand and crossed it over the lance to counter a blow from Samiel's scythe.

Of all the Horsemen, Samiel was the oldest and most powerful: a Seraphim, as well as the only archangel. He pushed Michael backwards across the slippery tile.

"Wither," Michael whispered in desperation.

A creeping mold spread across the snath of the scythe like frost. It proliferated quickly and moved from the weapon to Samiel's skeletal hands and wrists. In response to the devouring fungus, a thin layer of earth buried the voracious growth. Drained of any moisture, the desiccated bodies of maggots and worms fell to the floor, the only victims of the withering effects.

"We Four are the instruments of the Apocalypse, the threads

of Affliction sewn into the tapestry of the Creation after the fall of man," Samiel said. "We are immune to the gifts of our fellow Horsemen."

"Immune," Michael said, "but not invincible." He hooked the war lance and the katana inside the curve of the scythe's blade, braced against the sickle, and used all his weight to tear the weapon from Samiel's hands before rolling backwards. The reckless maneuver sent the scythe skittering thirty-feet across the floor.

A swell of water reared up from Momao Abai'Vonin. The tidal surge arced over Michael and struck Samiel in the chest. It flattened the Horseman. Lifting him from the floor, the river water hurled him across the chamber and slammed his body into the wall with enough force to shatter the marble. The impact left fractures around the indentation of his body.

There was no time for a victory celebration. Wyrmwood came at Michael from above, wings unfurled, brandishing her bow like a bōstaff. She hooked his ankle and brought him to the floor. On the inhale, she knocked the great katana from his grasp, and on the exhale, pinned the war lance beneath her boot. Nocking an arrow, she aimed for his face and released the shaft.

Michael deftly rolled aside to dodge the arrows. Bits of shattered tile flew at him, stinging his face, as arrowheads impaled themselves in the floor.

In a desperate effort to escape the archer, Michael kicked her in the knee to reclaim his lance. He spun it like a plane propeller and struck her in the chin with the spiked butt. It was enough to put some distance between them. In the footlists, space was an advantage against a swordsman. Against an archer of her skillset, it was deadly.

She drew back the string and launched volley after volley. Michael spun the war lance, deflecting the first two arrows, but he was soon overcome by the sheer number and speed. Crouching down, he bowed his head and retreated into the cocoon of his wings.

Wings? he thought, astounded.

Huddled beneath the gray, black bespeckled wings, Michael stared at the primary and secondary flight feathers and the silvery-white highlights between the pinions. Forgetting that he was in any danger, he leaned forward, using the lance for balance as the wings unfurled with a thought and stretched back across his shoulders, first one and then the other. A stack of broken arrows laid at his feet.

"The wings of an archangel." Out of breath, Raijin stooped to retrieve his katana from the floor and sheathed it in one fluid motion. "May you prove worthy of them. Maoffras restil, Son of Mikha'el – Famine."

"May you praise Him and that praise be immeasurable." Wyrmwood bowed her head reverently. "I welcome you, little brother."

"I don't understand," Michael said.

"This was your third and final trial, Michael – The Awakening." With a grimace, Samiel extricated himself from the fractured wall. "Maoffras restil, Son of Mikha'el, Son of God." Death gestured to the Fossegrim guards in the corner. "Release his Nightmare."

Maintaining a cautious distance, the house guards used catch poles to unlock the iron shackles. As the muzzle fell, Anaba pounced on them before they could flee. She doused them with brimstone to disorient them and ignited the cloud. Mean-spirited, but not fatal, the fiery blast was more concussion than flame, knocking them to the floor. Wheeling toward the Horsemen, she snorted in fury and charged.

"She's not taking this well." Raijin nervously thumbed the guard of the katana.

"Why would she?" Wyrmwood asked. "We locked her up and tried to kill her Rider."

"Subterfuge was necessary, Michael," Samiel said. "Anaba will not hear our explanation. If this is to end well, you must explain it to her."

"Anaba, no!" Michael flew to engage her, arms and wings outstretched to stop her rampage.

They bound me in iron! Muzzled me! The Nightmare slid to an abrupt halt, dragging her hocks across the floor to keep from colliding with him. *Tried to kill you!*

"Settle down, gunny!" Like blindfolding a spooked horse, he wrapped his wings around her head and shoulders to focus her attention on him. Ears swept back in confusion, she swung her head from side to side, thrusting her nose into his wings. "Hey! That tickles."

Michael pushed her nose back toward her chest. She shoved him back a step, glaring at the Horsemen. "Pissed, gunny? Yeah, my feelings are a little hurt, too. But this was my final trial. I passed."

Barely! she hissed.

"Settle down." He grabbed a handful of mane and with a flutter of his wings was on her back. "You know what this means, don't you?" He leaned across her neck and whispered, "We can fly!"

The Nightmare pinned her ears. Uncertain of herself, she walked three steps forward, then took a step back, rocking back and forth on her legs. Her hindquarters dipped precariously beneath him as she struggled to find a sense of balance.

"Trot on, Anaba!" Raijin said, slapping his thigh in exasperation. "For a Nightmare, flying is nothing more than an exaggeration of the Touch of Zephyr. Concentrate, girl!"

I'll concentrate on kicking your teeth in. Poised to charge at him, she relented when Michael gave her a kick in the ribs.

The Nightmare collected herself at a trot, lengthening her stride toward the wellspring. At the rim of the basin, she leaped into the air and continued at a canter, rising above the frothy waters. The movements of her neck and back became more fluid as she grew accustomed to flight.

Weaving between Tiamat's fossilized heads, she flew to the domed ceiling of the Momao Abai'Vonin sanctuary, and then descended. With a stumbling step, she came back to the mosaic floor and trotted toward the other Horsemen.

"And the Four shall be separate, but as One!" Raijin declared, nursing a bruised shoulder. "If every Nephilim has this potential within them, the Grigori are in for a rude awakening. This calls for a celebration!"

Michael grinned, slapping Anaba's neck. "I agree. Let's see what we have in the fridge."

CHAPTER 53

The mood on the grounds of the estate was festive, complete with Fossegrim fire jugglers and acrobats; artisans blowing crystal into wine goblets; and leatherworkers crafting hats and masks for the villagers who came out to celebrate. Culled from the wetlands, a feast of waterfowl and vegetables roasted over open hearths, and the pungent smell of *ubehla*, an indigenous wild boar, wafted from smoke pits near the kitchens.

Accompanied by lever harps, the melodies of 8-stringed violins resonated through the manor house. Haunted by the music, Michael listened from a furnished alcove. He brushed aside the sheer curtains billowing against his face and stared at the distant silhouette of the Citadel of Judgment.

Elijah was sitting alone on the outdoor veranda as dusk approached. He had been there for hours. For most of the evening, Michael had avoided him. Dreading the inevitable conversation, he picked up a couple of crystal goblets and a bottle of wine from a tray and went out on the patio.

"They call it Balzizras." Michael sat down and offered his partner a drink. "In Enochian, the name means judgment. The land you're sitting on is called DrunGer."

"Not exactly the Caribbean, but the view ain't bad." Absently plucking grass from the verge, Elijah tossed the blades into the pond and accepted the wine. "Sky's weird though. Wasn't expecting that." He squinted into the starless firmament. Veins of crimson bled through the asymmetrical patches of blue-green.

"It's not supposed to look like that." Michael poured himself a glass of wine. "I… kind of messed things up when I got here."

"Why am I not surprised? You always manage to take shit to the next level." His anger manifested itself in low tones, articulated in every accented syllable. "I really hate you, man."

"EJ–"

Elijah cut him off with a raised hand. "I was molested by a Hellhound this morning. It put its nose up to my crotch and sniffed my junk! Then it licked me like it wanted to fondle my balls!"

The image was too vivid. Michael laughed, unexpectedly snorting wine through his nose.

"That's funny, Mike?" Elijah punched him in the shoulder, spilling wine on the bench between them. "If I was asked to name the Four Horseman of the Apocalypse on a game show, I'd get it wrong. You know why? Because I'm on a goddamn, first-name basis with them! Samiel, Raijin, Wyrmwood, and *Michael*. Wrong answer! But it's not wrong, is it, Mike?" He slouched against the back of the bench. "I can't even believe I'm having this conversation. My partner, the man I trust with my life, moonlighting as some goddamn angel of the apocalypse! Seriously, Mike!"

Michael tapped his fingers against the crystal goblet. "If it's been so terrible, EJ, why did I see you kissing Dr Wyrmwood last night?"

"She kissed me! Get it straight!" Agitated, he sat up and jammed his finger into Michael's chest. "And let's stop pretending, Mike! She's no doctor."

"You slept with her?" Michael sipped his wine with a grin, knowing the answer. He felt his partner's narrowed eyes cutting into him.

"There are worse ways to catch an STD! Did you see that

dress she was wearing? She might as well have been naked!" Elijah crossed his legs, bobbing his foot in agitation. "She took advantage of my shock and jumped me."

"She jumped you?" Michael replied, feigning disbelief. He knew if anyone made the first move, it was Wyrmwood, but he played along. "Bullshit. I saw you checking her out."

"Like you haven't slept with Anaba!"

Elbows perched on his thighs, Michael interlaced his fingers around the goblet and shrugged. "I did."

Elijah's face lost all expression. "You lying sack of shit."

"Wouldn't lie about that, partner." Michael looked at him from the corner of his eye and snorted. He sat back and laid his arm across the back of the bench. "Round Two went a whole lot better than Round One did."

"Holy shit," Elijah whispered, shoulders slumped in defeat. "When I said we needed to find a pair of nice girls, this wasn't exactly what I had in mind."

Michael remembered the night of that conversation, sitting at a bar after one too many shots of J&B. He held his glass up for a toast. "I don't know, EJ, we could have done worse."

"Certainly couldn't have done any better." Elijah tapped his glass and drank with him. "Old girl put some moves on me. Took me to school. I could barely move this morning. My perception of angels has been changed *forever*!" Elijah looked over at him. "And Anaba?"

Michael smiled, remembering their first night together and falling asleep with Anaba in his arms. "I'm looking forward to Round Three."

Drumming his fingers against his thighs, Elijah shifted uncomfortably on the bench beside him. It was a nervous tick that Michael recognized as a sign of distress. "So what happened with McKabe? And don't bullshit me, Mike. I saw you and your *team* leaving the house this morning? McKabe was with you." His fingers ceased their fidgeting. "When y'all came back... he wasn't with you."

Michael scratched at the back of his head, reluctant to answer the question. "Remember the time we investigated that lady in the Florida Everglades? The one who believed her husband had been kidnapped by shadow people?"

"That crazy faith healer? Yeah, we found what was left of her old man a month later in snake shit. Poor bastard had been strangled by one of those feral pythons and swallowed whole." Distracted by the details of the old case, Elijah abruptly went quiet. "You fucking fed McKabe to a snake?"

Michael twisted his lips into a obstinate pucker to hide a conceited grin. "I gave him to Harvey, my Leviathan."

"You *what*?" Eyes blinking rapidly in disbelief, Elijah turned to stare at him. "You fed McKabe to a snake? Here in Hell? A snake named after that man-eating python in the Everglades?"

Michael tilted his head and shrugged. "Harvey's a little bigger than a Burmese Python, partner. About three *hundred* miles bigger."

He remembered how the Leviathan had answered his whistle, rearing up out of the pitch with its maw opened wide to receive its offering. McKabe had vanished into its mouth, his screams drowned out by the roar of the beast.

Burying his face in his hands, Elijah rocked back and forth in agitation and groaned. "*Jesus Christ,* Michael! Where's does this shit end?" He massaged the deep furrows in his brow as he struggled to cope with the news. "And it ate him?"

"Swallowed him whole."

Elijah shook his head in horror. "And here I thought Jonah had it bad inside that ole whale. What a way to go! Even for an asshole like McKabe."

"It's not quite that simple," Michael said in a prolonged sigh. "Samiel gave McKabe his blessing. He can't die." Michael met his longtime partner's eyes without remorse. "He'll be spending the next century *or two* getting ground up in Harvey's guts."

"You sadistic, sonovabit–"

"Can you think of a better prison for an angel? I don't think

Rikers Island is equipped for celestials, do you?" He folded his hands in his lap, sensing the strain on their friendship. "I needed to send a clear message to our boss, Rathan. One that couldn't be misinterpreted."

The sharp, protracted blast of a trumpet broke the night's stillness. Originating from Balzizras, vibrations from the sustained chord sent ripples across the surface of the pond.

Elijah wrapped his fingers around the hilt of the dagger Wyrmwood had given him. "What the fuck is that?"

The music and celebration festivities abruptly ceased. Michael's mind went blank, his limbs numb, as he stood up, compelled to answer the summons. He dropped the goblet, oblivious to the high-pitched pop as the crystal shattered on the stone walkway. Wyrmwood and Samiel hurried from the manor house. Their eyes fixed on the tower.

"Samiel?" Michael asked. "What is it?"

"When evil comes upon us, we shall stand before His house, and in His presence, and cry unto His Afflictions," Samiel said. *"One will shall bind the Four."*

"Is this the... the end of the world or something?" Elijah flinched as a second blast reverberated across DrunGer. Wyrmwood went to him, taking his hand.

"The signs are not in proper alignment for the Apocalypse." Raijin hurried towards them from the terrace steps. His elaborate gusoku armor rattled with every earnest step. "But no good can come of this."

"The Father is incapable of destruction. A Horseman has presided over every major disaster in the history of the Creation," Samiel said. "These tragedies have always been precipitated by the blast of a trumpet from the Citadel of Judgment. The greater the disaster, the greater the number of Horsemen required to accomplish it."

The deeds were outlined in an ancient codex Samiel had given to Michael as a gift. The accounts were beautifully illuminated in hand-painted renderings and lyrical prose written by Enoch, his grandfather. One illustration depicted the destruction of the cities of Sodom and Gomorrah, where Samiel and Raijin rained fire and death down on the inhabitants, sparing none but Lot and his wayward daughters.

Raijin's fiery katana brought the Tower of Babel to ruins, while Wyrmwood poisoned the minds of the men building it, so they would never attempt such a feat again. Michael was especially drawn to the gospels depicting the acts of his predecessor, who unleashed the Great Flood and later, Eligoriel who would bring about the destruction of the continent of Atlantis.

But when it came to epic disasters, none was better orchestrated then the Ten Plagues of Egypt. The Father's wrath required all Four Afflictions. It was initiated by Famine, who turned the waters of the Nile to blood, killing all the fish. Wyrmwood sickened the cattle and set a plague of boils on God's enemies. Raijin brought fiery hail and locusts, waging a war of nature. But nothing was as terrifying as Samiel taking up his scythe and, with black wings unfurled, passing over the land to reap the souls of the firstborn.

Despite the beauty drawn and recorded on each vellum page, there was an underlying terror beneath every story. The codex was the *Iliad* of Heaven, a lesson about the perils of rage. No story was more horrifying than the first, when the Four Horsemen were summoned for the first time to lay waste to *Mahorela* – the Garden of Eden.

Samiel closed his eyes as the fourth trumpet blast sounded. "The Father has called, and His Afflictions must answer Him."

Releasing Elijah's hand, Wyrmwood walked to the edge of the veranda. *"And I saw a white horse: and she that sat upon him had a bow, and with the noise of thunder she went forth conquering and to conquer with disease. I am the Herald of the First Seal, Lady of Anguish, Bearer of Malediction."* Summoning the recurve bow from the ether, she laid the weapon on the ground at her feet and took a knee. "I am Wyrmwood, the Angel of Pestilence, and I yield."

Armor rattling in the stillness, Raijin took his place beside her. *"There went out another horse that was red: and power was given its Rider to take peace from the Heavens, and the Earth, and the Pit of Hell, that they should kill one another. And there was bestowed unto him a great sword. I am the Herald of the Second Seal, Lord of the Conflict, Bearer of Strifebringer."* He laid the great katana reverently on the ground before him and took a knee. "I am Raijin, the Angel of War, and I yield."

Michael stood paralyzed, staring at *Balzizras* in a panic. He remembered the words of the homeless preacher he heard that night in Central Park when the body of Mary Klinedinst was discovered. A sense of calm overcame him. *"And lo, a black horse; and he that sat on her had the name Famine: and he was granted authority to balance the scales from abundance to despair. I am the Herald of the Third Seal, Lord of the Drought, Bearer of Bitter Harvest."* Michael summoned his war lance and laid it on the ground before him and took a knee. "I am Michael, the Angel of Famine, and I yield."

"And behold a pale horse: and his name that sat on him was Death, and Hell followed with him, he who would command the dead to rise and come forth to final judgment. I am the Herald of the Fourth Seal, Lord of the Barrows, Bearer of the Last Breath." Samiel laid the wicked profile of the scythe on the ground with the other weapons and took a knee. "I am Samiel, the Angel of Death, and I yield." Samiel stood again, taking up his scythe. "And the Four shall be separate, but as One. Rise, Heralds, it is time to ride."

Assistant Director Rathan stared through the blinds into the storm. The heavy deluge of rain hurled gigantic drops against the corner office windows. His heart was heavy, his emotions as indistinct and blurred as the cityscape.

"Are you certain, Nuriel?" Shivering against a chill, he coughed into a towel, scowling at the bloody phlegm. Angels were immune to disease, but not when the malady came from the hand of the Angel of Pestilence herself. Gonorrhea. Wyrmwood's idea of amusement.

"I saw it happen with my own eyes, Fifth Commander. Kokabiel is dead." Dressed in a dark blue sports coat and dress pants, the Grigori bowed her head. The FBI badge about her neck jingled at her chest. "He was badly injured, probably by the Nightmares. His wings were broken."

Rathan folded the soiled towel and wiped the sweat from his forehead and goatee. "How did they kill him?"

"I was keeping watch in DrunGer as you requested," Nuriel replied, "when I found where the Horsemen were holding him–"

"How *did* they kill him?!" Rathan thundered, his hands balled into trembling fists.

"Childs dropped him into the mouth of the Leviathan." Her lips quivered. "I am sorry, Rathaniel. There was nothing I could do."

"Arezodi, my old friend. May you find peace." He closed his eyes but refused to be humbled. "Kokabiel was my right hand. Without him, I am in need of another. You have distinguished yourself among all the others, Nuriel."

"It would be my greatest honor." She raised her head proudly. "What are your orders?"

"Send a company to pay a visit to Mikha'el's human whore. I want her dead. See to it personally." Rathan turned away from the window and threw the towel on the floor. "I shall lead the remaining battalion to the Nephilim sanctuary."

Nuriel's eyes widened. "You've found them?"

"The traitor Pagiel has been hiding them in a church." Rathan unwrapped a cough drop and plopped it into his mouth. "Thanks to Agent Rollins' excellent record-keeping, we traced a number of missing persons to that location. That's probably why you can't locate her. She will die with the rest of the vermin."

"By God's will." She nodded and retreated through the office door.

Rathan laid his hands on top of his desk, leaning over it as he stared at the man in the chair across from him.

Caim held a bloody handkerchief against the side of his face. Ravaged by Nightmare teeth, ragged flaps of skin hung loosely from his temple and scalp.

"I see that I am not the only one to suffer casualties. You've lost your man – Steiner?"

"Anaba settled that old score in the only way Anaba knows how. I've taken control of Steiner's assets, but they'll be of no use to you. Not with the Horsemen breathing down your neck." Caim stiffly got to his feet and stood, waiting for his bruised limbs to adjust. "I'm done."

Rathan coughed, slumping into his chair as the fit brought the taste of blood to his throat. He spat the discolored mucus into the wastebasket. "I will kill him, Caim. Famine will fall. I cannot promise any mercy for the Nightmare."

"Anaba will never accept me as her Rider." Caim hesitated at the office door before leaving. "Kill her, and I'll owe you a debt of gratitude."

Rathan nodded. "Consider it done."

CHAPTER 54

Riding four abreast in full armor, the Four Horsemen galloped down the Vestibule Road on an undulating tide of flame and shadow. Their Nightmares temporarily broke ranks and cantered single-file onto a dogleg trail. This nexus led into a veiled portal between the trees. They re-emerged onto an unfamiliar landscape, congested with thick gray smoke and flames of a different sort. The outlines of buildings, burning out of control, stood out prominently in the twilight darkness.

"Where are we?" Elijah asked, looking up from Wyrmwood's wings for the first time since leaving DrunGer.

"Whatever disaster was intended for this place is well underway." Raijin slapped the bight of the reins against Gyaku's neck to reprimand the spooked Nightmare.

Michael's heart kicked at his sternum. "This is my mother's farm!"

The two-story barn on the eastern side of the property was fully engulfed. Hundreds of alfalfa bales fueled the escalating blaze, which had spread to a nearby utility building. Explosions signaled the demise of tractors and assorted farm equipment stored inside. The flames licked up the walls of the stable and left the stone foundation smoldering.

Anxious horses cried out. Chased from the burning barn, they raced into the paddock and galloped in panicked circles.

With smoke still clinging to her flannel shirt, Stacia DeJesus ran after them with a carriage whip in her hand. Coughing between ragged gasps of air, she swung the pasture gate open.

A Grigori soldier pursued her, slashing her forearm with a short sword. Cursing at him, she hit the angel in the face with the buggy whip and slammed the gate into his shins. The steel livestock gate knocked him to the ground. He tucked his wings and rolled against the water trough to avoid being trampled as the horses fled into the lower pasture.

Bleeding from a head wound, Noah Childs attacked him with a pitchfork. The angel kipped up to his feet and swung at him, but he caught the blade in the tongs of the fork and disarmed him with a twist. Noah maneuvered himself between Stacia and the Grigori and drove the pitchfork into the angel's chest, pinning him to a fence post.

The angel snapped the pitchfork's handle in half with a malevolent grin and struck Noah in the face with the splintered handle. Noah collapsed at his feet. Before the Grigori could impale him with the shaft, Wyrmwood nocked an arrow and fired. The arrow struck the angel in the head. His limp body fell forward, torn from the fence, and tumbled into the water trough.

"Noah! Where's mom?" Michael shouted.

Reeling from the blow to the head, Noah sat up on his knees with Stacia's help. "The house..."

Elijah jumped down from Kali's back and drew a 9mm from his waistband. "I've got this, partner. Go find your mom."

Michael looked at the pistol skeptically. "EJ, I told you, guns don't work on angels."

"That one will," Raijin said. "It's loaded with mercurial-core bullets bearing the Mark of Azazel. It belonged to a wily CIA man." Raijin rubbed a finger across a bruise on his forehead. "If you want to win the war, bring the proper tools to the battle. Wyrmwood, cover them. I'll douse these flames."

Michael stood up in the stirrups as Anaba and Malis raced uphill to the farmhouse. A violent altercation was underway in the driveway. Armed with a longsword and a dagger, Gabriel fought off three Grigori swordsmen.

Pivoting on his heel, the archangel drove the bony tip of his wing into the Grigori's nose. Blood splattered across his white and gray feathers. He flipped the sword in his grasp and stabbed the second angel in the chest. A kick to the groin removed the corpse, and a clever feint penetrated the third Grigori's defense. He struck her in the forehead with the sword hilt, stunning the soldier, before he sliced her throat.

Raphael fought at his back with a pair of kalis blades. The curvy, metal shafts delivered jagged wounds, even in angelic flesh, without getting caught on celestial bone. He slashed at the first opponent and cut a long gash across the lower half of the Grigori's face. When the soldier recoiled, Raphael quickly brought both swords from left to right horizontally across his chest. Gouging through the leather breastplate, the kalis sliced through the flesh beneath it. As the angel dropped to his knees, Raphael stabbed him in the neck and kicked the body back into his companions.

Wielding a heavy pike with triple blades, another Grigori lunged at Raphael with the advantage of a fifteen-foot reach. The archangel threw himself backwards to avoid being impaled. Balanced on the tips of his wings, Raphael threw one of the kalis. The blade embedded itself between the Grigori's eyes, but before the corpse could fall, Raphael snatched the sword from his dead face.

"Michael, see to your uncles," Samiel said. "They won't last against those odds."

"My mother–"

"I will see to your mother." Samiel's Nightmare galloped three strides into the air and vanished into the darkness.

Gabriel grunted through gritted teeth when a longsword pierced his left wing. Had he not been in motion, the blade would have penetrated the center of his chest. He fell back against Raphael, who took a brutal punch to the jaw for his trouble. They were surrounded on all sides by a score of Grigori soldiers.

Anaba lowered her head and charged. Michael laid the war lance against her neck and couched it beneath his arm for impact. The Nightmare's approach was silent, heralded only by a cloud of brimstone. By the time she ignited the vapor, the signature warning of flames came too late. The momentum of the war lance severed the unsuspecting Grigori's spine.

With a catlike grace, Anaba dropped to her forehand, legs splayed almost parallel to the ground like a championship cutting horse. She sprang to the side at a 45-degree angle, nearly unseating Michael. He braced himself in the stirrups as the Nightmare pirouetted to counter a sword attack from the Grigori attempting to flank them.

Blinding the soldiers with a blast of brimstone, Anaba's molten flecks ignited a flash of vividly green flames. Caught in the explosion, the Grigori screamed as their eyes were burned out in the detonation. The rest scattered to avoid the Nightmare's fire.

"Michael!" Gabriel pointed to a pair of angels advancing on the group from the front of the house.

The Grigori soldiers reached into their pinions, appearing to pluck at their feathers. Michael saw a metallic glint between their fingers as they threw a volley of daggers in his direction. The blades whistled through the night air, honing in on their target.

Is that the best you got? The Nightmare tossed her head and neck, casting a fire shield with her mane. Lumps of molten metal fell at her feet. Ears pinned flat against her head, she rushed the angels, teeth bared and flames lashing from her mane. Trampling them to the ground, she exhaled a noxious vapor over them.

Their stricken faces turned green and then brown and then gray, finally blackening as their skulls were reduced to withering ash. She spun in a tight circle. Michael swept the war lance's blade between them and severed their emaciated skulls from their shoulders.

Winning hearts and minds, or removing them! Anaba hissed. *That's the Marine Corps way.*

"Where's my mother?!" Michael could hardly breathe, the fear in his chest crushing his lungs.

"She fled to your father's dojo," Raphael replied. "We tried to hold them off until they could find cover."

They? Ziri's with her?

"The boy wouldn't leave her side." Looking at his injured wing, Gabriel winced. "There's more than sixty Grigori here. The dojo was the safest place."

"She's trying to get to the safe room," Michael said.

Ignoring the path that wound around the side of the house into the garden, Anaba collected herself and leaped into the air. A blast of flame lifted her muscular body and held her aloft as she made the rooftop height, landed, and trotted across the wooden shingles to peer down into the meditation courtyard.

Ziri was surrounded. Three Grigori closed in for a kill with their blades out. Wearing an indigo turban that veiled the lower half of his face, the Tuareg boy stood his ground. A silver thumb ring flashed each time he drew back the string of a double-curved bow. With only his eyes showing from beneath the blue veil, he released arrow after arrow from the quiver on his back.

Despite finding their targets, the arrows had little effect. Undaunted, Ziri continued firing until his hand reached back and grasped only air.

"Iblis!" he spat. "Release her!" Drawing the bone knife from his belt, Ziri slashed at the closest angel. The Grigori recoiled in pain and retreated a few steps. The unexpected drawing of blood by a human gave the others pause.

"Finally, the prodigal son appears." Near the entrance to the dojo, dressed in silver, ceremonial armor, Nuriel held Serra Childs by the throat. She glanced up at Michael with a smile.

"Remember me from the alley, Son of Mikha'el? I swore you would regret murdering my brothers. Today is that day."

Serra struggled, scratching at Nuriel's hand, but was no match for the Grigori's strength.

Nuriel drew a dagger from her warbelt. "Fifth Commander Rathaniel ordered this happy homecoming for you, but I'm afraid you've arrived too early and ruined the surprise." She slowly thrust the dagger into Serra's abdomen, twisting it in her gut.

Serra stiffened as the blade penetrated her. Michael heard the anguished gurgling in her throat, drowned out by the Grigori's grip on her neck. Nuriel threw her body from the porch like refuse.

"No!" Michael dug his spurs into Anaba's flanks.

Like a valve bursting under pressure, the Nightmare charged from the rooftop. Her hooves dug into the wooden pavilion and sent flaming shingles into the air behind her. Headbutting an angel trying to intercept her, Anaba shattered the Grigori's skull and trampled him beneath her hooves. Gabriel and Raphael descended into the melee with blades spinning to clear a path to Nuriel.

Michael watched the swelling green glow of Anaba's flames reflected in Nuriel's eyes. Those flames would be the last thing the Grigori would ever see. Twisting her head sideways, Anaba opened her mouth as wide as she could and grabbed the Grigori by the chin. She did not flinch when the angel sliced at her face with the dagger.

With a guttural squeal, the Nightmare shook her head, like a hound shaking a rabbit, and broke the angel's jaw, crushing the mandible in her teeth. Flame and wrath carried the Nightmare and her quarry into the darkened dojo. Michael held on to the pommel of his saddle as she leaped the steps and crashed through the partially opened doorway. Her ravenous flames lit up the interior chamber with the infernal light.

Enraged, Michael stood up in the stirrups and raised the war lance over the Nightmare's coiled neck. He brought the blade-head down into the Grigori's unprotected throat, retrieved the lance, and sank the obsidian blade back into her flesh. Ignoring the spray of blood across his face he timed his strikes to the Nightmare's vicious efforts to rip the angel's head from her shoulders.

"Anaba, iyyăw diha!" Ziri's voice was broken with tears.

Anaba struck at Nuriel's corpse a final time before releasing her. Burning feathers fluttered in the air about her head. She pricked her ears in the direction of Ziri's desperate voice.

"What's he saying?" Michael asked, propping himself on her neck in exhaustion.

Your mother… Carefully picking her way through the ruins of the dojo's charred, wooden floor, Anaba trotted to the porch.

CHAPTER 55

Serra was lying on her back, surrounded by her beloved rose bushes. Stripped away by thorns, threads from her dress and wispy strands of silver hair hung like fraying tapestries from the broken branches.

Samiel stood over her. His black wings cast a long shadow across her body like a shroud. He bowed his head beneath the wicked curve of the scythe's blade and stared down into her face. "Are you in pain?"

"A little," Serra replied, struggling to breathe.

"It will pass."

"Samiel, what are you doing?" Michael swallowed. It was difficult to speak.

Summoning the blue fires of immolation, Anaba leaped from the dojo porch and galloped toward Death with every intention of trampling the Horseman.

"Anaba, abdad!" Ziri pleaded, bringing the Nightmare, half rearing, to a halt. He pressed his trembling hands against Serra's wound. Despite his efforts, blood seeped between his fingers, as tears fell from his eyes, dampening the indigo veil. "He's holding her spirit."

They were badly outnumbered and surrounded by enemies. Gabriel and Raphael fought off ten Grigori soldiers on the other side of the garden. Thirty more were converging on them from the rooftop. All were frozen in place, trapped in an acute state of slow motion.

"They cannot harm you, Michael. Or her," Samiel said. "We are temporarily out of time and beyond their reach."

"Out of time?" It was an ominous statement. Michael stumbled from the saddle, nearly falling as he dismounted.

"One of my vested powers is The Last Breath. My scythe allows me to temporarily extend the final moments of someone's life."

"Samiel, please. You can't let her die."

"I am honoring your mother's wish. I cannot go against my word."

"Y-you mustn't be angry with Samiel," Serra said. Her chest expanded spasmodically as she tried to take in a breath.

"This is what you were talking about at the ball, isn't it? That's why she looked so sad." Michael's fingers tightened on the war lance. "How could you betray me!"

"Michael." Serra coughed, weakly reaching up for him.

He fell to his knees beside her. "Mom, you've got to hold on. I can have a medical team here in minutes."

Serra shook her head from side to side. "I miss your father." Her eyes fluttered closed for a moment, tears falling from them. "This is the only way… we can be together."

"He doesn't deserve you." Michael leaned over her. She wiped away his tears. "Why wasn't he here to protect you? Mom, please. What does it mean to be a Horseman if I can't protect the people I love?" Taking her hand, Michael held her cold fingers against his cheek.

"Your father's disobedience came with a terrible price… for all of us. You must forgive him, Michael, and me."

"Don't talk about him." He brushed the thin sisterlocks from her face. "Save your strength."

"Michael… my roses…"

Withering with the hiss and pop of burning sap, the overgrown rose bushes were dying. Influenced by the swell of his emotions, the wilted boughs drooped and turned black, desiccated by the unnatural evaporation of the water within them. Vulnerable limbs broke off as the weight of the larger branches brought the plants to systemic collapse.

Michael willed the waters back into the dying plants. Summoning the excess rainwater, he imbued it with minerals from the soil to restore them. The revitalized bushes awakened from their stupor and verdant green buds sprouted and burst open with crimson bulbs that blossomed into hundreds of mature roses. The night air grew pungent with their fragrance.

"What was once lost and then forgotten must be found again." Serra raised both hands and held onto Michael's face, her voice fading with her strength. She stared into his eyes, unable to speak until a spasm of pain had passed. "Give the Nephilim what the Father could not… a home." She smiled, a pained expression. "Find them a refuge that is as close to Heaven as any of them may get, until they find their rightful place." She gasped, blood trickling from the corner of her mouth.

"I can't." Michael drew in a sharp breath. "Not without you."

"Michael, you are the key." Serra removed the silver band from her left hand. Carved into the likeness of a single feather, the ring cast an ethereal illumination that was not of the living world. She put it in his hand and wrapped his fingers around it. "Your father gave this to me as my wedding ring. It is his signet – the ring of an archangel. And now I give it to you to seal your birthright."

Michael stared into the night sky, but took no solace in the stars looking down to witness his tragedy. "Samiel!" he exhaled "I'm begging you!" Tears spilled over his hands and hers.

"I am sorry, Michael," Death said. "It is time."

"You're so much like your father." Serra's cold hand caressed Michael's cheek. "I will always love you." She closed her eyes.

"Mom! Mom, please!"

An earthquake shook the ground, an upheaval that loosened hardened sand, shifting gravel and rock. It grew in intensity until the powerful vibrations rattled the support pillars of the dojo.

Anaba pinned her ears. *Ziri, stay close!*

Samiel stared into the skies, his face visibly drained. "An Exalted One approaches."

An archangel cloaked in blue light descended into the garden. His armor was resplendent with a brilliance that banished the surrounding darkness. Six white wings buffeted the air, generating a wind as potent as the earthquake that announced his arrival.

"You have done the unspeakable!" Though soft-spoken, the Exalted One's voice was labored with the weight of his sorrow. "In His Name, be damned!" Uncradling the flamberge of lightning in his arm, he drove the great sword into the ground.

A shockwave radiated outwards from the blade, negating the effects of Samiel's temporal hold. Michael laid across his mother to protect her from the debris kicked up by the resulting blast. Anaba wrapped her neck around Ziri, shielding him with her body. Samiel stood, unmoving, seemingly untouched by anything more than a persistent breeze.

Thrown helplessly to the ground as if caught in a nuclear blast, the Grigori soldiers cried out in one, terrified voice. Desperate, floundering wings were scorched away; skin was flayed from flesh; and bone rendered to ash without flame. Anguished screams echoed into the night as the Grigori were judged by the Word of God and obliterated.

In silence, the Word and Death reigned.

"Maoffras restil, hoath, Samiel, Archangel of the Passover," the Exalted One said. "I bid you peace. Arezodi." His voice rang hollow behind a visor. "And you as well, true sons of the Lord God."

Gabriel and Raphael dropped to their knees in the ashes of their defeated foes. Sweating and panting, they bowed their heads in greeting.

Samiel nodded respectfully. "May you praise Him and that praise be immeasurable, Enoch, Prince of Archangels."

"My daughter has finally come to judgment." Enoch stared down at Serra's body. "Why do I sense her soul quivering within this broken shell?"

"I did what I could to ease her suffering, but hers is not a soul for my reaping. I held the last breath, as she requested. Your grandson, His Chosen, heard the last confession. All is as it should be." Samiel again bowed his head reverently and stepped back. "She awaits your escort to the Place of the Eternal Inheritance."

Enoch raised the visor of his red-plumed helmet and revealed a benevolent, yet stern, countenance. His eyes shone with all the starlight of the heavens.

"You!" Michael gasped. Though he had never met his maternal grandfather, he recognized the face from one of the darkest days of his life. "The Knight Marshal at the tournament?"

"Your father's legion were fending off an attack by Lucifer and his Black Seraphim on the day of your championship," Enoch said. "He could not be there with you, so I came in your hour of need, Michael."

"Then be here for me now!" Michael pulled Serra's lifeless body into his arms and rested her head against his shoulder. "Please… don't do this."

"The implications of your birthright are a burden. Shadows that will not be vanquished by any light." Enoch removed a gauntlet and caressed his face, wiping away his tears. "Will you accept that burden for a fallen people who may not deserve your sacrifice?"

"There is no greater drought than the famine in a man's heart."

Enoch's eyes widened in surprise. "You remember my words? But do you comprehend their meaning?"

Michael looked up at him. "I will do what I am supposed to. I will find a home for the Nephilim. But I won't do it for them. Not even for myself." He held his mother's hand against his lips and kissed her fingers. "I'll do it for *her*."

"This is why the Father exalts mankind above all else in the Creation, even His angels." With an anguished expression, Enoch took Serra's body from Michael's arms. "Gabriel, word of this sorrow has spread through the Father's house. Though it will come to good, it has not been well received. Go to Mikha'el and give him what comfort he will receive. Raphael, you will join me on the Vestibule Road." Knees slightly bent, Enoch leaped into the air. Even before his six wings unfurled, he was gone, a pinpoint of light among thousands.

"Why the Vestibule Road?" Michael said. "He's taking her to Hell?"

"*All* souls descend into the underworld to begin their three-day journey to Heaven," Samiel replied. "That is the Father's decree."

"Anaba–" Michael turned to call the Nightmare to his side.

But Samiel caught him by the arm and held him. "Anaba has caused more than enough mischief in the Kingdom of Heaven. More than any *one* Nightmare has ever caused.

"She'll be fine, Michael," Gabriel said, laying a hand on his shoulder. "*You'll* be fine." He held on to Michael's shoulder. "Your father trained you for this. You're ready for what lies ahead."

"If you doubt yourself," Raphael said, glancing to Anaba, "don't doubt her. Restil, nephew." He nodded to Samiel and flew into the night with Gabriel.

Sitting on his knees, Ziri pulled the veil from his face and rocked back and forth in grief. He clutched the double curve bow to his chest. His fingers were covered in Serra's blood. "She was teaching me the anăgad – the veiling – when they came. She told me to be mužeɣ – to be Tuareg… to be noble, yet I couldn't save her." Without the veil to absorb them, tears dripped from his chin. He laid his hands in the pool of her blood. "*Truth enters the soul like a thorn*. Har ažăkka."

"If you dare to run with Horsemen, you had better be armed like one." Samiel touched the tip of the bow. The limbs and string thrummed. "Speak its name and be judged, so that this weapon may serve you in this life and the next."

"Ulh-kereššet," Ziri said, his voice faltering. "Broken hearted."

"This bow will never miss its mark, but, being mortal, it will exact a terrible cost from you," Samiel warned. "Every life taken will bring you a day closer to your own death."

Michael got to his feet. Stunned with grief, he could do nothing except move backwards with the misplaced hope that by retracing his steps he might undo what had happened. Before his legs gave out, he bumped into something solid. He stood with his back propped against it. The object neither yielded nor pushed back, but remained resolute and supported him.

"Michael?"

He could feel Anaba's breath on the back of his neck, but when he turned to face her, she was in human form. Sorrow devoured what sensibilities he had left. Sobbing, he buried his face in her shoulder, desperately clinging to her. He feared that letting go might cast him adrift onto a distant night shore with no hope of ever finding his way back from the darkness.

Anaba wrapped her arms around him and ran her hands across his back to comfort him. When he fell to his knees, his strength gone, she went with him and held him up. There was no safer place for him to be than in her arms. He marveled at her strength and fought to absorb some small essence of it to fortify himself.

"I've got you," she said, pressing her cheek against his forehead. She kissed him. "I've got you."

CHAPTER 56

Michael opened his eyes. He was lying on his stomach on the quilted sofa in his mother's bedroom with no memory of how he got there. He breathed in the faint scent of Serra's rose water perfume.

Anaba caressed his face. "Michael?" Her fingers smelled of fire and roses.

Disoriented, he sat up, still clutching the silver ring Serra had given him. It felt unbearably heavy in his hand.

"Michael, you're spooking me." Anaba forced him to look at her. "Say something."

"Where is everyone?" he croaked.

She was visibly relieved. "Downstairs in the kitchen."

Michael stood up, taking her by the hand, and led the way down the stairs into the living room. He hesitated at the basement door, peering into the kitchen as the murmur of hushed voices fell silent.

Ziri sat at the breakfast nook between Samiel and Raijin. War was teaching the Tuareg boy how best to tie his veil and turban. Wyrmwood and Elijah were preparing coffee on the countertop. Noah was leaning beneath the center island light while Stacia dabbed at the bloody gash on his head.

"Mike?" Noah said quietly.

Michael's throat tightened, preventing him from speaking.

Looking at the faces around him, he panicked and hurried down the cellar stairs. Anaba closed the door behind them.

A thin layer of dust covered the recreation room, blanketing the furniture, a ping-pong table, and an air hockey game. Missing a leg, the latter was propped up with mythology textbooks. The pool table in the center of the room was buried beneath piles of out-grown clothes, boxed Christmas ornaments, armor, and old saddles. Over a decade, the room had gone from a family room to a storage space. In the wake of his mother's death, it was a mausoleum.

Michael scanned the familiar clutter like an untouched archaeological discovery, seeing his childhood memories as though they were antiquities buried under the dust. Rummaging in a box labeled *Pictures,* he pulled out a handful and chuckled through his tears.

"Someone looks pissed." Anaba studied a picture of very young Michael sitting, half buried, in a pile of fall leaves. His face was flushed from sobbing. "How old were you?"

"Three. My mother…" he stifled a sob through a deep breath. "We had just moved in. My mom spent a Saturday morning raking leaves. Later that afternoon, Gabriel convinced me to play soldier. We scattered those damn leaves all across the yard and made a mess of it." Michael brushed away a tear with the back of his hand and sniffed. "She threatened to sell my pony. That's why I'm bawling."

Anaba laughed. "What's going on here?" She pointed to the next curled photo in his hand.

Michael was sitting at a picnic table in the garden. No older than five or six years-old, he was scribbling on parchment paper with a feather quill. "My father insisted on teaching me written Enochian. But since he was never around, the duty fell to my uncles. But Uncle Raph was more interested in watching *Star Wars* movies. All Uncle Gabe wanted to do was play *Final Fantasy*. It never quite took." He rubbed his fingers pensively across his stubbled chin. "That's why

I didn't recognize the language when I saw it at the crime scenes."

"You were never very good at Enochian. Your mother intervened and decided it was not in your best interest to learn it," said a familiar voice. "Arezodi, my son."

Michael dropped the picture. Caught between grief and fury, he felt faint and leaned against the pool table for support. "You wish me no harm?" Michael spat, interpreting the Enochian. "It's a little late for that."

"Anaba, please leave us," Mikha'el said. "I must talk to my son."

"Not a chance," Anaba replied through clenched teeth.

"Anaba, niis!"

"You son of a bitch!" Michael spun on the ball of his foot to confront his father. "You may have forged her, but Anaba's bound to me, not you!" He could smell the acrid taint of brimstone. At a word, the Nightmare would have attacked, but he feared for her safety against God's greatest general.

Mikha'el was dressed in a white tunic beneath a silver cuirass decorated with an intricate gold inlay. Bracers of a similar design covered his muscular forearms. Shoulder-length dreadlocks were swept back from his face in silver rings. His eyes were bloodshot, the lids swollen and tinged with red as if he'd been crying for a prolonged period of time.

"We need to talk, Michael… civilly."

Michael had spent the last ten years imagining this reunion. Wondering what he would say. How he would say it. The decades-old staged rehearsals fell short. "What if I'm not of a mind to listen?"

"Then listen out of respect for your mother. If only this one time." The laugh lines of the archangel's face were evident, but now strained with an almost imperceptible sorrow that his handsome features could not mask. Retrieving the picture from the floor, he glanced at the image with a smile and placed it back in the box.

"You're stalling."

"I am," Mikha'el confessed. "This is more difficult than I imagined. Cherubim have always been better at martial arms, not words. The Father rarely sends me with messages. He usually sends Gabriel, who has a flair for such things."

"At least Uncle Gabe was here," Michael said. "You were absent. As usual. When she needed you most. When *I* needed you."

Mikha'el narrowed his eyes under the weight of the accusation. "I loved your mother. More than anything in the creation. But there was a price to be paid for that love."

"When did love become sin?"

"When it became a choice!"

Summoning Ah-Azarim Aziagiar, his hands firm at the haft of the war lance, Michael thrust the edge of the blade-head toward his father's throat. "Give me one good reason not to end you!" Calmly looking into Michael's eyes, the archangel made no movement in his own defense.

"You really shouldn't get your hands dirty," Anaba whispered. "Let me do it."

"Do you remember our home in Scarsdale?" Mikha'el asked. "The night we left and why?"

"I was three years old!" Michael replied. "How the fuck do you expect me to remember that night?"

"Think back, Michael. Remember," the archangel replied. "Why did we leave?"

The attack came in the middle of the night with loud, angry voices, accusations of disobedience and defiance. The charges were met by his father's authoritative voice, the one he used when the horses got loose and went galloping in the road. But with a belly full of milk and chocolate chip cookies, Michael was too sleepy and could make little sense of it.

Michael withdrew the war lance, staggered by the memory and took a step back and away from his father. His knees threatened to buckle beneath him. "The Grigori?"

Serra roused him from a warm bed and scooped Michael up in her arms. He was too old to be carried, but there was a sense of urgency in the way she held him against her. Leading Noah by the hand, she ran with them into the bathroom in her room and locked the door.

Leaning his weight on the war lance, Michael stared at the floor as the images replayed themselves through his fractured memories. "The Grigori had come to kill us…"

His mother was bleeding from a cut on her cheek. There was blood on the back of the door where she had drawn a symbol. The door bulged in as if a great weight pressed against it from the outer room. But it held.

There was a terrible racket beyond it, a dull thumping and the thud of wrestling like when Noah and he would play fight in the living room. They always got in trouble for it, sentenced to the outdoors for the rest of the day or to extra chores. He imagined his mother would be cross.

"They had come to kill me," Michael whispered.

Michael's father burst in through the bathroom door. He had a way of doing that – getting through locked doors with special drawings on them. "…too many of them… more coming…" he said. Taking Michael in his arms, he reached for Noah's hand, while Serra took the other and they fled as a family.

"I never abandoned you, Michael… or your mother," Mikha'el said. "I stayed with you as long as I could after the initial attack: teaching you, preparing you for the day I would not… could not be there." He stared up into the rafters with a fatigued sigh of resignation. "A day, which has finally come."

"Uncle Gabe and Raph were there too." Michael allowed the final moments of the recollection to wash through him. He saw snatches of the unsettling images: *his uncles dressed in leather and maille armor, their wings unfurled, fighting for their lives among overturned tables and furniture in his mother's living room. They held off five unfamiliar angels while Michael's parents fled with Noah and him into the night.*

"Do you know why I knelt before Adam, a simple thing made of simple clay? It was not to worship him as the Father asked. I pitied him and the life of woe that was to befall mankind." The archangel stared into Michael's grieving eyes. "The notion that free will comes without suffering is a lie. Every angel knew it. None more than Lucifer, who rebelled and paid for his insolence with banishment."

"Adam and Eve didn't exactly get off with community service," Anaba said under her breath.

"The original sin was not theirs. It was God's. His failure to see the terrible consequences of His actions. Adam and Eve's transgression led to a regrettable act of rage that severed mankind's connection to Heaven. Salvation came with a price. A Messiah to address the sins of man–"

"But not the Nephilim?! They were just left behind? Abandoned to roam the Vestibule Road?" Sensing Anaba at his back, Michael went face to face with his father. "You're going to tell me how to make that right!"

Michael was two inches taller than his father, forcing the archangel to raise his chin to look into his eyes. "As the Father gave his only son in penance for man's salvation, so I must give mine for the Nephilim."

In the Old Testament, the price of loyalty was blood. A theme that would bleed into the brutal sacrificial rites of the Egyptians, the Aztecs, and hundreds of other ancient cultures. Even into the New Testament. The wrenching revelation took the breath from Michael's lungs. He staggered back against Anaba.

"Everybody knows how the Son of God's story ended. *Badly,*" Anaba said. She fought to get past Michael, but he held her back. "If that's the script, it ain't happening. Not on my watch."

The archangel smiled sadly, looking over Michael's shoulder at her. "If one of His Apostles had been a Nightmare…" he shrugged, "…things might have gone quite differently."

"That's why you forged Anaba," Michael accused. "To make certain there was a different ending?"

"Nothing is certain, Michael, but the Father does enjoy irony. In every sin there is salvation." He looked through a box of holiday ornaments and took out a velvet bag. "When the Watchers learned of the Father's edict to eradicate their children, they turned to the only human who would listen. Enoch. He knew he could not save the Nephilim or humanity from God's wrath, but he was certain that his bloodline could purchase salvation for a few and their descendants."

"Noah, the original Noah, and his family?" Michael said. "There were Nephilim hidden on the ark?"

"Yes. Enoch made a covenant with the Watchers to safeguard some of their children, and kept that vow by allowing me to take his daughter as my wife." Mikha'el closed the box.

"Committing *you* to Enoch's cause and turning the Nephilim into pawns!"

Carefully opening the bag, Mikha'el removed a decorative star from the interior. He walked over to the Christmas tree stored beneath the stairs and set the star prominently on top of it. "The Father has put all of His enemies in one place. They have conspired against Him for millennia. Another war is inevitable. One that will encompass the whole of Heaven, and Hell, and the Earth." Mikha'el carefully untangled the ornament's cord. "Only this time, Heaven *will* fall. Without the Nephilim, the Father will lose. *Everything*."

Michael glared at him, infuriated by the manipulation of his life and the unjust fate of the Nephilim that hung in the balance of arrogance. "How can God expect the Nephilim to raise one finger to save Heaven?"

"Because you will lead them." Mikha'el plugged in the star. The silver engraved crystal lit up, refracting iridescent light across the walls and ceiling. "In Enochian, Qaaun means fulcrum. The Christ was one side of the scale. You are the balance."

"And who is on the other scale?"

"She has not yet been born. And when she does come, she will bring neither dove nor laurel, but a declaration of war." Mikha'el paused to let the weight of his words sink in. "No angel has ever been or ever will be as pivotal to the Father as you, Michael."

"Don't you mean half angel, a Nephilim abomination." Michael reached behind his back and took Anaba's hand.

"As I was just a Cherubim when the Father called for a general to lead his legions against Lucifer. Though my list of deeds is not nearly as extensive as yours." Mikha'el walked about the room, eyeing the dust-covered games and artifacts. "No angel has ever caused the great waters of Hell to run dry. Or summoned a Leviathan." Grinning mischievously, he stroked Michael's cheek and cupped his chin in the palm of his hand. "Or risked the wrath of Vanity by casting Lucifer from the dance floor."

"You were watching?"

"If pride is a sin, then let me be damned. I couldn't stop laughing. The look on Lucifer's face." Mikha'el wiped a tear from the corner of his glassy eyes. "I have seen many wonders over the millennia, but I would give a wing to see my brother's dour expression one more time." The archangel's grin faded. "Though I was disappointed when you broke your promise to your mother and touched the qeres. That was a foolhardy venture, my son. One that could have gotten you killed."

His father's laughter was infectious. Against his will, Michael felt a smile pulling at one corner of his mouth. The decades old knot of hate and abandonment unraveled in Michael's stomach. As an FBI agent, he understood the call of duty. From Anaba, he had learned the wrenching cost of sacrifice. He bowed his head and succumbed, submitting to reconciliation as Anaba bowed to the iron bit.

Mikha'el reached out and opened Michael's hand, running his fingers across the silver band in his palm. "Now you see why

I have strayed so far from the tenets of Heaven to assure your survival. The destiny of the Nephilim is tied to the prophecy of the Qaaun."

Michael closed his eyes, reveling in the touch that had been denied to him for ten years. "I suppose you'll be wanting this back?"

Mikha'el shook his head. "This is *your* holy signet, *your* sigil of power. If you choose it." He glanced at the star and its sparkling lights. "Talveh – family. I didn't name the family farm after my love of mankind, but out of my love for you, Michael. You are the key," he insisted. "The Grigori have risked everything to fulfill their edict. Even now, in his madness, Rathaniel is leading what remains of his battalion to the church where the Nephilim have taken sanctuary. He means to kill them all and anyone who dares get in his way."

"I'm not going to let that happen." Staring at the signet ring Serra had left him, Michael slipped it onto the index finger of his right hand.

"Maoffras restil, Son of Mikha'el, Archangel of God." Mikha'el hesitated near a set of steeply sloped wooden stairs leading to the backyard of the farmhouse. Gray wings materialized, unfurling across his back. "I will be watching," he said with a sad smile. Leaping through the opened bilco doors, he vanished into the night sky.

Turning to Anaba, Michael embraced her. "You down for this, gunny?"

"I'm offended you even have to ask." She rubbed her thumb over the silver band on his finger.

"Come on, let's warn the others."

CHAPTER 57

"EJ, call Father Patrick! Something's up at the church..." Michael hesitated in the cellar doorway. He held his arm across the threshold to keep Anaba behind him. The power was on, but the lights were out on the first floor of the house.

The Horsemen and Elijah were huddled in the darkened foyer, peering through the kitchen doorway. Noah had Stacia pinned protectively in a corner. She was holding a knife in her hand.

"Anaba, zăbbăt!" Ziri hissed.

The Marine instinctively dropped to a knee and pulled Michael down into cover.

Clutching his recurve bow, Ziri pointed to his eyes, the only visible feature beneath his blue veil, and then pointed into the kitchen.

"What did you see?" Anaba whispered.

"*Ăzayeǵ,*" he replied.

"A raven?" Perplexed, Anaba leaned back against the staircase wall to get a good look. "The same raven that attacked the Grigori in the carnival?"

The Tuareg boy nodded. He reached up along the oak frame and switched on an exterior light. Cast in shadow, the profile of a raven was projected onto the far wall through the glass. The bird sat on the flower box between the gossamer relief of the sheer curtains that framed the window over the sink.

A harsh caw escaped the raven's mouth. It tapped its beak insistently at the glass. The noise echoed in the emptiness of the kitchen. In a flutter of wings, it flew away.

Steeping his tea, Raijin sat down on the console table outside the kitchen. "I told the boy we were a bit busy for bird watching."

"He's been watching us. Listening." Ziri clasped the silver cross in his hand, absently stroking the talisman with his thumb. "The kel essuf are known to send portends with pied crows. It is why their necks are white to mark them as messengers."

Michael crept across the hall and turned off the lights. "Why does that make me really nervous? EJ?"

Peering around the corner into the living room, Elijah jumped back. "Damn, kid's right. It seems to know we're in here." He pointed to the multi-pane bay window. The raven's ominous silhouette darkened the wall, magnified by the glass.

Hiding behind furniture, Ziri slid across the wooden floor on his hands and knees. Crouched down behind the sofa, Wyrmwood caught him by the ankle before he could reach the front door. She gestured to him, twirling her finger, and they switched positions. Together, they moved into the shadows on the far side of the staircase.

"We've got company," Wyrmwood said, maneuvering her bow into position.

"More Grigori?" Michael whispered.

"Samiel and I will go round the back," Raijin said, "and gather the Nightmares."

"Wait." Michael slipped through the shadows beneath the staircase and made his way to the west wall by the windows overlooking the porch. He twisted his neck at an odd angle to get a better look through the sheer drapes. "It's Loki'el and the Black Seraphim."

Wings folded at their backs, Lucifer's personal bodyguards stood side-by-side in the driveway astride their mounts. The rangy, gaunt-looking Nightmares had hides that resembled spent charcoal after the flame had died. Their dull coloring provided a sharp contrast to the crimson armor that the fallen angels wore, which ranged from leather to maille to full plate. Despite the variations, the armor had one commonality: the icon of a black raven embossed on the breastplates.

"Ziri, on my signal, open that door." Wyrmwood waited for him to get into position. "Go!" As the Tuareg boy threw the front door open, she stormed through it with three arrows nocked in her bowstring. "You're not welcome here, Loki'el!"

Dropping the reins over his Nightmare's neck, the Seraphim held his hands up in feigned surrender. "Not to be rude, Wyrmwood, but... I would hear that from the master of this house, not a meddling guest." He winked at her, his mouth twisted in a sardonic grin.

"What do you want, Loki'el?" Samiel demanded. "We are pressed for need and time."

"By the Blood of the Christ! Does the Nephilim have no voice?" Loki'el clucked his tongue in annoyance.

Michael stepped out onto the porch with the war lance locked in his grip. "Like Samiel said, we're a little busy."

"By the looks of the place, you've had some trouble." Lowering his hands, the fallen angel looked out over the mottled sections of grass, blackened by the burning corpses of angels. "I give you my word, Son of Mikha'el, the Black Seraphim had no part in it."

"Maybe you've come to finish what the Grigori started then?" As his wings materialized at his shoulders, Michael shrugged aggressively against their weight.

Loki'el calmly dismounted, leaving his reins dangling on the pavement. Approaching the porch, he removed his gloves, and placed a foot on the lowest step. The Seraphim leaned across his thigh and slapped the gauntlets against his boot. The coy smirk on his face faded. "It's not often that I feel any form of regret. For anyone. But you have my sincere condolences for your mother. Had we arrived a bit sooner, things might have gone differently."

The Angel's sincerity was disturbingly genuine, and Michael believed him. "Thank you."

Loki'el narrowed his eyes. "You wear your father's ring? The ring of an archangel?"

"*My* ring," Michael replied.

"And lo, a black horse; and he that sat on her had the name Famine." Loki'el wagged a scolding finger at him. "I tried to warn you, Son of Mikha'el. The greatest plague God unleashed upon the world was His angels. Believe me now?"

Michael recognized the voice of the homeless preacher he encountered on the way to Mary Klinedinst's crime scene in Central Park. "That was you?"

"That was me," the Seraphim gushed with false humility. "Sent by Lucifer to keep you on the prophetic path to discovery."

"Is Lucifer working with Rathaniel?" Michael tightened his hand on the war lance. In no mood for the Seraphim's trickery, he stepped down, face to face, to confront him.

"Perish the thought." Loki'el winced in disgust. "Lucifer wanted – needed – to even the odds. Odds which were heavily stacked, and remain stacked against you." The Seraphim's roguish grin returned. "At the ball, there was no opportunity to properly present the Son of Mikha'el with a gift."

"A gift?" Wary of the trickster, Michael searched his eyes for signs of treachery, but strangely found none.

"Rumors in Hell suggest you are about to go to war. No celestial battle is complete without at least *one* Black Seraphim there to raise a sword. You will have all ten, temporarily."

"Four Horsemen and ten pompous asses against an entire battalion of Grigori?" Raijin snorted. "We'll need more than your insufferable arrogance to make up for those numbers, Loki'el."

"True. Such odds doom us all, but the offer of our skills is a mere token, a tribute to honor the new Famine. The real gift comes in the form of an Eophon de Okada."

Michael frowned. "A lamentation of mercy?"

"An official pardon," Loki'el corrected him.

"For what?" Michael growled. "Turning off the water? Painting the sky blue? Failing to housetrain the Leviathan? Bill me."

"The Prince of Hell must be daft," Raijin sputtered. "The Four are in no need of a pardon. Certainly not from him."

"The clemency is not for you," Loki'el said, rolling his eyes. "Cherubim can be so thick-skulled. The pardon is for *them*." He pointed to the skies above the farmhouse.

Covered in filth and grime from millennia wandering the Vestibule Road, an army of angels flew down from the night skies and landed in the yard behind the Seraphim. Emerging from the smoldering remains of the barn and the fence line, they converged on the farmhouse. Many were missing limbs, an arm or a few fingers. All were scarred and misshapen by their suffering. All had the same unhinged look in their eyes that reminded Michael of Mary Klinedinst's damned soul.

"There must be hundreds of them," Michael said, stepping off the porch with the other Horsemen.

"Barely a garrison," Loki'el replied, "but enough to somewhat even the odds."

"What trickery is this, Loki'el?" Samiel said.

The Seraphim shrugged. "So long as your name isn't Odin or Thor," he spat the names with malice, "I offer no tricks. Only truth."

"This is Lucifer's answer to the Grigori?" Raijin asked, his hand on the hilt of his katana.

"These wretches can never go back to Heaven, and Hell will not receive them. Indecision cost them everything, but Lucifer has summarily agreed to grant them asylum. *If* they consent to making a final stand for your cause." The Seraphim stared out at the motley assortment of apostate angels behind him. "There was no shortage of volunteers. So we had to get picky. They're mostly Cherubim." He glanced at Raijin, mockery in his eyes. "With a few Virtues and Dominations whose minds were still intact."

"And what does Lucifer want for this army?" Michael asked, not certain he wanted to hear the answer.

"His reasons are his own," Loki'el said, surreptitiously winking. "The enemy of my enemy is my friend."

"I have no wish to be God's enemy."

Loki'el laughed. "Give it time."

Discordant, agitated croaks came from the farmhouse's rooftop. Flapping its wings defiantly, the pied crow hopped across the shingles and shrieked at them. The white splotch around his neck stood out in the moonlight.

"Blasted beast!" one of the Black Seraphim growled. He held his arm up to recall the raven, but it refused to obey him.

"Tannin, can't you control that infernal bird?"

"Bastard has a mind of his own, Loki'el."

Ziri jumped down from the porch and craned his neck up to see the raven. "It *is* you." Slinging the bow over his shoulder, he clucked his tongue at it. "Amădray, iyyăw da. Come!"

The raven tilted its head from side to side, wavering between options. Hopping into the air, it flew down from the roof and landed on the ground at Ziri's feet.

"Careful, boy. That's no ordinary raven," Loki'el warned. "It was once a Guardian Angel named Malpas."

"An angel?" Michael asked, incredulous.

"The lesser spheres of angels that fell with Lucifer did not survive the Purge. They were the fortunate ones," Samiel explained. "Those that did not perish were changed, becoming beasts. Wolves, cats, and ravens, as you see there. Despite their transformations, they still possess their faculties and grace, as well as an insatiable affinity toward humans."

Ziri held up his arm and clucked again. With an appeased cry, the bird leaped from the ground and alighted on his wrist. The Tuareg boy winced as its talons dug into his flesh for purchase.

"Ziri?" Anaba moved toward him in worry.

He held up his other hand, preoccupied in conversation. Nodding solemnly, he turned to the Horsemen. "Malpas brings a warning from the other ravens to avoid the skies over the city tonight."

"That can't be a good sign," Elijah said.

"No, not when he was tasked with surveillance of the church where the Nephilim are hiding." Loki'el walked back across the driveway and mounted his Nightmare. "I suggest we go before it's too late."

CHAPTER 58

Emerging from the spectral shadows of the Vestibule Road, Anaba cantered across the empty street in front of St. Joseph of the Merciful Heart. She moved like a defiant shadow into the alley beside the convent and jumped the privacy fence in the rear of the church.

The Nightmare recovered on the other side and trotted into the garden, sweeping her head from side to side for signs of trouble. Michael took his cues from her alert ears. Seeing no movement that alarmed him, he tapped Ziri's leg. The boy slid down over Anaba's hindquarters and hunched down, hidden in the fullness of her tail. He then ran to the back of the main building and rapped on the door.

Raijin and Wyrmwood jumped abreast, guiding their Nightmares over the six-foot fence. Samiel and Loki'el followed. Like a soundless steeplechase from the darkness, the rest of the Black Seraphim made the leap and pulled up in the yard in front of the parsonage.

"Ziri!" Father Paige's exclamation echoed in the narrow, concrete accessway leading to the backdoor of the church. Still wearing a clerical collar, he hurried to join Michael with another priest at his side. "Ol tibibp, Son of Mikha'el. All my sorrow for the passing of your mother. Yours and your father's grief must be unfathomable."

"Thank you." Michael bit his lip. There would be time to grieve, after he dealt with Rathaniel.

Awed by Nightmares pawing in the dead grass, the younger priest made the sign of the cross. Like a frightened foal, he stayed at the senior priest's hip. "Father Patrick, is this the moment of tribulation you spoke of?"

"Steady on, Father Marcus." Father Paige took the priest by the shoulders to comfort him. "I told you we would not be alone in this dark hour. You remember Special Agent Childs."

"That's *former* special agent. I've been suspended." Michael jumped down from Anaba's back. "Though I'm not sure if it really counts when the man who took my badge is actually a Grigori. The FBI Assistant Director goes by his given name – Rathaniel. Do you know him?"

"The Fifth Commander. Hidden in plain sight all this time. The Father gave too much power to the Watchers." Father Paige shook his head. "Clearly, they were securing positions of power to fulfill their edict against the Nephilim without drawing too much attention."

Father Marcus clasped his hands in prayer. Ironically, he recited a petition to Mikha'el in Latin as he turned his gaze to the skies. Hunched like stone gargoyles in grotesque poses, the army of apostate angels gathered in the garden trees and on the church rooftops.

"What's your status here?" Michael asked.

"There's been some odd electrical interference this evening, more so than can be explained by an old building and its aging infrastructure. The landlines haven't been working for hours, and there's no cell reception. The neighborhood power grid went out for eight blocks in all directions."

"You don't look to be in the dark." Holding onto the pommel of his saddle, Loki'el gazed at the array of floodlights bolted into the old brick.

"Loki'el? Lucifer sent you here?" Father Paige looked at Michael with concern.

"Call it a humanitarian effort, Pagiel." Throwing his leg over the withers of his Nightmare, he hopped down from the saddle.

"The church has auxiliary generators. Primitive, but effective."

"All the better to see what needs to be done."

The leader of the Black Seraphim began barking orders to his subordinates, sending various members of his entourage inside the church to draw Lucifer's sigil on the front door. Like Michael's father's signature, the glyph was a potent ward of power, despite the Seraphim's fall from grace. Loki'el ordered others to organize the apostate angels they had brought with them. Flanked by three more, he went into the church.

Father Paige put his hand on Michael's arm. "No one willingly travels in the company of the Black Seraphim."

Don't look a gift horse in the mouth, Anaba said, swishing her tail.

Michael scratched her neck affectionately. "We were badly outnumbered at my mother's farm. We're expecting the same force or greater, so we brought reinforcements. I just hope it's enough."

Raijin dismounted beside them. "Sun Tzu said '*victorious warriors win first and then go to war, while defeated warriors go to war and then seek to win.*' This isn't like the time when one of your predecessors had to choose between bringing a drought to the Sahara Sea or flooding the Nile River."

Michael stared at him. "The Sahara Sea? Don't you mean the Sahara Desert?"

"How do you think it became a desert? Poor planning." Raijin's shoved his hands into his gloves. "Come, Famine, this is no time to dawdle. We've a battle to strategize."

Michael's last memory of the sanctuary was the night he left Manhattan to meet Samiel in Hell. He remembered changing into his practice armor in a darkened sanctuary, full of empty pews, yellowed hymnals, and the dimly illuminated face of Christ crucified on the cross. It had been a lonely place, as lonely as Gethsemane must have been after the Last Supper. But no longer.

The sanctuary was lit in every corner by chalice-shaped lamps suspended from the vaulted ceiling. Every pew was crowded with people. Michael recognized some of them from his previous visit to the dormitory in the basement level of the building, but there were new faces – frightened faces – of men, women, and children. They were disheveled and weary. Their eyes distant, like the vacant expression of the souls who walked the Vestibule Road. The nuns moved between them, serving water and snacks or offering a moment of prayer and comfort.

"Business is booming," Michael said.

"There's been a sharp uptick in numbers," Father Paige replied. "Especially with young Keisha being killed and the attack on Jesse. You can thank your Agent Rollins."

"Rollins?" Elijah said, catching up to them. "We haven't been able to reach her."

"She's been working out of my rectory. Using some list she compiled. She contacted many of the people here and encouraged others to seek shelter."

Michael chewed at his lower lip. "Does she know the truth?" he asked, following the priest by the large pulpit.

Father Paige smiled sadly and glanced over his shoulder. "Enough to put her life in danger."

"I'll go check in with her." Elijah exited through a side passage leading away from the sanctuary.

Father Paige stood on tiptoe, reaching for a pair of crossed short swords arranged in a display within a shield on the wall. As his fingers gripped the hilts, rust rained from the blades in a metallic shower. Hidden beneath, Enochian glyphs gleamed in the polished steel.

"Nice to see you haven't lost your teeth after living among

the sheep for so long," Loki'el said. "Hope the rust falls as easily from you, brother."

"They served their purpose, as relics to power my protection ward, but they will be best wielded as the Father intended," Paige countered.

Father Marcus extended a trembling hand to touch one of the swords. "May we not be cast adrift."

The Black Seraphim rolled his eyes, intercepting the frightened man's hand with a slap. "Our standards are low, but not that low. Professionals only. Don't touch the merchandise."

"But I want to fight," the flabbergasted priest said. "This is my church. My congregation – my responsibility." His face was troubled, his eyes wide with fervor.

"Go light a candle or something. We're going to need all the fool's luck we can get." Loki'el rebuffed him with a kick in the backside.

"Father Marcus, someone in authority will need to comfort the people when they take shelter in the subbasement," Father Paige said.

"That's a bad idea. This sanctuary is the safest place. If you take these people down into the sub-basement and the Grigori get into the building?" Michael shook his head, hands on his hips. "Rathaniel's not looking to take any prisoners. They'll be trapped down there. It'll be a slaughter."

"There's a tunnel that connects the bomb shelter to an abandoned subway channel," Father Marcus said, keeping his distance from Loki'el.

"A way out means a way in." Loki'el whistled loudly. He turned to one of his Seraphim, "Secure that passage. If any Grigori tries to get through, make certain they regret it." He gestured toward the human priest. "Take the human with you. He seems unusually eager to die."

Making the sign of the cross, Father Marcus brought the rosary crucifix to his lips and kissed it. "Everyone, attention," he said and waited for silence in the sanctuary. "Please move to your designated areas in the recreation room. Keep together and remember our drills." He led the Black Seraphim and the contingent of Nephilim downstairs into the basement.

Walking through an alcove housing a statue of the Virgin Mary, Elijah removed the 9mm from a borrowed holster and gave the weapon a quick inspection. "Rollins is good. When she couldn't reach either of us, she figured something was up. So she went dark, thinking we did the same."

"How many rounds you got left?" Michael asked.

"Ten. Gonna have to pull a Deadpool and make every last damn one of them count before I go all *Lord of the Rings* with my dagger."

"Another mortal eager to die. Is there no shortage of the absurd?" Crossing his arms over his chest, Loki'el sat down on the feet of the crucifixion statue. "You'd have a better chance at boring them with a Gregorian chant than killing them with that handgun."

Elijah hit the magazine release and held it up to the Seraphim's face. "The Mark of Azazel." He slammed the magazine home and racked the slide to chamber a round. "Three dead bad guys with fucking wings made me a believer."

Loki'el sat up with interest. Putting his fingers to his lips, he whistled sharply. One of his compatriots ducked his head back into the sanctuary with a quizzical look on his face. Loki'el pointed to Elijah. "This human actually has potential. Take him with you."

In the field they were partners, a cohesive unit. Michael never had to question if Elijah had his back – no matter the danger. But the current situation was different. The rules of engagement had changed. The perps were angels. The stakes higher. "Watch your ass down there, partner."

"It's all good, Mike." He slapped him on the shoulder. "See you when this shit's over."

Standing in the rear of the church with Wyrmwood, Ziri

hurried away from the Horseman toward a crowd gathered at the steps leading down from the choir loft. "Jesse!" he shouted.

"Ziri?! Is that you?" Jesse Parker sprinted across the near-empty sanctuary and jumped into Ziri's arms. "I didn't think I'd ever see you again." Her face was scabbed over with the indelible carvings of Enochian profanities. "Don't look at me," she whispered. "I'm so ugly." She pulled strands of her curly hair across her face. "Why are you still looking at me?"

"Fel-as igrâz-i… I look because it pleases me." His voice was muffled beneath his indigo veil. "Among some of the tribes of Mali, scars are a sign of a woman's strength and her maturity. These represent your bravery." Ziri ran his fingers across her face. "I'm sorry I didn't stop them from taking Keisha."

"I don't blame you. Neither would Keisha."

"I have so much to tell you." He took her by the hand and interlaced his fingers with hers.

"How revoltingly tender," Loki'el said, "but there's no time for it. Ziri, or whatever your name is, recall your raven and find out what it's seen."

Ziri held Jesse's hand across his heart, then let go and retreated up the stairs into the choir balcony with Wyrmwood. Suspicious, Michael watched Loki'el observing the girl, studying the Enochian profanities carved into her face.

"You there," the Seraphim called. He retrieved a curved dagger from his belt and held it out to her. The weapon was as beautiful as it was lethal with a sharpened gut hook crafted into the tip of the blade.

"Survival is a form of revenge," Loki'el whispered to her. "I should know."

"Not a good idea, Loki," Michael protested. He reached for the weapon, but Jesse snatched it from Loki'el's hand before he could take it.

"I can take care of myself." Jesse curled her forefinger over the guard. She was a natural despite no prior training. Like him.

"This one shows promise. Jesse, was it? Down to the basement with the priest, girl. I suspect you'll do more to protect your people than he can."

"She's just a kid!" Michael argued.

"As were you when your father put a weapon in your hand," Loki'el countered. "Think he did that for male bonding? No, he did it to redefine you. Just as the Grigori have redefined this girl." He winked at her. "Off you go."

Michael stared after Jesse as she raced into the corridor to catch up with Father Marcus and the other Seraphim.

"The Norsemen of old had a saying: *It is better to die as you lived,*" Loki'el said. "How have you lived, Son of Mikha'el, Son of God?"

Michael narrowed his eyes and replied with the FBI motto: "With fidelity, bravery, and integrity."

CHAPTER 59

"They're coming!" one of the Seraphim announced from the sanctuary's rear entrance.

Flanked by Samiel and Pagiel, Michael hurried through the connecting hallway and out the exterior door. The scene in the garden was measured pandemonium. The frenetic notes of an infernal composition fed by pure anarchy. Nightmares reared and galloped, biting at each other's necks and flanks. Clouds of brimstone rose as vapor. Ignited by molten flecks, it detonated and sent flames across their bodies.

Three of the Black Seraphim scrambled into their saddles and cantered away cloaked in darkness to take up key positions around the church. Hundreds of apostate angels fell into defensive ranks to secure the building, its rooftops, and the nearby streets.

Loki'el walked into this maelstrom, eyes closed, his lips parted in rapture. "I haven't felt such havoc since the final days of Ragnarok!" The Seraphim extended his arms out to his sides and drew in a deep breath. "Huldra, niis!" He waited for the Nightmare to gallop to him and mounted in one fluid motion.

Baring her teeth aggressively, Anaba herded the other Nightmares out of her path. Haunches low to the ground, she pivoted on her hind legs as Michael settled in the saddle and cantered back into the crowded yard. The night skies above the church undulated with the movement of a thousand wings.

"Hold!" Raijin called from the darkness beside the parsonage. "An emissary requests permission to approach!"

"Oh for fuck's sake," Loki'el grumbled. He dropped his reins in his lap and crossed his arms over his breastplate like a petulant schoolchild denied a treat. "They want to make nice before we kill each other? This is far too exciting to stop and talk terms." With an irritated gesture, he put his hands up to his mouth and shouted, "Let your emissary approach!"

Dropping down from dark skies, Rathaniel landed on the rooftop of the old convent across from the church. Dressed in a gray, metallic cuirass and leather accoutrements, he rested a hand on the hilt of his bastard sword. "Loki'el? Why am I not surprised to see you in the midst of this anarchy?" He coughed fitfully into his hand. His black skin glistened, even in the shadows, showing a heavy sheen of sweat. "You have no love of mankind. No more than your master."

"What's that, Rathaniel?" Loki'el retorted, cupping a hand over his ear. "Hard to hear your narcissistic bullshit over that awful cough. What in Hell is wrong with you? Come to war with a cold?"

"He's got gonorrhea. Compliments of Wyrmwood," Michael said.

"How now? The Clap? You jest! The cherry hanging from that branch is as ripe as the day the Father called it forth." The Seraphim slapped the reins against his thigh. "And they say the Afflictions have no sense of humor. What say you, Rathaniel? Soiled and sullied, but still chaste." A raucous chorus of laughter spread through the parsonage yard.

"I say only this." The Grigori's jaw muscles twitched in fury. *"That on the earth the Nephilim shall never obtain peace and remission of sin. For they shall not rejoice in their offspring, they shall behold the slaughter of their beloved; shall lament for the destruction of their sons; and shall petition forever, but shall not obtain mercy and peace."*

Rathaniel knelt down on one knee and stared at Michael. "These are your grandfather's words, Son of Mikha'el."

"Taken woefully out of context. Beware, Michael," Samiel warned, "he's goading you."

"I have pitied you, Childs," Rathaniel said. "Because of the sins of your father, you've lived between worlds – neither human nor angel. Never knowing peace. You have no sense of who you are."

"You've been at the FBI for over a year, you bastard. You could have killed me any time. Why didn't you?" Michael wound the reins around his fingers until they throbbed.

"You were a reminder. *Never* to underestimate my enemy. As the potential Qaaun, you were a means to find other Nephilim and flush them out, so the Grigori could cleanse the Creation."

Lowering her head, Anaba pinned her ears and chomped on the bit. Her furious pawing intensified the conflagration of flame rolling up her legs. She flicked her tail across the blaze and sent gouts of green fire into the darkness. *This fucker has a death wish.* Attuned to her agitation, the other Nightmares grew restless.

The Grigori stood up, hands gripping his warbelt. "I came to your home when you were a child. My plan was to kill your mother and you, sparing you this ignoble life, and then drag your disobedient father back to Heaven to atone for his indiscretions. I failed, but tonight is your reckoning."

"It's a bit early for victory speeches, Rathaniel," Loki'el said, grabbing Anaba's reins to help restrain the Nightmare. "We're not quite dead yet. Though being dead would be preferable to listening to your long-winded assery." He rolled his eyes. "I may bleed out in boredom."

"Despite appearances, your mother's story had a happy ending," Rathaniel said, ignoring the crude Seraphim. "I'm going to carve her rightful name across your forehead: ababalond. Whore. Then I will carve your traitorous father's name beside it."

"Now *that* was uncalled for." Loki'el released Anaba's reins. "I say kill the bastard."

Michael's wings sprang from his shoulders and unfurled. He closed his legs about Anaba's sides to urge her forward and held on as the Nightmare vehemently complied. Laying the war lance across her neck, he tightened his grip on the shaft until his knuckles cracked.

Loki'el and the Black Seraphim charged with him, their Nightmares leaping into the sky. A contingent of apostates rallied behind them. They were met by hundreds of Grigori soldiers, who flew down to intercept them.

Pulling up from a dive, a Grigori retrieved a trio of daggers from a slotted glove on his hand and threw them at the incoming wave. The knives were curiously small, a mere nuisance, not capable of producing mortal damage.

With a grunt of pain, an overeager Cherubim armed with a ranseur gasped when struck in the thigh. He fell backward, his clawed hands reaching for the sky. Wings flapping frantically, he landed in the street with a sickening crack of asphalt and bone.

Snatching a blade from his shoulder, a second angel went rigid. His muscles convulsed involuntarily. He arced his back, writhing in pain, and fell out of the sky while strangling on his own blood.

"The cowards are using qeres!" Loki'el shouted. He crossed the tips of his wings over his breastplate to reinforce his armor.

Anaba tossed her head, raising her crest to make herself a larger target. The third dagger embedded itself in her neck instead of Michael's chest. The Nightmare flinched, but was unfazed by the blade or its poison. Ears pinned against her skull, she lowered her head and continued her charge.

"Kill the Nightmare!" Rathaniel ordered. "Leave the Rider to me."

Michael braced himself in the stirrups as Anaba closed on Rathaniel. Before impact, he was broadsided. Three Grigori dragged him from the saddle. Desperate to hobble the Nightmare, another four tackled Anaba, driving her downward diagonally toward the church.

"Anaba!" Out of control, Michael spiraled through the air. He heard the whistle of arrows from the church rooftops and felt the impact of the shafts embedding themselves in the Grigori restraining him. He recognized Wyrmwood's craft as the virulent infection ravaged the angels, killing them with a prolific eruption of boils.

The violent noise of crossed swords and wind abruptly ceased, replaced with the roar of breaking wood and smashed brick. Michael and the corpses crashed through the rooftop of the carriage house behind the convent. Wincing at the sting of a split lip, he swallowed the taste of blood. It was acrid, metallic, and sour on his tongue.

The collision was painful enough, but a closed fist to the face rattled his senses. He crawled to all fours and got kicked in the ribs for his efforts. The force of the blow knocked the wind out of him. He fell, skidding across the floor among shattered bricks and roofing shingles.

"Mankind taints everything it touches, even the hearts of angels!" Rathaniel sneered. His voice was hoarse, strained with every syllable.

"But you knelt before Adam?" Michael said, wheezing to catch his breath.

"It was what the Father commanded!" Rathaniel spat back. "I saw no value in Adam nor in his progeny, who would repeatedly prove themselves unworthy of God's love."

"So it's not just the Nephilim you hate, but *all* of humanity?" Michael got to his feet, deftly avoiding another punch. "How are you any different than Lucifer? Fallen." He retaliated with a jab to the Grigori's face.

Caught unawares, Rathaniel staggered back a step. Dabbing at the trickle of blood running from his nose, he smeared it across his palm and drew his bastard sword from its scabbard.

Hissing against the inside of the sheath, the blade captured Michael's reflection in the burnished metal. "It was your father who delivered the order to wipe out the Nephilim." The Grigori commander spat blood onto the floor at Michael's feet.

"Save your breath and your lies. It was my father and Enoch who secretly conspired to save them." Michael sank down into a defensive stance, determined to ignore the baiting.

Swinging the lance across his shoulder in a feint, he lured Rathaniel to counter. The sword did not have the same reach. When the Grigori raised the blade to attack, Michael charged in a rapid, offensive thrust that penetrated his armor and sank deep into the flesh on the inside of his thigh.

The Grigori commander fled into the high ceiling, flying backwards to evade further injury. Michael persisted, thrusting rapidly in various directions to overwhelm the angel's defenses.

"No celestial was more enamored with mankind than your father. You would have thought he was a Guardian Angel rather than an archangel." Rathaniel landed on the other side of the attic. "He shared that weakness with the Father: a fondness for fragile things."

"You sound jealous. Did you ever stop to think why God favored humans over angels?" Michael tipped the lance upward to defend against a glancing blow. "It's because man was destined to become greater than the angels. Even in our imperfection, He loved us more."

"You dare speak to me of imperfection!" Grasping the sword in both hands, Rathaniel charged.

"The Nephilim committed no sin. God sent the flood to punish His wayward angels. To erase the evil the Elohim had brought into the world. But not all the Nephilim were tainted, a fact the Grigori commanders failed to mention in their report." Michael blocked with the war lance, arms trembling.

Leaning heavily on the lance, the Grigori commander locked the weapon on the guard of his bastard sword and kicked Michael in the chest.

Forced down on one knee, Michael timed a low thrust. Parrying the angel's retaliatory stroke, he retreated but not before thrusting the lance downward through Rathaniel's foot. With the sound of splitting wood, the blade-head penetrated through to the floor.

Rathaniel growled and leaped forward with a punch. Weighted by a gauntlet and the sword, his fist broke Michael's nose and sent blood spilling over his lips. Blocking the war lance and an attempt at his throat, the Grigori backhanded his former FBI subordinate.

Defiantly, Michael spat blood into the angel's face and grinned at him. *Play him for a fool and promote his conceit,* he remembered one of Raijin's aphorisms.

"Pride is a far greater sin than disobedience, which is why God has sent his judgment against *you* and not the Nephilim."

Rathaniel faltered. "His judgment?"

"Why do you think the Horsemen are here? We were sent to defend the Nephilim. Where do you think that leaves the Grigori?" Michael taunted.

Revelation erupted in a swell of anguished rage. Rathaniel charged, repeatedly driving the edge of his bastard sword downward in both hands. Michael blocked the reckless, but powerful strokes with the shaft of the lance. Forced to retreat across the room, he grappled with the incensed Watcher, his arms trembling as he struggled to hold Rathaniel back.

"With–" Cut off by a sharp knifehand strike to the throat, Michael gasped for air.

The Grigori grabbed him by the neck and threw him through a brick wall. Michael tumbled into a small laundry room, trailing a cloud of brick dust, and collapsed in the corner by the sink. Rathaniel stood over him, pressing his hand against Michael's face in an attempt to smother him. The porcelain basin shattered beneath their weight.

"You will die as the tainted Christ died," Rathaniel said. "Humanity's salvation was an unfortunate oversight.

There will be no redemption, no promised place, for the Nephilim."

Unable to breathe, Michael concentrated on the stream of water arcing above his head from a damaged pipe. The water twitched with sentience and lashed out like the tail of a scorpion, striking Rathaniel in the face.

The Grigori reared back with a bloody gash across his cheek. Before he could retreat, the watery whip coiled itself about his neck. The tendril constricted, biting into the folds of his throat, turning the water pink and then crimson with blood.

He fought to free himself, but the water slammed him from side to side within the narrow space. Veins bulging from his temples, Rathaniel drove his bastard sword into the floor in desperate fury. The act sent a shockwave of energy that erupted with such violence the wood beneath splintered. Structural cracks spidered up the carriage house walls. Creaking under the strain, the floor gave way with a roar.

In a cloud of stonedust and rotted wood, Michael and the Grigori commander fell into the darkness below.

CHAPTER 60

Angels were powerful creatures but even they had limits. Carrying the weight of a striking, biting Nightmare was one of them. In a writhing ball of smoldering wings and fiery hooves, Anaba and her assailants crashed through the weathered rooftop of the dilapidated convent across the alley from the church. Narrowly missing a row of spiked lightning rods, the Nightmare landed on her shoulder in the third-floor attic and slid across an inch of asbestos and insulation dust.

Blinded by a dense cloud of debris and disturbed cobwebs, she smashed through a brick wall, leaving a sizable hole. Desperate to regain her footing amid crumbling mortar and rotted wood, Anaba rolled with the momentum to protect her exposed belly from the flashing steel of the Grigori soldiers rising to attack her.

The Nightmare retreated into a cloak of darkness and used the silence and the shadows to evade them. A metallic ring of a sword missing its mark and striking stone rang out as the Grigori slashed blindly to find her.

She stalked them, pouring brimstone into the stale air. Molten flecks ignited the vapor in a condensed flash that negated the darkness. The startled angels fled from the deadly conflagration, flying above and beyond the radius of the flames. Hovering precariously, they regrouped and flanked her.

Armed with a heavy mace, the first soldier bashed the Nightmare in the forehead. Anaba squealed as the blow landed, leaving a gash above her left eye. Blinking rapidly to clear the blood from her vision, she reared and struck out with her front legs, but before she could land a kick, the angel's head whipped back abruptly. His body was ripped away from her and collided with a wall, harpooned by a long spear. Wings still fluttering, his body squirmed in its death spasms.

Runic symbols, illuminated by a pale yellow light, flashed along the weapon's shaft. Dangling a foot off the floor, the unlucky corpse still grasped the mace in his hand. Its spiked head swayed back and forth against the wall and left marks on the peeling dry wall. Anaba's flames reduced the corpse to ashes, but did no damage to the wooden spear.

A second angel charged at her, provoked by the death of his companion. Anaba dropped her head to the floor and swung around to kick him. Hunching her back for spring and velocity, she took aim for his face and launched both hind feet.

He gasped, an audible intake of fear, and dodged the Nightmare's wrath. To counter her, the Grigori swung a dagger in an underhand grip and drove the weapon into her right hind hoof. With a twist, he broke off the blade in the sole.

Penetrating the sensitive frog of her foot, the bloody tip of the dagger protruded through the horny, outer wall of the hoof. A squeal escaped the Nightmare's throat. White pinpoints of light danced before her eyes. When she stepped down in shock, the pain was excruciating. Anaba's knees nearly buckled. Fueling her fury with that pain, she balanced over her front legs like a gymnast and kicked the angel in the face with her good hoof.

Blinking against blood flowing from a gash between his eyes, the Grigori stumbled back. Anaba turned to face him. Wounded or not, she still had her teeth, and she was intent on using them. Before she could attack, the strange spear with the runes once again appeared and struck the angel in the chest. It lifted his body and carried him fifteen feet across the room, impaling the corpse against the tatters of a support wall beside a faded portrait of the Roman centurion Longinus.

Loki'el flew down through the hole in the roof. Hovering on black wings, the Seraphim held his hand out. The lethal spear vanished and reappeared in his hand, answering his summons. With nothing to hold it, the body of the angel fell to the debris-covered floor and was consumed in fire.

"Careful, Anaba," the Seraphim said, wagging a finger at her. "We mustn't add any more feathers to that crest of yours."

Grinding her teeth, she tried to put weight on the tip of her injured hoof. The pain shot through her hock and the rest of her hindquarters. Three-legged, she limped to a wall and leaned against it for relief. *Why's it so important to you?*

"Samiel didn't tell you?" Loki'el leaned the spear against the wall and reached for her wounded foot. "Death is such a hoarder of secrets."

Not in the mood for your bullshit, Loki! Anaba hunched her back and delivered a warning cowkick to his chest. *Stay the fuck away from me! I've got to get back to Michael.*

The Seraphim drew a dagger from his boot. "I would be happy to reunite you with your Rider."

Anaba spun away from the wall. Flames igniting from her hooves, she lined the angel up for a charge.

"That didn't come out quite right." Loki'el raised his hands up and held the blade out harmlessly across his palm. "We're on the same side, remember?"

I remember, but do you?

"Touch of Zephyr or no, you won't be doing any fighting on that hoof. A three-legged Nightmare is a soon-to-be-dead Nightmare." He tilted his head and kindly regarded her with a grin. "I learned much from my time with the master craftsmen of Asgard. A scratch of Æsirian runecraft, a squiggle of Enochian script, and some innovative farrier work will get you back in the fight in no time. And back to your Rider, whom I am certain, needs you."

Ears pinned flat against her skull, Anaba scraped her teeth against the wall. The incisors left deep gouges in the dry wall. It was a warning as the Seraphim approached.

"Steady," he whispered, cautiously.

Anaba did not resist when he ran his hand down her leg. He leaned against her haunch and carefully picked up the injured foot. She shifted her weight and leaned back, putting her weight on the raised leg to make it difficult for the angel to hold it.

"Seriously?" he growled, hitting her on the hindquarters with the hilt of the dagger.

The Nightmare caught him in the face with a scourging whip of her tail. He blinked against the sting as thin, reddened welts rose from his pale skin.

"This might hurt." Grunting with the effort to support the ill-tempered Nightmare's leg, Loki'el used his knife to cut away at the bloody sole. Though she tried to yank free of his grip, the Seraphim used his wings as leverage and locked her hoof between his knees while he worked to excise the broken dagger tip and repair the damage.

"You don't like Samiel, do you?" Loki'el said, winded by his labors.

I don't like you either. The Nightmare threw her head and suppressed the urge to bite him. A low white noise buzzed in her ears. She was going into shock, losing feeling in her extremities. The injury fired every nerve in her body, but the more the Seraphim cut and rasped with the edge of the blade, the less pain she felt. She took a deep breath and relaxed, relieving him of her weight.

"And here I thought I'd been so charming during our brief encounters at the ball."

You tried to get me drunk at the after-party.

"Just two old soldiers reminiscing over drinks about their days in the trenches."

You faked an emergency and came back, after transforming yourself into Michael. You tried to stick your tongue down my throat!

"Ah, there is that." He held the dagger in her flames until it glowed red, then pressed the heated metal against her sole. "What gave me away?"

Your stink. Anaba lowered her head to evade the acrid scent of burning horn.

"My good lady, I am wounded." He laughed as he readjusted her hoof between his knees. "I copied your master exquisitely. From his pouty, puppy eyes right down to his favorite cologne."

There's not enough perfume in the world to cover the stench of a fallen angel, Anaba retorted. *And Michael wouldn't have touched me the way you did.*

"Hmm, I must admit I *was* feeling a bit randy after we polished off that last bottle of Bacardi Millennium. So you knew it was me?" He put her foot down and slapped her across the flank. "Tell me you weren't tempted? A fallen Seraphim like me... a savagely gorgeous Nightmare like you? Think of all the Hell we could raise."

Anaba shifted her weight onto the injured hoof. It held solid. Able to bear weight on it, she trotted away from the wall to face him. *What is Samiel hiding?*

Arching his back to relieve the strain of being hunched over, Loki'el grinned. "So you were listening?" He wiped the bloody blade on his sash. "The Crest of Nanqueel is more than a pedigree, Anaba, it's a doomsday clock. The number of man is six. You are the sixth mount of the Horseman Famine. Six feathers completes the crest. You're three feathers away from triggering the Apocalypse."

That's why Caim Seere wanted me so badly.

Loki'el leaned licentiously against the wall. "Caim wanted leverage over Heaven and Hell, but he didn't have the stones to accomplish it."

But you do?

Studying his nails, the Seraphim shrugged. "I don't mean to brag, but when it comes to ending worlds... few have my extensive resume or real-world experience."

Anaba blasted him with a cloud of brimstone. Rearing violently, she struck out with her forelegs. *So your plan was to lure Michael to his death and then use me to end the world?*

Blinking rapidly to restore his vision, Loki'el threw his arms up to protect his head. Her hooves battered his bracers. "Anaba, wait! You've got it all wrong!" He grabbed the reins of her bridle and yanked at the bit, but she broke free, delivering a skull-rattling headbutt. The Seraphim was brought to his knees. "Lucifer sent the Black Seraphim to protect you and your Rider. We're here to *prevent* the Apocalypse!"

Why?

Loki'el jumped back as she charged, her teeth gnashing the air in front of his face. "By mutual agreement between the Father and Lucifer: neither party is eager to throw down the gauntlet and start a war."

Where does that leave the Nephilim?

"Collateral damage, I'm afraid."

But God sent the Four Horsemen to protect them? Lucifer sent you with an army of angels from Hell to fight for them?

"Lucifer's ragged army was to put a dent in the Grigori's military apparatus. The Horsemen were a warning to their commanders to stand down. The Nephilim were the bait." For a moment, there was a hint of regret in the Seraphim's pale blue eyes. "These are *fallen* angels, Anaba. Broken vessels. They're no match for the Grigori." Fingers splayed, Loki'el gently ran his hand across her face and nose. "But there might be a way to level the playing field… with your assistance."

I'm listening.

"The Grigori possess their full celestial grace." He laid his forehead against hers and whispered, "but if they were to fall…"

They'd be weakened, Anaba said.

"Evening the odds in *our* favor." He cupped his hands beneath her head and scratched the velvet fur beneath her chin. "That breastplate about your neck bears the Seal of Enoch. It cannot be countered *except* by the Word of the Father."

She didn't trust him, but there were no other options. *What do I need to do?*

"I was hoping you might ask that," Loki'el said, grinning mischievously. "The pyramid of power for a Horseman is his domain, his weapon, and his Nightmare. As I am no Horseman, I'll need a few substitutes." He reached into a pouch at his belt and produced a black, crystal vial. He unplugged the stopper and poured the watery contents on the floor in a circle around Anaba's feet. Ice shards formed within the creeping tendrils of steam that rose as soon as it made contact with the wood.

Water from the Cocytus? Anaba recognized the smell. It was reminiscent of the stench of mass graves she uncovered in the desert during her tour of Syria with the Marines. The frozen lake was nothing more than Hell's version of a body dump, filled with thousands of souls left to rot for eternity.

"And now a weapon." Loki'el retrieved his spear. He traced the glowing runes beneath his fingertips. "This is Gungnir, a little souvenir I borrowed from Odin."

What did Odin have to say about that?

"He didn't have a say. I made certain of that." The Seraphim laid his hand on her wither and gathered the reins over his thumb to mount.

Anaba narrowed her eyes and moved away, preventing his foot from reaching the stirrup.

"Now, now," the Seraphim chided, caressing her neck. "If the spell is to work, we need to get friendly. You're the most important piece of this diabolical recipe."

The Nightmare lowered her head to signal her compliance, and warily, the Seraphim put his foot in the stirrup and mounted. *Don't get comfortable.*

"Magnificent," Loki'el sighed, settling his weight into the saddle. "Now be a good girl and summon your immolation. One blast should carry the effects of the banishment spell and knock the Grigori off their glorified pedestals."

Anaba intensified her flames with clouds of brimstone until they burned blue.

"All we need now is a little blood to power the spell."

Blood? Anaba pinned her ears.

"The blood required for this ritual is my own." Loki'el removed a glove. Using the blade-head of the spear, he pricked the pad of his thumb. With a puckish curiosity in his eyes, he rubbed his bleeding finger across the Crest of Nanqueel and closed his eyes. "I invoke you, Enoch, Exalted Prince of Archangels, to pass judgment on those beyond this circle of shadow and flame. Having been born of nothing, let them *be* nothing. Strike their names from time, so that no record of them endures. Cast them down to be subjugated by your enemies. In the name of your true Father, banish them forever from the Light. Anaba, niis! Find us a road!"

The Crest of Nanqueel burned with a golden hue, shining between his bloody fingers. No longer under Anaba's control, the immolation field grew dense, heavily charged with a pale white miasma that reeked of burning metal. In a rapid pulse, the volatile flames blasted outward from the Nightmare, accompanied by a thunderclap loud enough to cause a modest trembler.

Suffering the distinct, gut-flipping sensation of free fall like parachuting from a plane, Anaba shifted uneasily beneath the Seraphim's weight. Something was wrong. *What have you done?*

Gloating over her, the Seraphim snorted. "Did I fail to mention that to banish an angel, one must banish them to a particular place."

Anaba gritted her teeth, hunched her back, and bucked violently. *You dirty bastard!*

Loki'el was thrown from the saddle and collided, upside down, with a wall. He slid down to the floor and landed on his head. Wiping a trickle of blood from his nostril, the chuckling Seraphim crawled to his knees. "By the Father, it was worth it." He struggled to his feet and picked up his spear. "Such power."

Anaba leaped to the ruins of the rooftop. The iconic New York City skyline was gone, replaced by an upheaval of dark blue and black skies. Having fallen from alignment, moons and planets collided in a cosmic catastrophe. Fissures of lightning arced across the broken horizon between shattered remnants of unnamed planets that drifted aimlessly.

St. Joseph's church, its convent and parsonage, along with a few other buildings sat in a desolate wasteland on the tapestry of a forsaken universe, torn apart at its seams.

We're in Hell?

"Not Hell. We're somewhere much worse." Loki'el flew out of the attic and took a knee beside her. Grinning out over the battlefield, he listened to the screams of falling angels as the sounds of battle gave way to wails of dire realization.

The Grigori had fallen.

"This is Mahorela, the Garden of Eden, or rather, what's left of it. If you're going to banish angels, I can't think of a better place." The Seraphim flew back out of reach to avoid a kick aimed at his face. "Now we've got a fighting chance. A chance to save the Nephilim." Loki'el drew his sword with a crooked smile. "So. Shall we find your Rider?"

CHAPTER 61

Michael landed on top of a 1957 Cadillac Seville parked in the carriage house. Kicking free of Rathaniel, he rolled across the smashed-in roof of the vintage car and fell to the concrete floor. Winded and dazed, he struck the Grigori in the chin with the butt of the war lance. His fingers went numb from the blow, but he risked spinning the shaft over the back of his hand and thrust the blade-head at the angel's throat.

Rathaniel blocked with his forearm and shoved the lance harmlessly away. "You are an inferior being, but you've got heart, Michael. That, I admire." Shaking blood from the curved, karambit blade in his hand, the Grigori disengaged.

Michael stared at the knife and then his forearm. He saw blood dripping from his sleeve, staining his maille. The cut was not deep, but it bled profusely. An amber oil greased the edges of the wound. "Qeres?"

As the cold perspiration broke from his pores, Michael recognized the familiar numbness coursing beneath his skin. It was followed by a burning that spread up his arm into his shoulder, assuring him the poison was in his bloodstream. He collapsed against the hood of the car. Constricting throat muscles worked at the lump rising behind his tongue.

The room shifted sideways, but it was not the room. It was him. He fell to the floor when his legs gave out to erratic spasms. The concrete reeked with the pungent odor of gasoline and old motor oil. It made him gag, which further irritated his throat. Lying on his back, he clutched at his stomach to stifle the pain of nails piercing his gut. The simple effort of rolling to his side left him panting. He tried to drag himself across the garage floor on cramped fingers.

"Do you know what qeres is? How it came to exist?" Rathaniel retrieved his bastard sword and sheathed it. "Believers do not speak of it in the Bible, and for good reason. While God's wrath is to be feared, it is His sorrow that is ever more terrifying."

Michael pressed his cheek against the cold floor. His shallow attempts at breathing produced a dull rattling in his chest.

"After the fall of Adam, the Father sent the Four Afflictions to destroy Eden. They made a ruin of his precious garden, annihilating everything within it. With one exception: the Tree of Life. God descended from Heaven to rip it out of the soil with His own hands, so that He could have the satisfaction of watching it die." Rathaniel laughed. "That was the day mankind lost the Eternal Inheritance. As the tree withered, so did the bond between the Creator and His Creation. In the aftermath, the Father wept. His tears formed a pool in the hole where the Tree once stood – Bahal'li."

"He… cried?" Michael whispered, translating the Enochian. The tears of God – it was no small wonder the substance was poisonous to angels.

Michael's desperate fingers clutched for the war lance. Rathaniel kicked it underneath the car with the toe of his boot. "Oh, ye rebellious son." He flipped Michael onto his back with a kick to the groin. Kneeling beside him, the Grigori caressed his cheek with the oily edge of the curved dagger.

Michael cringed as the qeres burned his skin, leaving blisters along his jawline.

"Tomorrow morning, your body will be found behind the Jacob K. Javits Federal Building. The story will take the lead on every news channel: FBI Special Agent Michael J. Childs –

killed by the sadistic serial killer he was hunting. The death of a hero will sufficiently bury the report of the tragic fire at St. Joseph of the Merciful Heart Church." Rathaniel shrugged. "No one will care about the deaths of a few hundred homeless people sheltering there."

The Grigori straddled him, spinning the karambit into an underhand grip. "But first, to prepare you for your life on the Vestibule Road. By carving your mother's name into your skull."

Michael threw his hands up and grabbed Rathaniel's wrists to defend himself. The karambit blade gleamed, the metal shining with the sheen of the qeres coating its edge.

"Anaba, ni–" Michael's attempt to summon the Nightmare was cut short by a punch to the jaw. He trembled with the effort to keep the tip of the blade from his face, but lacked the advantage of weight, leverage, and strength. It hovered inches above his forehead.

Rathaniel locked both hands around the hilt of the blade and bore down on him. "If she lives, the Nightmare will not arrive in time to save you. When this is over, I will find her and kill her too. To honor her and you, I shall cut out her heart and burn it on a pyre with your eyelids and tongue."

The ground shifted in a violent, seismic upheaval. Rathaniel was pitched forward off balance. Michael moved his head as the karambit slammed against the concrete. Sparks flew into his face.

Thin fissures fanned out like cataclysmic webbing across the damaged garage floor. Dust sifted from the beams supporting the carriage house's ceiling. A clap of thunder and a pulse of blue flame accompanied the trembler. The fire vanished so quickly Michael thought he had imagined it. *Nightmare immolation?*

Screams of anguish rose, muffled by the walls of the carriage house. The cries reminded Michael of those he heard from the damned who walked on the Vestibule Road. The sudden loss of strength in the Grigori's grip and the resurgence of energy in his was no illusion. Nor was the potent scent of brimstone in the air.

"Fallen?" Rathaniel said under his breath. "This cannot be. You are the ones who deserve to be abandoned!" He drove the karambit downward into Michael's face.

Readjusting his hands on Rathaniel's wrists, Michael pushed back. "What's wrong, Rathaniel? Getting a little taste of what it's like to be on the outside looking in?"

"No half-breed is the match of any angel, not even a fallen one!"

"Unless they happen to possess a Nightmare. Unfortunately for you, a Marine has just landed." Michael bridged up with his hips, forcing the Grigori forward onto his hands. When he heard the karambit blade hit the concrete, he hooked Rathaniel's arm and rolled with him, reversing the mount.

Punching the angel in the face, Michael got to his feet and extended his hand. The war lance materialized in his grip. He turned to the shadows as Anaba silently charged from a portal of darkness and flame. Michael clutched at the roots of her mane and leaped into his saddle. He rested the war lance across her neck and couched the shaft beneath his arm.

"You got him?"

Locked and loaded.

Rathaniel flew backwards in retreat, but there was no place to escape the Nightmare's charge. The war lance impaled him in the right side of his chest. Wings tangled, the Grigori collided with the garage door with enough force to dislodge the double hinges and springs. Aged and partially rotted, the door bulged outward under the violent impact and splintered as Anaba continued to gallop.

Grasping the war lance in both hands, Rathaniel clenched his teeth, but did not cry out, even when his back slammed into the trunk of a petrified tree. The war lance pierced him completely through and embedded itself into the dead wood, driven deep by the momentum of the Nightmare's charge.

Michael was breathless, his chest and rib cage bruised from the concussion. Still suffering the effects of the qeres, he leaned over Anaba's shoulder and vomited. The world shifted out of focus as the Nightmare slid to a halt and retreated. Releasing the lance, Michael tried to cling to the pommel of the saddle but his wrist was badly wrenched. In a halfhearted attempt to dismount, he fell to the rocky ground at Anaba's feet.

CHAPTER 62

A cold wind blew across Michael's face. Lying on his back on hard ground, he wanted to raise an arm to shield himself, but lacked the strength. He was tired and stiff. The stomach cramps caused by the qeres had subsided, and his breathing had eased. When the wind died down, he opened his eyes.

The Angel of Death stood over him, black wings unfurled like the walls of a sepulcher.

"Samiel?" Driven by panic, Michael tried to sit up, but could not move. "Is this the Last Breath? Am I dying?"

"I am truly sorry, Michael," Samiel replied.

Michael looked around him. Though there was no clarity to his immediate vision, the peripheral edges were fully in focus. Elijah was frozen in place, two paces away, reaching down for him. His partner's face was grim with the implications of the prognosis. Wyrmwood was on her knees. She had a belt in her hands and was strapping it around Michael's arm. Anaba had her teeth bared and was in the act of rearing at Rathaniel, who remained impaled against the tree.

He swallowed and stared into the dark skies overhead. "Are we in Hell?"

"Hell is a place where the Father puts things he can no longer stand to be in his sight," Samiel sighed. "Mahorela is where He puts those things he wishes to forget."

"How did we end up in the Garden of Eden?

"I sense Loki'el's mischief, but he lacks the sufficient prowess. A far greater power is at play here."

"The Grigori?"

"Not likely. They have fallen." Confounded, Samiel shook his head and frowned. "Their banishment worked in our favor. They have been defeated."

Michael reveled in the good news. He felt sleepy, but resisted closing his eyes for fear he'd never open them again. "The Nephilim?"

"Sheltering in the church."

"What was once lost and then forgotten must be found again," Michael mused.

"What is this riddle you whisper on your dying breath?"

"Something my mother said. Samiel, the answer is Mahorela. Eden could be a temporary home for the Nephilim. I'm the key." Michael held up the ring that signified his rank as an archangel. His sigil, Talveh, glowed vibrantly within the textured silver. "This is the price that had to be paid for the Nephilim to find redemption."

"Your life? For this ruin?" Samiel's skeletal hands rattled against the shaft of the scythe. "A poor bargain."

"Better than wandering the Vestibule Road. And the price is not my life, but the restoration of the garden that was lost. Release me from the Last Breath."

"Michael, Anaba will not be able to save you from the Vestibule Road this time."

"I don't plan on dying, Samiel. Not this time. The Horsemen may be immune to each other's vested powers, but not our own. That's why you are the only original member of the Four... You can't die. Now release me. I don't have much time."

Samiel's shadow grew heavy like a shroud of damp earth draped over Michael's body. His languid tongue rasped like sandpaper across the roof of his mouth. Dulled senses required concentration to attune them. Hearing returned first. Michael honed in on Loki'el's voice.

"There, there... be a good girl, Anaba... kill the bad angel. Damn the Apocalypse. It'll be worth it to see you tear the bastard to pieces." The Seraphim sighed, his irritation evident from the heightened nasal inflection. "Raijin, do get out of the way. I love it when she bares her teeth like that, especially when it's not at me."

With the whites of her eyes showing, Anaba lunged at Rathaniel. Pinned against the tree by the war lance, the Grigori flinched beneath the Nightmare's gnashing teeth. She arced her neck and exhaled a green-tinted vapor into his face. *God may forgive, but Marines don't.*

The creeping spores in the cloud adhered to exposed flesh and spread across the Grigori commander's skin. It darkened to the same black hue before turning ashen as the moisture-draining fungus desiccated and consumed the left side of his face. Revealing unusually angular bone and teeth, the withering claimed his earlobe with an audible popping before the entire ear sloughed off his head in a trail of ash.

"Brava!" Loki'el slapped his thigh, applauding exuberantly. "A Nightmare in a blood frenzy is absolute poetry."

Anaba pinned her ears at him. *You're next.*

"Anaba." Her name slipped from Michael's mouth in a whisper, but resonated like thunder in his skull. He drew in a sharp breath from the pain. The stomach cramps returned, twisting his gut into knots as the qeres continued to ravage his body. He curled into a fetal ball on the ground.

"He's back!" Elijah cried.

"Tighten that tourniquet," Wyrmwood ordered. "We have to slow the poison!"

"Forget the tourniquet. It won't work," Michael said. "I'm going to try something a bit more radical."

"Michael," she protested. "there's no cure–"

"EJ, get her back. Samiel," he pleaded, looking up at the

Horseman. “Keep them all back.” He glanced over his shoulder. “I’m going to use the power of my domain to remove the poison from my bloodstream.”

Samiel slammed the butt of his scythe against the ground. “Do as he asks!”

“Anaba?”

The Nightmare trotted to him, lowering her head. Michael pulled the reins over her head. He wrapped his injured wrist in the leather and grabbed the bight in his fist. “This is going to hurt like a bitch.” He took a deep breath, consciousness waning. “Hold on to me, gunny.”

I won’t let you go. Anaba grabbed the bit in her teeth and leaned back.

Michael pulled against her weight. Closing his eyes, he willed the water within him to dilate his veins. Excruciating pain lanced through him as nature complied. He instinctively drew back his arm to quell the agony, but Anaba held firm, dragging him until it was fully extended again.

Seeking the foreign globules of qeres that had infiltrated his bloodstream, microscopic tendrils of plasma latched on to the deadly oil and expelled it in a yellowish discharge that seeped through the bloody cut on his arm. The beads drifted through the air like suspended raindrops in a storm.

“Careful, Michael,” Wyrmwood warned, “if you drain too much, you risk killing yourself.”

Raijin removed the visor of his helmet. “I have never quite understood the Father’s preoccupation with mankind, but now I am beginning to appreciate His vision.”

The more severe symptoms resolved as the poison left his bloodstream, but Michael felt weaker than before, lightheaded and faint. He attempted to stand but fell at the Nightmare’s feet. Anaba lingered above him, brushing his sweaty face with her muzzle. Sinking to her knees, the Nightmare carefully laid down beside him. *I told Natalia I’d make the shore, dragging your ass behind me. I meant it.*

Michael grabbed a handful of her sooty mane and pulled himself up to her withers. He fought to throw his leg over the back of the cantle and crawled into his saddle. The Nightmare stood up, surrounded by thick globules of qeres-laced plasma. They spiraled about them like an emerging galaxy.

"This is no victory!" Rathaniel said. His voice held an unnerving lisp due to having half a face. "The Nephilim will never be safe, not here in Mahorela nor in the living world."

"You're right, Rathaniel," Michael said, his voice faint. He was exhausted, leaning lethargically over Anaba's neck. "Which means I need to make an example of you as a warning to anyone who threatens us." Michael nudged the Nightmare closer with his heels. Grasping the war lance, he gave the weapon a sharp twist and wrested it free of the petrified wood and the skewered angel at the tip.

Rathaniel fell to his knees, clutching at the wound. The Grigori's jaw muscles twitched in rage. He snatched the bastard sword from its scabbard and lunged at Michael.

Laying his hand on Anaba's shoulder, Michael splayed his fingers across the Crest of Nanqueel. He met Rathaniel's defiant eyes with a hint of sympathy. He knew the pain the angel had experienced was only a fraction of the agony he was about to inflict.

"Forgiveness is a kind of nobility, Rathaniel… God learned that from mankind, not His angels. That's what made us better."

Still encapsulated in plasma, the qeres linked together in a chain. It made a noose about the Grigori's neck and yanked him off his feet. Piercing armor and bone, the links burrowed into the injury at his shoulder and burst through his flesh like the invasive tentacles of an octopus, causing multiple wounds. Completely encapsulated within the water, the proximity of the poison was enough to inflict sores and blisters, but was not enough to kill the angel.

Wings helplessly pinned against his back, Rathaniel dropped his sword and cried out. His voice was drowned out by the roar of a fifty-foot geyser that shot up through the hardened surface of a dried-up riverbed beside him. The watery restraints bound his wrists and ankles, unnaturally contorting his outstretched limbs. Eyes bulging from his head, the Grigori wept in fury as qeres-laced tendrils carved Enochian obscenities into his flesh.

"I'm going to chain you to the Altar of Cain for all of Heaven and Hell to see," Michael said. "No one will hear your blasphemies above the roar of the River of Guilt. You'll be a reminder to everyone of what it truly means to be abandoned." The watery restraints retreated into the ground, dragging their prisoner with them. "Take a deep breath, Rathaniel. You're going to need it."

CHAPTER 63

Turning his gaze to the skies, Loki'el drew his saber from its scabbard. The sounds of renewed fighting cast a pallor over his face. He relaxed his stance and turned to Michael with a grin. "Hope you have a permit. Trespassing here has fatal consequences." He nodded to indicate the corpses of apostate angels tumbling from the heavens like falling stars.

Wielding a claymore of flame, an archangel descended amid the carnage. He landed with such velocity that he was forced to take a knee upon landing. A black maille shirt covered his upper chest, leaving a heavy leather gambeson to protect the lower half of his abdomen. A silver gorget encircled his neck and extended across his shoulders as pauldrons, allowing him freedom of movement with the great sword.

He pressed his large black hand into the muddy shores of the riverbed. Water was still bubbling up from beneath the cracked surface, filling in the stony channel. "Can this be? Mahorela lives again?" Staring at his muddy fingers, the angel turned to Michael. "I know those eyes."

Michael set the war lance against the tip of his boot, patting Anaba on the neck to keep her calm. The Nightmare chewed anxiously at the bit. "My given name is Michael, Son of Mikha'el. Arezodi."

"I am Uriel, the last remaining guardian of this forsaken place." He stood eight-feet tall with shoulders wide enough to carry the moon. His body blazed with a heavenly flame so intense the heat radiated from him in visible waves. "You are the Qaaun – His Chosen. Have you come to claim Mahorela in the name of the Nephilim?"

Michael looked to Samiel with uncertainty. "Yes."

"This is a day to rejoice; for what was once lost and then forgotten has been found! But Mahorela is a desecrated land where free will led to temptation and betrayal and the wrath of an inconsolable God. The way forward will not be easy," Uriel warned. "His swift judgment came with disastrous repercussions not only for mankind, but the Elohim. Healing wounds will take time."

"But it is possible," Michael said.

"The Horsemen destroyed this garden. It is only fitting that a Horseman restores it. A great wrong was committed against mankind." Uriel put his hand on Michael's shoulder. "Learn from those mistakes, Son of Mikha'el, Son of God, and do not repeat them." The archangel looked down at the small creek forming in the riverbed. "I am His emissary, and I will prepare the way." Uriel turned to regard Samiel with a respectful nod. "Maoffras restil, Samiel."

"Maoffras restil." Samiel bowed his head as the archangel departed, leaping into the sky.

Michael sensed the profound grief in him. "When was the last time you spoke to Uriel?"

"I have not seen my brother nor heard his voice since the fall of man." Samiel leaned on the scythe, wearily brushing the hood from his head.

"God punished you and the other sentinels for the fall of man?"

"We became the first apocalypse angels – the Afflictions through which the Father would punish mankind for Adam and Eve's disobedience. Uriel was the youngest among us. His sentence was to guard these ruins as a reminder of our failure."

He smiled sadly. "To look upon Eden again, as a home for the Nephilim gives me hope. Come, when I last laid eyes on Pagiel, he was fighting off Grigori in the sanctuary."

"No need to thank me," Loki'el announced, shoving his hands into his gloves. "Had it not been for my quick thinking and conjuration skills, you'd still be fighting a one-sided battle and losing."

Michael pursued the arrogant Seraphim through the remains of the parsonage garden. The privacy fence was down and marked a demilitarized zone between the church grounds and the barren, stony earth of Eden. "You tricked Anaba into helping you!"

"Yes," the Seraphim confessed, walking to the front of the ruined church. "I rather think she enjoyed it." He winked at the Nightmare. "I know I did."

"Loki'el, what you did may have worked in our favor, but look at the damage!" Michael pointed his war lance at the devastated church, its outbuildings, and the obliterated street. "How much damage was done in the living world?"

"I would imagine it's considerable."

"Wait!" Elijah swept his hand across the off-kilter landscape. "You can't put this all back where it was?"

"Clean-up is reserved for Servants of the Lord God," Loki'el replied with a shrug. "As you recall, I was sacked. Good luck with that." He turned in the direction of a low rumble of thunder.

On a trail of flames, ten gray Nightmares cantered abreast from the rear of the property. Riding among the Black Seraphim with his bow slung over his shoulder, Ziri sat astride one of the warhorses and led another by the reins. A pied crow circled in formation in the skies above him as they pulled up to a halt.

The smug expression on Loki'el's face fell away. "Would one

of you cretins please explain to me why this human is riding one of my angels' Nightmares?"

"Because Tannin is dead," one of the Seraphim piped up, wiping a smear of blood from his chin. "A few more of us might be had it not been for the boy. He handled himself well for a levithmong, and he certainly handles the bird better."

The eight surviving Black Seraphim stared at their leader, not speaking. Annoyed by their silent inquisition, Loki'el bellowed, "What?" He turned to one in particular. "What say you, Anubis?"

Anubis leaned over the pommel of his saddle. Scratching at his neck, he stared at the ground. "We think the boy would be a damn good replacement."

"A human?!" Loki'el spat. "To replace a Seraphim!"

"That bow of his is like Gungnir, Loki. It never misses."

"Have you all come to a consensus?" Loki'el asked, dumbfounded. "Without consulting me?"

Anubis pursed his lips together. "Yes."

"We're the Black Seraphim! We serve the Prince of Hell. Do you know what you're asking?" Loki'el glared at Ziri. "You're mortal. The peril here is abundantly real, *especially* for you."

"Enough, Loki'el. *We* voted. We like him, but it has to be unanimous," Anubis said. "All that bluster surely just means you like him, too."

"I am the grandson of an ălwăli, a friend of the kel essuf." Ziri pulled the indigo veil from his mouth. He dismounted between the two Nightmares and laid his hands on their necks. "I have walked with spirits from the moment of my birth."

"Maybe you didn't hear me," Loki'el growled. "Or worse, you didn't understand. This is me, trying to dissuade you from throwing in with these reprobates."

"He wasn't talking to you, Loki." Michael turned to Anaba, whose ears were pricked forward at attention.

Ziri tossed the reins to the closest Seraphim and walked to Anaba. "I would have you see me one last time as a boy," he said, avoiding any eye contact. Raising the veil to cover every feature except his eyes, he bowed to her. "You are the only mother I have ever known. I will not seek this path, if you think it unwise."

A sacred voice has been calling to you for a long time, Ziri ag Wararni. She rubbed her muzzle against his chest, tracing the outline of the Tuareg cross.

"The voice of my grandfather." He nodded as a tear fell from his eye. "I have heard it many times, but chose not to listen. Until now." He laid his forehead against hers. "I owe you my life."

And now I give it back to you. The Nightmare blew warm breath over his fingers.

Ziri drew his bone knife and cut a piece of her mane. The long strands fell away from her neck with a spark of flame. He reverently placed the lock in his gris-gris bag and wiped his tears away with the back of his hand. "Take care of her, Amaăwan." The Tuareg boy smirked. "Namărh. Nemensu."

"We're back to insults now?" Michael shook his head. "After all of this?"

He called you a Horseman, and he's giving us his blessing: to love each other and to forgive each other.

Ziri placed his hand over his heart and bowed. "What I wish for myself, I wish for you." He returned to his Nightmare. Mounting up, he held his arm out to allow Malpas the crow to land on his wrist. "Har ažăkka. Until tomorrow."

"How am I ever going to explain this to Lucifer?" Lokie'el rolled his eyes to the noise of the Black Seraphim cheering to welcome the boy. "Someone get me a bucket. I'm going to be sick." He reached for his stirrup and mounted his Nightmare. "Goodbye, Son of Mikha'el, may we never cross paths again." He narrowed his eyes, glaring at the rest of the Horsemen. "That goes for all of you." He winked at Anaba, pursing his lips to blow her a kiss. "However, I do hope to see you again, dear, sweet lady."

Sitting tall in the saddle, Loki'el turned to Ziri. "Send your bird to spread the message to our meager army. It's time to go home." He put a spur to his Nightmare and led the Black Seraphim away at a gallop. A throng of winged figures followed in their wake.

Elijah threw his hands up in exasperated despair. "Mike, this was the site of our investigation. We're responsible! How do we explain this shit back in the real world?"

"Take it easy, partner. I have an idea." Michael stroked Anaba's neck and ran his fingers through her mane. "Anaba, find us a road."

CHAPTER 64

It was seven o'clock on a rainy Tuesday morning. Maple Park Place Boulevard should have been empty, but the sidewalks were crowded with throngs of people. Shoulder to shoulder, they had their cell phones out, recording evidence of what had happened in their normally quiet, Bronx neighborhood overnight.

The quaint, sleepy street was jammed bumper to bumper with first-response vehicles, consisting mostly of New York City police cars, fire trucks, ambulances, and a hearse from the coroner's office. A dozen utility vans from Con Edison led the parked convoy. The flashing of blue and red emergency lights was enhanced by a low-lying fog that crept in from a sinkhole in the middle of the block where St. Joseph's church had stood for the last two hundred years.

Michael made his way toward the police barrier wearing leather and chainmail armor. The gold and green maille rattled as he walked through the crowd, receiving more than a fair share of strange looks from onlookers and the first responders on the scene. The situation called for a taciturn expression as he approached the disaster site. But it was difficult to suppress his pride in wearing the mantle of a Horseman so publicly.

Dodging a fire truck, Michael hurried across the street to elude the curious stares. He rubbed his hands together to restore feeling to his fingertips. The temperature in Manhattan was dropping as a wave of frigid air moved in over the city. The mercury was expected to dip sharply below freezing by rush hour.

"And lo, a black horse; and he that sat on her had the name Famine!"

Michael hesitated in front of the homeless preacher camped on the sidewalk. "Loki'el?"

"No, it's me. Marcuriel." Lucifer's messenger adjusted a tattered baseball cap on his head. The fallen angel grinned up at him with yellowed teeth.

"What are you doing here?" Michael asked, trying to keep his voice calm.

Marcuriel picked up the cardboard cash box and shook it insistently, jingling the assorted coins inside. "Appearances are everything, Son of Mikha'el, Son of God."

Michael rolled his eyes and tossed a $5 bill into the flimsy carton. The bill landed on a heavy-bonded envelope crafted from black parchment paper. "Another invitation?"

"Lucifer is hosting a private hunt at his estate," Marcuriel said, gleefully clapping his dirty hands.

"Let me guess, everyone who's anyone will be there?"

Marcuriel grinned, sharpened canines revealed against his lower lip. "Every Duke of Hell will be in attendance with their entourages for the festivities."

"Only one envelope?"

The fallen angel held his hand up and spread his empty fingers wide. As if shaking water from them, he flicked his wrist and three black envelopes appeared. He dropped them into the box. "And the Four shall be separate, but as One."

Michael shoved the invitations into his boot without breaking the waxy red seal. "RSVP by threat again?"

"Be there," Marcuriel said blissfully, "or... *be there.*" Retrieving his cash box, he got up and wandered down a nearby side street away from the swelling crowd.

Absently fidgeting with the silver band on his index finger, Michael took a deep breath and exhaled his fears. He had neither the time nor the energy to expend on wondering what Lucifer wanted from him this time, but he was certain it had to do with the Nephilim and his recent acquisition of Eden.

He made his way through the back of the crowd. Officer Larry Fitzpatrick paused while cordoning off the area with police tape. The cop shook his head in disgust. "Let me guess, Special Agent Childs, you're just coming home from the Crusades? Did you liberate Mecca?"

"It was Jerusalem that was liberated, Larry, not Mecca." Michael ducked beneath the yellow tape without showing his credentials. "I'm supposed to be playing the hero at the Renaissance Games in an hour, but I got called here."

The cop shrugged and tied off the end of the tape to a sawhorse. "FBI's investigating sinkholes now?"

"Loose ends," Michael replied. "My partner and I were here a few days ago speaking with Father Paige about some missing persons."

"Might be plenty missing people under all that rubble," Larry said. "Whole church went down, along with the garage, and the old convent. Gas company showed up and kicked everybody off the scene. No one's allowed in until they clear it."

"I can handle debriefing my partner, Larry," Elijah interjected. "Do you mind?"

Chided, the cop shrugged his shoulders and returned to his crowd-control duties.

"How's it looking?" Michael whispered. Con Edison, the city's primary power and energy provider, had taped off a no-man's land around the three-acre sinkhole where even cops were turned back.

"So far, so good, Mike. Just waiting for the climax." Elijah pretended to scribble in his notebook. "What's taking Anaba so long?"

"Special Agents Childs and Pope." Rachel Rollins flashed her badge at the policemen holding the line, but it was unnecessary. The team of SWAT members behind her was more than sufficient to grant her entry.

"Rachel." Michael was relieved to see her. "What's the word?"

"Promotion, Agent Childs – yours, at least, temporarily," she replied. "Assistant Director Rathan is MIA, so is Agent McKabe. The Bureau's looking at you to take the lead. It's your investigation after all." She tried to smile, the lines of her face drawn with fatigue. "What are your orders, sir?" She was playing the ruse well, considering what she knew. Michael was proud of her and determined to put her on the fast track to special agent.

He glanced over his shoulder to a parking lot that had been taken over as a command station by the NYPD. Samiel was standing beside a black SUV, dressed in his usual dark suit and hat. The Horseman tipped the brim at him. Raijin stood at attention and saluted Michael with his riding crop. Winking as she clutched a clipboard in her arm, Wyrmwood adjusted her glasses with a tilt of her head and waved.

Rollins laughed and shook her head. "Knowing who they are? Do you ever get over that?"

"Not really." Michael scanned the crowd of spectators and first responders, but could not find the one face he desperately wanted to see.

"What's the hold up?" Wyrmwood demanded of a passing utility worker. "There's a malaria outbreak in Belize, a new strain, and I'm dying for a sample. Let's get this show on the road. Where are the bodies?"

"That's the problem, lady," the Con Edison tech said, lugging a ground-penetrating radar device to the curb. "Bodies must be buried deep. Corpse-sniffing dogs can't find a thing. No matter how deep the city engineers probe, they keep coming up empty-handed. They're calling it an act of God."

"Nonsense! This is what I call an act of God." Wyrmwood pinched Elijah in the ass, making the agent jump in alarm.

"Dr Wyrmwood!" he gasped.

"Special Agent Childs, you might want to see this." Exiting a surveillance van with a laptop in her arms, a female agent set the computer on the hood of a cruiser. "Approximately fifteen minutes ago, the NYPD received a 911 call about a potential ten-ten: suspicious persons. Of course, the press were all over it before the cops could get there."

She turned the screen toward them, where a CNN reporter stood beneath an umbrella. Behind her, policemen were helping a seemingly unending line of men, women, and children through an opened cistern in the street.

"In an astonishing development to our breaking story," the reporter said breathlessly, "survivors of the sinkhole that swallowed St. Joseph's church have been found alive and well. The congregation was at a midnight prayer vigil when a mysterious quake interrupted their service. Fearing a natural disaster, Father Paige and Father Marcus led their flock into the old World War II tunnels beneath the parish in a daring escape as the entire structure collapsed."

The camera cut to the two priests assisting people out of the sewer and into the hands of paramedics with blankets and water bottles. "The Catholic priests led the survivors on a harrowing trip through the city's subway system. Survivors have suffered only minor injuries. As yet, no deaths have been reported."

"They found 'em!" Larry shouted, quelling the noise in the immediate area. "Holy shit, they found them!" He hurriedly made the sign of the cross and kissed his St. Christopher pendant as a cheer went up among the first responders on the scene.

"That's our cue," Michael said. "Rollins, gather a team and get down there with your list."

"I'm on it, Agent Childs." She slapped the tattered notebook against the palm of her hand. "Nice outfit by the way," she said with a wink, "but you might want to slip into something more suitable. The Deputy Director left DC as soon this news broke. Her plane lands in an hour."

"Noted." Michael again scanned the crowd, still looking for the one face that would settle his heart. This time he found her.

Watching him from across the street, Anaba lurked in the darkened windows of a coffee shop. The vendor was opening his doors early to capitalize on the surge of activity on the block.

Michael made his way across the street. "Anaba Raines?" he asked. "Gunnery Sergeant Anaba Raines?"

She brushed the heavy mane of dreadlocks from her shoulder. "Who the hell are you? And why are you following me?" the Marine replied, sticking to the script.

"FBI Special Agent Michael Childs. Just want to talk, gunny. Need to ask you a few questions. About a recent 911 phone call." He put his hands around her waist and pulled her close.

"What if I plead the fifth?"

Comforted to be reunited with her, Michael laid his forehead against hers. "What took so long? You had me worried."

"Arranging an extraction for a hundred civilians takes a bit of planning, Special Agent Childs," she countered. "The Vestibule Road is no place for the living, even with four Nightmares to protect them."

"I thought Marines were trained to improvise."

Anaba rolled her eyes and laughed. "I should have killed you when I had the chance."

Michael kissed her, his lips lingering over hers. "Any regrets, gunny?"

She looked up at him with a smile and kissed him back, running her hands through his dreadlocks. "Not one."

SIGIL KEY

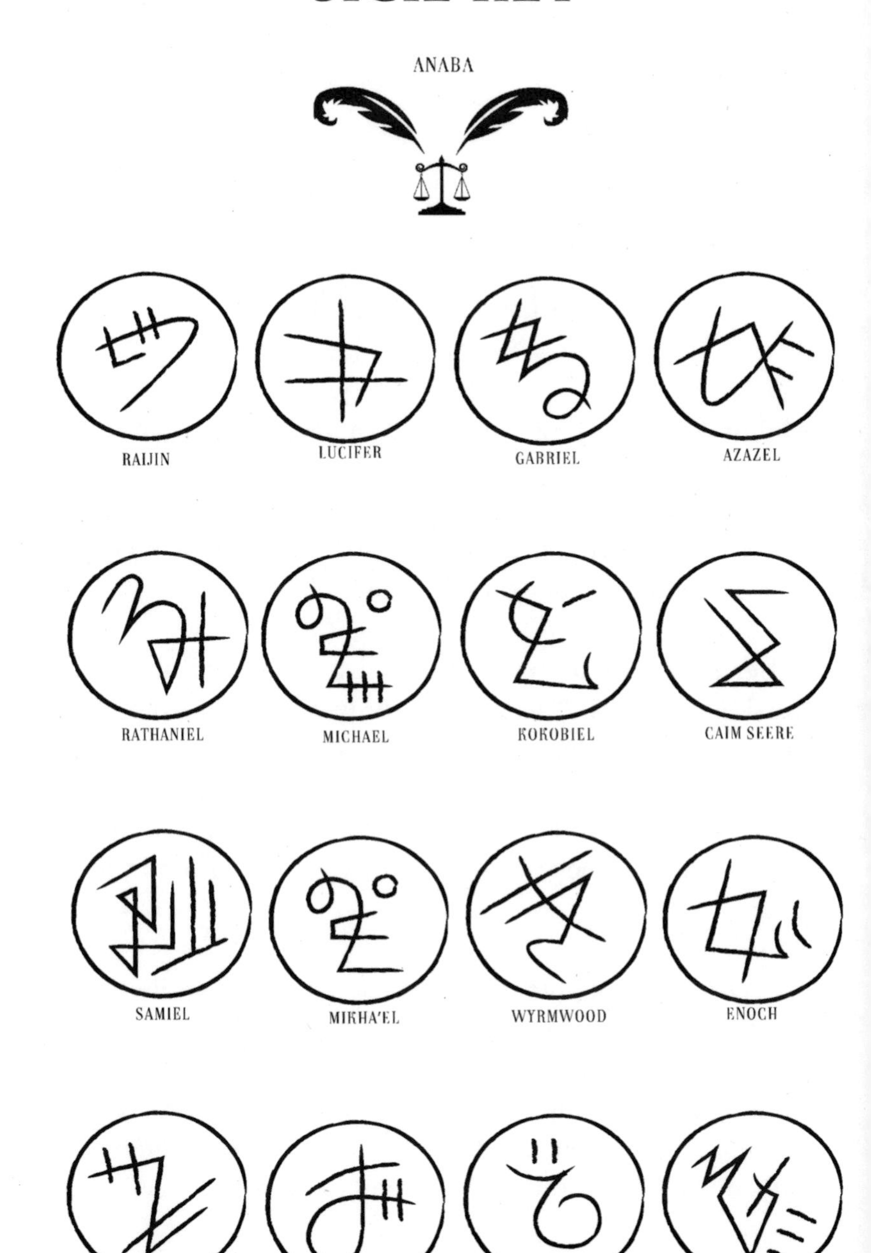
ANABA
RAIJIN
LUCIFER
GABRIEL
AZAZEL
RATHANIEL
MICHAEL
KOKOBIEL
CAIM SEERE
SAMIEL
MIKHA'EL
WYRMWOOD
ENOCH
RAPHAEL
PAGIEL
LOKI'EL
URIEL

GLOSSARY

Abdad [Tamasheq] – a command meaning to stop an action.

Ababalond [Enochian] – an insult referring to an action that is considered unclean; a person whose bloodline is considered tainted; derogatory term for a whore.

Acheron, River of Woe – the first river in Hell, the first crossing for souls. The water is brown in color with the consistency and odor of untreated sewage.

Adrpan [Enochian] – a disparaging reference to fallen angels who have been cast down; anyone exiled from their home.

Ah-Azarim Aziagiar [Enochian] – the phrase literally means *a bitter harvest*. It is the title bestowed upon a war lance forged by the Archangel Mikha'el. Used in the final battle against the fallen angel Lucifer Morningstar, the lance was left behind immemorial to the angels that died, on both sides, during the last battle to defend Heaven.

Ălbăraka [Tamasheq] – a blessing bestowed on another to bring good fortune, spiritual favor, or protection.

Ălfăsseq [Tamasheq] – an insult, meaning a hypocrite, generally a reference to a corrupt government official.

Altar of Cain – a crude stone altar used by the firstborn son of Adam and Eve to make offerings to God. After murdering his brother, Cain's altar sank into Hell, heavy with the weight of his guilt.

Amădray, iyyăw da [Tamasheq] – a Tuareg expression meaning 'younger brother, come here.'

Ămud [Tamasheq] – a simple prayer.

Anăgad [Tamasheq] – a reference pertaining to the ceremony of the veiling among the Tuareg people.

Ărdăɣ [Tamasheq] – a request to listen.

Arezodi [Enochian] – an Enochian term literally translated as 'I mean you no harm' or shortened to mean 'Peace.'

Ăssălam ăɣlekum [Tamasheq] – a Tuareg greeting meaning 'Peace be unto you.'

Ăɣlekum ăssălam [Tamasheq] – Tuareg response to a traditional greeting. The phrase means 'And may peace be upon you, too.'

Aɣrut [Tamasheq] – a pied crow. Though having the characteristics of a raven, these are smaller birds, easily recognized by a ring of white feathers around their necks and their glossy black feathers.

Ăzayeǵ [Tamasheq] – a raven.

Bahal'li [Enochian] – a pool of God's tears that formed in the ripped out roots of the Tree of Life in the Garden of Eden; the term literally means, 'He cried.'

Balit'ádh [Enochian] – a reference meant to wish someone good fortune or luck.

Balzizras [Enochian] – meaning judgment; a tower also known as the Citadel of Judgment. Situated in the center of DrunGer, it is a direct gateway into Heaven.

Bani [Tamasheq] – a wish for good health or peace.

Bărăd [Tamasheq] – the term means to 'Be brave.'

Benediximus [Latin] – the term for 'good luck.'

Bushido [Japanese] – a code among the samurai that provided guidelines in moral and ethical behavior.

Cocytus, River of Wailing – though usually referenced as one of the rivers in Hell, the Cocytus is not a river, but a lake at the very bottom of the abyss. Totally frozen over, the lake is the final resting place for sinners who betrayed their families, countries, or masters. Due to the shift in gravity, the depth of the lake is unknown.

Crest of Nanqueel – a brand found on the left shoulder of Nightmares, signifying that the warhorse has killed an angel. The more feathers in the crest, the more powerful the Nightmare's abilities.

Dods [Enochian] – to vex or annoy; diarrhea; (colloquial) to give the shits.

DrunGer [Enochian] – the term means 'the heart within'; the sovereign territory of God in Hell, comprised of the estates of the Four Horsemen of the Apocalypse.

Elohim [Hebrew] – a term used for God, but also collectively for His angels.

Enai [Enochian] – when used in deference, the term is a title, meaning lord or lady.

Enochian – the written and verbal language of the angels.

Eophon de Okada [Enochian] – the phrase means 'lamentation of mercy'; also used to described a written contract of pardon.

Essesnăn-kăy Măssinaɣ [Tamasheq] – an insult or rebuke meaning, 'May God cause you pain!'

Fel-as igrâz-i [Tamasheq] – a colloquial phrase or compliment, meaning, 'I look because it pleases me.'

Fetharsi [Enochian] – literally translates as 'Approach, I mean no harm.'

Fey – a collective term for supernatural or otherworldly elements; in this case, it refers to the Sylphs who serve the Horseman Pestilence.

Forging – the brutal practice of torturing a condemned soul with extreme forms of unction and forced confessions to transform it into a Nightmare.

Fossegrim – water spirits from Scandinavian lore, known for playing the Hardanger fiddle; often associated with stories involving the luring and drowning of unsuspecting children or people who get too close to their watery abodes.

Four Afflictions – another, lesser known, name for the Four Horsemen; associated with the belief that the fall of Adam and Eve brought the advent of war, sickness, drought, and death into the world to punish mankind.

Gusoku [Japanese] – a type of Japanese armor that emerged about the time when matchlock muskets were being mass produced.

Grigori [Enochian] – a corps of angels from all the celestial spheres, collectively known as the Watchers. They were charged with overseeing the well-being of creation after the fall of Adam and Eve. Two hundred of these angels transgressed, however, taking human men and women as their lovers. Their children and subsequent descendants are known as the Nephilim.

Gris-gris [African] – a protective charm; a prayer bag containing sacred relics or charms necessary for prayers and rituals.

Har ažăkka [Tamasheq] – a farewell salutation meaning 'Until tomorrow.'

Hoath [Enochian] – a true worshiper; faithful adherent (i.e. She is hoath).

Iblis [Tamasheq] – a vitriolic insult, meaning devil.

Ifrits – a type of volatile spirit in Islamic tradition, usually associated with fire; sometimes referenced as djinn.

Immînda [Tamasheq] – a saying that marks the conclusion of an act that is well done; literally meaning 'It is finished.'

Išenǵa [Tamasheq] – disparaging term for an enemy.

Iv'baato [Enochian] – an affliction.

Iviahe [Enochian] – a Song of Honor for a deceased person; requiem.

Iyyăw diha [Tamasheq] – a request, 'come here.'

Kakeukr [Enochian] – to wither.

Kel essuf [Enochian] – mischievous desert spirits, categorized as neither good nor evil.

Keys of Solomon – a sacred tome containing the names of every angel ever created, including the Fallen; also includes rituals to summon, command, or access the abilities of these angels through the use of their sigils or unique signatures.

Lethe, River of Oblivion – the first river in Purgatory, though not located in Hell proper; a tributary of the Lethe feeds back into Hell and contributes to the River of Guilt.

Levithmong [Enochian] – a derogatory term for mankind.

Mahorela [Enochian] – a translation for 'dark heavens'; the ruins of the Garden of Eden.

Maoffras [Enochian] – a literal translation for 'not to be measured,' meaning an act that is too great; a description for an act that is worth tremendous praise or one that is exceedingly immoral and/or unlawful.

Maoffras restil [Enochian] – a phrasing of greeting, wishing the recipient great fortune; literally means, 'May you praise Him and that praise be immeasurable.'

M-isem-năk [Tamasheq] – a question of introduction, 'What is your name?'

Momao Abai'Vonin [Enochian] – the literal translation is the Crown of Dragons; a wellspring surrounded by the five severed heads of the Babylonian Dragon Goddess Tiamat. The five great waters of Hell flow through her mouths and down into an abysmal basin to create the River of Guilt.

Mužeɣ [Tamasheq] – a statement of pride meaning 'To be Tuareg.'

Namărh [Tamasheq] – a blessing to 'Love each other.'

Nemensu [Tamasheq] – a blessing to 'Forgive each other.'

Nephilim – the direct descendent of an angel; usually born with twelve fingers and toes and a gift or supernatural ability referred to as grace.

Nightmares – infernal warhorses created from condemned souls through the forging, a process of extreme torture. The transformation breaks the mind and spirit, leaving many untrainable. All Nightmares are commonly sooty gray in color. Exceptional mounts will shed out to simple colors, white or white with a hint of green. A less common color is chestnut, and the rarest of all is black.

Niis [Enochian] – a word of binding/summoning, that literally means 'to come'; used by Riders to summon their Nightmares.

Noib [Enochian] – an affirmation, meaning 'yes.'

Od'a Es tria'noan tliob cirp'ca El [Enochian] – an affirmation of a statement; literal meaning 'And the Four will be separate, but as One.'

Ogăẓ-kăy Măssinăɣ [Tamasheq] – a blessing for good fortune and protection, meaning 'May God protect you.'

Ol tibibp [Enochian] – an offering of condolences, meaning 'My sorrow.'

Phlegethon, River of Fire – the third river in Hell, the Phlegethon is home to murderers and war-makers, who stand in the boiling river of blood as punishment for their crimes. Intermittent flames rise from the surface, scorching anything within the river's current or in close proximity.

Qaaun [Enochian] – a term for God's foretold Chosen, who would rise from among the Nephilim; also means fulcrum.

Qeres [Enochian] – a funerary oil used to purify a corpse before burial; a poison that is highly toxic to angels. Exposure through external contact or ingestion results in paralysis, convulsions, and death.

Querida [Spanish] – an affectionate term, meaning dear.

Ripir [Enochian] – an insult, meaning beast; someone who has no proper place, like an animal.

Ritual of Descarbia – a taboo ritual that permanently exiles an angel or angelic descendent from Heaven, damning them to walk the Vestibule Road for eternity. Victims are poisoned with qeres and then tortured through violent acts of mutilation (i.e. removal of the wings or partial excoriation of the back). The ritual calls for the removal of the eyelids and tongue, while the victim is still alive and awake. These items are burned in a clay jar and the victim is posed for display. Enochian obscenities are carved into the flesh, marking the victim as an outcast in the afterlife.

River of Guilt – is the largest waterway in Hell because it is fed by tributaries of the five great waters: the Acheron, the Styx, the Phlegethon, Cocytus, and the Lethe.

Siatris [Enochian] – literally translation, scorpion; the steward or head of a household who serves a Horseman and sees to the day-to-day tasks of running their estate.

Tagelmust [Enochian] – the veil worn by men of the Tuareg tribe. Women are generally not veiled.

Styx, River of Fire – the second river in Hell, the Styx is home to the wrathful and sullen souls, who have been damned to its inky, putrid-smelling waters or the marshes along its shores.

Sylphs – air spirits or winged elementals who can control wind and lightning, often attributed to fairies.

Talveh [Enochian] – meaning family or belonging.

Tamăḍrayt [Tamasheq] – colloquial term for sister.

Tamasheq [Tamasheq] – the Tuareg language.

Teknâ tihussay hullen! [Tamasheq] – a compliment, meaning 'She is really beautiful!'

Teẓẓ [Tamasheq] – a crude insult making reference to the anus; asshole.

Three Spheres of the Elohim – the categorization of angels; First Sphere (highest): *Seraphim, Cherubim, Thrones*; Second Sphere (middle): *Dominations, Virtues, Powers*; Third Sphere (lowest): *Principalities, Archangels, Guardian Angels*.

Tifinagh – the Tamasheq alphabet.

Toru [Tamasheq] – a term referencing the use of black magic.

Touch of Zephyr – the ability of Nightmares to walk above the ground or over water without disturbing the surface. This allows them to move silently, especially in darkness. However, when pressed into a hard gallop, the scorch marks of partial hoof prints are often left in their wake as evidence of their presence.

Ubehla [Enochian] – meaning stubborn; an indigenous wild boar found in DrunGer.

Ulh-kereššet [Tamasheq] – colloquial for broken hearted; a bow.

Urch(es) [Enochian] – literally translated as a confounding or insane angel(s); an annoyance.

Vaoan Dagger [Enochian] – Vaoan means truth or purity. Known for their razor-sharpness, these daggers are used in the Ritual of Descarbia.

Vestibule Road – the main route of travel throughout the whole of Hell; a nexus of portals and crossroads to various destinations within the abyss. The Vestibule Road is extremely difficult to navigate without a Nightmare or the proper maps and sigils.

Wăr ăksodăg wăla! [Tamasheq] – a declaration, meaning, 'I am not afraid of anything!'

Yari [Japanese] – a type of Japanese blade, usually paired with a staff to make a formidable polearm.

Zăbbăt [Tamasheq] – a request, meaning 'Get down!'

ACKNOWLEDGMENTS

To Mrs. Dorothy J. Beck for setting me on the path of a writer, reading the early ramblings of a horse-crazy little girl and feeding me a steady diet of dragons, unicorns, and Nightmares.

To my first Creative Writing class, specifically: Ariana Tomb, Veronica Mallens-Luttgens, Grace Miller, Isaac Embry, Susie Williams, Mohtaz Mahmuda, and Liz Steelman for encouraging me to bring this story to life.

Special thanks to Gabriella Tranchitella for challenging me to write fanfiction on WattPad and getting her friends to build my first readership. Love ya, kid!

To Wattpad for offering the very first Online Novella Contest, where the initial 20,000 words of this novel came together in a three-round sprint, earning second place in a crowded field.

To Nancy Springer for reading the first chapter and sending it to her agent to give me a push in the right direction, and then always being there to offer a word of advice.

Thanks to the first set of beta readers from another stunning Creative Writing class: Isabella Kostic, Kaylynn Keahtigh, and Silvana Iazetti, who listened to my zany ideas, chapter after chapter.

Many thanks to my best friend Gaylene Ponas, who never doubted me or the book.

To beta readers extraordinaire: Bobbi Billman (who read the

manuscript three times!) and Yari Rivera, who craved every chapter!

Special thanks to Mrs. Gretchen V. Blakey, my barn mother. "Make it happen, Patty!" will resonate in my mind forever.

Undying thanks to Sara Megibow of KT Literary. There's no room to tell the story, but the Universe placed me in the hands of a legend.

To the Angry Robot Books team for their diligence; Eleanor Teasdale for taking a chance on an old warhorse; Rose Greene for polishing it up, and Gemma Creffield for getting us to the show ring in style.

Last, but not least, thanks to my mom, Mrs. Dora L. Jackson, for indulging my horsey self. She stood ringside in the rain and cold and mud to watch me ride, despite being absolutely terrified of horses.

To the beloved Nightmares in my life: Amadeus, Clay, and Niko who carried me across ditches wide and fences tall… I will see you again. To my current Nightmares, Maya and Indy, thanks for uplifting my soul in dark times. This book would not have been possible without your lessons in love, humility, and acceptance.

And finally, thanks to every horse girl and horse boy out there. You know who you are! *You,* who understand the indelible bond that exists between horses and the humans who love them.

And finally, thank you, dear Reader, for coming on a wild ride to Hell and back again. I look forward to taking you back to the Vestibule Road one day soon in the near future.

Silent Hall
N.S. DOLKART

Among the Fallen
N.S. DOLKART
The Gods are drawing battle lines

A Breach in the Heavens
N.S. DOLKART
The end is nigh

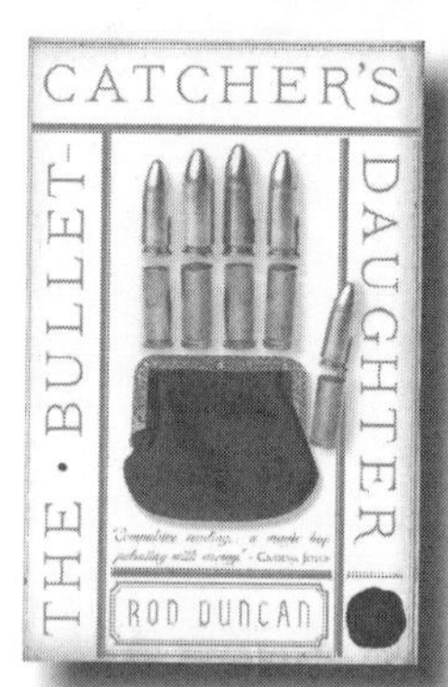
THE BULLET-CATCHER'S DAUGHTER
ROD DUNCAN

UNSEEMLY SCIENCE
ROD DUNCAN

"ELIZABETH BARNABUS WILL ENTICE READERS FROM THE FIRST PAGE"
- STEPHEN BOOTH
THE CUSTODIAN OF MARVELS
ROD DUNCAN

PAIGE ORWIN
THE INTERMINABLES

MOONSHINE
JASMINE GOWER

"RARE AND PRECIOUS... COMPELLING AND TRUE."
AN OATH OF DOGS
WENDY N WAGNER

Science Fiction, Fantasy and WTF?!

@angryrobotbooks 

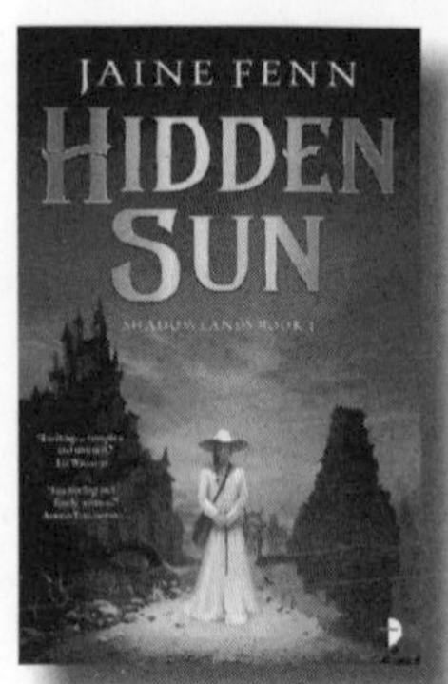